48 HOURS

BOOKS BY WILLIAM R. FORSTCHEN
FROM TOM DOHERTY ASSOCIATES

We Look Like Men of War
One Second After
Pillar to the Sky
One Year After
The Final Day
48 Hours

48HOURS

WILLIAM R. FORSTCHEN

FORGE®

A TOM DOHERTY ASSOCIATES BOOK
NEW YORK

48 HOURS

Copyright © 2018 by William R. Forstchen

A Forge Book
Published by Tom Doherty Associates
175 Fifth Avenue
New York, NY 10010

www.tor-forge.com

Forge® is a registered trademark of Macmillan Publishing Group, LLC.

The Library of Congress Cataloging-in-Publication Data is available upon request.

ISBN 978-0-7653-9791-1 (hardcover)
ISBN 978-0-7653-9794-2 (ebook)

Our books may be purchased in bulk for promotional, educational, or business use. Please contact your local bookseller or the Macmillan Corporate and Premium Sales Department at 1-800-221-7945, extension 5442, or by email at MacmillanSpecialMarkets@macmillan.com.

First Edition: January 2019

Printed in the United States of America

0 9 8 7 6 5 4 3 2 1

For the real "Darren & Darla" and so many like them who in any crisis will strive to make the moral choice. And of course . . . for Robin.

PART I

Some say the world will end in fire,
Some say in ice.
From what I've tasted of desire
I hold with those who favor fire.
But if it had to perish twice,
I think I know enough of hate
To say that for destruction ice
Is also great
And would suffice.

—Robert Frost, "Fire and Ice"

1

DARREN Brooks fumbled as he tried to slap the alarm clock into silence, knocking it off the nightstand. The two little bells on top of the clock, with a tiny clapper between them, slamming back and forth, continued to ring, its tinny sound nerve-jarring.

"Oh, for God's sake, Darren, turn that damn thing off," Darla moaned from the other side of the bed.

He leaned over, groped around. It must have slid under the bed.

"Darren!"

"Okay, okay, I got it," he mumbled, pulling back the heavy wool blankets and cursing softly as his feet hit the cold floor.

Getting down on his hands and knees, he reached under the bed and grabbed the annoying antique, jamming a finger between the clapper and bells to silence the little annoying monstrosity at last.

The switch—where was the damn switch? He poked around the back, feeling for the lever, then his finger slipped off the clapper and, though muffled, the damn thing rang again.

"Darren!"

A memory hit of all those old cartoons where Elmer, Daffy, whomever, tormented by an alarm clock, just threw it out the window. He found the switch and flicked it down, and the devilish machine fell silent.

He was still tempted to throw it against the wall, but wisely decided to just put it back on the nightstand. Now half-awake, he stumbled to the bathroom and out of force of habit flicked the switch.

And of course, no lights came on.

"Damn. Power is still off." He sighed.

"It's freezing in here," Darla said. "I kind of figured it's down again."

There was no need for lights to just relieve himself. At least the water supply was gravity fed from the town's storage tank—that was, as long as they pumped it full while they had power, which had been on for several hours the previous evening. He scurried across the freezing-cold floor and scrambled back under the covers, Darla muttering an affectionate curse as he pressed his cold feet up against the backs of her legs, but then she sighed as he snuggled in closer. She stood not much more than five foot two at a 110 pounds or so, and he was more than double her weight, six foot four, and bearlike. He wrapped his arms around her, the two nuzzling closer for a moment.

"Don't fall back to sleep," she whispered.

"Yeah, I know."

Absolutely content with life at that moment, he held her tight, kissing her on the back of the neck.

"You need a shave." She laughed softly as he rubbed his chin stubble against her upper back, a hint of a seductive note in her laughter.

"No, stop it," she finally said. "You've got to go to work."

"Later, then," he whispered into her ear.

"Promises, promises," was her sleepy reply as she pulled the heavy blankets back over her shoulder as he drew away, turned, and put his feet on the still-icy floor. He fumbled in the dark for his slippers, put them on, picked up his heavy bathrobe from the corner of the bed, and trekked out to the living room. The fire was still going. He opened the glass doors, fed in several more logs, closed the doors after opening the flue wider, then went into the kitchen, turning on the battery-powered lamp he had rigged up to the kitchen chandelier.

For southern Missouri in December, it was damn cold, well below freezing outside, frost glistening on the deck railings and on the cover of the hot tub, which they had shut down and drained three weeks earlier when the problems had started.

Always efficient and thinking ahead, Darla had set out the night before, a two-pound can of coffee and an old-fashioned percolator that had been stored in what they called their "prepper stash," down in the basement. Filling up the pot with water, Darren now spooned coffee into the basket to be placed at the top of the percolator, put the lid on, and turned on the kitchen stove. At least that still worked because it was propane. They used to have a tank topped off with five hundred gallons of the stuff, but in the weeks after power had gone on the blink, they had been far too profligate in burning it up with their home generator to power and heat their four thousand–square-foot house, figuring the grid would be back up soon enough. Once things got back to normal, they'd just order up a propane truck to come out and fill them back up again. But things had not come back to normal, and they realized they might be in for a long haul with a cold winter, and the fifty gallons left should be hoarded only for cooking. The woodstove could provide sufficient heat for the living room and kitchen area, and at least they could cook indoors, unlike more than a few neighbors who on cold evenings stood shivering outside, cooking on their barbecues.

In the last few days, Darla had even passed out nine buckets of freeze-dried food from their emergency supply to neighbors who were coming up short, each bucket with enough food to keep a family of four going for a month. They had always factored in a thought regarding their neighbors and friends in a time of crisis—that was just part of their nature—but they could only give out a few more one-month buckets of food before having to think about their own long-term needs. Surely, though, they both hoped the damage to the power grid and overall infrastructure of the region from the solar storm of three weeks past would be repaired and life would soon return to some semblance of normalcy.

Neither of them wanted to think about the grim mathematics of what might happen to their emergency food supply if things still were not repaired a couple of months from now, especially given the reports, starting yesterday, that another solar event might be brewing.

The water in the coffeepot heated up, and there was the first hissing pop as it began percolating. Darren loved the sound of it. It reminded him of his grandmother's home, a small farmstead, as if from another age, up in the back hills of the Ozarks. The soothing nostalgia-inducing sound from the coffeepot grew louder, the dark brew splashing up against the small clear glass globe atop the pot. When he spent week-ends at his grandparents' house, Darren always got the job of watching the pot until the coffee was jet-black, and they would then let him have a few warming sips, heavily laced with fresh cream from their cow teth-ered in the barn. The advent of the Mr. Coffee machines and then the little K-Cups had, in nearly all homes, resulted in relegating a percola-tor coffeepot to the basement or the trash pile. Buying one for use in an emergency had been one of many smart moves that were now paying off. And besides, he loved the sound of it, and somehow—maybe it was just psychosomatic—the coffee did seem to taste better.

He went back into the living room, taking in the vista offered by the two-story-high glass windows of their home. Their house, a log cabin of contemporary design, was situated atop a high ridge rising nearly two hundred feet above the Lake of the Ozarks. It faced southeast and at this time of year provided a perfect viewing point for the sunrise, which was beginning to unfold, the deeper indigos giving way to scarlet and brilliant shades of pink.

Darla shuffled out, bundled up in her oversized, rather funny-looking camouflage-pattern bathrobe with matching slippers—a Christmas present from him last year—went into the kitchen, pulled down two cups from the cabinet, and poured out their hot coffee, plain black, fresh cream no longer available.

She then shuffled into the living room, handed him one of the cups, and put her arm around his waist.

"Love you, Bear."

Bear, her affectionate nickname for him, pronounced on their first date when at her door he asked permission to kiss her good night, and she of course agreed. He effortlessly lifted her a foot off the ground, wrapped in his massive embrace, and gave her a good-night kiss that convinced her on the spot that though still gun-shy from her divorce, she would not let this one get away.

"Wish you'd quit that damn job," she announced. "We don't need the money anymore now that we've sold our business, and you know it. Perfect morning to watch the sunrise, throw some more wood on the fire, and then back to bed."

The way she said "back to bed" had a suggestive tone in it that made him hug her in closer.

She had been saying it nearly every morning of late, especially when what everyone was now calling "the Big Storm" had hit several weeks earlier. It had become a demarcation point, a dividing line between "before" and "after." The before time was one of ease and luxury. After had been a wake-up call as to just how dependent all were upon limitless electricity, always available at the flick of a switch, a world with a global connection to friends, family, entertainment carried in the palm of a hand. All of that now limited at best in the southern tier of states, and according to the occasional news reports they could monitor, still entirely off-line farther north, where the impact of the solar storm had been more intense. The refrain punctuating most conversations now: "Once things are back to normal, we'll . . ." But after three weeks that increasingly seemed like a fabled promised land that surely must return soon. Surely the ever-mentioned "they" had to get things back in order by the end of the year.

He sipped his coffee and looked down at her snuggled in by his side.

"Oh, come on. I was getting bored not doing anything. And, sweetheart, I'd drive you crazy within a month just hanging around here, and you know it. Besides, the benefits package is good—free medical insurance; you can't sniff at that—and it keeps me out of your hair."

"Still, given how things are now, especially over the next few days if that next storm hits, at least think about it. Okay? If things get worse, I want you here."

He didn't reply. It was ironic in a way to hear her concern. There was a touch of role reversal in their marriage. The military, police work, or security had been part of his life since high school. But Darla? Beyond her very feminine, petite exterior was someone with indeed a unique background. Definitely a tomboy raised by a single father who owned a gun-customizing business, she had taken it over in her early twenties after his passing and turned it into a thriving enterprise of providing customized weapons for the nation's elite military units. So her appeal was not one of a nervous at-home wife feeling a need for her bear of a husband to be a protector. If anything, she was the one providing protection around this house and was deadly efficient with a multitude of weapons that her family business had manufactured until the sale of that firm a year ago. He found it amusing to say that if ever there were a situation that hit the fan, he'd be the backup for Darla.

Quitting his job, especially now, struck him as an act of cowardice, which was never part of his playbook. He had a job that he could not just walk away from now.

The sun was just breaking the horizon, usually a favorite moment for him of watching the long shadows interspersed with red and golden streaks of light spread across the lake.

At times, though, this moment still made him think of how different it was from sunrise out on the ugly flatland deserts of Iraq. That glaring orb rising and within minutes the temperature soaring from a comfortable chill to another day of hundred-degree heat.

He squinted, staring straight at the sun as it climbed above the pine trees rimming the ridge on the far side of the lake.

It didn't look any different. Some people claimed that right at sunrise you could stare at it for a moment and see the spots, the building eruptions. He couldn't, and he finally turned away, blinking, spots dancing in his vision from having stared at the sun too long.

"Drink your coffee and get out of here," Darla chided him. "Bad example the head of security being late."

He drained his cup, handed it back to her, and leaned over to kiss her on the forehead.

He glanced at the sun again, squinting, but it still didn't look any different. But it was different. Just before going to bed shortly after midnight, they had listened to a BBC broadcast on a battery-powered shortwave radio and heard that another CME had exploded from the sun's surface, perhaps more powerful than the December 1 incident, and would strike Earth in less than three days.

Something was indeed going wrong, and holding Darla close, he felt a vague fear of what was to come.

PART II

Humanity has all but forgotten about the humanities on the way to Armageddon.

—Anthony T. Hincks

2

A MONTH earlier, maybe one person in a hundred knew what a CME was, shorthand for a coronal mass ejection, a solar storm that triggered an electrical disturbance so intense it disrupted—and in some places—blew the nation's power grid off-line. Everyone knew about the dynamics of it now. It had been one hell of an education over the last three weeks after a solar storm had hit with, as the lineup of experts on television were saying, "a near Carrington-level event."

Power grids, especially across the northern United States, had taken a pounding. More than a few cities resorted to martial law to keep order while the Department of Defense, FEMA, and dozens of volunteer agencies rushed emergency supplies to sustain the populace until full power was restored, and with it, a return to some semblance of a twenty-first-century infrastructure.

It was still just estimates, but the general consensus was that maybe twenty-five thousand or more had died from exposure, lack of medication, and the desperate need for clean, filtered water. At least farther south, where the impact of the coronal mass ejection had not been so severe, most power companies—though partially down with the loss of some high-transmission lines and even generating plants—were still able to deliver electricity as a rolling brownout or blackout to their customers for several hours each day.

As the sun rotated on its axis every twenty-four days, the region where the storm of December 1 had exploded from was now showing two more major disturbances building up . . .

Building with an intensity that with every passing hour became a source of far greater anxiety . . . and fear.

JUST before the December 1 storm hit, how the mechanics of it worked had been explained to the public by a popular television host, Mr. Science. His personality was sort of like a Mr. Rogers for adults, and the federal government had called him in and given him less than a day to put together a program to demonstrate just what the hell was going on with the sun.

Tall, skinny, horn-rim glasses, prematurely bald, and wearing a white lab coat complete with pocket protector, he was like a caricature of everyone's eighth-grade science teacher. The demonstration started with his usual nerdy grin and overly enthusiastic tone. "Hi, everyone! Mr. Science here for a lesson that this time is really serious, so listen up."

The camera focused on him pulled back to reveal that he was standing exactly in the middle of the old Astrodome at the fifty-yard line. Standing behind him was his equally nerdy assistant, Mr. Finfer, who, reaching into his lab coat, pulled out a large grapefruit, which Mr. Science took and held aloft.

"Now, let's say this grapefruit represents our sun, and down there, way at the end of the field, is Earth going on its usual business of orbiting the sun."

As he spoke, he pointed downfield, where a Super Bowl–winning quarterback stood in full gear, grinning at the camera focused on him. He held up a small blue-green marble as if it were an Olympic torch and then took off at a slow run, trotting around the vast perimeter of the Astrodome playing field.

The demonstration was so low-tech it was nearly comical, but it resonated and would score a couple of hundred million hits online, at least while the internet was still working.

"So I'm out here holding up this grapefruit, which represents our sun, and our star quarterback is running circles around me holding up that blue-green marble, which is us, riding along in our yearly orbit."

And then the lesson took a bizarre turn, which, when seen for the first time, left most of his audience wide-eyed since it was so totally out of character for the Mr. Rogers–like scientist.

"Mr. Finfer, put on my blindfold, please," he said with a dramatic flourish.

Finfer reached into his bulging lab coat pocket, pulled out a white blindfold, stood on tiptoe, and did as ordered.

"Thank you, Mr. Finfer. I can't see a darn thing now, and so technically we could say this is now a test in random probability. Okay, Finfer, now give me my CME projection machine."

Finfer opened his lab coat and pulled out a truly massive .44-caliber Magnum pistol from a shoulder holster that had been concealed beneath his lab coat, a genuine-looking Dirty Harry revolver. He nervously placed it in his boss's outstretched hand and then bolted off the field at a run.

Blindfolded and randomly waving the pistol around, Mr. Science continued the lesson.

"Okay, let's say that each bullet in this rather heavy gun represents a CME, a coronal mass ejection. For our demonstration today, those .44-caliber steel-jacketed bullets are CMEs, a massive burst of energy and radiation exploding off the surface of the sun at a speed of a million miles per hour or more, from the sun I am holding over my head." He held the grapefruit straight up.

"Storms are exploding from the surface of the sun all the time, and some of those explosions are so big, they are tens of thousands of miles across when they blow. They are packing a huge punch of radiation, and gamma rays are the bad guys for us. CME storms blow up from the surface of the sun and go off in random directions nearly every day, but then, every once in a while, one comes toward our little blue marble that is orbiting around me."

A second camera offered a quick visual of the quarterback, who had already completed nearly one lap around the perimeter of the field, still holding the blue-green marble over his head.

"Now, we do have an armor shield around our blue marble, sort of like the helmet our quarterback is wearing. The helmet around Earth is called the magnetosphere. It's out there several thousand miles above us. Remember, Earth has a molten iron core that is magnetic; thus, our magnetic north and south poles are two poles of a vast magnetic field that engulfs and protects our planet from nearly all solar storms, which allows us to live."

He paused a moment for effect.

"Because without that magnetosphere, radiation from the sun would have killed us off long ago; in fact, life never would have even started here because of the continual stream of radiation from the sun and, every once in a while, something that could really be nasty—a massive solar flare event. But we're not dealing with that today, just a regular CME.

"Now, these CMEs are happening all the time. Most of them aren't all that powerful, at least as far as solar storms go. Let's say the smaller ones have as much power as a BB or spitball. Those happen nearly every day. The big ones, sort of like the .44-caliber steel-jacketed rounds inside this hand cannon I'm holding—which I've named my CME Projection Machine—happen infrequently but often enough to be a concern for us."

And he held the *massive* gun up for dramatic effect.

"Which direction do they go? Well, that is all random, and that is why I am wearing a blindfold—to ensure that this little demonstration and test of ours will be truly random. So we have CMEs blowing off the surface of the sun, most with the comparative power of a BB or a .22 round. No big deal with those. But then, every once in a while, you got a huge .44 Magnum erupting, and the big question then is, just where in the heck is it going? Sort of like this!"

Blindfold still covering his eyes, he swung the gun up and turned around a few times, the camera going shaky for a second and someone behind the camera yelling, "Duck!" Then he squeezed the trigger.

The .44 Magnum let off with a roar, nearly knocking Mr. Science off his feet. As the explosion echoed within the domed stadium, there was the sound of glass shattering, and a camera turned its focus to one of the high-priced skyboxes lining the upper balcony of the stadium.

Mr. Science turned, raised the corner of his blindfold, and looked at the camera focused on him.

"What'd I break?" he gasped dramatically.

"You blew out a skybox window," a voice replied from off camera.

"Oh, great. How much will that cost us?"

"A lot."

"Hey, Doc," said the quarterback, "you never told me that damn gun was loaded for real!"

"Listen up, Earth, just stay in orbit—no ducking or stopping. That's what you're being paid for. Okay? Now let's continue with the demonstration," Mr. Science announced, pulling his blindfold back into place then turning around several times.

He raised the gun again, pointed it at random, this time in the general direction of one of the goalposts, squeezed off a round, quickly turned and let off another, then leveled it straight across the field and fired off two more.

"Damn it, Doc, that last one was pretty close!" the quarterback cried as he continued to run around the perimeter, holding the marble over his head.

Lowering the gun and still blindfolded, Mr. Science turned his attention to where he thought the camera was located; the man and woman crew behind the camera were flat down on the ground.

"You folks okay?"

"Yeah, we're okay. Just nearly deaf, that's all."

"You'll be all right. So now that we've had our exciting demonstration, it's time to do a little math here, which is the whole point of our demonstration."

He continued to hold the gun straight up, still blindfolded.

"What really were the odds that just pointing the gun around randomly in this huge stadium that I would shoot the blue marble out of the upheld hand of our heroic quarterback who, Atlas-like, is carrying our world and all of us on it? Now what do you think the odds are? Well, actually, darn near zero for any given shot. Some astronomers ran the numbers years ago and calculated it'd be, at worst, one chance in fifty thousand or more that on any particular day we'd get hit by a major CME, given how big space is and how small Earth is out there orbiting around."

There was a quick cut to the quarterback, who was still running and looking nervously toward the gun-toting lecturer.

"Hey, no sweat—one in fifty thousand I was going to hit you, isn't that right, Earth?"

Again the quarterback forced a grin but did not reply while continuing to run, now crouching down low.

"But—and there is always a *but* with these kind of problems—let's stretch time out for 150 years or so and fire the gun once a day; that would be 365 times 150," his face contorted up again for a few seconds. "Oh, around fifty thousand or so shots. We run some more math about how much space Earth occupies relative to the potential trajectories of those big CMEs flying around, and sooner or later, one of them is gonna hit us square on.

"So"—he sighed—"you see where this is going."

He paused.

"Hey, Earth! I got a question for ya!" he shouted.

"Yeah, what is it?"

"Did I fire off five or six rounds?"

There was no reply.

"You didn't answer me. Was it five rounds or six that I fired?"

"I don't remember, Doc. Five? Six? I'm not sure!"

Mr. Science grinned sardonically. "Okay, Earth, just tell me this."

A pause.

"Earth, do you feel lucky today?" he shouted, giving a bad Clint Eastwood imitation. Mr. Science leveled the pistol and squeezed the trigger.

It had indeed been five, and now the sixth one exploded out of the barrel with a thunderous roar. The explosion echoed within the Astrodome, overlapping a loud cry of pain and muffled cursing.

The quarterback was down.

Mr. Science drew back his blindfold, tossed it, and motioned for the camera crew to stand back up. Facing the camera, he smiled.

"Okay, folks, that's what's happening to us right now. We estimate that about every 150 years or so, the sun blows off a massive flare, like that .44 Magnum round. Our odds of it missing have run out, and it will hit us straight on. That is what's going to happen to us in about two days or so. We're going to be hit by the most powerful CME to come our way in over a hundred years."

He paused for a second, blindfold off, handing the pistol back to Mr. Finfer.

"Okay, Earth. This time they were only blanks, you can stop over-acting and get up now!"

The quarterback stood up, marble held out in his right hand, and went up to stand by Mr. Science's side.

"Don't worry, folks, everyone was wearing ear protection, and we just rigged that broken window up for some dramatic effect. Now back to our lesson for today. You now know how the odds of being hit by a CME work, but what happens when a CME actually does hit our planet moving at a speed of over a million miles per hour? Mr. Finfer?"

"Over here, sir." Finfer was shown coming up from behind a goal-post, where he had been cowering.

"Bring the balloon. So a CME blows off the surface of the sun. NASA has several new satellites named *Helios I, II,* and *III.* They're orbiting the sun from less than ten million miles above its surface, monitoring the weather on the sun 24-7 to warn us of just this kind of event.

"Late yesterday, we got a warning from *Helios II* that a CME, level five at minimum, more likely level six—it's the same way we measure tornadoes and hurricanes—had exploded from the surface of the sun and is coming straight at us. It will hit our magnetosphere in about forty-eight hours."

He took the balloon from his assistant, held it in his left hand, and then with right forefinger pushed in hard. The balloon quickly distorted and looked as if it was about to burst.

"So my finger represents that storm; it hits our magnetosphere, which is this balloon. The small ones barely dent it, but the one coming now can distort it so much that some of the energy, the gamma rays inside that invisible but potent CME, pushes right through our protective bar-rier and hits Earth's surface. It has been doing that every hundred to two hundred years or so since this planet first was formed billions of years ago. Never really bothered the dinosaurs—or us, for that matter. But then, back in the last half of the nineteenth century, something dramatic happened that changed everything and why we are now worried about this one. Geniuses with names like Edison, Tesla, and Westinghouse transformed our entire world. They harnessed the power of electricity and developed the means to generate it, move it, and power the vast, complex technological world we live in today.

"The downside for us at this moment is that nearly all of that system is susceptible to the overload of energy from a CME. If enough energy breaks through our magnetosphere and reaches Earth's surface, it can feed into all the millions of miles of wires that distribute electricity coming from thousands of generating plants around the world. And then? Just like a lightning bolt hitting the power line to your house, blowing out your brand-new eighty-inch high-def TV and every computer-driven component in your house, the CME can do the same thing globally. Its energy will hit millions of miles of power lines and surge through those lines in the blink of an eye, feeding into tens of thousands of high-energy transformers and from there into power plants, overloading them, and then *boom*. Our power grid is blown off-line.

"Now, add in something else that we've only had for several decades but has become part of our everyday lives in ways we are no longer even aware of—the internet. Nearly everything today is computer driven, and nearly all of that is hooked into the internet. So does that mean this is the end of everything as some overwrought people are screaming today?"

He shook his head for emphasis.

"Absolutely not. There are ways to limit that damage if we act together and we do so swiftly over the next two days before the CME hits our magnetosphere. What we have to do as a nation, in fact an entire modern world, is to do the same thing any prudent person would do if a huge thunderstorm was coming straight at their house. Go outside and pull the circuit leading into your home.

"Starting with each of you, we'll be broadcasting information how to shut down all electricity in your house and at what time you should do so just before the storm starts to hit. You will then, as well, pull the plug on every computerized component in your home. Beyond your own home or apartment, this is going to be a nationwide and global response. The best way to protect our electrical grid around the world and the internet is to turn off or at least power down every electrical component from inside where you live on up to the massive gigawatt power plants lighting up New York and Vegas. We have to power nearly everything down before the storm hits and then wait for it to pass. That is what we will start to do globally tomorrow if it looks like this storm will be as intense as NASA is telling us.

"That doesn't mean everything will be shut down. Fortunately, some of our electrical and computer systems are hardened against this type of thing, such as our military and crucial roles done by our government."

He paused again for dramatic effect and then sighed. "Yes, that includes the IRS, folks. They're going to get through it. Sorry."

That at least broke the tension a bit, the crew behind the camera chuckling.

"In an hour or so, our president will give us the details. I talked with him earlier today when he called me and asked if I could whip up a quick demonstration of what is happening. I was told it was okay to spill what he is going to talk about."

Again a pause, and his usual Mr. Rogers demeanor changed to one of absolute seriousness.

"There are already a lot of rumors out there, and I'm asking you now to listen and lighten up a bit. No, there will be no federal declaration of martial law, so let's kill that conspiracy theory right now. Okay? Local and state governments will retain the power to do that if some stupid people start getting out of hand and think this means a holiday from law and decent order.

"Folks, please cut out the panic buying of food we're hearing about. Just ensure you and your family and neighbors have enough to see you through for five days or so. Those in dire need can go to emergency facilities and shelters that your local governments will announce. Those of you freezing up north right now, hole up with neighbors and friends who have woodstoves, or again, local governments will have emergency centers. Hospitals are prepared for this, and if they don't already have hardened backup generators, the military is scrambling even now to help supply them.

"All airline traffic around the world starting at midnight tomorrow Greenwich mean time will be grounded. Rail traffic in America will stop at the same time. Get to your homes or where you can be safe and stay off the roads. Some people estimate that electric cars, hybrids, and even late-model cars might get shorted out due to all the computerized components in them, but we don't have an accurate read on that, so best bet is to play it safe. Store your car, and either do it yourself or get someone who understands what's under the hood and disconnect various electrical power lines.

"And finally, our government has been in contact with countries around the world—our friends and even some not so friendly. All have agreed to posture their military to defensive moves only. The United States, Russia, China, and NATO are in full agreement to keep careful watch, so again, let's all just stay calm."

He paused again for a moment.

"So that's about it for now. Depending on how intense this storm will prove to be—and we're not sure yet—power companies might shut their systems off completely. If not so intense, they will manage with lowering the power supply and then doing rolling blackouts so that at least you'll have electricity for several hours a day. Each power company will be releasing details as to possible shutdowns and what to do before, during, and after the shutdown over the next day or so. Now that's just about it," he said and then fell back into his Mr. Rogers voice for a moment.

"Any questions out there?" A pause, a smile, and a friendly nod. "Okay, that's it for today. See you in a week or so, I promise."

He looked over to the quarterback, who stepped closer to the camera and held up the blue-green marble.

"We're all in this together, folks. And maybe this is a good time to set aside some differences and work together. This might be a bit rough for all of us, but keep cool, help those who need help, and put some trust in your local governments. Don't let this turn into some kind of stupid sci-fi apocalypse behavior. Let's be decent neighbors, and we'll get through this just fine."

And then there was a bit of a reassuring smile.

"I'll see all of you at the Super Bowl in eight weeks, okay?" Mr. Science stage-whispered to finish the program on a lighter note, "Should I bet on your team getting there and winning?"

"What do you think?" was the reply, and then the program ended.

3

THAT broadcast had been nearly a month earlier and ran almost continuously on all networks and internet sources before the December 1 event hit. It had helped a lot with explaining to the public what was about to happen, and though there was some panic buying, especially in cities, most of the country and the rest of the world weathered it okay, the way people usually did when hit by hurricane, flood, and earthquake. Some went out of control, but most did what they usually did—took care of their families and helped others.

Most of the internet was still off, impacting financial systems, especially in a world where nearly all money transfer, right down to buying a burger and fries, was now done electronically. It was being reported that things were bad up north, especially places like Chicago, Detroit, and Cleveland, which were now experiencing one of the coldest winters in a decade or more.

For Darren, it still wasn't all that bad yet. Southern Missouri was cold but nothing like Chicago. For reasons that he kind of understood, the closer one got to the magnetic north or south pole, the more intense the impact on the electrical grid, so therefore they had only rolling blackouts there. To make sure he still got to work on time, he used an antique alarm clock rather than the soft music from his darkened cell phone.

A few radio stations were on, mostly local news and information bulletins and then what sounded a bit fishy to him, including a press statement from a NASA official confirming that a CME had exploded from the surface of the sun shortly after midnight eastern time and was forecast to hit at approximately noon eastern time in another two days. As with the prior storm, the same procedures would be followed yet again: global airline travel would be grounded come midnight London time tonight; twenty-four hours prior to impact, electric companies would start powering down; dusk-to-dawn curfews would be put in place at the discretion of state and local authorities; and then all the usual recommendations followed.

Even though this one might strike with greater intensity, it was as if the December 1 event had served as a drill, and there was no undertone of panic as with the last event, though how things were going in northern cities would certainly be made worse by this second blow.

What was troubling for Darren as he listened to the broadcast while driving to work was how the press briefing from Goddard Space Flight Center had ended when a question was thrown at the official.

"We're hearing rumors about another storm, not the one you just briefed us on. I'm asking about something named Sauron's Eye. Can we have a clarification about this?"

There was silence for several seconds, and Darren, wondering if he had lost the signal, turned the volume up.

"Ah yes, we are monitoring that situation, but our focus for now is on what we are calling *CME Two*. For now, there is no comment, and I wish to assure you there is nothing to worry about. Thank you."

The question was shouted again, this time by several reporters, and the program ended with "It is nothing to worry about for the moment, and I have no further comment," then went dead.

There is nothing to worry about. That rubbed Darren the wrong way. Maybe it was just a trigger phrase for him and the memory of the Bobby McFerrin song that he'd learned to hate, "Don't Worry, Be Happy." During the fight for Fallujah, one of his buddies played the damn thing over and over as a wonderful satirical statement on the insanity of their entire situation. It became a bit of a mantra for his unit when someone bitched about the situation they were in, and a reply would be shouted back, "Don't worry, be happy!" It was a joke until his buddy who had first used the line took one in the head from a sniper and was dead before his body even hit the ground.

As if reading his mind, the station he was listening to started playing that damn song, and he quickly switched it off, finding an FM station of easy-listening music, Sinatra's "Fly Me to the Moon."

Don't worry, be happy . . .

Darren took the exit from Route 64 onto Haywood Street, drove a quarter mile past the turnoff to the usual highway complex of a Hyatt, McDonald's, and gas station—which was closed, having run out of fuel last week—and then a right turn onto Limestone Avenue. He crossed over the double set of railroad tracks, and his workplace was straight ahead.

The weed-choked parking lot for when this place employed a couple of thousand in the quarry was of course empty. Straight ahead, the road passed through an outer perimeter of ten-foot-high chain-link fence, then a hundred feet farther on stopped, facing a vertical wall of limestone nearly fifty feet high, and, to left and right, finally curved around from view. On the left side that vertical wall flanked a massive hole carved into the earth, dropping off a couple of hundred feet. This had all been part of a quarry operation that had shut down more than thirty years earlier and now served another purpose.

He drove up to the outer perimeter fence to a gate that was supposed to be locked but was not, and it bothered him.

The excuse would be that the numerical keypad, which required a six-digit code to open, had shorted out in the first storm. Therefore, it meant you either had to post someone out there 24-7 to check IDs and manually open it or simply just leave it open. His midnight shift, which these last few weeks was down to but one person, had chosen yet again to not worry about the open gate. It meant yet another ass chewing, though frankly, down deep, he couldn't blame them. Certainly, the place needed security; when he had taken the job, he found out that he would be responsible not just for what was on the other side of heavy steel doors that were straight ahead but for what was reportedly tens of millions of dollars' worth of emergency supplies belonging to the state of Missouri.

He drove on through, got out of his jeep, walked back, and dragged the gate shut. The one man on duty, a young guy recently hired, came out from the security booth in front of the second inner steel door gate, pulling on a heavy parka.

"Sorry, sir!" he cried. "The director just came through and kicked up a bit of a fuss that it was closed and he didn't want to get out of his car. I ran out to let him in, and, well . . ."

"Yeah, okay, Tyrell, I know; this is the time of day if people are going to show up for work, they show up for work, and it's a pain in the ass to keep running in and out while the keypad is down."

"Something like that, sir."

Today, Tyrell was the only one. Most of his team members were having a hard time finding gas to get to work, and besides, those who did have gas—which, on the black market, was reportedly going for twenty bucks a gallon—could not see the sense of using it to commute to a fifteen-dollar-an-hour job as a night watchman. Young Tyrell at least lived within walking distance.

"You got a coffeepot in there that still works?" Darren nodded to the security booth.

"No, sir. We got power but ran out of the K-Cups yesterday."

"I've got some extras at home; I'll bring them in tomorrow."

"Thanks!"

"On one condition: tomorrow, I see you out by the gate, freezing your ass off, opening and closing it."

"Yes, sir."

"You make that mistake again, it's no coffee. Do you understand me?"

"Yes, sir."

The poor kid was obviously freezing and at least had stuck to his post in a small wood-frame booth that was no longer even heated.

"Go get your cup, son."

Tyrell went into the booth and returned holding a Styrofoam cup that had been used and reused. Darren took the cup, opened the heavy quart thermos Darla had filled for him before he'd headed out, filled the cup up, and handed it back.

"Thanks, boss."

"It's Darren, remember? *Sir* in front of folks like the director of this place and his assistant, but with the rest of us, it's *Darren,* okay? Not *boss.*"

He had always hated the term *boss.* As a kid, even though segregation days had died well over a decade before, it bothered him to see elderly black men still calling white men a third their age *boss.* Coming from Tyrell, a darn smart kid with a college degree in elementary education working as a security guard until a teaching job turned up, it just hit him the wrong way.

Tyrell smiled and nodded.

"Now open the main gate for me, at least."

Tyrell went back into the booth, carefully put down the brimming cup of coffee, walked over to the main gate, opened a gray circuit box to the side of what looked like a solid wall of steel, and flipped a lever.

Like the outer gate, the keypad system was shot, and they were relying now on the backup system to power the unit.

Darren sat back. Even though he had been doing this job for nearly a year, he still got a kick out of the gate opening.

The gate wasn't just any kind of gate; it was a heavy door of solid steel, with a clearance of sixteen feet and wide enough for two 18-wheelers to pass each other. As it opened, the steel door split down the middle into left and right halves that slowly rolled back into recesses. No matter how many times he watched it open, it always felt that it was like something he'd expect to see in a movie about NORAD—or better yet, the entryway into the lair of Dr. Evil. The only things missing were a handful of guards, clad all in black, faces concealed, weapons poised and shouting for him to show his ID.

Of course there was nothing like that. The state had installed the doors when they'd acquired several hundred thousand square feet of storage area inside. The arrangement struck him as a bit of overkill, but it at least offered some entertainment value for him whenever he arrived at work. The door parted to reveal a paved, wide, two-lane road carved straight into the limestone hillside. Directly ahead, he could see a gently sloping road going down into what had been, until thirty years ago, a massive underground limestone-quarrying operation. When open-cut mining had fallen into disfavor, the firm owning this rich source of high-grade limestone sought by builders around the country had simply tunneled into the hillside instead. After carving a two-lane road down a hundred feet deep to the rich layers they wanted, the miners began hollowing out the entire mountain, fueling the economy of Springfield, Missouri, part of which rested above the vast caverns.

When the veins of high-grade limestone finally played out, the operation folded up, with hundreds of jobs lost. Springfield was stuck with an abandoned, hollowed-out mountain, jobs gone, until a few investors came up with a brilliant idea.

Darren slipped his jeep out of neutral and drove through the steel-clad doorway. Directly overhead was a sign suspended from the ceiling, brightly illuminated:

WELCOME TO UNDERGROUND SPRINGFIELD INC.
Visitors Please Check In at the Security Office

The bright idea of the investors? An abandoned underground quarry of two and a half million square feet would make one hell of a good warehouse. Temperature a constant fifty-eight degrees, no bills for cooling in the summer when the world above was boiling at a hundred degrees or heating cost when the world above was freezing like today. No snow, no rain, no wind, and definitely no tornadoes. An abandoned limestone quarry had been turned into a gold mine.

The road sloped down at a gentle 3 percent grade until it reached the first galley a hundred feet down, illuminated by dimly glowing fluorescent lights. At least the backup power source to this place had been untouched by the CME.

Back when it was a quarry, the owners had decided to put in their own power source, and the new owners simply upgraded it.

That decision on somebody's part decades ago, based then on the fact that it would not be pleasant to be underground if all the power was blown out by a storm, was paying off now.

When the state of Missouri purchased over two hundred thousand square feet for "storage," as it was claimed, additional propane-fired generators had been added in for reasons they weren't supposed to discuss. The very visible touch signifying there was something important stored in the vast underground was the changing of the single main entry door of flimsy aluminum with the heavy steel barrier the state had paid a lot of money for.

As head of security for this facility, Darren had a good idea what it was all about, but that part of the cavern owned by the state, which was down a side tunnel, had been sealed off and locked. Once a year, a team from Jefferson City would show up, civilians along with a general and staff from the National Guard. They would go through the ritual of showing him their stamped papers for access, head off to the side tunnel for a day or two of "inventory check," then lock it back up. It was made clear to him that security was his ultimate responsibility, but it was never discussed what exactly he was securing.

Rumors, of course, ran riot. Local news outlets even tried to gain access but were turned away politely and told that it was simply emergency supplies in case of a major storm or natural disaster; they were forbidden to enter. Part of Darren's job was to ensure things stayed that way. Just before the December 1 storm hit, the team had shown up for an unscheduled survey and made some general comments about maybe needing to pull out some of the supplies, but then never followed through with that and just sealed the tunnel up and left.

The state of Missouri was only one of a number of clients within the Underground. The rest, several dozen of them, were farther down inside the mountain. Kraft Foods used two hundred thousand square feet as their primary warehousing and distribution center for a three-state region. It was an ideal distribution location for markets as far east as Saint Louis, northwest to Kansas City, Wichita to the west, and Oklahoma City to the southwest, all linked in by two interstate highways. The running joke was that if the entryway ever collapsed, everyone trapped inside could survive for years on all the Cheez Whiz, Velveeta, and Oscar Mayer wieners stored there.

There were several score other firms, from medical suppliers to auto parts wholesalers and a warehouse for a major furniture distributor to even just plain old traditional office spaces for a couple of dozen smaller firms. The first side tunnel to the right, which he was now turning in to after driving a hundred yards, was where his office was located in a large carved-out area, complete with parking spaces, and adjacent to the office trailer, there were a couple of restaurants, a convenience store, and even a pizza joint to feed the hundreds that came here every day to work.

The office for managing the facility was simply a double-wide trailer, his parking spot marked *Brooks—chief of security*, where he parked and got out, making sure not to forget his thermos.

After the frigid chill and wind blowing just a few hundred yards back beyond the steel gate, the fifty-eight-degree weather inside was absolutely balmy, like a beautiful spring day. He unzipped his jacket and walked into the administrative center, wondering what awaited him today, the worries of the outside forgotten for the moment.

4

DR. RICHARD Christopher Carrington V jiggled the mouse on his desk, drawing a circle on the main screen in the conference room around what appeared to be a black hole on the surface of the sun, edged with swirling arcs of red-hot plumes of fire.

"This is the origin point of the CME that will hit our magnetosphere in approximately forty-eight hours."

He clicked the mouse a couple of times, the image dropping down in magnification, pulling back from close focus on the sunspot until the one hundred–inch 8K screen was filled with the fiery orb of the entire sun.

He then shifted the mouse and drew another circle around what at first appeared to be a secondary sunspot, just over ten degrees to the left of center, of the sunspot from which the CME had blown nine hours earlier. The second was a tight, pulsing, spiraling circle that had been expanding rapidly over the previous twenty-four hours. Opening up wide, pulsing, closing in, almost like the iris of an eye when adjusting to light and darkness. It did have the vague appearance of a human eye, and over the last day, Richard had casually referred to it as looking like Sauron's Eye from *The Lord of the Rings*. The name had stuck, and somehow usage had drifted through the rumor mill of Goddard into the lexicon of the media over the last twenty-four hours.

"So that's it, the second one," Richard said softly, zooming in until it filled the entire screen and appeared to be gazing malevolently at them.

"Richard, you stand by your analysis?" He could hear the tightness in the voice of Judith Cooper, assistant director of Goddard.

"Look at the screen to the right," Richard replied, nodding toward a secondary monitor beside the main one, a stream of data scrolling down, smaller images posted to the side of Sauron's Eye as seen in different wavelengths from ultraviolet to an enhanced visual in green of X-ray bursts emanating from the anomaly. Then a click of his mouse brought the image up on the monitor to the left of the main screen, this one showing proton bursts pulsing out of the center of the "eye."

Judith was silent as were the dozen or more gathered in the Helio Observation Center, which was Richard Carrington's domain.

Another burst exploded, the high-energy level of it overloading the monitor and causing it to white out, the image in visible light range displayed on the center screen breaking up for several seconds and then stabilizing again.

Richard glanced over his shoulder at the tech team who were responsible for the hardware aboard *Helio II*, which was orbiting the sun from ten million miles out, along with its siblings, *Helios I* and *III*, placed into solar orbit a year back to get a closer view of the sun for just this kind of event.

Don Jamison, head of that tech team, shrugged and offered an attempt at a reassuring smile. "It can handle the overloads; we factored that in," he said casually, "and I stand by the data our instrumentation is reading down there. We've run full analysis checks, five times over the last day as you requested, and all come up identical."

"We lose *Helio II*, we lose our primary monitoring," Judith interjected.

"It'll hold up," Jamison replied, now sounding a bit insulted by her concern. He had worked on the instrumentation package for twelve years, having endured a budget cut from a previous administration that had gutted NASA and delayed deployment of the solar observatories for five years. Fortunately, the current president's push for increased spending had finally seen "his" system launched, enabling Richard and the Helio Observation Center to be at the forward edge of solar analysis— an analysis that had left him sleepless for the last two days.

Richard turned to look back at the three monitors, clicking and adjusting the view, shifting through several visual displays before again dialing up a visual for proton ejections.

Judith turned away from the screen.

"Our friends with the EU, Russia, and China?" she asked.

"They're on it as well. I just got off a conference call before asking you to come down here, Judith." He sighed and took off his glasses. "This is not another potential CME as was being reported earlier this week. We are definitely looking at a major proton event, a full-blown solar flare, and they agree. We're allowing them access to our data feed, and they are coming up with the same answer."

Judith looked around the others gathered in the room, the four other members of Richard's Helio Observation Center, the tech team responsible for the hardware on the *Helio* satellites, and Goddard's head of public information.

"Before we take another step," Judith replied, "I want all of you to take another look at the data coming in on this Sauron thing. We've got to get it right before taking another step."

"Judith, I've been monitoring it ever since the energy levels started shifting three days ago. The numbers don't lie, and I've already gone over it with Don and his team repeatedly; it is not a malfunction in the hardware on *Helio* or our software down here. What you are looking at is the harsh reality we have to face and make public. Space.com was posting the data until they were shut off from the flow early this morning, and more than a few out in the public sector who looked at that data are already running about and broadcasting their analysis."

Judith glanced over at the head of public information, who firmly shook his head.

"And set off a panic? No way," was the sharp reply.

"It's already leaking." Judith sighed. "We got hit with that at the press briefing this morning. A lot of folks, at least those who still have some kind of internet, are tapping into our data. At least up until now, public attention was focused on the CME, but in the last few hours, as you know, all our offices are getting flooded with queries about this Sauron thing."

Richard leaned back in his chair and waited for their responses.

One of the interns for the center, without prompting, went to the coffee machine and put a cup in for Earl Grey. Coffee was all but gone, but there were still plenty of K-Cups for tea in the room. A minute later, he brought the Styrofoam cup over to Richard, who nodded his thanks and took a sip.

"At least you Brits still have your drink," someone said, but Richard ignored the comment while listening to the arguments breaking out.

"So what do we call this?" someone asked from the back of the room. "Sauron's Eye? Conjures up fantasy and lacks gravitas given what that bastard might do to us. How about the Mega-Carrington Event?"

Richard turned in his chair, putting his glasses back on, the room going silent. Those who worked directly with him knew that he was proud of his illustrious ancestor whose name had been carried on across more than a century and a half down to him. But with the twin CMEs of this month, the name *Carrington* had taken on something of a sinister meaning for the general public. Several days earlier, some wag had even posted a picture of him titled "Dr. Doomsday" on the door into the center. If this damn thing unfolded as he feared, the last thing he wanted was for history—if there continued to be a history—to remember it with his name.

Richard Christopher Carrington V was indeed the namesake of his famed great-great-grandfather, at least famed in the small realm of solar astronomers. It was his ancestor who, back in 1859, pioneered the practice of using the new technology of photography and applied it to taking images of the sun. He was the first to photograph sunspots and an image of an explosion bursting off the surface of the sun, a solar storm eruption.

The sunspots that his illustrious ancestor had observed were so significant and pronounced that on a September morning of 1859, in London, when the atmosphere was thick with smoke—or what would one day be called *smog* and *air pollution*—it allowed one to look directly at the sun. What thousands in London saw that day, and which the first Richard Carrington had photographed, were visible with the naked eye as dark splotches on the surface of the sun. Later that day, an extra edition of the London *Times* reported on the phenomena and proclaimed, with all due proper respect, that even the Queen had seen them. Of course it had to be true, for never would *The Times* call into doubt the word of the Queen herself.

Across the next several days, Richard Christopher Carrington Sr. kept observing them. But it was what happened three days after the storm erupted from the sun's surface that there was a true connect-the-dots moment with the realization that beyond just warmth and light, the sun could have other impacts on Earth as well.

In 1859, there were two other new technologies transforming the world and driving the great Industrial Revolution of the nineteenth century: telegraphy and railroads. Three days after Carrington photographed and witnessed an explosion bursting off the surface of the sun, telegraph stations in Europe and American started blowing off-line, several of them spontaneously bursting into flames.

The telegraphy system of the day was powered by massive and extremely primitive batteries, with signals transmitted over copper wires. Telegraphers started reporting strange interferences on their systems and sparks shooting out of telegraph keys; some stations experienced their batteries overloading and bursting into flames while wires linking the stations smoldered, sagged, and then just melted off the poles.

The intensity of what was happening was demonstrated as well by railroads. Wooden railroad ties bolted to the iron rails cooked as well, smoke rising from them and even bursting into flames. Curious onlookers incautious enough to touch the rails reported they were hot; the onlookers even burned their fingers as if touching the surface of a hot stove. Others reported a strange tingling and in some cases outright electrical shocks. Anything with a long stretch of metal, especially something as highly conductive to electricity as copper, emitted crackling sounds, sparks, and even flames.

It was astronomer Richard Carrington Sr. who was the first to explain it as a storm exploding from the surface of the sun with an electrical influence that could impact Earth several days later and that conductive surfaces on Earth were absorbing that energy. Another ef-

fect that was now understood as to causality was the concurrent eruption of the aurora borealis. A common enough sight over northern
Scotland, Scandinavia, and Iceland, the northern lights ignited across
the night sky of London and over every major city in Europe, with reports
eventually coming in that it had been witnessed as far south as Florida
and the Caribbean islands.

The spectacle had proven to be a once-in-a-lifetime experience for
tens of millions, so intense that *The Times* reported one could read a
newspaper by the light emanating from the surreal event. More than a
few priests and ministers thundered forth from their pulpits come the
following Sunday that it was indeed a portent of the end of times.

To the relief of most and the always present disappointment of a few,
the world had not ended in that September of 1859. When Carrington Sr.
was asked why no one had ever linked storms on the surface of the sun
to the spectacular solar event and the strange electrical disturbances, he
pointed out with some pride of course that photographing and recording what happened on the surface of the sun was a new science; in
fact, he was at that time one of the few practitioners in the world doing
it. Second, objects made of long stretches of conductive metal were all
but nonexistent even fifty years earlier, and it required such long surfaces to absorb enough of the energy from the storm on the sun's
surface to cause them to melt or catch on fire. And finally, with a well-
deserved touch of pride, he was the one who put the two together and
came up with the answer.

But the next question was the really troubling one. When would it
happen again, and could it even be more intense? And there was no
answer . . . yet.

The first Carrington pointed out that to actually have a statistic that
could answer that question required accurate and detailed observation
of more than one event—in fact, observations of dozens of such events
across years, more likely decades or even centuries—before any kind of
predictions could be made.

The years passed, the incident all but forgotten while telegraphy companies quickly replaced the melted wires and overloaded batteries, and
the business of business continued on. Railroad companies pulled out

the burned ties and replaced them, and within days, trains were back on schedule. The nineteenth-century technological infrastructure, primitive as it was, had been damaged, but not all that seriously.

Carrington, who for a few days had been the focus of so much attention, had what would later be called his fifteen minutes of fame with the new media of daily newspapers linked together by telegraphy and railroads, and within weeks, the whole thing was pretty well forgotten. Back to his solitary pursuits, Carrington Sr. spent the rest of his life watching and photographing the sun. As the years passed, a few others picked up his work. Some observatories dedicated solely to watching the sun were built, though nothing much exciting happened, and the technological revolution rolled along.

Single strands of telegraphy lines soon had more wires joining them on the poles. Before the century was out, hundreds, then millions, and then tens of millions of miles of telegraphy, telephone, and electrical wiring were put in place.

There were solar storms, to be certain, observed nearly every day, but rare was one that went straight at Earth. It was found that electrical systems closer to the magnetic poles in higher latitudes were more susceptible to power fluctuations from solar activity than their neighbors farther south.

A fairly big one hit early in the twentieth century; there were some disruptions and wires melted and a few weeks of press excitement, then it was back to business. Another big one impacted Quebec in the 1980s and took the grid of eastern Canada down for a few days. There was some concern and excitement, but then it was business as usual, stringing yet more wires. By the late 1980s, small computer relays called SCADAS were being added to control and direct the electrical infrastructure, taking over tasks that once had to be done manually. SCADAS by the tens of millions were soon replacing people whose jobs used to be manually opening and closing valves, switches, relays, and vents; all were now directed by computers. All the SCADAS being installed at first were highly susceptible to a sudden electrical surges, such as those generated by a solar storm, a coronal mass ejection.

Carrington? His name would crop up occasionally, especially from the keyboards of what most people said were overwrought sci-fi writers, and the name had even been linked to describe what one author called an "electrical Armageddon," or a "Carrington-level event," a CLE.

For Richard Christopher Carrington V, it was all part of his family history. He learned about his illustrious ancestor as a boy growing up near Greenwich, England, emphasized when his father had taken young Richard to Greenwich for an event honoring the hundredth anniversary of his ancestor's passing.

The director of the observatory was captivated by the wide-eyed enthusiasm of an eight-year-old boy named for a distinguished ancestor (at least as far as the solar astronomy community went), and Richard soon became something of a regular companion and student of that mentor. The young boy soon gained the affectionate title of "Richard V" as those on that storied campus came to call him. By the time Richard was twelve, his career choice was set.

After earning his Ph.D. in astrophysics at MIT with a specialization in solar astronomy—of course—rather than return to England where research opportunities were limited at that time, he had first taken a teaching position for several years at Purdue, then a fellowship to the solar observatory at Kitt Peak in Arizona. NASA finally snapped him up to help oversee the instrumentation development for the *Helios* series of satellites and management of their solar observatory facility at Goddard. Along the way, there had been a loving marriage that heartbreakingly ended far too early because of cancer—a marriage which, however, did leave him a son and grandsons to carry on the name.

Since the death of his wife, Margaret, Goddard had nearly become his full-time home. Many were the nights that cleaning staff would run into his short, rotund form shuffling down the hall, wearing carpet slippers. His physical appearance combined with a pronounced London accent resulted in some claiming he bore a resemblance to Winston Churchill, which to him was, of course, a compliment. But rather than a cigar, his treks outside at all hours of the day and night were to sneak a quick smoke with his pipe and then to shuffle back inside to sometimes be found by members of his team, asleep on a cot in his small private office at the back of the Helio Center.

As he waited for the assistant director's response, he was filled with a craving for such a smoke and a good shot of scotch in his tea. She remained silent, just standing before the wide-screen monitor, quietly asking for shifts in data across the spectrum and then a comparison of energy output from previous days up to the most current read.

She studied the screen for several minutes until there was another surge of high-level X-rays that when displayed as visible green light by the computer was a near-blinding flash that lasted for several seconds.

"Those bursts are two full magnitudes higher than what we were seeing only twenty-four hours ago," Richard announced softly, "so you know where I am going with this if it continues to increase energy output at the same rate. The incredible gravity of the sun, up until now, has been bending it back, containing it. But if energy levels continue to increase at the same rate . . ."

He fell silent as Judith turned away from the screen, nodded to him, then took out her cell phone—one for official use only inside the facility, of course—and made a call.

"Franklin, this is Judith. You got an hour right now?" A pause. "Cancel it; I think it is important you come down to the Helio Center right now. Yes it is and you need to see it. Thank you sir."

She turned away and looked at the group standing behind Richard.

"The director will be here in five minutes. Get your data and interpretations of that data ready, and let's not go off half-cocked."

Several looked at Richard, shaking their heads. Goddard, like all research facilities, had gathered into its bosom several distinct personality types. There were the hard-core conservatives whose response was nearly always: "We need more research," unless the data on something had been replicated half a dozen times. There were a few others, upon whom the public relations office had to keep a close rein, who might publicly blurt out something fantastic that the media would of course jump on, such as that a planet identical to Earth had just been found and there seemed to be a radio source in that same solar system, or a more recent flap when a rock that the latest Mars unmanned explorer had stumbled on really did look like a fossil.

Richard fell into neither category, but he was the type that would stick his neck out with an interpretation of data that seemed like a leap at the time, though, after forging the way, others would prove the validity of his thesis.

He did take Judith's advice, scanning through several pages he had printed out. An intern popped another K-Cup into their machine—at least there was no shortage yet of Earl Grey—and Richard nodded his thanks when a steaming cup was handed to him. It was, of course, a bit of a British affectation.

He used to smoke a pipe in the office as well until the tobacco police banned smoking not only inside buildings but across the entire Goddard campus and inside any vehicle on the campus. The "lepers," as they called themselves—and Richard was one of the ringleaders—knew little culs-de-sac and well-hidden places where one could sneak a smoke, and his colleagues in the Helio Center, deferring to his seniority, did not comment about the scent of pipe tobacco clinging to him when he returned from "just a quick stroll."

Whenever there was some significant solar activity at a level that might affect satellites, the space station, or the private ventures trying to establish manned bases on the moon and Mars—all of which could be highly susceptible to a major solar storm—the center was manned 24-7 until the event had passed. Of course, over the last couple of months, ever since this surprise surge in solar activity starting with the December 1 event and now a second, even larger CME due to arrive in little more than two days, the Helio Center had been a beehive of activity.

There was a bit of nervous small talk as the minutes ticked by, all eyes glued on the monitors. Another burst, a high-energy release of X-rays, caused another flash when the computer displayed it as a visual while the overall energy output of the anomaly continued to tick upward. Long, twisting coils of plasma soared up tens of thousands of miles in a demonic-like dance of fire and then arced back down as the immense gravity of the sun pulled them back, even as another explosion soared upward, each high-energy spiral capable of engulfing a hundred Earths.

The door to the Helio Center swung open, and there was a slight rush of outflowing air. Any of the rooms that had arrays of high-end computers and/or sensitive equipment in their offices had extra filtration systems built into their ventilation and were slightly overpressured—not enough to pop ears but enough to keep ambient dust from entering from the corridors.

The director of Goddard, Dr. Franklin Massey—followed by a nameless but ever-present assistant, a young man from public relations—entered the room. Massey definitely had a photogenic presence with thick, well-groomed gray hair, bushy eyebrows, a face that usually appeared to be deeply tanned, and a body still narrow, trim, and ramrod straight.

He had been an astronaut back in the days of the shuttle, with three ventures into space as a mission specialist, one of them for a three-month rotation on what was then the new International Space Station, only to be grounded when the ever-hovering flight doctors picked up persistent high blood pressure while preparing for his fourth mission. He had been forced to take a desk job. Being a grounded astronaut with a Ph.D. in astrophysics put him into a far higher stratum in the world of NASA, which propelled him to eventual head of Goddard and a regular television presence, a function that had been overloading him this last month.

There were friendly enough nods, a few polite exchanges of hellos. Richard had found that Massey was usually an approachable enough leader. He had a good management style of trying to get out of his office for at least an hour a day, picking one of the buildings on the campus and just wandering around, saying hello, asking how things were going, anything he could help with and showing genuine interest. Over the last month, he had been personally dropping by the Helio Center nearly every day.

Now in his sixties and still holding the appearance of someone who put in the obligatory half hour a day at the gym, he had changed profoundly in the last month since the first CME had blown and the realization that one far stronger was developing. As he entered the room, Richard was surprised by Franklin's features, which were pale, eyes red rimmed, shoulders slumped from exhaustion.

Washington-based media had been showing up frequently since the CMEs started—Goddard, of course, being the closest and most accessible NASA center for them—and Franklin, with an excellent camera presence, was the man they wanted to interview. But with the obvious exhaustion he was now suffering from, it was being advised that he not appear on camera, this morning's briefing being handed off to one of the staff in public relations.

Franklin looked around the room, nodded a greeting, shook several hands, and then approached Judith.

"Judith, what have we got here that is so important?"

"Take a look at this, sir." She pointed to the screen.

"This latest CME?" Franklin asked wearily. He sighed. "If that is what you called me down here for, Judith, I'm sorry, but I've got to get back to my office. I might have to go to the White House in a few hours."

There was a rare note of anger his voice over the fact that he had been dragged out for something that was obvious anyhow, another CME, a magnitude more powerful than the December 1 event.

"No, sir."

"You mean this Sauron's Eye thing?" he replied cautiously as he quickly glanced at the screen displaying the latest data. "The press secretary at the White House was chewing my ear about it just before you called, saying they're getting some rumors from the NSA about what the Chinese and Russians are whispering among themselves. So give me the update if that is why you called me in here."

Without further comment, Franklin pulled a chair back from the desk next to Richard's, sat down with a sigh, then looked over at Richard and at least offered a wan smile. "How are you doing, Richard?" he asked.

"Not good, sir."

He looked away from Richard and turned to those standing behind him. "I would have been down here even if you had not called. I'm suddenly getting overloaded and needed to escape from the office and get a personal update," Franklin announced. "Besides the White House, I'm getting swamped with calls from the Senate as well about rumors. Beyond that, the Office of Management and Budget just announced behind closed doors an estimated damage to the economy so far of over a trillion dollars with a definite negative GNP to be announced from the December 1 event. Estimated repair cost at least five hundred billion and a year or more to do. It has totally screwed the national budget for years to come. Now they are crapping themselves with this new storm; estimates of damage another couple of trillion at least." He looked away for a moment, shaking his head.

"Okay, Dr. Carrington, with that in mind, please don't pile more bad shit on top of me this morning." He glanced over to Richard. "But I suspect that is exactly what you are about to do."

The room was silent, Richard looking from Franklin to Judith, who gave a subtle nod to go ahead.

"This is my analysis, sir, but it is being backed up by the data reviews I had with our counterparts in Russia and China. And yes, I know, the NSA was most likely monitoring those calls so please remind them that until a security lid is put on this, we need to compare data with them as we have in the past when it comes to solar weather."

A pause, Franklin shifting in his chair, staring directly at Richard, sensing it was going to be bad.

"Go on."

"Sir, we are looking at a very high probability of a major solar flare in approximately forty-eight hours at the latest."

"How bad will it be? I got a gut feeling what it will be so just say it straight out, no beating around the bush."

"Sir, it is my conculsion that we are facing a potential ELE. An extinction-level event," Richard announced, voice trembling, wondering if this was how a physician felt when conveying a death sentence to a patient.

Franklin, features pale, took that head-on news without any display of emotion. He just continued to stare at the center monitor, which was again focused on the anomaly. "It really does look like a burning eye," he said and then was silent for a moment. "Now tell me why this is happening."

Adjusting the mouse, Richard nodded to the main screen that dominated the room, blowing up the eye to maximum magnification, then pointing out data and secondary information on the screens to either side.

"As you know, sir," Richard began, "we're fairly certain that several solar cycles are overlapping—the standard eleven-year, then a longer-term, four hundred–year like the Maunder maximum, and now perhaps even a larger cycle that might be tens of thousands of years in length. All are converging like sine waves on a graph piling up one atop the other. This is the result—a maximum-level coronal proton explosion, what some would call a solar flare but this one is unprecedented in recorded history and even long before that. If you look at the data on the side screen, energy output from the sun is surging; even visible light has increased by nearly 1 percent over the last forty-eight hours, that outflow originating from Sauron.

"There have been major solar flares, coronal proton ejections in the past, of course. Hubble One and now Hubble Two have recorded a number of them on other stars. The type of energy release, traveling at upward of 90 percent of the speed of light, would impact our magnetosphere in less than twelve minutes.

"Around A.D. 775, there was almost certainly such an event. Historical records in China record a frightful brightening of the sun. A few Western records describe the sun looking as if an arm of white fire had burst from it. So why are we still here after that last one?

"The usual sequencing of a coronal proton ejection, or CPE, is the high-energy release of hundreds of billions of tons of protons—which is damn hard to conceptualize—accelerating up from the core of the sun, similar to a volcanic eruption here on Earth. The CPE reaches escape velocity from solar gravity, then, minutes later, if the eruption is aimed at us in our orbit around the sun it hits our magnetosphere. Nearly all the time, as long as the magnetosphere is intact, we survive. But here is the key difference, sir."

"Go on."

"It seems the standard sequence of events is that when a CPE—or what can be called a solar flare—erupts, it is often followed afterward by a secondary storm—a CME—which we are now all familiar with."

"Therefore? The difference this time, Richard?"

"It's backward this time, the sequencing of events. This time, the sun has first thrown off a CME, and in a little more than forty-eight hours, that CME will hit with such force that it will peel back the magnetosphere, cracking it wide open like an egg, leaving Earth's surface fully exposed—"

"To that thing"—Franklin added, motioning toward Sauron's Eye—
"which is following just behind it, exploding while the magnetosphere
is still disrupted."

"Precisely. Our shield is down, disrupted for twelve or more hours
up to two to three days. If a high-energy proton ejection happens just
behind that, Earth's exposed surface will be hit by a high-level radiation burst of catastrophic proportions—potentially thousands of rads per
square meter in the initial burst, followed by a continual stream of high-
energy radiation for hours more likely days afterward."

"How many rads of radiation will kill you?" The question was blurted
out by the now-shaken public relations person who had followed Franklin
to this meeting.

"A six hundred rad exposure is 100 percent fatal," Franklin replied.

"How long will it take to die?" the public relations man asked, his
voice shaking.

"You don't want to know," Franklin snapped angrily, annoyed by the
interruption.

"If you really want the answer, at the levels we're talking about,"
Richard interjected, "it will be quick, very quick—a matter of minutes."

"Direct exposure and Earth's rotation?" Judith asked. "If we're on
the far side, facing away from the sun, does that mean we miss it and
China is the one to get it?"

"Could be a factor," Franklin replied, "but that depends on how long
the flare is erupting." He looked over at Richard for backup.

"Precisely. A short-burst flare could do that, impacting only a limited part of the Earth's surface, but based on what we've observed with
this type of event with the Hubbles, it could continue to erupt for several days or more. Even the way the magnetosphere is distorted will impact dosage; some of it can even be bent by Earth's magnetic field and
strike the far side of the planet."

"And others are backing you up with this analysis?"

Richard looked over his shoulder to the rest of his team. "Any dis-
sent?"

No one spoke.

"This morning, I talked to Stanford, Kitt Peak, and, as mentioned, our counterparts in Russia and China, and the consensus is nearly universal: in forty-eight to seventy-two hours, there will be a massive solar flare erupting just behind the CME already traveling our way, a CPE with our magnetosphere already bent back and no longer protecting us."

He paused and then whispered, "Sir, it will be beyond anything witnessed in recorded history and could very well mean the end of civilization as we know it."

The room fell absolutely silent. One of those gathered started for the door, stifling a sob.

Franklin saw him and barked, "Damn it, stay put."

Again a long silence, and then Franklin slowly rose to his feet. "The odds. Are you betting the house on this?"

"Yes sir," Richard replied.

"Richard," Judith asked quietly, "exactly what are the odds?"

"When it comes to space and eternity," Richard replied, voice a soft monotone, "the odds are that sooner or later, shit happens. It doesn't matter what the odds are other than the fact we are the ones about to experience it."

"Complete lid on this! Do all of you understand that?" Franklin snarled. "I've got to carry this to the president now, so not a word of this outside of this room. Send the data to my secured server and prep a briefing for me to take to the White House."

Franklin's features were deathly pale, and though still standing, he swayed, grabbing hold of a table for support.

"I think I'd better get back to the office, call the White House, and . . . I think . . ."

Judith was first up to his side as Franklin sagged and then collapsed.

The heart attack was massive, and mercifully, he was dead before the EMTs had even arrived. The head of Goddard, Dr. Franklin Massey, could be defined as the first casualty of what was about to come.

PART III

And, lo, there was a great earthquake; and the sun became black and the moon became as blood . . . And the stars of heaven fell unto the earth. And the kings of the earth, and the great men, and the rich men, and the chief captains, and the mighty men, and every slave and every free man, hid themselves in the dens and in the rocks of the mountains; And said to the mountains and rocks, hide us from the face of him that sitteth on the throne, and from the wrath of the Lamb. For the great day of his wrath is come; and who shall be able to stand?

—Revelation 6:12–17, King James translation

5

DARREN'S cell phone chirped, and from the unique ringtone, he knew it was the director. At least the internet installed throughout the underground city and the phone system linked into it still worked. He picked up the call.

"Hey, Darren, you got a few minutes?" There was something in the man's tone of voice—normally so businesslike—that was different and stressed.

"Sure, what's up?"

"I just got a call and need to talk with you about it."

Picking up on something like that was part of Darren's job, and he was so damn good at it. A subtle change of tonal inflection on a phone might indicate stress, and of course eye movement and facial expressions were so often giveaways when it came to the shock and perhaps anger of someone falsely accused versus someone putting on a show because they were as guilty as sin. And then there was that other sixth sense that any good combat soldier or cop could not put exactly into words, but it was there, and more than once it had been the dividing line between being quick and being dead.

It was a short walk down the hallway to the director's office. This, of course, was not about life or death; it was just about dealing with his boss, Roger Rauch. He was one of those basically good guys; he was decent to his employees, and he could defuse the usual stresses that happened when hundreds of people worked in what was most certainly a unique facility, each firm renting floor space inside the millions of square feet of the Underground, all having different needs and demands. Roger was an upstanding member of his church and on its board of elders. Some would define him as that type of guy who would pitch in on any task if asked and exert a calming influence, but was there anything that really stood out that would make him memorable? Short at five foot seven compared to Darren's towering bulk, he did have the sad affectation of combing his hair over his large forehead to vainly try to cover the receding crown. He was twenty-five or so pounds overweight, not rotund but not fit, given to sport coats and slacks purchased off-the-rack at Walmart that never fit quite right, and he spent his weekends glued to a television, watching whatever sport was in season and talking incessantly about the game the previous Sunday. To Darren, he was just one of those average joes that made the country run without any real flair or fanfare.

Darren liked working with him, but would he have followed him into the alleyways of Fallujah and trusted that he was heading in the right direction—and if it hit the fan, would Roger stay calm and cover his back? Hell no.

The door to Roger's office was open, and Roger waved Darren in. It was a typical office of an administrator for a midlevel operation, with a slightly oversized desk with two flat-screen monitors on it and a bookshelf with photos of his four kids, who were now scattered around the country. Roger definitely seemed troubled as he gestured for Darren to sit down.

"What's up?" Darren asked, figuring it was best to skip the small talk and get straight to the reason for the summons.

"Darren, I just got a call from the governor's office."

That surprised Darren.

"Yeah, it's weird. It wasn't actually the governor, of course—one of his assistants, their liaison to the National Guard. He said that someone will be showing up within the hour, and you're to take him straight to that secured space the state set up a couple of years ago."

Darren took it in. "Must be about the CME. It's looking a lot worse than the last one."

"Most likely. Anyhow, whoever it is sounded all fired up. Not the usual 'call a week in advance and drive down' type of visit; they're coming in by helicopter and want someone to meet them out front with a vehicle."

Helicopter? More than a few were still being repaired from the last CME with some or most of their electronics blown. Functional helicopters were most likely at a high premium right now, so whoever was dropping in must have had a fire put under his butt by someone.

"You'd better be waiting outside to greet him."

"On my way. Anything else?"

"It must be something important about that tunnel and cavern owned by the state. Just let me know what it is all about."

In other words, try to find out why the state of Missouri is all so hush-hush about why they outright purchased and not just did the usual rental agreement on two-hundred-thousand square feet of the Underground, but not even the director of the facility, let alone the head of security, is allowed into that side tunnel.

Roger's desk phone rang, and he picked it up. "Yeah, okay," he said and then hung up. "Helicopter's landing now."

Darren walked out of Roger's office, stopped into his office to put on a parka, and was out the door. Within a few minutes, he was at the heavy steel door, which was already opening, having called ahead for Tyrell, who had stayed on when his replacement had not shown for the regular day shift, to open it.

The chopper was just settling in on the helipad on the far side of the outer-perimeter fence, and Tyrell was running up to the chain-link fence to open it.

Darren drove through, cracking the window to shout a thanks and to tell him to keep both the outer gate and steel door open. He drove the hundred yards to the pad with the window rolled down, and as always, the sights and sounds of a Black Hawk landing immediately triggered a rush of emotions—some good, some very bad.

He wasn't sure who to expect, but he was absolutely startled when the side door opened and he recognized Jackson Perry, a two-star general in command of the state's National Guard, followed by a captain and two sergeants, all ducking low against the rotor blast of the chopper.

During Darren's deployment to Iraq some years earlier, Perry had commanded Darren's battalion for several months before taking a chest wound that was so serious he was evacuated all the way back to Walter Reed. Perry was highly respected by the men under his command, and his removal from action was lamented, especially when his replacement was a colonel who was never on the front lines, never there to get a grunt's-eye view of what was happening, and who sat safely back in an air-conditioned HQ while his troops sweated it out in 120-degree heat. Perry was respected by all who served with him as a man who led from the front and asked nothing more of his troops than he himself was willing to give.

Darren knew that Perry had shifted from regular army to become the commander of the state's National Guard and had seen him from a distance at several ceremonial functions, but this time it would be face-to-face.

The wind kicked up by the chopper was absolutely numbing, but that did not stop Darren from coming forward with a bit of a smile, coming to attention and offering a salute—which, by instinct, Perry returned and then hesitated, looking at Darren questioningly.

"Do we know each other?" Perry asked, his deep voice rich and Southern.

"I was a staff sergeant and weapons specialist with Echo Company. Served under you at the first battle of Fallujah."

Perry's dark features visibly brightened as he extended his hand, which Darren gladly took.

"How the hell are you, Sergeant?"

"Well, at the moment, freezing my ass off, sir. Let's get out of the cold." He gestured to his jeep.

It was a tight squeeze in the back for the three staffers after placing small duffel bags in the storage area behind the back seat, while Perry of course squeezed his large frame, nearly the size of Darren's, into the front. There were quick introductions and polite handshakes, but the three seemed tense, all business, as Darren turned his vehicle around, drove through the outer-perimeter fence, and continued through the open steel door and into the complex.

"Where to, sir?" Darren asked.

"If you could give me a quick tour first. Then down to where Kraft has their warehouse, then finish at the tunnel the state of Missouri has purchased. That would suit me just fine."

Darren offered some small talk—asking about the general's recovery and whether he missed returning to the field—but the answers were merely short and polite, and within a few minutes, Darren could sense the general's mind was elsewhere. From long training and habit, when a general was preoccupied, it was best to just shut up and drive.

Glances to the rearview mirror showed him that the two sergeants, sitting to either side of the captain, had cameras and not just cell phones up and were filming everything. The captain hunched over an open laptop, the computer of military grade.

When they reached the vast area owned by Kraft Foods and pulled in to the parking area, his staff was immediately out of the jeep, cameras out, acting like awed visitors to a famed tourist location. The entire section rented by Kraft was a hundred and eighty feet below the surface, filling up a vast cavern occupying nearly six acres. Most of it was dark, with only the area around the entryway and the front office in a double-wide trailer illuminated by fluorescent lights fastened into the limestone ceiling twenty feet above them.

The general was silent, just pacing around a bit, taking it in.

"Sir, mind if I ask what this is all about?" Darren asked.

"In good time, Sergeant, in good time."

Darren fell silent, not following when the general walked over to his captain, and he overheard talk between the two about square footage, getting a full inventory, blueprints, and finding out if any additional inventory was coming in by the end of tomorrow.

He then turned back to Darren. "Is the manager of this here today?"

"Easy enough to find out," Darren replied, motioning for him to follow. There was a chain-link fence marking off the entryway into the open-air warehouse, and the gate was open. The firm's own security person was on duty, already coming out of the office.

"Hey, Mary, is Barry in?" Darren asked.

"Ah, no, sir, he's stuck at home with no gas." She looked a bit wide-eyed at the entourage around him.

"Mary, is it?" Perry asked.

"Ah, yes, sir." It was obvious she was a bit overawed by their visitors, her job normally that of just checking the paperwork of 18-wheelers coming in and leaving, sometimes upward of thirty or more a day, before passing them on to the crew at the receiving and shipping docks. But today, like all the days since the December 1 storm, it was eerily quiet. Kraft's main computer systems had taken a bad hit, and the vast complex infrastructure of food shipments had yet to come back to normal. The only traffic since the storm was several 18-wheelers a day showing up to pick up food, but no new shipments had been coming in.

"Would you mind showing my people to his office? We need to check up on a few things," Perry asked.

"Ah, sir, procedure is with outside visitors that I have to get permission from higher up and . . . ," she began nervously, looking to Darren as if appealing for guidance.

"Ma'am, just please take my people in; we need to start checking your inventory and don't have much time to visit."

"Sir, I'll have to check with my manager on that if I can even reach him by phone. My orders are that no one other than employees and drivers with proper authorization are to enter the facility."

She continued her appealing look to Darren.

"General," Darren interjected, "Barry O'Donnell is the manager of this facility. Like Mary said, he's been stranded for several days now."

"How far away?" Perry asked.

Darren wasn't sure and looked to Mary.

"He lives down in Branson, twenty miles away, and said he can't find gas."

Exasperated, Perry simply looked up for a moment as if appealing to heaven for patience. "What about an assistant manager?"

"Sir, I'm sorry, but the only people here today are a couple of the forklift operators. We got a call from corporate headquarters that no trucks are moving, and everything is going into lockdown until after this next CME thing is over, so we're just to stay here and keep an eye on the place."

"Is there anyone who can get us into the computer inventory?" Perry asked, increasingly frustrated.

"I'm kind of it, sir."

Perry sighed. Darren remained silent. This was not the army, where a general just had to look even mildly pissed and everyone jumped to respond.

Perry finally looked back up and gazed off toward the darkened cavern. "Mary, can you at least turn on the lights so I can see all of this place?"

"All of them?" she asked, still looking at Darren for help, and he simply nodded.

"Yes, Mary, all of them, please."

She turned about and went back into the office. Darren could see her through the open door, fumbling with an oversized control box, opening it, and hitting several switches.

The humming of hundreds of industrial-size fluorescent lamps echoed in the chamber, coming half to life and then suddenly bursting to full brilliance.

Darren was used to the sight, but he could see it certainly impressed Perry and those with him. In the vast underground cavern that had once been a quarry, the cave lit up like midday, just over two-hundred-thousand square feet that stretched out for nearly a quarter mile in length and as wide as a football field. Two perfectly straight roads bisected the facility, which was lined nearly to the ceiling with storage racks that would be familiar to anyone shopping in a big-box store.

"It looks half-empty," Perry said softly.

"All the traffic since the storm has been outflow," Darren replied. "I would guess the food processing plants that supply us might still be off-line, and so they are trying to keep stores stocked with what is warehoused here."

"Damn," Perry whispered as if to himself. "I was told there'd be a lot more."

He turned away from Darren and walked off as if to be alone for a moment. "Captain Harrison," he finally barked, and the young officer who had accompanied him snapped to attention. "Take Sergeant Freeman to the manager's office and see if you can somehow access the inventory and then report back to me."

"Sir?" Mary stood in the doorway to the office, obviously anxious. "Ah, sir, the computers are down—at least I think they are, and I don't have the passwords anyhow."

"Damn it," Perry said.

Darren made eye contact with Mary and gestured as if to indicate she should just stay out of it.

"General, maybe I can help, but first I have to understand why you are here, sir, and the reason for this request."

"Later, Sergeant, later," he replied sharply and then turned away. "Captain Harrison, if you can't crack the computer, then damn it, find a way to get ahold of somebody at Kraft's regional headquarters who can. Do you read me, Captain?"

Harrison called for Sergeant Freeman to get their duffel bags out of Darren's jeep as he headed to the trailer that served as an office.

"Now over to the state-owned facility, please," Perry announced as he climbed into the jeep.

"Look, General, I do have the responsibility of overseeing security for this facility. If you'd share with me why you are here, maybe I can be of better assistance."

"I'm here under orders from the governor's office to do a quick look-see for myself and leave people here to start an inventory check."

"Is this because of the next CME, sir?"

"Something like that."

A long pause.

"Anything else, Sergeant? You want to see authorization papers, call the governor perhaps? I'll give you his personal number."

"No, sir, that will not be necessary. I'll take your word for it," he paused, "I always knew it to be good when I served under you in Iraq."

There was an ironic tone in his voice but Perry did not react.

"Fine, then. So let's cut the bullshitting," he replied as he pulled back the sleeve on the parka he was still wearing and glanced at his watch.

"Damn it, I'm already running late, so if you could just give me a little cooperation, Sergeant, I'd appreciate it. I need to do a quick check on the facilities here that are owned by the state."

Darren did as ordered, figuring that any questions asked would be turned aside politely until the general was ready to explain his presence.

It was a rather long drive from the Kraft area at one end of the vast underground labyrinth to the tunnel that the state had purchased. The entry tunnel to the state-owned section was blocked off by a chain-link fence. A couple of security cameras kept watch, the fence plastered with several signs announcing it was state-owned property, that no trespassing was allowed and violators would be prosecuted.

"Let's drive in," the general said, and he got out of the jeep and pulled out a key chain that had about a dozen keys, each of a different color and marked with a small ID tag.

"I've got this," Darren announced, since he had a key to every lock in this facility. Drawing out his own key chain, a heavy one with thirty or more keys on it, he found the one needed and snapped the padlock open. At least doing that made him feel he was reasserting some small sense of control over the situation, whatever the hell the situation was.

The general offered a polite thanks as Darren pushed the gate back. Darren hesitated for a few seconds, not sure if the general was going to hassle him about entering; this would be the first time he would actually step foot inside the state-owned facility. There was no indicator either way from Perry, so Darren got back into the driver's seat and put the jeep in gear.

It was a short drive of less than a minute from the gate into the main cavern. Darren had to turn on his headlights along the way, since the corridor was not lit. Once into the open area, Darren got out, held up a flashlight, and looked around until he found the circuit box mounted to a wall. He then went over, opened it, and threw the switch for lights. Dozens of overhead-mounted fluorescent bulbs hummed and seconds later began illuminating the cavernous room.

Perry, out of the truck, stood silent, hands on hips, taking it in.

Far down the entire length of the space were scores of shipping containers, each stenciled with PROPERTY OF THE STATE OF MISSOURI and then warnings in smaller print beneath that to tamper with or attempt to steal the contents was a felony punishable by up to ten years in jail.

The containers had been brought into this cavern long before Darren had become head of security. When he'd asked his boss, Roger, about it on his first day of work, he was told that neither of them had a need to know other than that the gate was to be checked daily to ensure no one had tampered with it.

Joe, the owner of the pizza shop, eventually filled him in. For weeks after the state acquired the vast cavern, 18-wheelers pulled in nearly every day, dropped off shipping containers, and then simply drove off.

The team that had shown up just before the last CME to check on the facility had been led by a captain. Today was indeed different with the head of the entire National Guard for the state arriving like this, and Darren knew there was a lot to read from it.

Perry turned to the sergeant accompanying him and handed him the bundle of keys. "Okay, Sergeant, you've got your work cut out for you. Sorry we couldn't get a few extra hands for you to help on such short notice. Just do what you can until we start coming in tomorrow."

After an exchange of salutes, the sergeant opened the back hatch of the jeep and pulled out his duffel bag. Setting the bag down, he opened it, drew out a military laptop from a side pocket, and turned it on.

Perry watched him for a moment and then turned to Darren. "Okay, we're done here for now, Sergeant. It's Brooklyn, isn't it?"

"Brooks, sir, Darren Brooks. I'm head of security for this facility." He pitched his voice to try to sound calm and unruffled, but within, he was getting a knot in his stomach. Just what the hell was going on here?

He backed the jeep around and took the short tunnel out to the main two-lane corridor and stopped.

"Where to now, sir?"

"Back to my chopper." As Perry spoke, he made the deliberate gesture of yet again pushing back the sleeve of his winter parka and checking an old-style military-issue wristwatch.

Darren looked at him intently, then put the jeep into park and turned the engine off.

General Perry looked over at him intently. "You're going to ask a lot of questions now, aren't you, Sergeant?"

"Sir, yes, sir, and by the way, I am retired and no longer a sergeant. You can call me *Chief,* if you'd like."

"How about I just call you Darren?"

"Fine, then, call me Darren, and I will just call you Jackson."

The general bristled. "Fine, then, Darren. Ask your questions, but realize I am late, and it is extremely pressing as to where I am expected to go to next."

"Sir, it will take you a good ten minutes to walk out of here if you don't feel like talking, or I can drive you back in two minutes. Let's cut a deal of five minutes talking and then I drive you back to your chopper."

"Then one question to you first, Darren."

"And that is?"

"Do you mind if I smoke?"

"What?" That had caught him off guard.

Without waiting for a reply, Jackson reached into the side pocket of his parka, pulled out a pack of Dunhills, no less, and lit one up, inhaling deeply.

If this doesn't beat all, Darren thought. Years ago, the military started making smoking more and more difficult for anyone going for higher rank; it was a definite strike against because the actuaries claimed that promoting such a man or woman to high rank was a bad investment.

The general offered one to Darren, who shook his head.

"After I got wounded at Fallujah, a month or so after you got yours, I wound up in Walter Reed as well," Darren said. "I met my wife there, and a condition of marrying was I quit smoking, so I have."

"Smart move. Is she a good wife?"

"The best. Sir, you are trying to eat up the time, so let's stick to my questions, okay?"

"Yup." Perry took another deep drag.

"Just what in the hell are you doing here at this particular place, now, at this moment?"

"Running an inventory check."

"Inventory check? A job the captain you left at Kraft can handle. Why you? And checking what and why?"

"The state stockpiled a lot of emergency supplies back down that tunnel two years ago. We are going to need it, so I was asked to come out here and a few other places around the state, drop off a few National Guard personnel at each, and eyeball things in general. I must say, Darren, this underground city is really quite impressive."

"And that's it?"

"That's it, Darren." He took another drag and meaningfully looked at his watch.

Darren's years as a chief of police had taught him a lot about interrogation, and with this man, he knew all he was going to get were vague answers without substance. He was half tempted to tell him to get out of the jeep and walk back on his own.

No, that would be foolish; it would only serve to piss him off, and one does not piss off a general, especially the head of the state National Guard, without the risk of some real blowback.

"Okay, sir, I get it; you can't talk. That's it."

"No insult, Darren, but yeah, that's it, and I do have to get a move on. I'll be back tomorrow with a lot more personnel that are being mobilized today, and you'll get a full briefing then."

"Just one more, and then I'll drive."

"Okay."

"Why are the sergeant and captain getting dropped off first at Kraft Foods? I can maybe get it regarding checking state property. So why Kraft?"

Jackson just stared at him for a moment, took another drag of his cigarette, opened the window, and tossed it out. "Okay, straight answer, and then that's it for the Q and A. The governor is about to issue an executive order to seize the food stored here for the duration of this crisis. And that had damn well better stay just with you, Sergeant. The governor's office has already contacted their corporate office with that news."

"Seizing the assets?"

"Come on, Darren, damn it, the food. We thought there was enough food back there to feed ten thousand or more for months. I'll report back that there's half of what we'd expected, but that should still be enough."

That so startled Darren that it was his turn to go silent.

"Okay, Sergeant, time's up. You made a deal; now get me to my chopper. You and everyone working here will get a full briefing on it all by 1200 hours tomorrow when I get back here."

"One more, damn it," Darren replied sharply. "You said 'duration of this crisis.' From news reports so far, it will be like the last one, maybe worse, but that's it, isn't it? This is about another CME coming our way, isn't it? Nothing else?"

Jackson sighed, leaned back in his seat, and looked up at the ceiling of the jeep.

"I'll give you an answer, Sergeant, because I am going to need your help—a *lot* of help from you over the next few days. Several hours ago, the governor got a call from our senator—you know, majority leader, no less. He told the governor to start moving now on some things, and that is it. And that, Sergeant, is my final answer to your questions. Got it?"

Darren knew he had received just half an answer, but a warning as well that all this was about things from further up, even beyond a state commander of the National Guard, and he was to definitely stand back and out of the way.

Not another word was exchanged on the drive out to the chopper. General Perry punched in a call on his phone said just three words— "Fire her up!"—and by the time they were out through the steel gate, the chopper's blades were already a blur.

Darren pulled up, and the general got out, and then turned and looked back at Darren and offered his hand, which Darren took. The general's grip was deliberately hard, and he held on to Darren for a few seconds.

"Sergeant, I just wish I could tell you more. And to tell you the truth, I don't know much more than you do. Just work with me. Okay?"

"Yes, sir." How else could he have answered?

The general gave his hand an even tighter squeeze. "You got any kids?"

"Yes, sir, Darla and I both have one from previous marriages, but they're full grown."

"Where do they live?"

"One's in California, grad school. Other in the military, the navy. Not sure where she is at the moment."

A slight frown and then a nod.

"This stays between us, Sergeant. Call it a suggestion to an old comrade from Fallujah. Think about bringing your wife to work tomorrow. Okay? You say anything to anyone beyond that and my foot will be so far up your ass you'll be staring at my shoelaces." He paused, still holding Darren's right hand in a tight grip. "Do you read me, Sergeant? Mouth shut and get your wife here."

Another squeeze of the hand and then the general let go, ducking low as he trotted to the chopper that lifted off as soon as he was aboard.

Darren turned his vehicle around, floored it, breaking the speed limit of ten miles an hour by nearly triple that as he went through the gate to first stop at his office where he snatched up his coffee thermos. Less than fifteen minutes after the chopper had lifted off, he pulled in to the center of the compound owned by the state and got out with the thermos in hand.

The sergeant that had been left there already had three shipping containers open and was standing just inside the third one as Darren approached.

"Sir, I really don't think you should be in here. This area is supposed to be sealed off."

Darren offered a friendly smile. "Hey, we never were introduced. I'm Darren Brooks, head of security here, and the general said it was okay if I brought you some fresh coffee."

The sergeant hesitated but then politely shook Darren's hand while holding his laptop and a manila envelope that had been pulled out of a plastic holder mounted inside the door, the papers within undoubtedly the manifests for what the container held.

"Okay. I'm Danford, Sergeant Bill Danford. And yeah, some fresh coffee would be nice. They packed me off here with some MREs, but you know what that coffee tastes like."

"Yeah, shit."

"Something like that. I heard you say you served with the general at Fallujah?"

"Yup, I copped one in the gut about a month after he got hit. I was a stupid asshole; it was a 115 freaking degrees, and against orders, I took my body armor off."

"I'll confess I'm glad I missed all of that crap," Danford replied. "Yeah, I was in the 'Stan for one tour, but just doing this—glorified inventory clerk checking off supplies as they came in. Kind of makes me feel guilty at times for wearing a campaign ribbon, but we all got one for being there."

"No problem. Hell, after what I saw, I would have traded jobs with you in a heartbeat. So anyhow, here's the thermos. If you want some real food, we've got a pizza joint in here; just walk up this tunnel, turn right, second tunnel, then to the left."

"Thanks. In fact, I'm starving. I got pulled out of my office by the general, handed a duffel bag with rations, a sleeping bag, and this computer already loaded with data, and now I'm here."

"Care for some pizza now?" Darren asked.

There was a moment's hesitation. The sergeant looked down at his laptop, the unopened manila envelope, and then at all the other shipping containers lining the walls of the compound, which would take well into the next day to review.

"Oh, what the hell. Sure."

"Come on, I'll give you a lift."

Again hesitation and then a nod of agreement.

"So what is going on, anyhow?" Darren asked casually as they drove the quarter mile to the restaurant area of the facility.

"I most likely only know just about as much as you do. I got pulled from the general's office in the state capitol building not more than three hours ago. It scared the crap out of me when the general came in, pointed to the six of us who were there, and told us we were coming with him and no questions asked."

"But only three of you got out of the chopper."

"Yeah, the other three just took a short hop to a small complex like this one just outside Jefferson City, got dropped off, and then down to here."

"Is it because of that CME?"

"I would guess so. Yeah, a lot of paper pushers in the capitol building were really upset, you know, and crying, 'Oh no, not another one, this will really screw Christmas for the kids,' that type of thing.

"Saw more than a few of the top-dog types heading out the door and driving off, though. A friend of mine in the attorney general's office told me that she heard her boss on the phone talking to his wife, yelling at her to start packing, to tell the kids to get their asses home, then he was out the door. 'Packing for what?' I was asking myself," Danford said, obviously as ill-informed as Darren.

"Then the general walks in, I get drafted, and now I'm here. No time to call my wife or anything."

"Yeah, he did seem in a hurry."

"You aren't kidding. He was taking calls the whole way down here. A couple were from the governor; I could hear him answering those with 'Yes, sir, no, sir.'"

"Any idea why the hustle, what this is all about?"

The sergeant looked over at him and hesitated. They pulled in to a parking spot in front of Joe's Pizza, and Darren shut the jeep off, looked over at the sergeant, and offered a reassuring smile.

"Hey, I am as confused as you are. I'm just trying to figure out why all this running around. Any clues you can share would sure help me. That general left me a laundry list of things to do. Can you give me some help with that?"

"Well, he was on the phone a lot with the governor's office and then someone at the Pentagon. A lot of the usual jargon, you know what I mean? He kept repeating something about CG and ELE—you know, military acronym talk. When that came up, I could see he looked real worried; he replied with something like, 'You're shitting me. Is this really it?' Normally, he is unflappable; you know, since you served with him. Whatever it was about really got to him. My friend said the same thing—something that his boss was saying was an ELE whatever that is and therefore the CG was starting."

Darren had no idea what that meant, but he stored those two terms away to check out later and shrugged as if what the sergeant had told him was no big deal.

They walked into the pizza joint, which was nearly empty, but the owner, Joe, was, as always, behind the counter.

"Hey, Darren, what's new? Vicki down at the furniture warehouse just came in a few minutes ago and said you were driving some big brass around."

"Yeah, I guess they're just trying to get some things organized."

Darren nodded to his companion, introduced him, and told Joe to put whatever the sergeant wanted on his tab.

The sergeant ordered a meat lover's special. Joe apologized that he had run out of sausage and pepperoni days earlier, the delivery never arriving, but said he could at least put some bacon and hamburger on it.

Even as Joe took the order, Darren was heading to the door.

"Hey, Darren, what gives? Where are you going?" the sergeant cried.

"Just to my office—got to make a few calls. I'll be back to join you for lunch in fifteen minutes, but go ahead and start without me if you're really hungry."

"Ah, Darren, maybe I should—"

But Darren didn't wait to hear more. Back into his jeep, he drove off and headed straight back to the state-owned compound. A minute later, he was inside the third container, where Danford had carelessly left his computer. Darren snapped it open and shook his head. The guy hadn't even done a full shutdown, no need for a password, and so he scrolled through files that were still up on the active screen.

"What the hell?" he whispered a few minutes later.

It was a long list, dozens of pages of numbered containers, their entry codes, and the contents of each. Containers 4 through 7 held hundreds of collapsible bunk beds complete with rolled-up memory foam mattresses, portable chemical toilets with cases of toilet paper, and even signs marking them as for male or female use. Container 11 held partition walls, desks, chairs, desk lamps, and even a bookshelf. He had skipped the header at the top as he quickly scanned the listings. He tried to take it all in as quickly as possible. If that sergeant had caught on that he had been scammed, he would have been able to run back there by now.

Darren scrolled back up to the header for container 11. It was marked *contents for governor's use only.*

"Hey, Darren, just what in the hell are you doing?"

And it was indeed the sergeant, approaching from the dimly lit tunnel and out of breath.

Darren did not even wait to offer a reply; he got into his jeep and headed out of the compound, flooring it, poor Sergeant Danford cursing and giving him the finger after jumping out of the way.

Darren cleared the steel door a couple of minutes later and then really floored it. He picked up his cell phone, hoping against hope, and clicked it on. *Damn, no carrier at all.* He clicked it off. He turned on the radio and punched through the stations; all of them were linked to their network centers. The news was of course about the approaching CME, but that was it aside from an announcement that the president would address the nation that evening at 8:00 P.M. eastern time.

Darren hit Route 65, but rather than turn south for home, he turned north and then off at the exit for Springfield's National Guard armory. He had a few friends there, and if anyone was in the office, maybe they could fill in the blanks.

Twenty minutes later, he was out of that office, an MP coming out behind him and yelling for him to stop. Darren ignored the order, hit the gas, got on the highway, and headed south with pedal all the way down to the floorboard. Given Darla's contacts from the business she had just sold last year for quite a few million, maybe she could find the answers. His very short visit to the armory and the reaction to the few questions he'd asked told him that something was going wrong, *very* wrong.

6

"NERVOUS?"

Richard Carrington looked over at Judith, who stood nearly as tall as he did at just a bit shy of five foot eight. She had barely enough time to change in her office into a more professional-looking business suit from her usual Goddard attire of comfortable slacks and a sweater. Someone in public relations had found a blue blazer for Richard, which did not fit all that well, and a red necktie just before the helicopter arrived to take them on the ten-minute flight to the White House.

He didn't answer her question directly but simply asked it back. "Are you nervous?"

"Damn straight I am. Bad enough dealing with what happened to Dr. Massey." She paused for a moment, struggling to hold back tears. "It should be him doing this, not us."

She fell silent and turned away for a moment, taking deep breaths in an effort to get control of her emotions.

"Ma'am, are you all right?" asked Alice Naguro, one of the White House staff from their public relations office. She looked vaguely familiar to Richard, and he remembered that on occasion she stood in for her boss at the daily press briefings when it came to issues of science and technology.

Judith nodded but said nothing.

"It's okay if you need to sit down or use the restroom for a moment;

we're five minutes early. A lot of us knew Dr. Massey. We had a lot of respect for him."

"I'll be fine. Just give me a minute."

Alice turned her attention from Judith to Richard. "I know this is short notice, Dr. Carrington, but the president wants a straight-up briefing from someone who is on top of the situation and can explain it clearly and concisely."

"Understood." He felt a tremor of nerves.

"Protocol is simple. The president, advisors, and some key personnel are already in there." She nodded to the closed door nearby.

It was Richard's first time in the White House, and he expected that somehow things would be more ornate or, after the long elevator ride down to this conference room, that it would have more of a look from a spy thriller or old Cold War movie. The corridor from the elevator seemed no different form a typical business office—nameplates on doors, average beige carpet, illumination from fluorescent lights overhead, a few history-oriented prints on the walls, no high-tech feel to it at all.

"I will escort you to where you will sit at the front table; there will be several large monitors behind you. We've already loaded up the latest images from *Helio II* as they are coming in, and there will be a technician on duty—you'll see her in the corner, sitting at a terminal—who is hardwire linked into your facility at Goddard and can pull up any image, data, or video you need within seconds. After I've settled you two in, I'll go sit by the technician to assist when needed."

She opened the iPad that she had been carrying so that they could see the screen loaded with large icons. "These are the latest images coming in from Goddard even as we speak. You don't have to prompt me; just keep on talking, and we'll do the rest for you. Okay?"

They both nodded. Goddard was good at this sort of thing, knowing the old line that a picture was often better than a thousand words, and Alice had obviously been receiving the latest downloads from his office. That was at least a bit reassuring.

"You'll be introduced," Alice continued. "The president will be sitting at the other end of the conference table, flanked by whomever has been invited. Questions will come from him first, then follow up from others in the room. When done, he'll thank the two of you; that will be the signal that it is time for you to leave. It's usually his style to get up and shake hands with whomever has spoken, and the Secret Service agent assigned to you will lead you back out, and that will be it."

He nodded, and though he had never answered Judith's question, he was indeed nervous.

"Usual advice from me?" Alice continued. "Just stick to the question asked; don't wander off. He can have a fairly short attention span when things are tense, and he wants answers quickly. He wants concise, clear answers in laymen's terms, not long-winded technical meandering."

She paused, and he felt a slight touch of insult in that as if she were about to add in, *No lecturing professor routine; just stick to the basics.*

"You're cleared by Secret Service." She nodded to the agent who stood in front of the door, features placid and obvious intent on the two of them.

The agent offered a friendly hand. "Allison Minneci, sir."

The manner of introduction surprised him. He assumed that Secret Service agents were above such behavior of being polite and were meant to somehow intimidate. Allison seemed absolutely unassuming—petite, brunette hair cut short, eyes a pale blue and sparkling, made more noticeable when contrasted to her southern Italian olive complexion. She did not fit the stereotype of a Secret Service agent, and perhaps that was usually her mission when the president was out in the world, with her blending into a crowd, perhaps passing as a schoolteacher or even a student.

Richard offered her a bit of a nervous smile and a nod. He got a nod of acknowledgment in return.

"Hate to have to run down a few more things; it's just the usual routine. No emotional statements, no gushing with 'Oh, Mr. President, I am so honored to meet you' type stuff. If he shakes your hand, just return the handshake; don't use your other hand for some sort of two-handed thing. That gesture does make our security people a bit nervous. Hope you understand."

He again looked at the agent, who offered a slight reassuring smile. He found himself wondering what nearly everyone wanted to ask about when actually meeting a Secret Service agent face-to-face: *What gun are you carrying, and where is it hidden?* But he refrained from doing so.

"Sorry to have to go over that, but you'd be amazed at some of the stupid things people say and do when meeting the president and then expect to brief him. They ask for selfies with him, autographs, some souvenir to take home to their kids. It gets weird and happens more than you think." Allison looked straight at Richard. "You'll do okay, sir."

Allison touched her earphone and then replied, "We are coming in now." Richard could hear the door's interior lock snapping open.

"Drs. Carrington and Cooper, you'll do just fine," Allison whispered. She opened the door and gestured for them to enter. Richard stepped aside for Judith and Alice to go in first, and then he followed.

He did have to pause for a few seconds and blink; his first few steps were a bit hesitant since the lighting was turned down low. The primary illumination was from the large monitor dominating the far end of the room. The image on it was a live feed from *Helio II* aimed at the emerging CME—which, since its explosive launch from the surface of the sun approximately sixteen hours earlier, had already traveled nearly twenty-five million miles straight at where Earth would be in its orbit in less than two days.

Richard had not seen any live feed of what was happening since being whisked out of Goddard, an experience that had an almost surreal quality to it. Within minutes after Dr. Massey's body had been taken out of the room by the EMTs, Judith following them out and leaving all in the room in a state of shock, a call had come in informing Richard he was expected in the director's office immediately.

That office was a maelstrom of confusion with Judith in the middle, motioning for Richard to come to her side even as she continued to speak softly into a landline phone. Hanging up, she simply said, "We are ordered to the White House ASAP. They're sending a helicopter out to pick us up."

From there, someone in public relations had run him to an adjoining office, looking around frantically and finally ordering a staffer to take off his blue blazer and loan it to Richard, along with his necktie. It didn't fit all that well, and that barely done, he was run out the door to where a military Black Hawk was landing.

And now here in the basement of the White House, with heart racing, he took a few deep breaths trying to steady his nerves. He stopped to look at the image up on the main monitor and scanned the data stream of numbers cascading across a smaller monitor to the left of the main one.

"Dr. Carrington." Allison's softly spoken words prompted him to just keep moving to where he was supposed to sit and definitely not stand about like a gawking tourist. Alice was already at the far end of the conference table gesturing for where Judith was to sit, politely drawing the office chair back for her and then motioning for Richard to take the one to her right. As he settled into the chair, he realized he was sitting dead center at the end of a long conference table. At the far end of it, twenty feet away, sat the president of the United States.

"Drs. Cooper and Carrington," the president began without preamble, "thank you for joining us at such short notice."

Richard froze up for a few seconds. Born a Brit and still a Brit at heart, he somehow was expecting something more formal—introductions and perhaps even a slight inclining of his head as if in the presence of royalty. He knew that was absurd and followed Judith's lead of not saying anything yet.

"I wish to extend my personal condolences to you and the entire Goddard team for the tragic passing of Dr. Massey this afternoon."

"Thank you, Mr. President," Judith replied.

"Our time is short, so excuse me if we get straight to the point of this meeting and hear the information I need from you now."

"However we can help you, sir," Judith replied.

The president shifted in his chair and leaned forward, and though the room was dimly lit, Richard knew the president was looking straight at him.

"Dr. Carrington, I understand that you are the head of the Helio Center at Goddard?"

"Yes, sir."

The president paused, looking down at several sheets of paper in front of him. Richard surmised it was some sort of background information about him. The president looked back up at him, gaze intent. "And that you are considered one of our top experts on all things related to solar activity?"

Richard hesitated, fearful of sounding egotistical. "I have headed up the observation center at Goddard for five years," he replied, not responding to the comment about being a top expert. There were a lot of experts when it came to the sun, and a lot more so-called experts who had been dominating the media with sometimes inflammatory claims on one side or derisive dismissal of the potential effects on the other side since this out-of-control solar cycle had begun back in late November.

"Fine, then, Dr. Carrington, now straight to the point." The president gestured toward the screen behind Richard. "Tell us just what the hell is going on at this precise moment—the threat level, how much time we have to react, and how we should react."

Richard was taken aback for a moment by the bluntness of the request and how it was delivered. "Sir, I have been out of the information loop for well over an hour," Richard began and then paused, and fortunately Judith jumped in.

"Mr. President, Dr. Carrington and I left the Helio Center nearly an hour and a half ago and don't have the current update."

"We do." It wasn't the president but someone sitting to his right in an admiral's uniform. Richard recognized him as the head of the Joint Chiefs of Staff, Admiral Brockenborough, who, when there was a flareup of yet another military crisis, was put in front of the cameras to utter some highly quotable pugnacious comments.

"Latest update," the admiral announced, looking down at a printout, "is that it will start hitting the magnetosphere in approximately forty-two hours, full intensity within an hour afterward. Regarding energy level, we've just gotten a call from our so-called friends in China; they are predicting a full-out level six or more, at least a magnitude stronger than the last one."

Richard took that in.

The admiral continued, "What pundits are calling a CLE—a

Carrington-level event." He added with a touch of sarcasm, "Named after you, I assume."

That rankled Richard. Either the admiral was supremely ignorant or was just trying to knock him off edge a bit for the hell of it. Several in the room chuckled softly at his comment.

"No, sir," Richard replied, trying to keep his voice calm. "Named after my great-great-grandfather who first observed and recorded the explosion of a CME in 1859 and its impact on Earth's fragile electrical infrastructure of that time."

"Almost a family franchise of disaster," the admiral said sotto voce.

Richard felt the admiral was indeed trying to unbalance him, but then the president interrupted.

"Doctor, do you think the Chinese assessment is accurate?"

"Sir, I can't answer that yet."

"Why not? Do they have better information than us or not?" the admiral asked. He was getting on Richard's nerves. But then again, maybe that was what he was supposed to do—put the pressure on and see how he would react.

"Sir, they are very good at data analysis. The feed from our *Helios* system is as available to them as it is anyone else. There is no need for encrypting since it has no military function whatsoever and is observing our sun for just this kind of event—the same way we obtain data from Russian and Chinese monitoring satellites."

"So this data is out there, available to the public, even as we speak?" the admiral interjected.

"It was until just after midnight when, for a variety of reasons, the feed from our end was cut to all unsecured public agencies. I understand we are allowing a select few to have secured access, but that is it."

"Given what else we have to address, Mr. President," Brockenborough replied, "I urge you to shut the entire thing down now, because in short order, there is going to be a worldwide panic."

"Too late for that." Richard thanked God the woman sitting directly across from the admiral had stepped in. "We've been sharing data like this for years, interlinking with the Russians, Chinese, and EU; as Dr. Carrington mentioned, it's not as if it is military related." Richard realized it was Dr. Janet Lindstrum, the national security advisor. Fluent in five languages, including Mandarin, she had been a noted historian before being recruited by the president and was considered the intellectual of his inner circle. "We're all looking at the sun that we share in common. Yes, we cut the public access to internet sites like Space.com and others; it was being picked up and run with, and rumors were exploding as witnessed at the NASA press briefing this morning. But I think Dr. Carrington would agree that backup analysis from experts in China and Russia will not hurt. And besides, sooner rather than later, it will have to be publicly addressed."

It was obvious to Richard that the president respected her opinion. Brockenborough started to reply, but a gesture from the president stilled him.

"Mr. President," said Alice, "I just feel I should remind everyone here that all news outlets are expecting the president to make a public statement in less than four hours." She fell silent, not elaborating on what should be said or how.

The president turned his attention back to Richard. "Dr. Carrington, what do you think I should say?"

"That the shit is about to hit the fan," someone muttered.

Richard was not sure how to respond.

"Doctor, I need your advice now!" The president was more insistent.

Richard remained silent for several more seconds. Why question him on what they already knew? Printouts of data were in front of everyone there; for him to comment was simply redundant, and if time was so precious, this was a waste of time.

"We're waiting, Dr. Carrington," the president said, and Richard felt a growing impatience. From the corner of his eye, he saw Alice and Judith looking at him nervously, and Alice leaned forward as if ready to fill in.

"Mr. President, what we are facing far transcends the CME issue," Richard finally said. "The data on the CME is obvious, and you don't need my reiterating it yet again. I must assume I am here to clarify the assessments regarding the potential of a coronal proton ejection from what some are now calling Sauron's Eye?" Richard felt it best not to lay claim to the fact that apparently he had given it that name and it had stuck.

There was a stirring in the room.

"Doctor, you are indeed perceptive. Yes, the CME is a given; I need to hear straight from you what this other storm is all about."

"Sir, given you want an accurate up-to-the-minute analysis, can I have just a minute or two to check current data?"

"Go ahead."

Richard turned to Alice, rattling off requests for images and data, while hushed conversations started around the room.

After the first minute, Judith leaned over in her chair. "I can tell by your expression," she whispered, "you don't like what you are seeing."

He looked straight into her eyes and nodded. Absorbing the data and projections was no longer information related to just national or global interests. This was about his life as well—his son, his two young grandchildren, his entire world that held all that he loved or could love past, present, and future.

He whispered for Alice to shift the images he wanted up to the main monitor. When the view shifted from the CME to what he was there to focus on, the room fell silent, all eyes on him.

"Go on, Dr. Carrington," the president said softly.

Richard turned to look at the screen, the data on the secondary monitor, then back to his audience and just felt so damn awkward with the back-and-forth shifts that he finally just stood up and went to the lectern set to one side of the room, which gave him a better view of the monitors.

"Mr. President, that swirling mass the image is focused on is approximately fifteen degrees to the left of where the current CME exploded from, which means, given the rotation of the sun on its axis, starting in approximately forty-two hours, it will be aimed straight at us."

He nodded back to the screen and its current image. Since he had last gazed into that nightmare less than two hours earlier, it had expanded in size, the borderlines of energy swirling in and pulsing out of it rapidly increasing.

"Dr. Carrington, this is your show now," the president announced, "and everyone here is to remain silent until you are done. Tell us what it is and what, if anything, can be done about it."

"Sir, according to my analysis and also that of some of my counterparts in Russia and China, we are looking at a CPE, not a CME."

"Differentiate, please."

"A coronal proton ejection of a magnitude we believe not to have occurred in eons."

"Again, tell us what the difference is."

Richard so wanted to get into a detailed analysis but decided it was best to cut to the chase. "It could kill us all. It most likely will be an extinction-level event, the shorthand term is ELE."

The room erupted until the president shouted for everyone to shut up.

Even though his vision was now out of focus with his glasses off, Richard could sense that the president was staring straight at him, waiting for more.

"A CME is something that has been on our radar for years, and fortunately, in the last few, there have been some steps to ensure the survivability of our electrical and electronic infrastructure." He turned momentarily to look back at the screen. "A coronal proton eruption, a CPE, is different—frightfully different. It is a different energy level, mostly protons but also highly energetic X-rays and gamma rays bundled together, exploding from the surface of the sun in a vast ball of energy tens of thousands of miles across. And unlike with a CME, some of that energy is within our visible spectrum, and we will actually see it, the intensity of sunlight doubling, tripling, then going blindingly intense in a matter of seconds."

"In other words, a supernova?" someone asked.

"No, definitely not that. If it were a supernova, it would mean that planets clear out to Jupiter would be vaporized. No, this is different, but the potential danger is nearly as bad. A flare, like the one building up in what is being called Sauron's Eye, will explode with a release of energy across a broad spectrum, including visible light, so that for a few seconds, it might look like the sun is exploding."

"Has this happened before?" the president asked.

Richard looked back at the screen, gazing into Sauron's Eye before answering. "Yes, with other stars. We've managed to observe several across the last few decades thanks to the two Hubbles. But from our sun? Some historians of astronomical observations believe there was one around A.D. 775. Records in China, which are without doubt the best long-term continual history of astronomical events, record a sudden brightening of the sun for more than a day that, if gazed at directly, would all but blind you."

"So if that is true," the president asked, "why didn't it have the impact back then that you are predicting now—an extinction-level event, as you are calling it."

Richard turned back to his audience, who gazed at him in silence. "Because for starters, we of course don't know how intense the energy outburst truly was back then. Next, just like with a CME, it has to be aimed straight at us when it blows, if not it misses us completely and life goes on as usual. Even if it does come our way, usually, thanks to our magnetosphere, the radiation does not penetrate through to Earth's surface. Our magnetosphere truly is a blanket that protects our world from so much that out beyond its protective shielding is deadly. Without it, it is highly doubtful life ever would have evolved on this planet."

"It's in God's hand," the president said softly. The president's deep faith was well known. Several around the room nodding in agreement.

"Precisely, sir. Usually, when a CPE blows, an aftereffect—like a thunderstorm after a tornado has passed—will be a CME erupting in its wake. This one is shaping up far differently, with events in reverse. In forty-two hours, we will be hit first by a CME. That, as we all now know, will peel back the magnetosphere and its role as a protective blanket. Several hours later, if Sauron's Eye explodes as I and others are predicting it will, the high-energy radiation from that explosion will hit Earth's surface, and without the protective layer of the magnetosphere, the result will be a highly lethal burst of radiation that could very well bathe the surface of our planet for hours and perhaps even days."

He paused again, attention focused on the president. "An extinction-level event," Richard announced.

"You're talking about radiation." It was another officer sitting to the right of the admiral, a three-star in the army. "How much and for how long? Could it be minimal, requiring just taking some basic shelter and precautions for several hours?"

Richard felt like an oncologist now, discussing a frightful diagnosis with a patient. "Sir, given the amount of energy we are seeing within that building storm, my projections are that if it does indeed hit us while the magnetosphere is broken open by the CME, we will be facing an instant dosage of thousands of rads per square meter. With a duration of even a few seconds, it would lead to unconsciousness and death within a matter of minutes. This is far deadlier than a nuclear weapon, though, because unlike that instantaneous burst of radiation from a nuclear explosion which lasts for only a few microseconds, the radiation from this event could and most likely will last for hours at the very least.

"The downside for people retreating to the basic type of shelters from Cold War days? Even if the shelters they are in cut the radiation dosage by 90 percent or more? You would get a lower dosage, but across several days of such bombardment, unlike a burst from a nuclear bomb, it would still be fatal. Unless people are secured in very deep and shielded facilities, those exposed will eventually reach the six hundred–plus rad exposure and die anyhow."

"Merciful God in heaven," the president whispered.

There was numbed silence for a moment until the NSA director finally ventured a question, her voice tight, strained. "But by the time that damn eye lines up, the CME will be over and the magnetosphere will be back in shape to protect us, won't it?"

"If it only traveled at the same speed as a CME, my answer would be yes. Unlike a CME with a velocity of a million miles per hour or more, a proton flare travels at nearly the speed of light. From explosion off the surface of the sun to impact would be from ten minutes up to thirty minutes at most."

He looked at Alice, wondering if she had some graphic loaded, but it was obvious to him now that up until he spoke up, she had come prepared only to deal with the CME and assumed that was what the briefing was about. She was looking up at him, features drawn, stunned. Judith, sitting beside her, just gazed off, perhaps still in shock over the death of her mentor and friend, or now overwhelmed again by what he was presenting and she had been fully aware of for several hours.

Richard put his glasses back on as he stepped away from the monitor and back to the edge of the conference table.

"How long will this radiation strike last?" the admiral asked. "I mean, if we are on the nightside, that means China is facing the sun when it hits and . . ." He grinned slightly, which sickened Richard.

"My God, what are you implying?" the head of the NSA shouted back. "Where is your humanity? It is still half the planet with billions of people. Or, for that matter, suppose it is us facing the sun and they are on the dark side. We're then the ones to get cooked; it's a fifty-fifty chance."

The room exploded again until the president stood up slamming a balled fist down on the conference table. "Everyone shut up and let Carrington finish." Nodding to Richard, he asked, "What the admiral just presented . . . is that possible?"

"One, or the other." Richard sighed and shook his head. "Mr. President, it comes down to the duration of the flare. If it is a major burst but of very short duration—say, a few hours—then yes, the side of our planet facing the sun will get a direct and very high dosage of radiation, but even what would be the nightside of our planet could very well be impacted indirectly as what is left of our magnetosphere bends some of that energy into patterns that will encircle the earth. But odds are, sir, it will last for hours at the least and more likely days—perhaps longer— until the rotation of the sun on its own axis eventually points it away from us."

"I am hearing a lot of obtuse answers, Doctor. I want you to give us your exact read on what you believe will happen."

Richard deliberately turned to gaze into Sauron's Eye and then at the data scrolling down on the secondary screen. "I can't give you exact numbers yet. I'm nearly certain that we are about to witness a major solar flare. If it lets go a day early, it misses us. Four days later, it misses us, and concurrent with that, the impact of the CME is lessening and the magnetosphere is resuming its regular protective shield around us. We don't have much to build a probability model on."

"Damn it, your estimate, sir," the president snapped. "I have to make some decisions, and damn soon, Dr. Carrington. Your analysis may well decide what I tell the nation and the world tonight, and I have only a few hours to decide what to say."

"Don't say anything," Admiral Brockenborough interjected. "Shut down access to *Helio II* to absolutely everyone—especially the Russians and Chinese—and we stay silent, sir."

"The cat is already out of the bag, sir," Dr. Lindstrum replied forcefully.

Richard added, "Even up to a day ago, the threat potential was there but not truly significant. The probability of this happening only soared upward within the last eighteen hours."

Dr. Lindstrum stirred and this time politely cleared her throat, and Richard fell silent. He was glad to let her carry the ball to the next decision.

"Maybe we should have shut everything down earlier in anticipation, before that late-night radio guy did his program and really got things riled up," Lindstrum said. "But that is the past, sir. We have to deal with the now. Therefore, Mr. President, you have to make a clear statement this evening. It is the moral thing you must do."

"Moral?" he asked.

The NSA head turned back to Richard. "Doctor, is it possible to survive this?"

"With deep enough shelters and caverns, yes."

"Right there, sir. At least give people some chance to try to prepare. Every hour is precious."

"Mr. President?"

The president turned to his left, to the Senate majority leader, Hawkins of Missouri, who was standing. "Go on."

"Rumors are already out there, sir, and some state governments are reacting."

"And I wonder who tipped some of them off—like your home state of Missouri, for one?" Lindstrum snarled.

"Are you implying something?" Hawkins replied sharply.

"Yes, I am. As usual, there are leaks, and the governor of your state is already moving full bore on their CG plans."

"Enough!" The president slapped the table. "I agree there have been leaks; there are always damn leaks, but now is not the time to debate that. The point at this moment, given this latest update from Dr. Carrington, is that across federal, state, and local levels, we have to initiate our continuity-of-government plans now, immediately, today. Missouri and a few other states have jumped the gun, but we can't argue about who leaked now. Every hour is precious."

There were murmurs of agreement around the room.

"I'm of the opinion that continuity-of-government plans should be initiated starting this evening. Is there concurrence on that?" He looked around the room, and Richard could see that there was full agreement.

"And what about the day after it is over?" someone asked.

The president turned and looked to an elderly bent-over man halfway down the length of the table. "Some of you know Dr. Van Buren, our secretary of the interior. I asked him to attend for precisely the question of what we have to anticipate after this nightmare event has passed. Please go ahead, sir."

Van Buren slowly stood, looked at the projections on the monitor, and then focused on Richard.

"You call this a potential, and I quote, 'extinction-level event,' do you not, sir?"

"Yes."

"Define that term."

Richard felt out of his league now, assuming he was about to be jumped on for the use of that term that did sound alarmist and out of some bad sci-fi disaster movie.

"If the duration extends for several days, it means nearly every square foot of the surface of our planet except above the Arctic Circle will receive direct exposure to fatal overdoses of radiation."

"And therefore, all animal species on the surface, exposed to such radiation might very well perish?"

Richard nodded.

"Our good prophet of doom here," Van Buren announced, "might know of the Rancholabrean extinction?"

"The what?" was the response from more than a few.

"Dr. Carrington, are you familiar with it?"

"Vaguely, sir. If you study solar weather, sooner or later, you come across the thesis that a solar event approximately twelve thousand years ago triggered a significant extinction."

"Closer to thirteen thousand years ago," Van Buren corrected. "But what is a millennium, more or less?"

"Gentlemen, would you please clarify this for the rest of us?" the president interjected.

"Mr. President, approximately thirteen thousand years ago, there was a significant die-off of a vast assortment of animal species, especially larger mammals. The old thesis used to be that they were being hunted to extinction by an increasingly more agile *Homo sapiens* armed with bows, but a recent theory is that it was a major solar event, what our good prophet here calls a CPE. Evidence in some radio carbon dating supports this thesis."

"Therefore?" the president asked, and Richard sensed a rising anxiety from the president.

"Sir, even if some people survive, what kind of world will they find when the storm is past? The potential of nearly all domesticated animals dead. Most wild animals except those who by random chance are deep underground—say, because they are hibernating. Potential impact on plant life, even potential impact on climate."

"Not climate change again," someone said.

"Oh, this will do it far better than mere mortals can ever do, though whether that means another Ice Age or the polar caps melting and coastal areas eventually washed under is a topic of debate," Van Buren replied. "Therefore, I think we'd better address some of these concerns today and see if there are any contingency plans for long-term survival in such an altered world that survivors, if any, might have to face."

Van Buren looked around the room, waiting for a reply. There was none.

"Sorry, Mr. President, but felt I should raise my own concerns in my field. Maybe our precious redwoods can hack it; I'll have to check if a study has ever been done on what radiation level they can survive. But as for everything else?" He did not speculate further and simply sat back down.

"Doctor?" Lindstrum asked. "Do you have any additional thoughts on this as to how such a storm will affect Earth's environment long-term?"

"I think it would be best if Dr. Carrington just stayed within his field for right now," the president interjected. "Doctor, we are running this on a lot of assumptions and what-ifs, are we not?"

Richard nodded. "Yes, sir, but you asked me for my analysis, and that is it."

"Tell me, Dr. Carrington, what are the odds, the actual *real* odds of this happening? Overall probability seems incredibly low regarding what we are facing now; otherwise, statistically, this should have happened long before our species first appeared."

Richard smiled ruefully. "Sir, we have a saying in my business. When it comes to eternity as a measure of time and all of space as a measure of habitable planets, odds no longer matter. Sooner or later, it will happen, and it looks like our planet is about to get it." He paused for dramatic effect. "The only thing that matters is that it happens when you are alive to witness it and most likely will wind up killing you."

His words were greeted with silence. There was a subtle gesture from the president, and Allison went up to Judith's side. Judith—who, strangely, had never been pulled into the discussion—leaned over and whispered to her and then turned to Richard.

"That's it for now," Allison whispered. "We're being asked to leave."

A bit surprised, Richard stood up, not sure what to do.

The president, who was leaning over and huddled with the secretary of the interior in a whispered conversation about what he should say to the public in a few hours, paused and looked back up.

"Drs. Carrington and Cooper, thank you. Dr. Carrington, I need you to stay here at the White House for the time being. Dr. Cooper, I need you back at Goddard; you are now in charge there."

And that was it; there were none of the handshakes and thanks Alice had said would most likely happen.

Allison led them out of the room, closing the door behind her as they exited. "Do you think this is really going to happen?" she asked once the door was closed.

"Yes." Richard could not say more because his emotions were overwhelming him.

PART IV

And those who expected lightning and thunder
Are disappointed.
And those who expected signs and archangels' trumps
Do not believe it is happening now.

—Czeslaw Milosz, "A Song on the End of the World,"
in *The Collected Poems 1931–1987*

7

DARLA stood up, walked across the room, and turned off the small battery-powered television. Their cable system was down for the moment, and it had been nearly an entire day without electricity. The station they had been watching was broadcasting out of Springfield, picked up via an antenna pointing north, which she had rigged to the outside porch; she'd run the wire inside to the television resting on the kitchen counter.

They looked at each other in numbed silence.

"Well, at least we won't have to worry about those capital gains taxes from selling your business," Darren said, staring into the now cold cup of coffee he had been clutching for the last half hour while listening to the president's address.

The sad attempt to lighten the mood was at first met with stony silence from Darla.

"It felt like a half-truth," she finally replied. "This different kind of solar storm might hit, it might not—best to be prepared, stay in place, and seek shelter?" She shook her head.

He had to agree. He had voted for the president, trusted him far more than the last one, and yet he felt that the man had not been completely forthright. The explanation of a different type of storm coming from Sauron's Eye confirmed the rumors spreading from earlier in the day. But then the president had offered reassurances and suggested that people just simply continue to prepare as they had already been doing for the arrival of the CME, which was projected to hit in less than forty hours. He had then added that governments were going to take additional steps to ensure that all would function smoothly in the days ahead and were now preparing emergency shelters for key personnel in order to guarantee public safety.

The speech ended with reassuring words that he would update the nation the following morning as to the situation, signing off without taking questions from a frantically shouting press as he left the East Room.

Darren put several more logs into the fireplace, pausing for a moment to stand in front of the stove and soak in the radiant heat.

"I don't know, Bear," she said, coming up to his side and putting her arm around his waist, "but my bullshit detector is off the charts between that and what you told me about that general and the way you damn near got detained at the National Guard office."

"I think I'd better go back to work tonight," Darren finally replied.

"To do what?"

"Keep an eye on things? I don't know."

"Gut feeling?" she asked.

"Yeah."

"I think we both want some definite answers after that speech. There's a lot more behind it. Something is in the works, Darren, what with his comment that he will address the nation again come morning. A lot can happen between now and then. I'm going to make a call or two."

That surprising idea caught him off guard. "Maybe a bit of a risk for them if they answer," he offered. "That is, if you can even can get through."

"Nothing ventured . . . ," she replied as she walked into her office, switched on a handheld flashlight, and fumbled around a bit at a bookshelf. She returned a minute later with a three-ring binder thick with paper. Turning on the battery-powered light that hung from the kitchen chandelier, she opened the binder and started flipping through the pages.

Darren went to her side, and she looked up at him, grinning slightly.

"You never had security clearances, so you're not supposed to look at this folder," she said. "Don't make me have to shoot you."

Of course, she was joking, but deep down inside, it did touch a nerve. When they had first met, it became obvious that this wonderful person knew a lot more than she had first let on or that he would ever find out about. They had met while he was still laid up at Walter Reed with a bad gut shot, with an intestine that had to be resectioned.

His roommate was a marine gunny sergeant, a Navy SEAL, torn up pretty badly, gut shot like he was, with several shell fragments perforating various other parts of his body. They had gotten to know each other fairly well, making jokes about some gorgeous nurse rather than a male corpsman changing their colostomy bags. About five days after he had been checked in and was just starting to come out of the deep haze of anesthesia from several surgeries and the painkillers being pumped in via an IV, there she was, a chair pulled up by the side of his roommate, the two of them chatting away.

His first instinct was that she must be the guy's girlfriend. But even with that, there was just something about the way she looked that hit him, and he stared at her with eyes half-closed.

After several minutes, he finally stirred and deliberately let out a little moan to signal to the two that he was awake and could listen in on what they were talking about.

"Hey, you okay?" his roommate asked with obvious concern.

"Yeah, sure. Just a bit hazy. What time is it?"

Darla got out of her chair and turned to face him, her gaze dropping to the military-style watch on her wrist and then back up at him with an answer. He didn't even hear it; her pale green eyes had just gut shot him.

He remembered little of the conversation, for he was still in more than a bit of a drug-induced haze so that he finally drifted off.

Was she a dream? he asked himself when awaking again in the middle of the night.

That was answered the following morning when she was back in the room at 0900, ostensibly to visit his roommate, only later to admit that the way he looked into her eyes had absolutely caused her heart to trip over.

The days passed, and it turned out that she wasn't the SEAL's girlfriend or anything close to that. She had done some work with him and his unit as a private contractor. She and her soon-to-be ex-husband owned a firm started by her father that customized weapons for special purposes.

She and the SEAL were good friends and had known each other for years, but the visits—at least with him—were for business purposes as well, saving her a trip out to the Middle East to review how her company's products were holding up and what modifications were now being asked for.

The SEAL was finally transferred to another facility to start rehab, but the following day, she was back to sit at Darren's bedside for several hours.

A year passed after those first meetings. He was already divorced, having learned that his ex had drifted off with someone else while he was overseas, but that had been evident to him long before he had deployed, and it was no surprise when the farewell letter—followed by the paperwork for a divorce—arrived as he squatted in the heat of Iraq. Darla was then going through the same process as well, and she made it clear that until it was finalized, she still felt married and was morally bound to honor that. It drew him to her even more; she was an honest person who believed in honoring vows and promises—an increasingly rare anomaly in his world.

They were both from the Ozarks, which would prove to be a wonderful coincidence. Discharged after recovering from his wound, he returned home to take a job as chief of police for a small town outside of Springfield. They had stayed in touch, phone calls and such, with her mostly on the road, and then nearly a year later, she had just walked into his office, smiling and offering to take him out to dinner. A month after that date, they were married.

It was indeed a curious marriage that resulted—a wife with a security clearance, who still managed a company she'd built up to a dozen highly skilled employees, her ex having finally just sold the firm to her, taken the money, and disappeared on a thirty-eight-foot sailboat to the Caribbean, not be heard from again.

The one thing that continued to bother Darren big-time after their marriage was that every few months, she would pack a duffel bag—no suitcases for her—announce she would be "on the road" for a few weeks, kiss him passionately, and then just disappear and upon returning kiss him even more passionately but not being able to tell him where she had been.

Three years earlier, she had returned from such a trip, shaken, and wouldn't talk about it; she woke him up several times over the next week, crying. Something had happened, and she suddenly just announced that if it was okay with him, she was going to sell the firm and get out.

Okay with him? He had been the absolute model of circumspection, never questioning her professional life or ever doubting in the slightest her absolutely loving devotion to him at home and when on the road.

The profits from the sale of that firm had enabled them to build a magnificent house overlooking the Lake of the Ozarks, and after Darren had a close call on the job, it became quid pro quo. He quit as chief of police because she repeatedly said, "I am more worried about some bastard strung out on opiates far more than some damn terrorist getting through the gate when I was at a forward base in the 'Stan. At least out there, I was surrounded by thirty or so of the toughest killers in the world with enough of an old-fashioned sexist view that they would protect me to the death. But you, dear Darren, the only one watching your back makes Barney Fife look like Dirty Harry."

He had to agree, thinking about how that routine traffic stop turned into a shoot-out with an idiot wasted on meth. Boredom, however, settled over him within days. To keep up to speed, and simply because they both liked the work, they'd occasionally rent themselves out as a security team for special events and to help cover a nearby popular preacher when he did a large rally. In his case, there really was the concern that some nutcase might just wander in someday, as was all too frequently happening with churches and schools of late.

Now, sitting by the fireplace with the three-ring binder in one hand and holding a flashlight with the other, she thumbed through the pages of the binder, paused, and studied some names and contact information. She shook her head, then thumbed back.

"George Atkinson, for starters. If anyone knows what the hell is really going on, it'll be George."

Darren peeked over her shoulder at the information she was examining. The man was listed as a Navy SEAL, in command of a counterterrorist reaction force based in D.C. The name jogged a memory, but he wasn't quite sure of what.

She went back into her office. He could hear her opening the small safe located under her desk. She returned several minutes later with a cell phone, and not just a standard one; it was military grade and appeared to be capable of satellite uplink and downlink.

Darla clicked it on and smiled as the display indicated a 100 percent charge.

"See, that's why I keep preaching all electronics should be kept in a proper Faraday cage and recharged every three months when in storage!"

He smiled, leaned over, and kissed her on the forehead. "Should I just go to the other end of the house and find something to do?"

She smiled and shook her head, reaching out to pull him down to sit by her side, then reading off a long number string from the printout in the binder.

"This info is three years old," she announced. "Let's pray this thing still uplinks to a functioning sat, that George still has this number, that he has a phone on him that works, and that he picks it up."

She hit the Send button. Silence for a moment, then a burst of electronic noise, and seconds later a voice answered.

"Hello?" A pause. "Darla, is that you?"

"Hell yes it is, George."

"After three years, why are you calling me now? Especially tonight?"

"Sir." Her tone shifted from casual friendly to dead-on professional serious. "Colonel, I have a couple of deep and troubling questions tonight and figure you will give me a straight-up answer."

"Everybody has questions tonight." He paused. "Okay, for you, a few answers if I can. I'm giving you two minutes, Darla, and that's it. Things are really stressing out here at the moment."

She looked at Darren, nodded, and flipped a switch to speakerphone.

"George, you remember my husband, Darren, don't you?"

"Yes. And he is a lucky bastard." His tone relaxed slightly. "Darla, you know I wanted you too. Can that son of a bitch hear me?"

"Oh yes." She chuckled.

"Hey, you bastard, are you still shitting in a bag?"

That totally caught Darren off guard until he connected it all together. The man on the other end was the Navy SEAL who had shared a room with him at Walter Reed years earlier.

"Oh my God," Darren replied. "How the hell are you, sir?"

"I'm doing just fine. No time now for small talk with you two. Darla, you are down to ninety seconds."

"George, the president's speech. Felt like some things were being held back."

"Of course some things were being held back; they always are. So what is it that you want to know?"

"George," Darren interjected. "I'm head of security for a two-and-a-half-million-square-foot underground facility here in Springfield, Missouri."

"Yes, I know of the place," came a quick reply, which surprised Darren. "You do?"

"Yeah, of course I do. It's on more than a few listings. You're down to sixty seconds."

"Sir," Darren replied, "this afternoon, the commander of the National Guard for this state, General Perry, arrived for a quick inspection and left some people to inventory a huge stockpile of food stored by Kraft Foods along with state equipment stored there."

"So?"

"I heard some jargon—you know, military talk. What is *CG*? I know it's pilot shorthand for *center of gravity* on a chopper or plane, but that doesn't seem to fit for whatever is going on."

"It means *continuity of government*. The states and feds are taking control of places like yours starting at midnight tonight."

"For what?"

"Forty-five seconds left, Darren, and I am sorry, but that's a question you should be able to figure out on your own. Continuity of government. All across the country, government officials are getting set to evacuate to deep underground shelters starting tomorrow. Once that is in place tomorrow morning, the rest of the country will be told what is coming next. Thinking was to get CG rolling first without panicked mobs getting in the way. So you figure the rest out from there."

"George, who is getting evacuated?" Darla interjected. "Why and to where?"

"Just all those who it has been decided are so indispensable for our country that they will go underground to survive so they can come back up topside and run the government after it is over. Now is that it? Damn it, my ass will be in the wringer if this gets traced. I'm doing it only because I had a crush on you, Darla, and beyond that, a hell of a lot of respect for both of you. Next question, and make it quick."

"What is ELE?"

They heard an intake of breath from the other end. "Where did you hear that one?"

"One of the staff traveling around with General Perry said he overheard Perry talking about something called ELE with the governor."

There was an extended silence, and Darla picked up the phone and looked at the screen to see if they were still connected.

"Five minutes on the internet will give you the answer," George finally replied.

"Damn it, George, we don't have internet," Darla growled. "Most of the country doesn't have internet; that's why I'm calling you, so please just give me a straight answer!"

"Extinction-level event."

"What?"

"You heard me. Now listen up, you two. Tonight, the president said about as much as he could without triggering a full-blown panic. This CME storm hitting the day after tomorrow is only the start, like a one-two punch. A couple of hours after that hits us, this thing, this Sauron's Eye, is set to explode. When it does, the radiation from it will be like a million nukes going off. No blast, just radiation. Enough radiation to kill you within minutes. That's what is going down. It was decided to at least get some things in place before spilling out the rest of the news as to what will happen. Across the country, continuity-of-government plans are kicking in. By tomorrow morning, at least several hundred thousand people—military and federal, state, and local government types—will be moving into shelters."

"That's it?" Darren cried. "George, I've got millions of square feet of deep shelter that I'm responsible for. A hell of a lot of food down there as well. Beyond those the state of Missouri is sending there, how many people can I expect? Sure, I get it regarding government types, but what about everyone else?"

George's laughter had a sad, exhausted sound to it. "Come on, you two, wake up! Anyone who has pull, a friend, a connection gets in to the deep shelters. Big donors to the right party, political friends, friends of their friends, mistresses, lots and lots of self-important bureaucrats, we all know the type. They get in, then the doors get closed. Do you read me on that?"

"George, there are tens of thousands of civilians living in Springfield directly above those caverns. What about them after all the state government people move in? What about everyone else?"

"Fuck 'em," George said wearily.

"What?"

"Darren, did you hear me? Extinction-level event. The select have already been selected. If this thing is as bad as I'm being told, those with the right tickets will scramble in and then lock the doors."

"There's enough food in the tunnels to feed ten thousand or more for months."

"Which ten thousand, Darren? Think about it! This ain't some *Titanic* fantasy of lifeboats for women and children first. This is captain and crew and their families first, then afterward tell everyone else the ship is sinking. The rationale, the balm on their souls? Why, it's all about continuity of government and 'Gee, sorry, folks, no more room down here; just head to your basements, or dig a hole, or sit back on the surface and have lots of 100 SPF sunblock.'"

"And you are going along with this?" Darla interjected angrily.

There was an audible sigh. "What else can I do, Darla? I'm in command of a security team being deployed to one of the sites for D.C.—which one, I will not tell you. They want to get the CG in place and secured for everything federal, state, and local first before really letting on just how bad it most likely is going to be."

"Worse than what the president said?"

There was a long silence, and when George spoke again, they could hear his voice was breaking. "Yeah, I'm selling my soul by going along. The balm? Do it, and my wife and kids go with me. Refuse, and they die. As for you two? Darren, if you can get to your kids, grab them, take Darla, and get them into that shelter now, tonight, before the government takes it over. That's the bottom line. Do it now."

Darla asked, "George, are you the same man I worked with and respected for so many years?"

"I tell myself it is about my wife and kids. I pray God forgives me," he whispered, and the signal went dead.

Darren and Darla looked at each in silence, and it was finally Darren who broke it. "I haven't had a drink since I got shot. I need one now."

Darla went into the storage area set aside for prepper supplies and came out a few minutes later with a dust-covered bottle of single-malt scotch. She took two coffee cups, opened the scotch, poured out a very stiff dose for both of them, and sat down by his side. Staring at the fire, she drew closer to him as she sipped the scotch, and he could tell that she was trying to conceal the fact that she was shaking and in tears.

"Do we believe him?" Darren finally asked, coughing and gasping after he took a long gulp of his drink.

"Yes. He did two more tours in Afghanistan, got a mustang promotion and became my chief contact person for developing contracts. His word is gold. That's why I picked him and prayed he would answer our call. If he says this is it, I believe him."

"So that's why the general told me to get you and bring you back to the Underground. He was doing both of us a favor."

"How so, Bear?"

"The good state of Missouri is going to move into the Underground tomorrow. That storage area they had purchased was stockpiled with material for living quarters like I told you, complete with an office to be set up exclusively for the governor. They'll be moving in likely thousands of people. It's why checking out Kraft was first on his list, to see how much food was on hand."

He took another sip of his drink.

"I could see he was upset with how it was half-empty, but still, there was enough to feed thousands, and then add in whatever the state has in its tunnel as well. That can keep thousands going for months. They might be moving in even now. They'll most likely deploy the local National Guard unit of military police to secure the perimeter. That explains why they damn near detained me when I went into the armory and tried to ask too many questions. Their commander overheard me and started yelling for them to shut up and for me to be held."

"Which means?"

He got up, opened the door to the fireplace, threw in a few more logs, and then sat back down, leaving the door open, wanting to experience a fireplace the way it used to be with the actual sound of crackling wood and that wonderful scent of oak, maple, and hickory burning.

"Get their people in, then seal it up until whatever is going to happen with this Sauron's Eye is over with, one way or another."

"George was scared just now. I could hear it in his voice, and that is one man who doesn't scare easily," Darla added.

The scent of the firewood drifted toward him when a downdraft hit the chimney, a cold wind howling outside. He closed his eyes for a moment, the drink and that scent, the radiant heat at least relaxing him a bit.

The sun and solar weather had been an increasingly major topic in the news over the last six months or so, long before the big CME of early December. Stations like the Discovery Channel and others that long ago used to actually do science and history before the damn reality show crazy took them all over had been putting out some informational programs for a change. Some of them were sensationalistic crap—alleged experts predicting the sun was about to blow up; that, with the planet's magnetic poles shifting, weather on Earth would be affected; even that Earth's poles were going to flip, which would screw up a whole host of things. Talk of supernovas, explosions from stars up to fifty light-years away that could wipe out every living thing on the planet. Flares and superflares.

It had, of course, become numbing to be taken too seriously or for one's own emotional well-being just ignored until the first CME hit. It had been tough these last three weeks, but society had not collapsed into a postapocalyptic world. But now? This? According to a man that there was no reason not to trust, this Sauron's Eye thing was the end-game for humanity . . . except for those who got to the deep shelters first.

On the other side, Darren's fundamentalist friends had been predicting for years that the end-times were at hand. Now he wondered if indeed they were right.

"Bear? What do we do?" Darla asked softly, her voice nearly breaking.

He looked down at her. "What?"

"Just that. What do we do?"

He stared back at the fire. "If we just leave this place now, we could be to the Underground in less than an hour. Once inside, we'll be safe. As head of security, I doubt that General Perry will kick us out if we help him."

"Are you comfortable with that? Just drive up there, don't tell our friends, our neighbors? Just drive up there, get our tickets to survive, and that's it?"

She looked up at him as if seeking guidance, though he inwardly admitted that so many times it was he who turned to her for the right answer.

He sighed, leaning forward, and picked up his empty coffee cup. Looking at the bottle of scotch, he was sorely tempted to get drunk, get absolutely shit-faced drunk and wait until morning to figure it out. But that thought just turned his stomach. It was not how he lived his life or how she lived hers.

"We should at least try to reach our kids, give them a warning," she said.

He nodded.

She picked the satellite phone up, punched in an access code, and then tried the numbers for both of their children, their cell phone and landlines. All four times, the reply was the ever-annoying high-pitched tone and a computerized voice announcing that all circuits were busy and to try again later—the same thing they had been hearing since the start of December.

She filled up with tears and snuggled in by his side, an arm around him, and he felt her hugging him tightly.

"Bear, now what?"

He stood up as if to put yet another log in the fire but then just walked around the living room, stopping to glance at the various photos of children and grandkids that Darla had merged into a wonderful display of both sides of their families that their marriage had joined together. The room was still just illuminated by the fire and created a warm, pulsing glow so that the photographs had an almost haunting quality.

He walked over to a gun case in a corner that held not just current weapons; in it was an M1 given to Darren by his grandfather, who had carried it when he went ashore on Utah Beach. A battered Sharps rifle from the nineteenth century was beside the M1, the gun from Darla's side of the family, connecting them generations back to the Civil War. Objects, things, mementos, current photographs of the living, gazing out of the photographs into a future that might very well be at an end. Photographs of their own parents, grandparents, and in turn their grandparents. Lives in the past across generations of half-remembered stories, of faded images locked in tintypes from 150 years ago, resting alongside a just-arrived picture of a new granddaughter held by a proud son and his wife.

Then things from the lives that he and Darla had merged into one. The honeymoon to Alaska, a place they had always wanted to visit but never managed to until finally meeting and falling in love. Their honeymoon was four weeks of camping, fishing, hunting, and nights staring up at crystal-clear skies and auroras that back then seemed to be so harmless and wondrous but now might be the harbinger of the end. The end of all of this?

He walked back around the room, taking in the memories in a moment that filled him with a profound insight. It was not just his life, her life; it was all their lives, including the lives of those who had died long ago but lived on in the two of them that hung in the balance. The thoughts now were about a future, how to try to create some kind of lasting future.

He looked back at her and finally understood what he would do. He told her what thoughts were forming from deep within. She stood up, tearful, and embraced him.

"I love you, Bear, and that is exactly what I was thinking we should do."

8

THE White House was turning out to be a disappointment for Richard, ensconced in a communications center several stories beneath ground level. It felt like any government office area. The chairs and desks were standard government issue, slightly faded blue or gold with a leather backrest but at least not government-issue gray. The snack area was well stocked, even with tea, and the small cafeteria had a chef who gave him a perfect omelet. One story farther down, there was a sleeping area and a long corridor; the room assigned to him was utilitarian, six foot by nine, with just enough space for a twin bed, small dresser, and an adjoining private shower and toilet.

The whole thing was making him damn claustrophobic.

Allison, apparently the Secret Service agent assigned to be his guide, had led him straight to the room after he'd left the conference with the president. The pictures on the wall were typical hotel decorations, most of them of a historical scene, and the entire facility was 100 percent non-smoking. It didn't matter, because in the rush to bring him here, pipes and tobacco had been left behind at his office in Goddard.

After getting him oriented as to where the cafeteria was located as well as a small conference room where a computer link had already been set up to Goddard, she told him to be in his room, the café, or assigned office since he was now on call when needed. After handing him a White House identification card that he was to wear at all times, she left with the suggestion that he at least try to get a little sleep.

He sat alone in the room for several hours, trying to do just that with no success. Too much was boiling up inside of him. He wanted to be at Goddard, monitoring the situation as it unfolded, not stuck here, his only communication link tethered to a standard office computer. His post should be there, he reasoned bitterly, able to observe on the 8K wide-screen monitors what was shaping up to be the greatest and most frightening event in the history of solar astronomy.

He finally wandered down to the small conference room where he had been assigned a workstation, and there, along with several other staffers, he watched the president's 7:30 P.M. address. It did surprise him that the president had only revealed a half-truth, a warning, and not the full reality of the situation. He could understand why. The president had decided to put the information out in two packets. The first to give the military and government at least some lead time to prepare before the general populace learned the full reality, when panic most likely would set in. But still, to keep citizens in the dark bothered him. The staffers standing about whispered nervously, for within the White House, the inevitable leaks had quickly sprung, and most knew the full extent of what was coming. Fortunately, no one recognized who he was to then bombard him with anxious questions.

Returning to his room after at least enjoying an omelet in the cafeteria, the first meal he had eaten since early morning, he finally managed to doze off, only to be awakened by an insistent knocking on the door to his room.

"Who is it?" he muttered wearily.

"Agent Minneci, sir. Please open the door."

"Who?"

"Allison Minneci, sir."

Groggily, he sat up on the side of the bed. "Just come on in."

"Sir, I prefer you open the door."

He sighed, realizing the usual protocols were in place when it came to a member of the opposite sex entering a room, especially someone's sleeping quarters. He stood up, feeling rumpled, mouth sticky, rubbing his scratchy chin, and cracked the door open.

"Sir, please come with me immediately."

"Why, for heaven's sake?"

"Sir, you'll find out."

He awoke more fully. "Has something blown?"

"No, sir. Now would you please come with me?"

He gazed at her intently for a moment. Maybe twenty-five, twenty-eight or so at most. No ring on her finger, about the same age as his daughter-in-law. Brunette hair cut short, just a touch of makeup, trim figure mostly concealed by the "uniform" of business-style blazer and slacks.

An overwhelming thought hit him as he gazed at her. *I've had a life of just over sixty years; what of yours if this is truly the end?*

He realized he had been staring at her, and he felt a flash of concern that she might interpret it the wrong way. "You're about the same age as my daughter-in-law."

There was no reply, just a polite nod.

"If we're going to be working together, it's Richard. Okay?"

She offered a faint smile. "Sure, Richard, now will you please come with me?"

"Is it okay to call you Allison?"

There was a friendly smile, and she nodded.

"Now, what's up?"

"It will be apparent in a few minutes, sir." A pause. "Richard, sir."

He went to pick up the necktie he had taken off and tossed onto the top of the dresser.

"No need for that, sir." Another pause. "Richard. Just the blazer will be okay."

"Can I at least brush my teeth?"

She chuckled softly. "One minute, that's it." Then she directed him to put on his ID tag as they finally headed out of the room.

She led him down a labyrinth of corridors, and within a minute, he was totally disoriented and knew he'd need a guide if he wanted to get back to his room. One elevator took them up, stopped, then out of that and down another corridor to a second elevator, which went up just a couple of floors. Out of that and then a final turn to where a Secret Service agent stood watch at a closed door. The agent immediately opened the door, and Allison whispered for Richard to go into the room, the door closing behind him.

Entering the room, he found himself face-to-face with the president.

It was a heart-stopping moment. The day before, the president had been a slightly shadowy entity at the far end of a conference table, nearly the kind of setting in which one would expect to see a president during a high-level and very tense meeting. This was different. Rather than sitting behind a desk, the president stepped forward and extended his hand in greeting.

"Dr. Carrington, how are you? Sorry to roust you out at this hour, but I'd like to go over a few things with you. Did you sleep well, at least get a little rest?"

No sense in lying, he thought. "No, sir. Maybe dozed a bit, but not peacefully."

A slight smile creased the president's features. "Same here. Twenty-minute nap and that was it."

He stood several inches taller than Richard at just under six feet, his pale blue eyes were piercing, and Richard felt as if the man were looking straight into him, searching for something.

"Let's sit down and chat," the president said, motioning to an oversized leather chair placed opposite to an identical chair. The room was comfortable—no windows, bookcases lining two walls. Richard glanced at them as he sat down. Mostly history books, several he had read as well. When entering a room like this, Richard had always felt that a quick scan of the bookshelves could reveal a lot about who he was meeting with.

It became apparent that the books were not just decorative touches; more than a few had faded, worn covers. There were quite a few biographies, mostly of political leaders of the past, an interesting span of history, and even some works of literature—mostly American classics. Seeing what the president might read was a positive for Richard.

There was a decidedly masculine feel to the room, the bookshelves laden with serious works, the leather chairs, several historic paintings of the American West—one of them he thought might be an original by Frederic Remington—and several heavy cut-crystal decanters on a side table. Furnishings were along the lines of something designed by Frank Lloyd Wright. As a boy and young man growing up in England, he had seen rooms similar to this in most upper-middle-class and upper-class homes, though usually with antique furnishings, the ubiquitous family portraits dating back several hundred years, and a proper display of old firearms mounted on the wall.

Richard would never admit that he had not supported the candidacy of this man sitting across from him, but there was something to his presence that he liked. Richard had never gone for American citizenship; at heart, he'd always felt that his sojourn in America was temporary, even though he had married an American and raised his family here. Therefore, he had tried not to pay too much attention to American politics and the rise of this man who had come out of nowhere as a moderate compromise candidate in the last election—which, like all the elections of this century, had become fraught with accusations, counteraccusations, investigations, and endless screaming and wrangling. Not that English politics were any better; it was just that up until the last few months, being a solar astronomer was a life relatively free of angst and worries, so why upset that by following politics?

He realized that while he was contemplating these thoughts, the president was sitting in silence, gazing at him, his eyes revealing that he was indeed exhausted.

For several seconds of this silence, the president seemed to be sizing him up, and under his gaze, Richard glanced to a dark walnut side table with several magazines on it, including a *Scientific American* published several years earlier, in which Richard had coauthored an article about the rapid increase in solar activity ahead of the usual solar maximum cycle of eleven years. His theory was that the sun having several different cycles of energy output, beyond the well-known eleven-year alternating solar maximum and minimum and across several hundred years what was known as the Maunder Cycle and that something beyond those two cycles was approaching. He and his coauthor postulated that a cycle perhaps thousands of years in length was now happening for the first time in recorded history.

Next to the *Scientific American* rested a paper copy of an internet article speculating that the sudden die-off a large number of species and rapid ending of the Ice Age thirteen thousand years ago might be linked to a solar flare, the same event mentioned by Secretary Van Buren at the afternoon meeting. Though the article was not written by Richard, he was familiar with it.

The president noticed what he was looking at. "Yes, I've been doing a lot of studying the last few days. You write clearly and concisely, Dr. Carrington."

"Thank you, sir."

"Doctor, let's just relax a bit, okay?" His smooth, well-modulated midwestern voice was appealing. "Would you care for a drink? There are a couple of good scotches available and a well-aged American whiskey." He nodded to the sideboard.

"I think I'll pass on that for now, sir. To be honest, if I have a drink at this moment, it will knock me out."

"Wise decision. I'm refraining, as well. How about something else less dangerous? You name it, they have it in this building."

"A tea would be nice, sir."

"Earl Grey, isn't it? One lump, no cream?"

That startled Richard, and the president chuckled softly. "It always gets some people when they find out how much is researched about them before we even meet. I know it is creepy to some; hope it doesn't bother you."

Richard didn't know how to reply.

The president touched his phone resting on the side table. "Tea for the doctor, coffee for me, please."

He focused his attention back to Richard. "Dr. Carrington, can we go a little less formal here, sir? How would you like to be addressed?"

"Richard is just fine, sir." He did not dare to ask if he could call the president by his first name. As a very young man, he had attended a ceremony at Buckingham Palace honoring the director of Greenwich, where his mentor would be honored with a knighthood to be presented by the beloved Queen. Richard had been invited by his elderly friend to stand nearby and would then be presented to Her Majesty as a direct descendant of the first Richard Christopher Carrington.

The drill beforehand, given to him by a palace advisor, on protocol when meeting the Queen had been extensive and frightening for a twelve-year-old. How to enter the room, where to stand, to speak only if spoken to, how to respond if the Queen or others of her entourage offered a hand. He feared he was going to get sick to his stomach as he entered the room, but when it was all done, he had found her to be kind and charming. She expressed what he felt was a genuine delight that he wanted to follow the same career path as his illustrious ancestor. She had even presented him with a splendid book, an illustrated history of Greenwich, with her noting that an entire chapter was devoted to his forebear.

Now he was sitting with the president of the United States, but it was nothing formal, more like two gentlemen chatting in the lounge of an upscale club.

If I can get through an audience with the Queen at the age of twelve, I surely can get through this next half hour or hour without making a fool of myself.

"I was hoping you would be comfortable with my addressing you as Richard," the president continued, interrupting Richard's thoughts. "It does get to me at times all the various titles people expect and how they get fussed up if not addressed that way."

Even as he spoke, a side door opened. A young man approached, balancing a small tray with two cups, and set it down on the side table without comment or ceremony.

"Thank you, Peter." The president nodded to the cup of tea, while picking up his own cup, taking a long sip, and setting it back down.

"So I am willing to bet you're wondering why you're here and what I want."

"Well, honestly, sir, yes."

"Fine, then, let's get started. I'm getting updates at least every hour, but I want to go over everything again with you, one-on-one, with no one filtering in between us. What is going to happen and when? Start with the CME."

Richard set his cup of tea down, shifted nervously in his chair, and told himself to ignore the fact that this man was the president; he was just someone who wanted to know the straight answer. *Don't hold back.*

"Sir, I have to confess I was napping in my room when I was requested to come here."

"I'm jealous." The president sighed. "Every time I try to lie down, there's another call or meeting. I asked for the job, so I shouldn't complain." He shrugged and tried to smile. "When was the last time you looked at your data."

"Sir, what time is it?" Richard asked.

The president looked at his wristwatch. "12:40 our time."

Richard hesitated for a second. Was it A.M. or P.M.? He had not passed a window since coming here.

"Just past midnight," the president added with a smile.

Richard took another sip of tea, needing a caffeine jolt with the realization of the time and the need to be sharp. A blessing of his choice within the field of astronomy was that he worked during the day, rather than sitting up night after night. When doing his graduate work, he had endured many a long night of yawning and downing numerous cups of coffee or tea. That had ended when he had gone full-time into solar work, and therefore, he rarely was awake much after nine in the evening.

He took another sip of his tea, but it had yet to bring him fully awake and into focus. "Sir, last time I looked at the data was shortly after nine in the evening during a review of it via a teleconference with a friend of mine in China. I feel asleep after that. Has anything changed significantly within the last three hours that you are aware of, sir, and I am not up to speed?"

The president shook his head.

"If that is the case, the CME will begin having an effect by approximately eleven tomorrow morning. What hits first is like a bow wave, a disturbance in front of a ship. Full impact follows shortly thereafter, hitting fully by noon tomorrow—approximately thirty-five hours from now."

"A Carrington-level event," the president offered with a slight smile, which Richard returned wanly. "You don't like it being called that, do you, Richard?"

"To be honest, no, sir. Family name linked to such an event."

"Okay, I'll make sure we stop calling it that."

"Thank you, sir, but it is already out there."

"I know. My press secretary tells me the bloodhounds of the press are already announcing to the world that the president of the United States is huddling with Dr. Carrington, the world's expert on solar storms, who the CME is named after, and they can't wait to hear what we've talked about."

"Oh, merciful . . ." He held back.

"Merciful God, you wanted to say. And yes, it is frustrating. Though this building is one of the securest in the world, it is still a fishbowl, and it nearly drives me crazy at times." He took a sip of his coffee and forced a smile. "An ant can't break wind in this place without someone reporting on it, and half the time the story gets so twisted up it's reported that a small nuclear weapon was detonated."

The president laughed ruefully at his own joke. Richard found it to be more than a bit surprising but also disarming, which he realized it was meant to be.

"Don't worry, we are very secure and very private here, though, for your information, the famous Oval Office is not more than a hundred feet from here. When I want to meet someone privately with nobody knowing, I come here to this quiet little room. This room is where Jack Kennedy used to have his midday rendezvous with Marilyn Monroe, and yes, where that other president used to play with his intern. It serves better as a library retreat, don't you think?"

Richard did not know how to reply. The president lowered his head slightly and shook it, a gesture that made Richard think a devout Baptist was telling an off-color joke and then worrying about what the reaction might be. So this man really was a straight arrow, and Richard now realized that information that was ballyhooed throughout the campaign that he was a man with true personal morals was not just for public display to win votes.

"Now to the core of it," the president finally continued. "Sauron's Eye, as everyone is now calling it. It will be a near-extinction-level event, won't it?"

Richard picked up his tea to take a sip and buy a few moments of time. To his dismay, he realized he was trembling, his hand shaking.

A terrible memory hit him. The day he sat beside his mother as she calmly asked the doctor to be honest, that the cancer had returned and would be terminal. The way she asked, there was no fear, instead a tone of calm acceptance, and it was she who did the consoling when he broke down after leaving the doctor's office. It felt the same now.

The president was slightly hunched over, arms resting on knees, hands folded in front, head leaning down but eyes gazing up intently fixed on him, the same as his mother's once was.

"Sir, we have a lot of models, but we have no prior data from other events to compare it to. But the way the energy within the anomaly we're calling Sauron's Eye is building up, the sun's gravitation field will eventually no longer be able to contain it. Unless things have changed profoundly in the last few hours since I looked at the data . . ." He was delaying with laying the god-awful truth out in the open and both of them knew it.

"I was just talking to my secretary of the interior; you might remember him—Dr. Van Buren. He said the data is following your projections."

"Then, sir, it will blow within the next thirty-six to forty-eight hours."

"That's a straight answer, Richard. Thank you. You said an ELE at the meeting yesterday. Did you still hold to that?"

"That, sir, I cannot give you an absolutely straight answer on."

"Why?"

"There are variables, as I told you yesterday afternoon. What we are dealing with here is something unprecedented for us."

"Fine, just give it to me again. Straight out. I want a rundown of the variables as you see it, without anyone interrupting us."

Richard wondered if that was a reference to the admiral who was all too eager to jump in on the briefing.

"Timing is the big one," Richard said. "If it blew right at this instant, its probable trajectory would miss us. Even if it did blow before noon tomorrow, our magnetosphere, not yet distorted by the CME, would absorb most the blow. But it might not blow in a straight-line trajectory. Remember the gravity and magnetic fields of the sun are so intense that years ago Einstein's theory was proven by observing how light from a star was bent—" He paused. "Sorry, sir, I was drifting, and I know your time is precious."

"It's okay; it's a complex topic, and I'm trying to wrap my brain around it."

"The gravity and magnetic fields of the sun might affect trajectory, just bend it by several degrees as it blows out, making a huge difference when it arrives and passes through our orbit."

"Got that. Okay. Next?"

"The center of what is building up is nearly on the equator, and the sun turns on its axis, same as Earth does. Starting midday tomorrow, it will be like looking down the bore of a rifle aimed straight at us."

"And as you just explained, if the magnetosphere has not yet been impacted by the CME, we have a good chance of survival."

"Yes, sir. The crisis will be after the CME starts to hit." He took another sip of tea. "Ironic, sir. In and of itself, the approaching CME will have an impact on our electrical and electronic infrastructure far worse than the December 1 event, potentially well into the trillions of dollars of damage and years of work to recover from. I know the government has been deliberately vague on the impact of the last event. Just how bad is it in places like Chicago, New York, Boston?"

"At least fifty thousand dead according to the latest report," the president said softly.

"My God."

"Yes, my God. Civil order really disintegrated in Chicago and parts of New York, Philly, even here in D.C. With this cold snap, it's been far worse. In and of itself, the December 1 storm has proven to be the worst natural disaster in the history of our nation. Kind of ironic isn't it?"

"How so, sir?"

"What has already happened will pale to insignificance if the worst happens tomorrow. Even if it does not, and we are simply hit by this CME, that will really knock us off balance for some time to come."

Richard remained silent.

"At least, if that is all we have to deal with, we'll eventually recover. But you don't see it that way, do you?"

"No, sir."

"What are the variables? I've been getting a heck of an education on radiation effects, shelters, and such over the last day, but I need to hear it from you."

"The actual level of radiation in the initial explosion and duration of event will be the factors. Relatively low radiation of short duration, we might actually get through it, though there will be casualties; if short enough, it could even be localized to just one part of our planet."

"Like what Admiral Brockenborough was chortling about yesterday that just part of the earth gets hit and he hopes it is China."

"Yes, sir. Or it could have a long stream behind it, a tail blowing outward for hours, even days, in a wide enough burst that even as the sun rotates on its axis and we continue to move in our orbit, we'll still be getting radiated. If so, the entire planet gets dosed, perhaps some regions get two or even three days of exposure."

"I now understand there are a couple of ways of defining that in what are called rads, or sieverts."

"Mr. President, I prefer rads. Best-case scenario, a burst hitting for short-duration hits with an intensity of rads into the high hundreds of total exposure. Worst case, the first seconds of burst could expose someone out in the open with thousands of rads, followed by a continuing and far higher dosage spread out across a couple of days."

"Extinction level for anyone or anything exposed." The president sighed.

"Are those the variables you asked for, sir?"

"There is another variable as well," the president added, and there was a flicker of a smile, but his features were cold, intent.

"I think you are about to say, Mr. President, that I and all the other experts are dead-on wrong about the whole damn thing—there is no solar flare; we simply get hit by the most intense CME in more than a century and a half. A disaster in and of itself, but nearly everyone will survive it, at least short-term."

"Exactly. And then all who were running around buying into your projections will look like total assholes. There have been plenty of ex-amples in the past and not-so-far-distant past of people and even entire governments buying into bad science."

"So your question then is, sir, is this bad science?"

"Yes."

"I assume you've heard from more than a few disputing my thesis and that of quite a few other solar astronomers?"

"Yes, more than a few."

"I have no answer to you, sir, other than the fact that I trust my work, I trust my team that built the algorithms for analysis. Dr. Chen's team in China, using algorithms independent of ours, have reached the same conclusion, though they narrow the window a bit to twenty-four to thirty-six hours from now. We and the Chinese, though, are in full agreement that the CME starts affecting the magnetosphere at 11:00 A.M. eastern time and will reach full intensity by noon eastern time tomorrow."

"Thirty-five hours from now."

"Yes, sir."

"And you will hold to your projection and that of the Chinese re-garding the flare?"

"Yes, sir, unless the data starts changing significantly, which is always a possibility."

"So I have a bottom-line decision to make, and I damn well better make it soon, very soon."

"Which is?"

"Did you hear my address to the nation last evening?"

"Yes, sir."

"You knew of course I was prevaricating. Still using words like *possible* and *probability* and *maybe*. I assume you disagreed that I did that?"

"I understand your position, sir."

The president smiled. "Diplomatic answer, Richard. You see, there was no holding back the data any longer; too many sources were onto the threat from Sauron's Eye. I had to say something and at least give some warning, but I did not say straight out just how catastrophic this will most likely be."

Richard had no reply. He picked up his cup of tea, saw that he had drained it off, and set it down. The president did not notice it was empty, and Richard had no desire to ask for more at this moment, though he felt he desperately needed it, along with a good shot of scotch and a pipeful of tobacco.

"Reports already are that panic is building. I know you might disagree that I did not fully lay it out just yet."

"But those who needed to know, at least as you define it, are fully aware and acting even as we sit here talking?"

"At the moment, I saw it as the only way I could go. Government officials in all fifty states, the governors, commanders of the National Guard, those in charge of emergency services are setting their plans in motion. The same, of course, is true at the federal level."

"Continuity of government, I think that's what you call it?"

The president was silent for a moment, noticing their cups were empty. He tapped his phone and asked for refills. He remained silent until more tea and coffee was brought in, took a sip, and then finally continued.

"What should have been the moral choice? You yourself said there are variables, that it might not happen as you say it will." He offered a sad smile. "Perhaps such a variable means that Lot finds the tenth virtuous man."

"Sir?"

"Remember your Bible? I assume you were raised Anglican."

"Yes. But when it came to Sunday school, I'll confess I often slept through it."

The president chuckled. "So did I, but still that particular story has been surfacing in my mind over the last few days. It's when God decided to smite Sodom and Gomorrah. God tells Abraham of his intentions, and Abraham begins to bargain with him. I always liked that story. Abraham negotiating with God—call it a plea bargain. Used to think of it when I was a judge and some lawyer was trying to talk me out of a stiff sentence even though his client was guilty as hell. Abraham opens the bid with asking God that if fifty righteous men can be found in the cities marked for destruction that God will change his mind. God agrees.

Then it is, 'Okay, God, how about just five fewer? Can we make it forty-five righteous men?'"

The president openly chuckled. "Old Abraham was a darn good negotiator—don't jump to the bottom line all at once; just lead it along step by step. So from forty-five, he gets God down to forty, then thirty, and finally wraps the deal up with 'Let me speak just once more,' knowing he was pushing his plea bargain to the edge, and closed the deal with 'What if only ten can be found there?' and God answered, 'For the sake of ten, I will not destroy it.'"

The president sighed and took another sip of coffee. "You have your way at looking at the odds, the algorithms; mine is that story. Are we really doomed? Maybe this is all a warning from God."

He looked intently at Richard. "Or even if it is just an uncaring universe, devoid of reason, and we are at the hands of random probabilities, it could still turn out that we are spared the killing blow—or maybe it really is that a tenth righteous man has been found and, for his sake, the rest of us can go on living. And I would like to believe if we do go on living, we'll have a far different perspective and grasp of what is the meaning of it all. There is nothing like getting the crap scared out of us, individually or collectively, to wake us up to what we should be doing with our lives rather than what we simply are doing often without thinking."

Richard had no answer. Yes, he actually did struggle with the same question. Was there a divine purpose to this universe? At times, especially in his profession, where one would be so overwhelmed by the sheer vastness of the universe, it seemed utterly illogical to believe in some story hatched in the infancy of our race that there was a benevolent, all-seeing, all-knowing, and all-loving father keeping watch. But then at other times, the opposite thought would form that surely there was a logic, a higher something that had created this incredible wonder of a universe and of one's own life. At this moment, he envied the faith that had just been expressed by the man sitting across from him.

"I wandered a bit with that, Richard; I'm sorry. Perhaps I should take us back to the point I wanted to raise. I made a decision yesterday to at least offer some fair warning. In contrast, the Russians and Chinese have

been silent at the official level, only offering warning and directives regarding the approaching CME, while their governments scramble with
their own CG plans. And yes, I'll confess that I recoiled at the thought
of laying it all out, up front, and tell the world what you and other experts predict. But then suppose you are wrong—and you will admit that
is always a possibility, will you not?"

Richard nodded.

The president stood up and paced back and forth, head bowed, hands
clenched behind his back. "So I tell the full truth. Then what? True mass
panic? What is left if civil order collapses? But on the other side, the rumors are only out there, and rumors always run with the worst case
possible, never the best. I promised the nation I would personally give
an update first thing in the morning. What would you do?"

That was startling. Richard wanted to refuse an answer, but the president had stopped pacing, now standing before him, gaze intent.

"And I do expect you to give me an honest, full update a minute before I go in front of the cameras."

"It will most likely be the worst-case scenario, sir."

"Therefore? What would you say?"

"Don't people have a right to know? We're supposedly a free people,
not children to be lied to."

"Go on."

"Sir, I hate to sound maudlin, but back when things were at their
worst during Dunkirk and afterward, Churchill just told the truth, my
people faced it as eventually did yours. Hold it back or lie? Well, sir, in
less than thirty-six hours, no matter what is said, it will happen, so I'd
want to know the truth. Certainly, there will be panic and, heaven help
us, civil breakdown in some places."

"So let's just say I give it out straight and it doesn't happen? A lot of
people could die from the ensuing panic."

"But if you don't make an official announcement with the full truth
and it does happen, a least a few people who might be able to survive—
at least short-term—will die needlessly."

"Short-term?" the president asked.

"Sir, we can't even begin to estimate what a post-flare world might look like a year later. Which animal species, if any, will survive. Your secretary of the interior raised that very effectively, along with what might even happen with plant species and environment."

"Are you saying that even for those who do survive, the planet has been dealt a deathblow and all are doomed?"

"Sir, I'm not the expert on that," Richard replied cautiously. "I'd suggest personnel from Department of the Interior would have a better handle on that."

"That conversation was troubling," the president replied, leaning over again, elbows resting on knees and hands clasped. "He urged that we prioritize what he calls *doomsday survival,* says that Norway had been doing something like that."

"I'm not sure I follow you, sir."

"Some years back, they built a deep vault; inside it are stashed seeds by the billions, DNA samples of thousands of species, data storage of damn near everything from all our recorded histories and such."

"Do we have that?" He felt at least a small surge of hopefulness with the thought.

The president did not even bother to look up. "Survival of government in the event of nuclear war, bubonic plague, things like that? Oh yes, we spent hundreds of billions ever since World War II. We most certainly thought of that going back to Truman, having a deep shelter put in here when the White House was remodeled in the late 1940s, to Eisenhower just so happening to ensure that the Site R bunker complex as a fallback position for the Pentagon was built a five-minute drive from his Gettysburg house. But to think longer-term—about all of humanity. Looks like the Norwegians and, according to rumor, the Swiss and even the Israelis thought of that while we did not."

"Can we do anything now?"

The president shook his head. "Secretary Van Buren was pressing that we find places where domesticated animals, cattle, sheep, pigs, goats, and such can be driven to, for starters. Nice idea, and I did not reply with the answer of a realist. We've got what, thirty-six hours to try to organize that? Then imagine that little rodeo going down while millions of people are in a panic, desperate to break into those same places?"

He fell silent, and Richard could see that though farsighted, there would not be enough time. Even if they'd had a week or a month, it would be impossible. Explain to a desperate mob outside a gate that cows go in but they cannot?

"I asked the secretary just how it could be done. Beyond that, the millions of species of animals, even plants, what of them? The old man had no answer, of course. Muttered about line items in the national budget that tried to address these things that were always mocked and then cut in committee. He was a sad, broken man when he left here an hour ago. He offered a chilling closing comment on the way out the door. Something about how Earth itself will survive, some things will survive, most in the ocean will survive. If eventually none of us do, Earth will still be here and will survive."

He looked back up at Richard. "I'd like to believe that maybe the story of Noah is literally true. Eight people survived on that boat—Noah, his wife, their sons and wives, along with all those giraffes, pigeons, and lions. Maybe that is how it will be. Maybe the Norwegians and their doomsday bunker will one day reseed our world. Some hope there, at least, even though we in this country failed to do so."

The president remained silent for several minutes after that and then touched the phone on the side table asking for yet another cup of coffee and of tea, which was brought in a few minutes later, neither having spoken during the interval.

"I can arrange to have something added to that," the president said as Richard gratefully took a sip, hoping the familiar custom of drinking tea would settle his nerves a bit.

"Don't tempt me, sir. I think you'd prefer me clearheaded for right now."

The president smiled and nodded a thanks.

"May I ask a question, sir?"

"Certainly; this isn't just a one-way street here."

"This talk about CG—what does it entail? What is happening now?"

"Continuity of government goes back to the start of the Cold War and involves what to do if nuclear war breaks out. Starting right after the Second World War, the government eventually spent billions constructing vast underground shelters—places like Site R—to serve as fall-back positions for the Pentagon, deep shelters at Camp David, a huge complex under a hotel in West Virginia for Congress."

He took a long sip of coffee. "It just kept morphing through the years. Eventually, state and even local governments started building them. There's one hundreds of feet deep for the mayor of New York; nearly every governor has one. Everyone was saying we needed to ensure the government continues even if there is a full-scale nuclear war and we blow half the planet apart. Once the dust clears and the fallout settles, government will continue. Believe it or not, there's even a facility for the IRS."

"Who goes and who doesn't?"

"Key personnel—at least those who draw up the plans—were of course the ones who defined who exactly are 'key personnel.' Top government officials and administrators were of course given the nod, folks like that."

"Anyone else?"

"Oh, if there is time to pull in others, there are lists of additional personnel. The usual candidates—scientists, doctors, essential personnel for post-disaster survival, they call them."

"What about families?"

"What do you think? I wouldn't give two cents for someone who takes a slot in such a place and leaves his or her family behind. One of the briefings a new president gets when he comes into office is about CG. I asked the same question you did and got a lot of blank stares. I insisted immediately families henceforth be included. Lot of complaining about expanding facilities, and heaven help me, I haven't followed up on it since then and have to assume that, so typical of bureaucracies, they are still 'studying the concept.'"

"And I assume along with families of top officials, as you call them, if there is enough time before disaster hits, friends of those top officials, people with political pull, all of them with their families and such?"

"You sound cynical."

"Just a realist, sir. And now, tonight? How many have been—how is it said in America?—tipped off?"

"All top levels of the federal government are already moving personnel. There was some sort of leak earlier on into this; I suspect our beloved senate majority leader called a few friends, so some folks got a jump start in his home state and a few other places, but by noon tomorrow at the latest, state and local governments will be inside or in transit to their fallback positions. Total number? I'd estimate at least several hundred thousand people are already on the move."

"What about the rest of the public?"

The president sighed and lowered his head. "You just clinched the argument for me. Do any of them stand a chance if given early enough warning?"

"Sir, again, ask your specialists with the Department of the Interior or experts when it comes to radiation. All I can give you are the estimates of how big a dose will hit, and I do know that in the worst-case scenario, those out in the open will die within a matter of minutes."

"Will it be bad?" the president asked softly. "I mean, you are talking about death from radiation. From everything I know about it, it is a ghastly way to die."

Richard shook his head. "I know what you are thinking—like those poor souls who died after Chernobyl that lingered in agony for weeks. No, you get hit with several thousand rad all at once, you collapse and go unconscious within a few minutes. But those who might be in partial shelters, cutting the radiation dose down, could survive if they have enough shielding. The cutoff for a 50 percent death rate from exposure is around three hundred rad. But even then, those that survive such a dose only do so with intense medical intervention."

"Even for those that survive? How do they survive if nearly every living thing on the surface is wiped out?"

"Unless you are down deep with a hell of a lot of food to rely on for months, perhaps even a year or years, survivors coming out of shelters will be scrambling for whatever food can still be found on the surface."

"Nightmare," the president whispered. "Maybe those who crawl out alive in the days and weeks afterward will wind up envying the dead. I asked myself that. During the Cold War, some theorists argued that in the event of an incoming attack, no warning should be given to the civilian population. The logic was to let them have their last minutes of life in peace. And besides, those that did survive would eventually envy those who did not."

"Do you believe that, sir?"

"No, of course not. It is just that the scenario you paint and that Secretary Van Buren spoke about . . ." His voice trailed off. "If my wife were still alive, and maybe on a trip thousands of miles away, I would want her to have the chance to get back so we could then face it together. Wouldn't you?"

"Yes." Richard was unsure if the president knew that, like him, his wife had lost her fight with cancer two years earlier.

"Then that decides it. Regardless of the chaos, all people should have the chance to decide how they will face the end. For many, it will be fear and panic, but I daresay, most will want to embrace those whom they love." There was a flicker of a smile from the president. "Thank you for your time, Richard."

Richard felt as if that were a dismissal and began standing, but then the president reached out, touched him on the arm, and motioned for him to sit back down.

"I want you to stay very close; in case there is anything you feel I should be updated on, you'll be given a priority code number that will take you straight to me in less than a minute. I plan to address the nation again at 7:00 A.M. eastern time, and it will reflect what you and I have talked about. Okay?" He held Richard's hand firmly. "People have been coddled and lied to for far too long. They are going to hear the truth, and I believe most folks will actually hold together." He smiled sadly and looked off. "The better angels of our nature."

"Sir?"

"Abraham Lincoln, the closing lines of his first inaugural. It was an appeal for peace; he prayed that all of us would finally be moved by 'the better angels of our nature.' I believe him. It is part of my faith in man and in God, Richard."

9

"IT looks like we were right," Darren announced as he turned their Tahoe off Highway 65 and onto the Haywood Road exit. A vehicle, a Humvee with military markings, was parked at the exit ramp but not blocking the road. Darren gave the driver a friendly wave as if his arrival were just routine, and he did not slow down as they turned east on Haywood and then onto Limestone Road to access the Underground. Going around the bend on Limestone Road, he could see in the early-morning twilight half a dozen more Humvees and a couple of trucks parked in front of the entryway. Fortunately, none were blocking the access road.

Maybe, just maybe, he prayed, they could pull it off with complete surprise and no one would get hurt.

Three cars, a small caravan, were sticking close behind him as ordered. Ten people—six of them the entire police force from the town where he'd served as chief of police, a lone sheriff's deputy whose home address he knew and could locate at two in the morning, and his very sleepy-eyed pastor with a couple of deacons from the church. All of them were armed.

"Assume the worst," Darren whispered as he approached the perimeter fence and slowed down.

"I always do," Darla replied as she chambered a round into her M4 and then slipped it down between the door and the seat on her side so it was out of view.

Turning the final curve in the road, he sighed. "Damn it, a Black Hawk on the helipad."

"General Perry?"

"Yeah—would have preferred he not be here."

"That doesn't change anything, does it?" Darla asked.

"Not now. At least I hope not, but it might not be as easy as we would like with him inside."

The steel door was open, the roadway in clear.

"At least the door isn't blocked," she whispered.

"Stupid on their part. We stick to the plan."

They passed through the chain-link fence gate. Half a dozen MPs were near the steel door; he could see that one of his people, Tyrell, was with them.

An MP moved to step in front of the Tahoe, bundled up in a heavy parka—no weapon out, thank heavens—holding a gloved hand up for them to stop even as Darren rolled down the window.

"Identification and your purpose for being here," the MP barked.

"Good to see you guys are securing this place," Darren replied conversationally as he held up his opened wallet, displaying his ID card as head of security for the Underground and, beside it, his old chief of police identification—expired, of course, but who would notice at this moment?

"Is General Perry inside?" Darren asked.

"Yes, sir. Why do you ask?"

"Good; he asked me to get back here with some employees to help you guys out."

"Sir, I've not been told to expect you, so please park over to the side. I'll call for the general to come out and meet you." The MP motioned for him turn aside from the entrance.

"What, and freeze our asses off out here?"

"Sir, I'm ordered that—"

Typical MP following orders exactly. A couple of them were wandering over.

"I bet Perry is down in my office. He called me a few hours ago, and I was supposed to meet him there ASAP, and I'm late."

"Sir, I have my orders, and they are—"

Darren didn't let him finish. He still had the Tahoe in low gear; the first thing the dumb-ass MP should have ordered him to do was to turn the engine off. He floored the gas. The Tahoe leaped forward, and he nearly hit one of the approaching MPs, who jumped back out of the way. He drove straight through the access way into the Underground, thanking God the steel doors were still open.

Those behind him did as he had briefed them, and all three followed. He drove a hundred feet down into the Underground and slammed on his brakes. The next car skidded to a stop beside him, thereby blocking both lanes while the other two in the caravan skidded in behind him.

He left the engine running, shifted into park, and slammed down on the parking brake while leaving his headlights, thus illuminating the tunnel and partially blinding anyone that might be approaching from inside.

"Ready? he said, looking over at Darla.

"Of course, Bear," she replied and gave him a tight-lipped smile.

He could see she had slipped into another mode—features calm, icy. The short-barrel M4 she had concealed down by her right side was already up as she yanked her door open, jumped out, and went into a semi-crouch with weapon shouldered and aimed down the tunnel.

Darren, Glock out, sprinted back up the road and went into a crouch, weapon raised, while behind him, his coconspirators piled out of their vehicles with weapons drawn.

Several of the MPs ran in after them and then froze at the sight of what they were confronting.

He prayed nothing stupid, nothing tragic, was about to transpire.

"Listen carefully!" he shouted. "I am head of security for this place and a combat veteran as well, like some of you. No one gets hurt. No one gets hurt if you follow my orders. Just back up outside the steel door. Do not draw your weapons! Keep your hands up and visible."

"What the hell are you doing?" the MP who had first stopped him shouted as he fumbled to open his parka.

"You open that parka and I see a gun, you are a dead man!" Darren shouted. "Back outside now!"

As Darren spoke, he advanced toward them, Glock held in a two-hand grip, pointing straight at them. The three MPs were joined now by three more who had been standing to one side of the door, one of them with an M16 out and half-raised.

"You with the 16! Drop the gun!" Darren shouted as he continued to advance.

The MP took one look at him and dropped the weapon, which clattered to the frozen pavement. He held his hands up.

"We don't want to fight, mister!" one of them gasped.

"Excellent. Now just back outside, hands over your heads, and no one gets hurt."

They backed out as ordered, Darren following to just short of the entryway. Keeping his gaze focused on them while holding his pistol with his left hand, he edged to the right side of the entryway, reaching out to fumble for the control box for the steel door. Finding the switch box, he pulled it open and slapped the switch down.

The doors began closing, Darren keeping a sharp watch on the startled MPs until the doors slammed shut. He then darted over to the small side door and locked it as well.

"Darla?"

"Nothing yet!" she shouted.

"Hey, nicely done, Darren!" congratulated his preacher, who approached his side, shaken by what he had just witnessed.

Darren nodded a thanks and realized that his hands were trembling slightly. Absolutely the last thing he wanted to do was to kill one or more of the MPs. He was ready to do it if need be, but he dreaded that prospect.

"Jim, Charlie, there's another access door to the outside off to my left, a couple of hundred feet down that side corridor behind you. Just make sure the lock is closed. Beyond that is a big door that used to be an access for trains when this was a quarry. It hasn't been opened in years, but I want you to double-check that all the switches in the circuit box are down. That will override anything from the outside. There are a few more personnel hatches at the far end of this facility, but we'll worry about those later."

"We've got company!" Darla shouted.

Headlights were coming up the tunnel; he recognized them immediately as a Humvee, high beams flipped on.

"Everyone get behind your vehicles," Darren ordered as he ran back down the access road inside the tunnel, moving to the left side of their Tahoe, taking position behind the open driver's door, Darla on the other side.

The Humvee stopped thirty or so feet away, its passenger-side door opening. Thanks to the glare from the headlights, it was impossible to see who it was or whether the person had a weapon out.

"Just what the fuck is going on here, damn it!" General Perry's baritone voice was clear and obvious.

"Sir, it's Darren Brooks, security here, remember?" Darren shouted back.

"Answer me! What the fuck are you doing?"

"Sir, have your driver turn off his vehicle and douse his lights. If he doesn't, I'll shoot them out in five seconds! Then step out in front of your vehicle so I can see you."

"And if I don't?"

"You'll be a dead man in five seconds, General, if you don't do exactly as ordered!" Darla shouted back.

Darren ventured the risk, stepped out from behind the Tahoe, turning his Glock aside but still holding it where the general could see that it was not pointed at him but could be in an instant if provoked.

"Sir, I've learned never to argue with my wife," Darren said, lowering his voice as he approached. "She really is a dead-on shot, so please do as requested."

The general wisely kept his hands visible, leaned back to tell his driver to turn the engine and headlights off, and then stepped forward, lowering his hands to rest on his hips.

"Sergeant Brooks, you are in a world of shit with this stunt," the general barked.

"Sir, actually we are all in a world of shit."

"I want you to clear those vehicles and reopen the doors now, Sergeant!"

"No longer in your army, sir. It's just Darren, and my wife still has a bead on you, sir, so please be polite to her."

The general slowly raised his right hand and touched the brim of his hat politely. "Good morning, ma'am."

The gesture did trigger a smile, the display one of bravado and trying to appear calm and in control.

Darla, however, did not reply.

"Okay, Darren, whatever it is you two are planning, let's cut the nonsense. You move your vehicles, unlock the door, and we'll let this thing between us pass."

"No, sir. You, your driver, and any other personnel in here are free to leave, but the door stays locked."

"What are you doing?"

"Seizing this place, sir."

"Okay, Brooks, if you and yours want to stay, fine, but cut out this bullshit Rambo act. Secure your weapons, and then let's talk. Do it now, or my mood is gonna turn really ugly."

"General, remember an old Bible story about Noah?" Darla shouted in reply. "Frankly, though I am a devout believer, I never could quite buy all the millions of species of animals on this good earth jammed into that one boat without them killing and eating each other before the forty days were up."

"Ma'am, just what in the hell are you driving at? You can give me your Bible story later, but first put those damn weapons down before someone gets hurt."

"Let my wife finish, please," Darren said. "It is a wise move to listen to her when she gets like this."

"Go on. Get your damn speech over with."

"My husband and I made a decision last night. We asked some friends and neighbors along with our minister about it, and they all agreed."

"And what decision is that?"

"We're changing the plan for this place."

"Okay, I get it. You two and your friends behind you figured it out that this Sauron's Eye thing is the end-times or whatever you want to call it, and you want in. So okay, you and those with you are in. Now get out of my way; in a few hours, this place will be chaos, and I've got to get things organized. You stay, and if you help, I promise passes for all of you."

"Don't insult us, General!" Darla cried, and Darren could hear by her tone that calm professionalism was giving way to insult and anger. He hoped Perry could pick up on that as well and not piss her off any further. "Who are they? How many and why?"

"Two thousand, for starters, most likely four or five thousand more by tomorrow."

"Why them?" Darla demanded.

"To keep the government running. The governor, top officials, staff, people like that."

"To keep *what* running?" Darla interjected, her voice filled with scorn. "From what we've learned, anyone on the surface tomorrow afternoon will be toast. Who chose some to live while damn near everyone else dies? Answer me that!"

"Come on, you two, somebody has to be in charge once this is over."

"Why them, damn it?"

"Because—"

"Because they selected themselves, that's why!" Darla roared. "And you are pimping for them."

He bristled, and Darren looked over at her, surprised.

"So you two get to do the choosing instead, is that it?" Perry finally replied. "What are you gonna do? A lottery, maybe?" His voice was edged with sarcasm. "Let me guess—form a committee and talk it over? Look, you two. Given the amount of food still in the Kraft warehouse and what the state has stocked here, it's been figured maybe ten thousand can last out here during the storm with enough reserve food to see them through afterward until spring. So what are you gonna do instead?"

"It's an ark."

Darren looked over his shoulder, startled that someone else had spoken out. It was his minister, who had quietly slipped up behind him.

"Will you three stop arguing and throwing insults and just get to the facts? Time's being wasted," the minister added.

Darren nodded in agreement and looked over at Darla. "Go on, Darla," he said, looking over respectfully at his wife.

"As I was about to say, General, we are seizing this facility to turn it into an ark."

"An ark for what?" Perry asked, confused.

"Children only."

"What?"

"You heard me right, General Perry. This facility will be for children only. Not us, not you, not the governor and all those clinging to his coattails. Just children. An ark for the future of humanity if anything is left out there when this is over.

"Yes, there'll be some adults as well, but not any of the folks the governor and those who planned for this place might have on their list. No big donors, no token gestures of a few people with special skills who got on that list because they have friends in the state government. The only adults let in will be those the community decides.

"Teachers, for starters. Parents can help us decide. Only the best teachers and not some damn education bureaucrats from Jefferson City who couldn't teach an idiot how to pour pee out of a boot with the instructions written on the bottom. Doctors and nurses, to be certain, but let the folks of Springfield tell us who are the best and most respected, not some medical board appointed by the governor.

"That's who will get in, General, and not one person more. That means parents will bring their children here, make sure they are safe inside, and then they must turn around and walk away. There will not be enough room here for all of them, so no lottery crap, no special appeals and exceptions. We take in children, those who they will need to help them survive if there is any way of surviving after this is over, and that's it."

There was a long silence as Perry gazed at the ground and then finally back at Darla and Darren. "You're both crazy, you know? How will they survive after it is all over?"

"We aren't sure ourselves," Darren said. "But at least they'll have a chance at it, unlike what you are now part of."

"They deserve that chance, General," Darla said. "That is the decision my husband and I made last night, rather than what you are planning."

"You're both crazy."

"Yes, I think we are," Darren replied with a smile.

"Do you think you can really hold this place?" Perry asked. "Like it or not, I know what the governor's reaction will be. We'll bring down even just a company of combat infantry, a few Bradleys, and one tank, and we'll take this place back. You force my hand and that will be the reaction."

"Then go try it," Darren said sadly.

"But when you do," Darla interjected, "it will not be just us inside. Word is already being passed through the community; we already set some people to do it. The message? Bring your children here and they will be safe. Bring them, pack a bag of warm clothes, a sleeping bag, maybe a favorite toy or stuffed animal—"

Darla's voice broke, and Darren knew she was thinking of her two grandsons they could not reach.

"Bring your children here, kiss them goodbye, hug them one last time, pray with them, then send them in. After that, we're asking parents to stand armed guard outside until one way or another God decides whether to give our world what it most likely deserves or to spare us. If spared and there is no solar explosion like what is being reported, at the end of three days, we will open the door back up, surrender, and face what I assume will be a firing squad or the rope given that martial law is in effect. But if not, I think even you will admit the right decision was made."

"If you try to take this place back," the minister interjected, "may God forgive you, because you'll most likely have to kill every parent standing guard outside."

"You're crazy!"

"Yes, I guess we are," Darla replied with a smile.

"You're free to go now, sir," Darren interjected. "We have work to get to now."

Perry stood silent for a moment.

"No argument will change our minds, General," Darla said. "You are free to go."

Perry nodded and motioned for his driver to get out of the Humvee. Darren escorted them to the side door, looked out through the re-inforced glass panel to the side of the door to make sure the MPs outside were not waiting to ambush them if the side door was opened, and flipped on an outside loudspeaker.

"We are letting General Perry out. Stand back as far as the chain-link fence, no display of weapons. Do it now."

The MPs, still bewildered, stepped back as ordered.

"There are still a dozen or so personnel down inside," Perry said. "None of them are armed—that is, unless they have opened up one of the shipping containers, which we haven't done yet, so I'd like to think you'll just let them go."

"We will."

"The officer with them, Captain Harrison—I'd suggest you just keep him here. There's going to be a confrontation over this, Darren; we both know that. You can use Harrison as a go-between when that time comes. Okay?"

"If he tries anything, you know what it will force me to do," Darren replied.

"He's not an idiot."

"All right, he stays but will be kept under guard."

Perry nodded.

Darren cracked the door open, Perry's driver making a quick exit at a near run and the general following him out into the cold light of early dawn. Perry turned and looked back. "Darren, you know what I have to do in response."

"Yes, I do."

"God forgive you."

"No, General, it is the other way around. May God forgive you."

PART V

What shall bring the doom | of death to Othin,
When the gods to destruction go?

—Selection from the Vafthruthnismol, *Poetic Edda*

10

THE signal on the radio drifted for a few seconds, the president's voice sounding tinny and then coming back in clear.

"May God bless all of you and be with you. Not just we of America but all of us who he placed here on this earth, our good earth. Let us pray that this crisis shall speedily pass away and leave us spared. But that is His will and not ours. I just now ask that all of us take guidance from the words of Abraham Lincoln, who, in an appeal for peace, asked his fellow citizens to be motivated by the better nature of our angels.

"Whether in fear or acceptance of what is to come, whether it does come or does not, I ask that all of us look to one another and to let our hearts be touched by the better angels of our nature."

The president paused, his voice on the radio wavering again, crackling with static so that Darren wondered if the speech had actually ended.

"May God be with you, and let us together face what is coming with calmness and with faith."

It sounded like a click in the carrier wave, and then the familiar voice of a noted television correspondent came on.

"Without responding to questions, the president has left the Oval Office. His message is indeed confirmation of rumors that have been sweeping the world these last few hours—"

Darren switched the radio off and looked around his crowded office, and there was silence broken only by the muffled tears of a few.

Those jammed into his office and out into the hallway were trying to take in all that the president had just said—that beyond the CME impact that was absolutely certain to start hitting at eleven the next morning, something far more overwhelming would transpire within minutes or hours at most after the impact of the CME: the solar storm called Sauron's Eye would erupt toward them with such intensity that only minutes later it would wash Earth's surface in a deadly bath of fatal radiation.

He had not pulled any punches; he'd laid it out clearly, asked for people to stay calm, mentioned that perhaps some preparations might be of worth if the storm turned out to not be as strong as currently anticipated, and that each must face this future as their faith and character might guide them.

There had been no mention of deep shelters like the Underground other than an oblique reference to certain personnel who could help guide the recovery afterward and to ensure that the nation survived.

Regardless of Darren's appeal for calm, several in the crowd in his office and out into the corridor of the Underground's office started breaking. Over the last hour, he and several of his old team from the Fairfield Police Department had rounded up the dozen soldiers still inside the complex. Fortunately, none had resisted. Strangely and without mention of General Perry's suggestion, Captain Harrison had suggested that he stay as a means of perhaps helping to negotiate once the next crisis hit, for surely the general would react. Darren had agreed, though he quietly ordered one of his fellow officers to stay constantly by Harrison's side and to stop him by force if need be if he tried to wander off. Why did Perry suggest Harrison stay behind?

Beyond the team he had brought with him, nearly two dozen employees of the Underground were inside when he had taken the place. Some of them were from the night shift, and many were people who had taken to just staying at work after the December 1 storm. After all, living conditions were comfortable, there was plenty of food, and with gasoline supplies so short, it spared them from worrying about commuting.

Now, in the wake of Darren and Darla seizing the place, and the full realization of the truth just delivered by the president, their moods were decidedly different. One cried that his family lived in Saint Louis and that was where he would be heading, and he fled from the building and out into the tunnel that led up to the gate.

Darren had a solid team of guards posted there; the steel gate would not be opened, but they had already been briefed that if anyone wanted to leave, they should open the small side door and let him or her out.

He hoped, though, that most would elect to stay, at least until the next day. They were the ones most familiar with the complex and what was in it, and they could be of tremendous help in the hours to come.

There was unease from that first cry of panic, which Darren could sense building into a mad rush to get out.

"Listen up!" he cried. Most looked his way, and a few shouted back at him to shut up. "Either we work as a team or this turns into chaos."

His request was greeted with cries of panic, anguish, rage. Darla climb up onto a chair—thus elevating her five-foot-two height to over six feet—drew out her Glock from her shoulder harness, raised it up over her head, and fired.

Darren winced. They were in nothing more than a double-wide trailer tucked inside a limestone cavern. The bullet went straight through the ceiling, and there were cries of alarm but no screams of pain. At least the round had not ricocheted back in. The shot did get the attention of those around her and out in the hallway.

"Now let's calm down, people, and please listen up," Darla announced while still pointing her Glock toward the ceiling.

"I'm not working with any of you!" a woman cried. "Screw it all! I'm going home, at least be with my family. I don't have any kids, but I do have elderly parents that you bastards won't let in. We work here; we should have the right to at least bring our families in."

Darla held her hand out for calm. "Listen up, people. Anyone who wants to leave is free to go. No one is keeping you here. Just walk out the hatchway next to the steel door, and you are free to go."

"My car is parked in here!" the angry woman shouted back.

"I'm sorry, ma'am," Darla replied, "but as long as those troops are outside the door, we cannot open it."

"Screw you, bitch. Thanks a lot."

Darren bristled but remained quiet, projecting a calm demeanor. In his years as a chief of police, he had endured hundreds of insults far worse to which he could not reply.

"That's the way it is, Margaret," Darren interjected. "If the troops outside pull back way beyond the outer gate, maybe then."

"Surely, the rest of you can understand what my husband just said," Darla said. "We wish we could open the door, but if we do, chances are those outside will rush us, and then this plan is lost, and a lot of people will die as well. We don't want that. I hope the rest of you can see that and speak up in agreement."

Good, Darren thought. She was making an appeal now for others to step in on their side.

"Darren Brooks, just who the hell do you think you are taking this place over?" snarled Roger Rauch, the manager of the facility who had stayed on throughout the night and had openly helped the National Guard personnel begin setting up. During the first minutes of the confrontation when Darren and Darla were seizing this place, Roger had remained conveniently out of sight. But now? Darren inwardly sighed as Roger shoved his pudgy form through the tightly packed room.

"Everyone, you know me as the manager of this facility. In that position, I knew some of the plans that the state government has for this place."

If so, Darren thought, *as head of security, it would have been nice to have been briefed on that when I first took this job, rather than "The state owns that corridor; I don't know anything beyond that, so just make sure it stays locked."* He said nothing, knowing it was senseless to argue that point now.

"Listen up!" Roger cried. "The plan was that as long as employees cooperated with the government in the event of an emergency, they and their families would then be allowed to stay. Your so-called friend here just screwed that for you. If you side with him and aren't killed in the process, you'll be kicked out. Those of you who refuse to help this terrorist still might have a chance to stay if we open this place back up and surrender."

The mood in the room now shifted, and angry glances turned Darren's way.

"Darren, you are fired as head of security," Roger raged, voice quavering. "I am ordering you and your criminal companions to leave this facility immediately—and as you do so, unlock the front gate."

"Too late for that now, Roger," Darren replied sharply.

"I don't give a damn what you think or say. You are fired—now get out of here! As for the rest of you, join in with him and you are breaking the law, and when this is over, you will be arrested and face serious consequences. Those who help me will be noted and allowed to stay."

"Roger, you have one of two options. You can stay and work with us to save a lot of children, or you can kiss ass like a self-serving coward, try to kick us out, and then let the governor throw you and those who follow you a crumb. Choose which way it's going to be."

"I suggest you leave now, Roger," Darla said, her tone icy and clear that the debate was over. Her gaze then swept the crowded room. "Any who feel the same as Roger, I suggest you leave now." It was not a suggestion; it was an order. The way she spoke reminded Darren of an age-old paradigm that in any dispute, right or wrong, if only one has a gun, that person will be the winner.

But what if those who agreed with Roger just stayed put and attempted to block or sabotage what he and Darla were doing? He did not want to use force, but he knew he would have to if driven to that extreme.

With the president's open admission of the true extent of the crisis, it was no longer just a rumor for the general public and a concealed fact held by a few in government. Everyone now knew this would truly be life or death for all of them and not just some emotional display about children. Once the crisis had passed, most would look at their civil disobedience as a noble act.

There was a tense silence. Darren looked over at Darla, who was now nearly at eye level when perched atop the chair. Would they be willing to kill folks that had just been his coworkers a day earlier?

Arguing again broke out. Then Darren saw Captain Harrison edging his way through the crowd and pushing his way forward to stand in front of Darren.

Oh, shit, Darren thought. The guy had that look. He was going to completely screw things up, and then what? He was tempted just to knock the officer on the side of the head, but that would set off a panic. It was at a razor's edge, and Darren looked over at Darla, who he felt just might take the stronger action of firing off a few more rounds to intimidate, at least he hoped just to intimidate. Before either of them could react, the officer held a hand up and shouted for attention.

"Listen up!" he cried. "My name is Captain Harrison, an aide to General Perry."

Darren tensed up. It was better to knock him out than have Darla shoot him; a bit earlier, she had told him that she was so committed to their plan and that if need be, she would shoot to kill if the troops outside tried to storm the place.

"I agree with these two people!" Harrison shouted. "Listen to me. They are right."

"What the . . . ?" Darla whispered, looking over at Darren.

Harrison turned slightly to look straight at Darren. "Just tell me what you want me to do, and I'll follow your lead." He offered his hand to Darren.

Darren took it, grasped it hard enough so that Harrison could not pull back. He leaned in close. "You'd better not be bullshitting us," he whispered, looking straight into Harrison's eyes.

Their gaze held for several seconds.

Harrison did not blink or let his gaze drift aside. "Just let me explain why. Okay?"

"Do it." Darla stepped down from the chair and offered it to Harrison, who nodded his thanks and climbed up to take her place.

Darren gave Darla a look that asked, *What are you doing?*

She leaned in close to him. "He's got us. What else can we do?" she whispered. "But if he double-crosses us, I think I'll shoot him. Don't worry; I'll just kneecap him."

The small crowd fell silent as Harrison introduced himself again, his rank, and the fact that he had come to inventory all food stored and, until more troops arrived, ensure it stayed secure.

"You should be following orders, not following these two," Margaret snapped back.

Harrison paused and gazed down at her. "Your name, ma'am?"

She hesitated. "Why do you want to know?" before finally offering her first name.

"Listen closely, Margaret. You tell me I should just follow orders, is that it?"

"Yeah, why?"

"Only following orders," he said softly, and then his tone turned angry. "Only following orders!" He spat the words out with disdain. "Yeah, I had additional orders beyond just doing inventory down here. Before General Perry drove up to meet you two this morning, I was with him. He anticipated that some people might try to take control down here before additional troops could be moved into place. My orders were that if anyone did try to take over, I was to stay behind, try to undermine it, talk you people out of it, or find a way to rush the door and open it. I was more than ready to do that until I heard why you are seizing this place. Those were my orders, and my moral defense later would be, 'I was only following orders.' How many times have we heard that before? Do any of you remember history? The perpetrators of nightmares crying out that they were 'only following orders,' and therefore not guilty, not guilty for My Lai, not guilty for the Holocaust. 'I was only following orders!'" This time, he snapped the words out with venomous disdain.

Margaret lowered her gaze.

"Those of you who served in the military know that in the military code of justice, officers are required to refuse an illegal or immoral order. They must refuse, and if they do not, they bear responsibility. I am doing that now. After hearing the president's speech a few minutes ago, I now realize my orders were immoral in the face of what these two people have decided to do instead."

"Why are your orders immoral?" asked Tyrell, one of Darren's security team who had been chewed out just yesterday morning about leaving the gate open. And either with calculation or because he was just plain being lazy, he had left the steel doors open that morning also.

"This is what I know about what is supposed to happen here," Harrison announced. "You already know that the state of Missouri, acting on the orders of the governor, has seized this entire facility. The governor, sometime yesterday, had already received a tip from one of our senators in D.C. that this Sauron's Eye thing would prove to be deadly."

"Some already knew?" Tyrell asked, his voice tinged with disbelief.

"He's right. I got that word last night from an old friend in special ops," Darla announced. "That is when Darren and I decided to do this."

"Most of you by now have heard the acronym *CG*. It means *continuity of government*. This underground facility was quietly planned several years ago to become the primary center for continuity of government for Missouri if things ever went really bad—nuclear war, pandemic, that type of thing. Of course, no one thought of this scenario, but there it is nevertheless. Underground Springfield becomes the continuity-of-government center for Missouri."

"Why not the caverns under Kansas City or Jefferson City?" Darla asked.

"In the event of nuclear war, both cities would obviously be targets, but it was felt Springfield would not be hit. Plus with Kraft Foods down here, millions of rations would automatically be in place."

"So why is that so immoral?" Margaret argued.

"Don't you get it, lady?" Harrison retorted sharply. "Who gets in here? The governor and his team, of course. All the top-level government officials, then their staff and so on. To govern what, damn it?"

The room was silent.

"Don't you get it? Our elected officials and their staffs get in here and live. Who else?" He paused, and no one replied. "Every political crony, every hack, every person who can call in a favor or bribe, and all their families and then extended families. Every corrupt person in this state with political pull is most likely flooding the governor's office with their appeals and told to just come here and their asses will be saved. That's who gets in here. Oh yeah, they'll make an all-so-emotional statement and offer to keep the rest of us quiet until it is too late. Of course, specialists with certain skills get in to help rebuild our wonderful fine state afterward. And who are they? The best doctors, the smartest engineers, and such? Yeah, right! They were preselected because they have a friend who has a friend with the right connections. But who chooses those who do the choosing?" His emotions were all but ready to boil over. "Do you, the people, get to choose? Oh yeah," he snarled sarcastically, "maybe if there's enough time, they'll have a lottery for additional slots. That would be fair, wouldn't it? To have a lottery and the winners get inside this place along with the governor and the rest? But suddenly, it's 'Oh, we're sorry, folks; there just isn't enough time to do that. Just trust us; we're going to save some great leaders that you elected, and they'll choose a couple of thousand more, and after it's over and you are all dead, at least our glorious state will continue to run as usual.' Of course, they can't forget some of their best friends from their country clubs, that cute staffer who's somebody's mistress, and given how rotten politics have been, anyone who is the supporter of the party in power and made the usual donations come election time. Human nature being what it is, there might even be payback for those who opposed them in the past. 'Sorry, we should have told you that list has been changed and you and your family are no longer on it.' That is how low our politics have become in this century. 'We live, and you people against us get what you now deserve and die.' The ultimate political payback. In a few hours, those are the people who will come flooding in here while your children stand outside waiting to die."

He fell silent and lowered his head, and Darren could see he was in tears.

Should he interrupt? He instantly knew not to. Harrison was articulating their position far better than he ever could.

"And at the end, just before that Sauron's Eye thing blows, it will be 'Oh my God, of course we planned all along to let some of your kids in and even some of you dear good local citizens; just give us a few more minutes to get organized.' But then when it blows, the gate slams shut, and only then, just before you die, do you realize that you have been conned and screwed for one final time, the same way most of us have been getting screwed for years. That is why I am refusing to follow orders," he said, his voice breaking. "These two are offering the moral choice, the ethical one to a society that still craves morality and ethics but has seen damn little of it of late. Your children—give them the chance to survive. And then maybe, after all of us are gone, they can one day remake the world as we once dreamed it should be when we were so young. And maybe this time, they will get it right. Give them that chance; we've had ours. And whether this thing is God's will, or it becomes proof of an uncaring, random universe, at least let's face it proudly knowing our final act was the right thing to do. I've said my piece; now if you want to riot and maybe kill these two, you have to get through me first."

Finished speaking, Harrison stepped down.

Darren took a deep breath and waited for what those gathered around him would do next.

Even before the sun dawned on the West Coast, reached its zenith on the East Coast, and was setting over Europe, cities began to burn.

Every person must eventually face their own mortality, and many try to avoid dwelling upon that until the moment is near at hand. Even then, for most, it is viewed as an abstract, "Someday, I am going to die," not as a true reality of "I am going to die today," as a prisoner must face when, at the approach of dawn, he will face his end. For nearly all, that moment of mortality is usually faced alone or at least with the ideal of quietly slipping away with beloved family and friends to comfort, and to comfort them in return.

For nearly all, there is a source of inner peace that comes with the belief that something of you goes on even if death is indeed the final ending. If not personal immortality, at least children and grandchildren or lives that you have touched will remember you after you are gone and be thankful that you had shaped their lives for the better. There is even some source of comfort, with thoughts of a tearful memorial service filled with words of love and thankfulness that you had been part of their lives that will continue on. For some, the thought was expressed by a bard a thousand years ago who wrote that at least what remains behind is the memory of glory once won.

At times, others are with you in that moment when mortality is faced, those locked in battle who see the end is at hand but will die with beloved comrades, perhaps to then go to some warriors' Valhalla together. Or even for those who stood naked in the snow of Auschwitz, with truth of their fate dawning at last, at least there were so many with them, and at least they could reach out to take the hand of a stranger to comfort each other in that final moment and recite together a prayer thousands of years old.

But to hear your entire world might face death in little more than a day? What then for comfort? What would be the actions not just of individuals but of all, of billions when that final day is at hand?

So cities were beginning to burn, flaring high across America, in Europe, and beyond. And for some, it was indeed the last holiday, the last orgy of gratification.

Within minutes, neighborhood stores were attacked, ever-growing mobs taking what was wanted—usually liquor to help fuel the frenzy—and then just walking out. A few shopkeepers pursued, for after all, it was their earthly things that should have been sold for profit: a six-pack of beer, a bag of chips, bizarrely in several such places even lottery tickets. And then and there, the killing started. Thief shot in the back, shopkeeper knifed or shot in retaliation, then the mobs would truly loot the store and set it afire in a bacchanal celebration of destruction.

But for some? Many a shopkeeper, after hearing the unvarnished truth that the world as they knew it would come to an end in just one more day, stood in shock, but when they saw the mob beginning to approach, openly laughed, threw open the doors, and invited them to take it all if that is what they wanted in their final moments. And as the mob looted years of sixteen-hour-a-day work, the shop owners, feeling truly liberated, walked out the door to go home to their families.

Others fought with a primal frenzy. They had not labored for so long for their meager earthly treasures just to see them disappear at the end, such as a convenience store owner in Greensboro, North Carolina, killing fifteen before being beaten to death and then immolated along with his shop.

In most places, at least for a few more hours, the police would show up shouting about martial law and would shoot and be shot. But for many wearing blue, as the hours passed, especially for those with families, their own inner questions took hold. Is this worth dying for anymore? To protect someone innocent, sure, but to kill and be killed for a lousy case of beer or *wide-screen television? And they would just shut down their sirens and flashing lights, turn about, and drive home to their families, who, in what might be the final hours, came first in their hearts.*

And so the looting spread in so many places—the big cities, of course, the warrens of poverty, fear, rage, and despair long before today now exploded. But it was not just cities; out-of-the-way towns and back-road villages all have such who would see the coming of a final day to be a day of final opportunity to indulge in their darkest desires.

Liquor stores and gun stores quickly became favorite targets. The first would fuel the panic, the other giving power to sustain it. And therefore, within a few hours, thousands were dying.

There was a thriving business for some entrepreneurs, at least until their strung-out clientele realized they didn't have to beg, and mere paper money was useless anyhow. So why not just take from those who had once forced them to pay for their hours of oblivion? Take it all and really shoot up this time. Therefore, thousands of addicts and their dealers were dead or dying within hours. Take it and just mainline it all! Take it and smoke it or inject it for the ultimate high, and it was indeed their final and ultimate high. More than a few who saw them decided to join in on that final trip to drug nirvana, at least a few wondering why they should stick around for what was to come.

Bizarre places that most would not normally think of were being looted as well. Exotic car dealerships were soon overrun. More than a few dealership owners were told as the glittering windows of their display rooms were smashed in, "If I'm gonna die, I'll do it in a Lamborghini!" And like the shopkeepers, some fought, more died, and some laughed and walked away from what had been a lifetime of building a business to go home to what they realized was most important of all.

So Lamborghinis, Porsches, Jaguars, Corvettes, and Humvees were roaring up and down roads, those within laughing, crying, drinking, and more than a few dying. But what the hell? they thought in those last seconds. I'm gonna check out in that Porsche I always wanted, like Viking chieftains of old buried in their longships.

Even airplanes. More than a few pilots just opened their hangars—no need to call control towers for directions, permission to enter the active runway and clearance for takeoff. The towers were all shut down anyhow. Freedom, total freedom of the skies as so many pilots dreamed of. No government on the ground to tell them what to do up there, where they could fly, where they could not. Throttle up, turn onto the runway, and fly like they had never flown before! Buzz an old girlfriend's house at two hundred miles per hour and five feet off the ground. Why not? But then not quite making it up over that hill a few hundred yards beyond. But what the hell, it would be a great way to go. For others? Heavenward, to loop and dive to punch through clouds and to chase the winds aloft and for some fueled on the Zen of flying in their old biplane or recon war bird to "reach out and touch the face of God." Perhaps to curse him, but for most a chance to ask why, or for some, one more chance to see the world as angels see it before the end.

But for each of those who robbed, looted, burned, killed, raped, drove off cliffs, or pulled a plane into a spin that would spiral down to oblivion, there were so many others reacting in so many different ways.

More than a few high-end restaurants and even fast-food places opened their doors and told anyone who wandered in to order the best, enjoy, and forget the tab.

Some indulged thus on lobster and hundred-dollar bottles of wine. Just some. Why let it go to waste? Some wandered into high-end stores and walked out in stylish furs. Even a place like Tiffany's was not immune when their own security people, of course paid a barely livable wage that was now meaningless, walked off the job, and customers, once so sophisticated, decided that a hundred thousand–dollar brooch they had been planning to buy would be a pleasure to wear today with zero payment down.

But for most—in fact, the vast majority?—there was but one thought . . . thoughts of those whom they loved.

The tottering phone network of America, damaged by the last CME, finally collapsed within minutes after the president's speech that laid out the reality of what was coming. Parents immediately tried calling children living in faraway places, and children called parents, perhaps getting a few words of love in and weeping until the overloaded circuits went down completely. What then? "I want to be with them; we just might have enough gas to get there . . ."

In less than an hour, in spite of so many cars damaged in the last solar event and the shortages of fuel deliveries and service stations unable to pump gas, the highways were jammed into gridlock. Driving to get a daughter back home, others who were blessed to still have that one family gathering place, Grandma's and Grandpa's place, the place of reunions, the place of celebration of Thanksgivings and Christmases, of weddings and christenings, of celebration and of mourning, and instinctively for those lucky ones, that would be the place to drive to with the hope that others were going there as well.

Young lovers rushed to find each other to then embrace passionately and to share that bliss for what might be just one more night. Elderly lovers, some of half a century or more, quietly went to bed, held each other, looked into each other's eyes and would spend that day and the night to come whispering, laughing, crying, and remembering the blessings of so many years together.

And more than a few estranged from their one true love, their twin flame in life, would realize something, would break through the folly, the foolishness of what had driven them apart, would seek each other out, race into each other's arms, weeping, asking forgiveness, kissing, and be as both young lovers and old.

Friends, so many friends to reach out to but one more time. A knock on the door, those within hesitating at first to open because of the chaos that might be erupting in the streets below, finally opening that door and there was an old buddy, a roommate of long ago, that one girl you could always get advice from and know it to be good and true, holding up a bottle and suggesting one more drink together, then spending the day laughing and remembering as well.

And there were even some who would think of enemies or those once harmed. For a tragic few, that would then become a target for a final payback for a prior offense, real or imagined. But to the surprise of more than a few, there would be a knock on their door—hesitation, even fear when the door was first opened—to then be greeted with a request for forgiveness and a hand extended in reconciliation. For most, the hand was taken for what was their anger of old compared to what all might be facing now.

Friends and enemies, a beloved teacher or student, parents and children,

children and parents, lost love estranged or love shared for a lifetime, that was the instinct that now filled so many. If we all but had twenty-four hours more to live, what would we do? And for nearly all, the answer was "Spend it with the ones I love."

Amid that, there were many who believed it would not happen—that there were examples enough from the past to believe that such learned people could indeed be wrong. They scoffed at the panic, locked their doors, loaded a weapon, and waited for what might come next.

Make a shelter, others thought. If the storm is of such intensity and I pile up X amount of dirt atop my basement, we can get through it. Many now clung to that hope and would in a frenzy labor through the day and night to come.

Others thought to the next step. If it happens and if I live, what then afterward? How will we survive? And thus markets and places that still had food on the shelves were looted clean, the wiser managers telling their staff to go home and be with their families, and they walked out of where they had labored for years to build that all-important career and left the doors wide open as they departed.

In such places, quite a few would die as they snatched for a weapon on the wall, a box of ammunition behind a smashed-in counter.

Outdoor supplies and sporting goods stores were quickly overrun as well. A sleeping bag, a solar stove, an extra parka was worth fighting for and dying for.

For those who called themselves preppers before all of this had come, the vast majority just quietly prepared. Those who had thought beyond themselves going to friends and neighbors, at last their words of "let's work together on this," accepted as more than just fanciful dreams or nightmares and together tried to prepare or reinforce the shelter place they had prepared. But for some, those twisted up with anger with years of waiting for "the big one," who were motivated by hatred of all around them, or who were self-centered just thought of themselves, there was concealed hideous laughter as they crawled into their shelters, weapons in hand, and waited for it, even cried out for it to come.

And what of the faithful or those who did not believe? Churches filled up as the hours passed. For some, there was the crying out that indeed this was the end-times, the fulfillment of Revelations and almost a sense of re-joicing. For others, a crying out as well, appeals to God to not extend his angel of death and to spare them. For yet others, almost dark laughter that at last they would together witness the punishment so long overdue, to the unbelievers, the ones who thought differently, to the unnatural ones who loved not as they should, and that the Lord's fire would sweep them away and render the land clean for those who were righteous and for who believed. Of course, those who prayed for such would be among the "select" and spared.

If this was the end, then so be it. If it was but a warning and the cup did not come to their lips, then so be it as well.

And therefore the churches and synagogues filled.

Sadly, so twisted and tragic, more than a few of faith that differed turned on each other, one or both sides crying that it was the time to kill to prove their faith, or to avenge past wrongs, or that this was indeed an end-time long prayed and called for, and they must now do their part. In the Middle East, Israel was under siege within hours in a frenzied wave of attacks. In other parts of the world, Hindu killed Muslims, and Muslims killed Hindus, and though more than a few of their brethren recoiled from the horror, it continued to spread.

A woman of wisdom once said that when enemies learned to love their children more than hate each other, there would be peace. So amid the fear and rage, parents hovered over their children and in some cases at least protected the children of their enemies. If there was leadership left any-where, some still struggled to bring order out of chaos.

11

"HEY, boss, something's up."

Darren went up to Tyrell's side and, bending over slightly, looked through the small rectangular view port that was thick with reinforced glass.

Of the approximately fifty people who were in the Underground when this confrontation started, nearly half had left. Some, like Margaret, cursed everyone as the small access door was opened for them to leave. Some left with heads bowed, unable to look Darren in the eye, and more than a few left saying they were going to try to find a safe spot where they could dig in and be with their families.

It was, as well, the opportune moment to implement the next step of the plan.

Sitting down with those who lived locally, he had drawn up a list of recommendations. If the plan was to work, it would, of course, not have to be just children. They would need teachers, good ones known and respected by the community. At least some adults would have to be admitted . . . but who?

James and Belinda Connors, who ran the old-fashioned diner inside the Underground and had been there for longer than anyone else could remember, had been the first to offer names.

"Jerry and Helen Green," they both announced almost simultaneously.

And from the other locals, there was a universal nod of agreement.

"Why them?" Darla asked.

"Everyone in Springfield knows them. Between the two of them, I bet they've served our town for—what?—maybe darn near a hundred years total. They started out as teachers in the poorer section of town; Helen taught our eldest when he was in fourth grade. Jerry coached him in high school and pushed hard for his scholarship to Mizzou. By the time our grandkids started school, Helen was principal of that school, and Jerry was principal of Central High. Jerry was even offered the job of superintendent and laughingly turned it down, saying he wanted to stay working with 'his kids.' In turn, they can tell you which are the best teachers we need to get in here. Not the drones, the educationalist types with their ridiculous theories; we want teachers who can teach and are also respected by both kids and parents."

"And no one will object to if they are let in while everyone else still must stay outside?" Darla asked.

The two looked at each other and then back to Darla and nodded. "If Jerry and Helen say they're okay folks, nearly everyone else will believe them and accept their decision." Belinda added.

"Anyone here know where the Greens live?" Darla asked.

A couple of hands went up, and they were tasked with finding them and getting them back here as quickly as possible.

"Medical?"

The names of Drs. Sarbak and Donkervoet immediately came up.

"Sarbak was a miracle worker for my wife," one of the employees from the furniture warehouse announced. His pronouncement was met with nods of approval from others, and a volunteer was sent out to find and recruit him. Another volunteer agreed to go out and find Donkervoet, a well-loved physician admired for doing house calls in an emergency, imbued with a manner that automatically elicited confidence from all who know him. He and Sarbak would be a team the community would trust.

Then other checklists. At least a couple of personnel familiar with the engineering aspects of keeping the Underground functioning. Fortunately, electrical for lighting and ventilation, at least for a while, could be handled by the internal generators. When engineers were digging out the quarry decades earlier, springs had been hit and dammed off and could be tapped into for a water supply. No one had an answer for sewage yet, but hopefully someone could be brought in to solve that.

The priority now was to get their messengers out to round up the personnel they needed and to let the larger community know to start bringing their children in.

Getting them out was easy enough. This was the first step of Harrison proving his usefulness. Stepping out through the side door, he called to the MPs at the chain-link fence, said that some folks were leaving, and asked if they were free to pass. Cleared, the messengers went out first, along with several additional volunteers who would, if need be, go street by street spreading the word to parents to bring their children. The minister volunteered to make a try with the local radio stations who were familiar with them and put the word out on the air as to what was happening.

Once they cleared the gate, got in still-functioning vehicles, and sped away, Darren released those who just wanted out.

As the last of them departed, Harrison stepped back inside, shaking his head. "General Perry is out there. He wants to talk, and, Darren, a reaction is building. I could see several trucks off-loading troops—I think your local MP unit."

"I'd be shocked if he wasn't going to try something," Darren replied.

Darren tried to switch on the exterior public address system linked to a control box by the side door. *Damn, it finally shorted, or someone on the outside cut the wires to the loudspeaker.*

Looking through the observation window, he could see Perry, in his usual pose of balled-up fists on hips, standing by the open gate of the chain-link fence.

"I'm going out to meet him," Darren said, looking down at Darla.

"Don't. For all you know, the moment you step out the door, you'll have a sniper's crosshairs aimed at your chest."

"That's why I've got Kevlar on underneath my parka, sweetheart. It's military grade."

The supplies the two had spent hours packing into their Tahoe before driving up here had included a mini-arsenal; from .50-caliber bolt-action sniper rifles, highly modified AR-15s and M4s, and a varied assortment of other weapons, along with over ten thousand rounds of ammunition—all of it once part of the Darla's former business. And along with the sidearms and shoulder weapons, they had packed along a good assortment of tactical gear, including what Darren now wore—a high-grade Kevlar vest.

"Bear, they might figure you'd be wearing one and go for a head shot."

"That's so hard it will bounce off. Besides, I don't think General Perry would sink that low," he replied, trying to smile. He kissed her on the forehead, cracked the access door open, and stepped out.

The sun was nearly at midday, covered with a light scattering of high stratus clouds so that he could almost look directly at it. He gazed at it for a moment, wondering if one could actually see what was going on with the naked eye. He had to turn his gaze away after a couple of seconds, unable to discern any difference, and then slowly walked halfway up to where Perry waited for him just in front of the gate through the chain-link fence.

"Okay, Darren, you've had your moment; now let's just finish this. Open up, let us in, and you and your wife will then be free to stay or go, along with the other folks inside there with you."

"Or what?"

"An M1 Abrams tank is on its way here and should arrive within the hour. A couple of shots of armor-piercing and then high-explosive will blow that door off its hinges and the game is up."

"I'd suggest holding back on that, General. We are fairly well armed, and if anyone approaches with hostile intent, I've already got guards posted; there are access ports from which they will shoot to kill. Beyond that, maybe you didn't see the inventory listing in the state-owned cavern. There is a crate of RPGs we're unpacking now. You bring up the tank and fire a round, and it will be one hell of a fight. I've got more than a few vets in here who know how to use them and what to aim for on a tank. There are at least a few I've sent out by side escape hatches, ready to nail anything heavy in the flank or rear."

"Are you finished with your threats, Darren?"

"Just figure I'd give you fair warning. It will save a lot of bloodshed."

"Don't bullshit me," Perry growled.

It actually was bullshit. There was a container full of weapons, to be certain—just older M16s, Glocks, and ammunition, all of it little better than surplus that had been packed up for storage years ago, and he did not have a single person set up outside as a reaction force. But how was Perry to know for sure?

"You've undoubtedly pulled the background checks on my wife and me by now," Darren continued. "Know what her business was. We came here with quite a few mementos of that business and passed them around to those supporting us, which now includes the captain, who is on our side."

"You can tell Captain Harrison for me that he'd better pray that damn Sauron's Eye thing blows. Because if not and this thing with the sun doesn't happen, under martial law, once inside this place, he will face a military court, and then believe me, he will be executed."

"It was his choice to stay, and he knows the consequences, which he felt were better than the moral choice of siding with what you want to do."

Perry stood silent for a moment.

"Darren, a convoy with well over a thousand people from the government is heading here as we speak. More will be arriving by tomorrow morning. They'd already be here were it not for the fact that the highways are getting gridlocked. The governor will be flying down later as well, and by God, he expects this place to be secured. If you don't open up by then, the order will be given to blow the gate open and then, if need be, shoot to kill. This facility has to go online today and start getting organized. That will give about a day to manage some sense out of the chaos that is starting to unleash."

"I'm sorry, sir, but no, sir."

"You've got about thirty minutes before the tank arrives, and then all bets are off."

Darren did not reply.

Perry gazed at him intently and then shook his head. "Got your Kevlar on, don't you?"

"If you were in my shoes, wouldn't you? We both learned that at Fallujah, didn't we, sir?"

"What?"

"It was so freaking hot both you and I took our Kevlar vests off."

Perry allowed a faint smile to crease his features. "Yeah, we did."

"And both of us were in direct violation of orders. Orders from on high, which came down to you, and you passed on to the rest of us. Taking your body armor off in a combat area, regardless of heat or discomfort, would be a disciplinary offense. So tell me, General, why did you disobey your own order?"

"Come on, Darren—or is it *Sergeant* again? What's your point?"

"Just that. You disobeyed your own order and wound up with a bullet a fraction of an inch from your heart. Why'd you take it off?"

"Because it was so damn fucking hot, that's why, and you know, you did the same damn thing."

"Get my point, sir?"

"Go on, enlighten me."

"Was the order logical?"

"Yeah."

"But was it realistic? Was it a realistic order?"

Perry did not reply.

"That's my point, sir. It was take the damn thing off or pass out from heat stroke. Yeah, we might get hurt worse. We made the choice, and we paid the price."

"Stop trying to put some sort of lesson on me; you are running out of time."

"We are all running out of time, sir. All of us, damn it!" Darren raised his voice loudly enough so that troops deployed just on the other side of the fence could hear him. He glanced beyond them to the parking lot. Several hundred people were gathered out there, apparently held back by a cordon of military police, proof that word of what they were trying to do was spreading.

He pitched his voice even higher so that it could carry beyond the parking lot on the far side of the fence. "All of us—you, me, the troops over there who can hear what I am saying—I am appealing to you,

General Jackson Perry, to make a moral choice. Disobey your order from the governor that only he and government officials will find refuge here. I and my friends are holding this place because we believe only our children should be sheltered here and let them survive what is to come. General Perry, a higher law is in play now beyond your orders from the governor. Children must come first, and to hell with your damn continuity of government." He fell silent, gaze fixed on the general.

"You son of a bitch." Perry sighed. "You certainly know how to grandstand it, don't you?"

"It is you, sir, who now has to make that choice, not I. Explain it to all those people who are watching and the families with children who will soon start flooding in here."

Without waiting for a reply, Darren drew himself up and offered a salute.

"I'm saluting the memory of a colonel I proudly served under, sir, and pray that man is still inside you." He turned and walked back to the steel gate, slamming the access shut behind him.

12

RICHARD wondered if the man sitting at the other end of the conference table had slept at all in the last thirty-six hours. At least he had managed to grab a catnap after staying up until 7:00 A.M., monitoring the situation and then briefing the president just before he spoke to the nation. After the presidential address, Richard was finally able to retreat to his small room until Allison—who it seemed had been assigned to him on a somewhat permanent basis—knocked on the door, informing him he had fifteen minutes to get himself together and there was another meeting to attend.

He staggered into the tiny cubicle of a bathroom, finding the toothpaste and brush—the usual hotel courtesy packet for guests—that had been placed in his room, got rid of the gummy feeling in his mouth, and was out the door five minutes ahead of schedule.

Allison led the way at a swift pace back to an elevator that took them a long way down, opening to the same corridor he had been in a day earlier. There was no waiting at the door this time. He was shown to a seat toward the opposite end of the table from the president. A laptop was already set up at his place, linked directly to the Helio Center at Goddard. He figured out how to use it within a couple of minutes, started scrolling through the latest data, took it in, and sat back in his chair. None of the data was good.

The president was already seated, whispered conversations going on with several standing around his chair. He seemed deep in thought, shaking his head several times. When he saw Richard gazing at him, he offered a nod of recognition and then was back into the quiet debate.

Admiral Brockenborough entered the room, followed by what Richard assumed were the army and air force representatives of the Joint Chiefs of Staff. The three went to the far end of the conference table where Richard had stood so nervously the day before, and the president broke away from the whispered conversation, saying, "Let's get started."

Computer images were instantly up on the screen behind the officers, providing a global overview. The army general spoke first, providing a rundown of military assets currently deployed around the globe. The largest cluster was, of course, in the Middle East.

Next came the air force, providing a posting of data as to which units were nuclear capable and what weapons were placed with them.

And then the navy. Brockenborough stated that what was about to be discussed required the highest level of security clearance, and Richard thought he had shot a glance at him.

"Everyone here is cleared," the president replied, tone a bit sharp, "if not formally, then by me now." He waved his hand vaguely as if mimicking a priest offering a blessing. "You are all allowed by my command to hear this."

There were several polite chuckles in response. Richard, watching the president, wondered if he was hitting the point of absolute exhaustion.

"All right, then, Mr. President. By your command and authorization, I will proceed."

"As if what General Patterson here and I just reviewed wasn't of equal importance?" the air force commander demanded.

"Gentlemen, just get on with it; every minute is precious, and decisions have to be made immediately." The president sighed.

"Of course, sir. Now first, our carrier groups," Brockenborough announced. A few seconds later, numerous flashing blue squares were up on the computerized projection. He briefly ran down the assets of each and current reason for deployment. The rest were in port for refit and could not deploy before the next day.

After a moment of hesitation, he quietly intoned, "Our nuclear-armed boomers now deployed."

Six more squares appeared, these flashing red—two in the Pacific, two in the North Atlantic, one in the Indian Ocean, and the other above the Arctic Circle.

Two additional dots flashed on the screen. "We have two more boomers that were preparing to deploy from Bremerton next month to replace the two currently forwardly deployed in the western Pacific. They are scrambling now and will leave port by 0400 tomorrow eastern time and be running deep and well over 160 miles from port by 1200 hours tomorrow. All eight will be shadowed by attack submarines deployed in defensive posture."

Blinking green lights appeared near each of the so-called boomers.

"Are the two going out tomorrow fully operational?" someone asked. Richard realized it was the head of the NSA.

"Some of the crews of both were on Christmas furloughs; replacement personnel were located. One is at 80 percent of full complement, the other at 90 percent. They are fully operational, sir. As with the other ships already at sea, those deploying each carry a full complement of launch systems, each topped with between six to ten multiple reentry warheads. Combined, that gives us a strike capability of over fifteen hundred thermonuclear weapons."

Richard sat back, awed and then sickened. He wanted to shout out a protest, that they were potentially at the end of all things and yet the conversation was about fifteen hundred nuclear weapons, each capable of annihilating an entire city.

"Dr. Carrington?"

Richard did not hear the president the first time, and his name had to be called twice before he realized the president was addressing him and therefore all in the room were gazing at him.

"Mr. President?"

"Doctor, you seemed surprised—upset, even."

Richard looked around the room and felt it best to say nothing.

"Well, are you?"

"It is surprising that we are talking about this now, sir. Given the information I am looking at, the probability of a full eruption, according to our algorithms, is continuing to increase."

"And if your algorithms are wrong," Brockenborough argued, "while everyone is breathing a sigh of relief, we will still be getting clobbered by a global CME that, regardless of this Sauron's Eye thing, is already going to put us in a world of hurt. Suppose in all of that, Russia, China, or some rogue with even a few nukes decides it is the perfect time to launch a preemptive first strike?"

There were nods of approval from more than a few.

"And suppose I and other experts around the world I agree with are right regarding Sauron's Eye?"

"Yes? And then?" the admiral retorted.

"Perhaps the subtext here is that if it does happen, we make sure of our so-called opponents by nuking the shit out of them afterward? Is that on the table as well?"

"It seems that you types locked away in your ivory towers have little grasp of real-world politics, because that is precisely what is being discussed right now, this moment, in Moscow, Beijing, Tehran, and elsewhere."

"Gentlemen, both of you." The president interrupted.

Richard looking at the president in surprise, feeling that the man whom he had come to trust over the last day had set him up to be a foil.

The admiral started to reply.

"Gentlemen, both of you, not another word." The president stood up, slowly, wearily, all eyes back on him. "I agree with Dr. Carrington's viewpoint."

That caught Richard off guard. Looking around the room, he saw mixed reactions, from angry disagreement to nods of approval.

"I've been on a conference call for the last hour with my counterparts in Russia, China, India, Pakistan, Israel, England, and France—at least those nations with nuclear weapons who were willing to join me in a conference call. I have proposed that all of us offer some sort of guarantee that our nuclear forces will go into lockdown, a stand-down in place. That no weapons will be launched unless there is absolute verification that someone has violated this agreement. And that whomever does launch a preemptive strike will receive a terrifying retribution from all other nuclear powers, regardless of prior alliances or agreements."

"Mr. President—" the admiral began.

"Let me finish, please. This stands whether we are hit by a solar flare or not. If we are hit by a solar flare as Dr. Carrington claims is increasingly probable, then God save us, what use will nuclear weapons be after it is all done? As was once said during the Cold War, we launch against each other just to make the rubble bounce? If we do that, we truly deserve the fate of annihilation.

"If that solar storm does not hit us, we will still have to deal with a major CME. Many of us will lose most if not all of our satellite and ground-based monitoring systems. In that case, someone going panicky, thinking they are being attacked, will preemptively launch back at whomever they suspect. The result? We're spared a solar storm but pretty well kill ourselves off anyhow."

"India and Pakistan? Israel and Iran?" the head of the NSA whispered, daring to interrupt.

"Yes, yes, I know," the president replied wearily. "I made it clear to all four of those parties that if any of them take advantage of the crisis, be it with or without a solar flare, the United States will side with the other and act accordingly."

That caused a stir, several nearly in unison saying, "You would hit our ally Israel?"

Another weary pause. "As a man of my faith, I would be loath to do it, please believe me, but I had to make that threat and make it believable to convey to the other powers my stance. I trust the prime minister of Israel, and he fully understands why I will be putting out a declaration shortly after this meeting, clearly stating that intent. I have his absolute assurance Israel will not launch first, no matter how difficult the situation is, and I believe him and trust him fully. Whether we are hit by a flare or not, whether nearly all of us are alive this time tomorrow, or but one in ten, one in a hundred, we will not push those who are left into the grave."

He paused and sat down, hands shaking slightly he poured a glass of water for himself and drained half of it. No one now dared to speak.

"Any questions, Admiral?"

There was no reply.

"Starting at the time Dr. Carrington feels the risk level is at the highest, all nuclear-weapon-carrying submarines are to go deep and there remain for . . ."

He looked at Carrington, who nervously cleared his throat.

"I would suggest at least ten days, sir. The ocean is an excellent shield, but to be on the safe side, at least a thousand feet down."

"Then you heard that, Admiral. Chances are our extremely low-frequency communications system will be off-line, knocked down by the CME regardless of the flare, so they will not know for ten days what has happened. I will order that at the end of ten days, they are to surface and attempt to reestablish communication. If any of us are still here, and we have some communications back up and running, they can take their new orders then. If not, well, then, most of us will be gone. I think the world would be a better place without nuclear weapons, at least for a thousand years afterward if anyone manages to survive a year or two. Regarding the nuclear-armed submarines, my orders are that, upon verification that the flare has hit and that no one has launched a nuclear strike, they are to then disable their warheads, return to port, and start trying to rebuild if there is anything left to rebuild."

"Sir, with all due respect for your position, you are wrong, sir," Brockenborough said. "If that astronomer's predictions are true, afterward is precisely when those who are left will need those weapons."

"For what, damn it?" the president barked.

"Some will survive. You signed the orders yesterday to start instituting our continuity-of-government plans. There will still be a United States government alive even if that flare kills off damn near everyone on the surface. There will still be a remnant left."

"What, a few hundred thousand bureaucrats?" the president replied with a sigh.

"Maybe more, many more. If only we had built more shelters years ago as quite a few in the Pentagon called for over and over, we wouldn't be in this fix."

"Maybe so, but that is the past. I'm thinking of the future, though according to some of Carrington's figures, if that flare hits us hard enough, nearly everything on the surface will be wiped out. Those in shelters? They come back to the surface and then what? Even if they can survive, I highly doubt a nuclear weapon will be of much use to them."

"I cannot agree with you, sir."

"Last time I checked my Constitution, I am commander in chief. Therefore, sir, you have the option of obeying my order or resigning!"

Richard glanced at the admiral, who stood with mouth open, features going pale.

"Do I have your resignation, sir, or your compliance with my orders?"

Brockenborough lowered his head. "Yes, sir."

"I see this as the only rational path left to us," the president said softly, but with gaze intent as Brockenborough stepped away from the lectern and sat down. "Yes, it is a risk, but it is time humanity took a few risks for a change. I always liked President Reagan's statement as he was trying to wind down the Cold War—'trust, but verify.' Well, this time, we are going to have to just trust each other for once, because sadly, I do not have the time left to verify."

There was no response.

"We reconvene in six hours."

PART VI

Of all the wonders that I yet have heard,
It seems to me most strange that men should fear;
Seeing that death, a necessary end,
Will come when it will come.

—**William Shakespeare**, *Julius Caesar*

13

"DARREN, it's coming."

He did not need to be told. Even through the steel door, he could hear the high-pitched turbine whine of an M1 Abrams tank. It was a sound he and his comrades often prayed for when pinned down at Fallujah; it meant the armor guys were coming up, offering shelter, and then blowing the crap out of the enemy.

But this time? This time, it filled him with dread, for unless something radically changed, their brief defiant stand was about to end.

Over the past few hours, maybe upward of a thousand or more local civilians had arrived with children in tow. A perimeter of MPs was holding them back out on the far side of the chain-link fence and parking lot.

Some locals who knew how to get in had slipped in via the three escape hatches at the other end of the facility, but even those had been sealed off in the last hour. The few who had gotten through reported that the tension between the military police and parents who wanted to get their children in was about to explode.

He turned to face those who had agreed to stand with him and Darla. "I want all of you to get back. Get all the way down to the first level. When that door blows, the projectile will cut right through it; that and the debris will be deadly. I've seen what it can do; there is no standing up to it. When they storm in, drop your weapons. Don't try to fight them; it will be futile."

He heard the tank's engine go into idle, and he looked back out through the view port. The tank had stopped just inside the barrier of the cyclone fence. The two Bradleys lined up behind it.

It was an older M1 relegated to the National Guard years earlier, its main armament a 105 mm rifled barrel. A single armor-piercing round from that gun would cut clear through the steel door, and followed by a couple of HE rounds, it would be blown apart.

There was no stopping it. The game was up.

"Everybody back down the tunnel now!" Darren shouted. "I want you beyond the first turnoff—and wait there!"

Some hesitated.

"No debate; move it! If he fires, everyone here is dead. Move it!"

Captain Harrison added his voice in agreement, physically shoving several of the men standing near him, and finally the group began responding, more than a few calling for Darren and Darla to come with them. Darren did not respond, attention still focused on the view port as the turret of the M1 lined its gun up on the door, making a fine adjustment so that it was aimed dead center.

Darren looked over at Darla. "Sweetheart, please go back with the others."

"Like hell." Darla unslung the M4 at her shoulder and held it up to the ready position.

"Oh, for God's sake, Darla, we can't stop them with what we've got."

"I'm sick of it, Bear, and I am not going to surrender. Let everyone see just how far we are willing to go and what they have to stoop to for what they want."

He nodded, took her hand, and squeezed it tight. There was no way he was going to force her to leave his side and go back, so they might as well face it together.

The first minute passed, and then a second. Nothing happened, the tank remaining in place, engine still idling.

Why was he waiting? Darren looked back over his shoulder to make sure everyone had cleared the tunnel. All had done as ordered except for Harrison, who was standing right behind him. There was a flash of mistrust with the man startling him like that.

He could have a concealed weapon, Darren realized, *shoot us in the back and then open the gate with reputation redeemed!*

"I'm staying with you," Harrison said, words spoken not as a request but as a firm statement.

"Why?"

"In for a penny, in for a pound—wasn't that the old line?"

"Yeah, something like that."

"He wants you to come out," Harrison stated. "I know him. End it peacefully."

"There's very little that's peaceful about him," Darren replied bitterly. "When we were pushing through the cemetery at Fallujah, literally fighting headstone to headstone, he told us that as long as CNN wasn't watching, take no prisoners, kill all the bastards."

"We are not the Taliban," Harrison said. "I'm going out there."

"What?"

"He wants to trying talking one more time."

"It's futile," Darren said coldly.

"Isn't it worth the try?"

"Bear, he's right," Darla interjected. "Let's at least try."

Without asking for permission, Harrison unbolted the access door and opened it. Darren looked down at Darla, who nodded and shouldered her M4.

"No, sweetheart. You are staying here in case anything goes wrong."

"Bear, if anything goes wrong, I want to be with you. Now let's go."

He looked down at her, M4 slung to her shoulder, tactical web gear on, Kevlar vest covering her chest, accentuating the natural curves of her body. He smiled and then shook his head, holding the door open politely so she could go through first.

"Damn it, Darla, there are times I wish you were a little more traditional."

"For that, you can kiss something later," she replied, looking back over her shoulder, "as punishment or reward, you decide."

The wintertime sun was halfway between horizon and zenith, and though the air was chilly in the high twenties, it felt like there was some feeble warmth from it, partially concealed behind a thickening layer of stratus clouds He glanced up, squinting, and this time he thought he could see the black dot of Sauron's Eye, a dark threatening blemish.

They walked the hundred feet up to the tank and then stopped, none of them sure what to do next other than to just stand in front of it as a final protest.

"Bet we look like Tiananmen Square," Darla whispered nervously.

"Very dramatic, even poetic." General Perry's deep voice startled them as, stepping out of the Humvee that had rolled up behind the M1 and two Bradleys, he approached them, shaking his head. "Now will you just step aside? Your protest has been noted."

"No, sir," Darren replied. "No, sir, to the colonel I once served under and respected."

"Look, Darren, I respect what you are trying to do here, but enough is enough." He looked back to the far side of the parking lot, where a crowd was gathered on the slope, held back by a thin cordon of military police. "Violence is about to explode back there, and it *will* explode if you continue trying to hold out."

"Can you blame them?" Darla asked. "This is about their children."

"I know, I know," Perry replied wearily.

"As the hours click off," Darla said, "you know as well as I do they will become desperate and finally act."

"Listen to me. Twenty busloads of government personnel, many with their families, and a couple of hundred cars are stacked up in the Hyatt parking lot and from there all the way to Route 65 with a hell of a lot more to follow. It is a regular damn convoy, and in a few more minutes, they are going to start rolling in here. You cannot change that. There's also another company of military police and a field medical unit. I've got my orders to either see that door opened peacefully or blow it off its hinges and time is up."

"No!" Darren shouted back. "Order your MPs to pull out and let children in first, and if there is any room left by tomorrow, then we let those drones in. Because that is what they are. I'm surprised they even lowered themselves to ride in buses. Bet there are more than a few limos out there waiting to get in."

Perry had no response.

"The governor and his bevy of hangers-on?" Darla asked. "Are they out there?"

"They are flying down by chopper tonight."

"So he sits in the capitol for now, faking that he is still at the helm. How many know he is about to run for this bolt-hole? And those are the ones you are taking orders from?"

"For God's sake, be realistic!" Perry shouted back, dark features reddening from frustration. "It is the way it is, and we all know that."

"Only if you allow it, sir." Harrison surprised Darren, who, up until that instant, was still not completely sure of him.

"Captain, no matter how this turns out, you are in deep shit, and I advise you to just step away from these people now!"

"Sir, it is you who are in deep shit. Sir, I have served under you as an adjutant for over a year now, and I know your soul, sir. I know who you are far better than these two people I am standing with. Sir, you are wrong, and you know it."

"I have my orders, Harrison, as did you."

"Do I have to go through the whole moral-versus-immoral orders yet again?" Harrison replied. "I already had to explain to these people here why I went to their side. I know the orders you have are immoral, given what is about to happen."

He pointed to the lowering sun shining dimly through the clouds and, nearly in the center of it, the menacing gaze of Sauron's Eye was indeed visible. "Your call now, General, but I know what is in your heart, sir. And, sir, if that doesn't work for you, then I will ask what history will say of you if indeed some children survive to one day write that history."

"Damn you." Perry turned to look at the sun.

"The children or the governor, General?" Darla said. "It is up to you now. You know it can't be both. The rule is children only; the only exceptions will be for just enough teachers and medical personnel to help them survive. If we allow those self-important bureaucrats to come flooding in by the thousands, what will happen? So far, we have parents cooperating, ready to help us, but if they see all those government types getting exceptions, this whole thing will break down into chaos. And when it does, you'd better be ready to order your military police, this tank, and anything else you have to open fire and slaughter people by the thousands—and the kids will be caught in the cross fire."

"General," Darren added, "yes, there are supplies down there to *maybe* keep ten thousand or more alive for a year, but we're still not even sure of that or how long they will have to stay underground. You most likely have a better picture than I do of what this world will be like when the storm has passed and the die-off has ended. Sir, what then? Who do you want left? Our kids? Because they will represent all our kids."

He looked at Darla. They had no means of reaching their own children and could only hope for the best, slim though that chance was.

"Those kids out there represent the best of what we are, General. Give them a chance to start things over, and maybe the next time truly do it right."

The general was silent, shading his eyes, gazing up at the sun for a moment, then lowering his head as if in prayer.

Darren took Darla's hand and held it tight, for his heart told him that in another minute, they would be dead.

The general stepped away from them as if clearing the way for the tank to fire, walked back to his Humvee, and leaned in to the vehicle to speak into a handheld comm unit.

Seconds later, the turret of the M1, which had been pointed so menacingly at the steel door, began turning, and seconds later, it had rotated nearly 180 degrees, barrel pointed back toward the access road and the highway beyond. Far up on the hill overlooking the entryway to the quarry, Darren heard shouting and saw the military police stepping aside as the crowd witnessing the confrontation pressed forward.

General Jackson Perry turned to face the three. "You win."

Darren felt as if his knees were about to buckle and all that was holding him up was Darla's fierce, loving hug even as she cried.

"I've ordered the crew of the M1 to guard this gate," Perry announced. "Bradleys will deploy to either side. Only children will be allowed past them, so open up that damn steel gate and get your so-called ark ready."

"God bless you!" Darla cried, breaking away from her husband to hug the general fiercely.

He stood as if stricken, confused and overwhelmed with what he had just done. "It will go bad before all this is done," Perry said. "The governor is going to have a shit fit when he hears about this. I think my people and your local National Guard MPs will stick with me, but before this is done, he will most likely bring up something else—perhaps even appeal for federal troops—and that could go very bad."

"If he does, what will you do, sir?"

"Tell him to kiss my ass and if need be fight to hold them back. Frankly, I never did like the son of a bitch anyhow."

Darren smiled, but Perry didn't.

"My MPs will hold the approach open. You didn't know this, but there must be three or four thousand people gridlocked back by the highway, and it has been damn near a riot for the last couple of hours. And yeah, I saw their desperation, so it wasn't just you three who threw me this curveball. It was hell hearing their cries, their appeals, many of them holding up their children for me to see, especially when all those buses with the ones chosen to be part of this damn continuity-of-government team lined up to drive on in. I couldn't look them in the eye. We'd better start figuring out how to organize this, because it will be chaos."

"We, sir?" Darren asked.

"Yeah, damn it. *We.*"

14

ALLISON opened the door and gestured for Richard to walk in. He hesitated. The president was sitting in the leather chair, head lying back.

Richard stepped back out the door. "He's asleep," he whispered. "Let's leave him to rest."

"No, I'm not, just dozing. Come on in, Richard, and Allison, ask someone to get me a coffee, the usual. Richard, do you want something?"

He was tempted to request a damn-good single-malt scotch but knew that would be stupid at this moment. "The usual, sir. Earl Grey, one lump, no cream."

"What time is it, Allison?"

She looked down at her watch. "It is 6:15 P.M. eastern, sir."

"Fine, Allison, just come get me at 6:55, and unless something really bad happens before then, like the world blowing up, just tell my chief of staff to hold all calls, and don't interrupt me. Got that?"

"Yes, sir." She closed the door.

"Come, Richard. Sit down. I want to talk a bit more with you."

Richard did as requested. There was a moment of silence as the president stood up, stretched and yawned and then went over to the bookshelf and scanned it. He pulled a book out and held it up. It was Thucydides' *History of the Peloponnesian War*. "Did you ever read this book?"

"I was supposed to, sir, for a first-year history class at Cambridge."

"Supposed to?"

"Well, sir, I'll confess there were cheat sheets, study guides, and most of us just did that, sorry. At the time, I couldn't see why someone who would major in astronomy had to read history. Kind of see things different now."

The president shook his head, suppressing a yawn, and then laughed softly. "Those required to read it usually hated it, but a few like me loved it. Read it half a dozen times across the years. Just wish since I became president I could have several days uninterrupted to read it again." He sighed, staring down at the book. "Maybe that's what I'll do . . ."

His voice trailed off, and he looked back to Richard. "In a way, it's what got me into politics, this and some other books about tragic failures in history. I was a history major at first. This book is complex reading, of course—all those Greek names and places you had to figure out before understanding the deeper plot of how the Greeks tore themselves apart in a war that went nearly thirty years. A period worth studying. After reading it for the first time, I even thought about going on to grad school majoring in ancient Greek history. Euripides' plays about the war, Aristophanes' satires, Plato, who as a student of Socrates, got in a hell of a lot of trouble. But it took me into politics instead."

"Why did it lead you into politics, sir?"

The president smiled. "Wish I had the time to give you the full answer, but we don't." He set the book down on the side table just as Allison entered the room with two steaming cups and set them alongside where the president had just placed the book, the president nodding a thanks as she withdrew and closed the door.

"Oh what the hell, it's worth the time to think about," the president said with a smile and with obvious affection he leaned back in his chair.

"The Athenians, supposedly a true democracy, are fairly close to winning the war after more than a decade of bloody fighting. But the stress of it, the pressures, the decisions, and put into that mix the seekers of profit or glory or both, all turn upon each other. One of them, Alcibiades, would definitely fit into today's political world with the way he could switch sides and almost always come out ahead. It reveals so much, that in order for a democracy like that to truly survive not just in good times but in crisis, it must be led . . . no, not led—it must be *guided* by men of ethics or moral character. But once the demagogues"—he sipped his coffee—"interesting word, that. Greek of course, it means 'people leader,' but not in a good sense. Demagogues hold power by inflaming the passions of the people to their own ends rather than as the ideal of leading to policies based upon higher ideals and moral decision-making. It's why someone like Socrates, who actually fought in the war but then was publicly denouncing the collapse of ethics and moral decision-making by his leaders, was finally told to shut up and handed that cup of hemlock."

He fell silent, taking another sip of coffee. Richard drank his tea, more than a bit curious as to why the president had summoned him and for what purpose other than to talk about Greek history.

The president started cracking the book open but then sighed and set it back on the table. "Wish we had time to go through it, talk about just this book for a few hours; it is really fascinating. Just switch some of the names out to our country's current leadership and it is damn near all the same." He looked at the book affectionately, actually patting its cover. "Hmm, where was I?"

"How reading that led you into politics."

He took another sip of coffee and sat back for a moment, head lowered as if about to drift off to sleep. "You and I are of about the same age, Richard. Remember the times when we were going through college? It was becoming such a new age with powerful new tools for demagogues to rise up using those tools: instant mass communications, twenty-four-hour-a-day news, billions of dollars being thrown out—or should I say thrown up?—into each campaign. I saw that and thought of old Thucydides as those so-called leaders urged their self-righteous mob on, shouting, 'We are right, you are wrong!' and led that mob in their frenzy, crying out, 'I am fighting for you!'"

He looked down again at the book. "Fighting for you? Fighting for what? If fighting that ultimately means someone within our own ranks is an enemy that has to be destroyed and the demagogue would, once elected, purge our good nation of all the sins of those they were fighting against. Thucydides wrote of incidents where a demagogue would whip a mob up to have someone purged and executed, or a city that was thought to be an ally was really full of traitors and to go burn them to the ground. Then within hours, the mob of Athenian citizens would be swayed the other way by a rival demagogue to lynch the guy who had been urging them on earlier that day. It's the same here. From election cycle to election cycle. 'I'm fighting for you' was their constant refrain. 'I'm fighting for you!' Those other bastards are destroying our country, or are so damn ignorant, or of course the old fallback that they are just stupid people who need 'us' as right-thinking people to lead them. Then, of course, comes the next election, the job of setting the country straight was never really done—more enemies to fight against, more billions need to be raised for their cause—and thus it went on and on, from election to election, and from decade to decade."

Richard did not reply, sensing that his job at this moment was to just sit in silence and allow this man the opportunity to vent.

"Logic therefore leads to what? Be it in front of the Parthenon in Athens or here. If both sides are screaming the other side is the enemy to fight against, the enemy therefore has to ultimately be ourselves. The enemy is someone we just plain disagree with and must be crushed rather than working united as we once could do at times. For that and other reasons, after doing a stint with the army, I found myself in law rather than history. Thought that rather than study and teach about what was, maybe I could do something about it instead and therefore went into politics and law."

He chuckled, shaking his head. "Yeah, crazy I guess. I can imagine the dark humor tonight of how many lawyers should be saved when this is over with, and frankly, I must agree.

"I was simply aiming for a seat as a judge. Figured at least I could do something about law and justice in my community from the bench. I think that was just about my happiest time. Got elected as district judge where I grew up, my office and courtroom in an old nineteenth-century courthouse in the town square. Sarah and I—" He looked away for a moment.

He cleared his throat. "Our daughter was born while I was a district judge, and then, well, you know how it goes. Ambition starts to take hold. 'Sir, you should run for state office; think of what you could do as attorney general, from there to governor.' Then after that, 'You could run for president; you'd be the perfect compromise if those two damn idiot front-runners don't get a majority at the convention.'"

He chuckled softly. "So here I am now, sitting with you, contemplating Thucydides, and the world might be coming to an end. There is a big parallel to what we are facing now versus back then during that war or most wars of the ancient world."

"How so?" Richard asked, not seeing the leap from a squabble between city-states of a few hundred thousand people and what the world would most likely face the next day.

"Back then, what happened if you lost? If your city lost? More than one city-state that ran afoul of Athens would be put to the sword, the war spiraling out of control to a conflict of annihilation. Rome and Carthage . . . how many Carthaginians were alive when that hundred-year conflict ended? Mongols versus China. Back then, a guard standing in a watchtower sees a cloud of dust approaching, and suddenly the realization is that before nightfall, everyone you love and ever knew will be dead. Your city wiped out, your people erased from history. Is it any different now?"

"Sir, there is the question of scale, isn't there?" Richard asked.

"Really. For you personally? The end is coming for you, your family, your world because back then your village, your town, was just about the entire world. If that moment is coming, what did they do when they knew the end of their world was at hand?" He sighed. "What do we do? What do *I* do?"

He finished his cup of coffee and remained silent for a moment, leaning forward in what Richard had learned was a characteristic gesture of forearms resting on knees, hands clasped in front, gaze finally looking up at him with eyebrows furrowed.

"The old line is appropriate here. Exactly why did I call this meeting?"

Yes, the question was there. Here he was sitting with the president of the United States, still considered by many to be the most powerful man alive, and out of anyone this man wanted to talk to him.

"I would guess you want the technical updates and evaluations from me, rather than secondhand through your staff and advisors."

"Yes, that, of course. But there is something else as well."

Richard felt it best to remain silent and wait for the answer.

"You are outside the loop, Richard, and I need that. A president—for that matter, *any* leader—had better be damn realistic as to who gets closest to him and why. Even the most trusted friend of old can be blinded by the power of such an office. It is human nature, and it is human nature for most to advance their agenda. Even if they think it is altruistic, it is still an agenda with a subtext."

"And you believe I don't have one?"

The president smiled. "There is a lot about you and I that is similar."

"How so?"

The president picked up his cup of coffee, which was now tepid, and drained it. "We are both absolutely dedicated to our work. At least with yours, there is objective truth. With mine, I look to history to try to model a response.

"Take Admiral Brockenborough, for example. A good man even if I can sense you and he have little affection for each other."

Richard smiled and nodded.

"I have a lot of respect for him, and at times his bellicose manner was necessary. You know that biblical statement, 'The meek shall inherit the earth.'"

"Of course."

"But is it true?"

He had never thought about it much, but when growing up, the memory of the Second World War was still alive in England with contempt for the appeasing meekness of Chamberlain.

"The definition of the word has shifted across the last several hundred years. In early translations of that phrase, the English word *meek* had a different meaning from today. What it meant four hundred years ago when first translated was that there was wisdom in being the biggest son of a bitch in the neighborhood but, in Christian compassion, to keep your sword sheathed. To not be the aggressor. A lot different meaning in that versus rather just being a lamb, bare your throat, and hope the wolves decide to be meek as well.

"Brockenborough gets the first half—that it is best to be the biggest bastard in the neighborhood, but to be meek with that power? At this moment, he doesn't get the second half of that meaning. In response to the admiral, every person around me, the vice president has already been evacuated to an underground site in Pennsylvania and no matter what happens will most likely still be alive a month from now. If something happens to me I know she shares my convictions as to what to do if anything survives and I do not and how to keep the admiral on a short leash.

"Every person in those meetings has their agenda and is eager to give me an earful of them."

"And I don't?" Richard asked.

"Yeah, kind of like that. Politically you are outside the loop on that. It gives me a few minutes to sit here, think, pray, remember what I learned and believed in decades ago, and I can freely talk about those ideas with you. When your director at Goddard—who would have been the one advising me—died, pitching a massive coronary, that said something to me about how serious this is. It was therefore suggested that both you and Judith come to the briefing. I could tell immediately that poor Judith was rattled, obviously distraught over the death of a man I was told had been very much a father figure for her. You, however, came across as—how shall I say it?—phlegmatic." He smiled. "A good term, that—reflecting the old belief that our health was about balancing our humors."

"So I'm phlegmatic?" Richard asked, trying to smile as he sipped the last of his tea.

"Something like that. Read your file before you arrived. Like me, you are a widower, your wife passing almost at the same time mine did and from the same kind of cancer. Strange, but call that a bit of a bond; unless someone has been through that fiery trial, they simply would not understand." He sighed and looked off, gaze unfocused. "Still hard to grasp at times, especially when I wake up early in the morning. Not because someone is waking me up with the phone ringing and my first thought is *Oh my God, what is it?* No, instead, that early-morning drifting awake, and for a brief, blissful moment, you think she is still by your side, perhaps already awake, looking at you and smiling."

He fell silent and Richard could sense he was struggling to hide his emotions, that he was nearly on the point of tears.

"I understand," Richard replied, voice near to breaking. He felt an urge to reach out with a reassuring hand, but the barrier of who this man was stopped him.

The president looked up at him and offered a weak smile, sensing what Richard was feeling as well. "You have a son," the president asked, voice a bit husky.

"Yes, sir. Same as me, family tradition. Teaches astronomy at a small college in Missouri.

"Have you been able to talk to him?"

Richard shook his head. "Phones in his area are down."

"I'm sorry. I put out a request to try to have him, his wife, and your grandsons located and seen after, but no luck; they had already left their home, and no one knows where they went."

Richard looked at him with surprise. "Sir, I did not ask for that," he said a bit defensively.

"I know. That's why I did it."

"Thank you."

The president spoke softly into the intercom by his chair, and the two were silent a minute later as cups of coffee and tea were brought in.

"Your daughter?" Richard asked, hoping he was not crossing a boundary.

The president nodded. "Ultimately, I'm only human, Richard. They're in my old stomping grounds in Iowa; some friends will be taking care of them. Maybe I should feel guilty—and as a president, I do, but as a father, I don't."

There was silence between them for a couple of minutes, each sipping his drink, each in his own thoughts until finally the president stirred.

"Richard, I assume nothing has changed?"

"Changed?"

"Sauron's Eye."

"The storm is intensifying, and probability of it exploding as predicted is increasing."

"At least according to your algorithms?"

"*Ours* meaning NASA, the EU, and the Chinese—yes, sir. Russia has gone silent, which tells me they are getting the same results, but the feeling is they are staying silent so all their leadership and cronies get into safe hiding first."

"That's the analysis from the CIA," the president replied. "Every top official and their families in Moscow are being evacuated to deep shelters outside of Moscow built back during the Cold War."

"Our only hope now is that the storm is of such intensity that it blows prematurely and travels at near the speed of light to race right through the CME, which will indeed start to impact at shortly after 11:00 A.M. tomorrow. If it does, that there is really no telling what it might do to the CME. Regardless of the concern about the CME, the model is still the same as I've outlined to you before." He looked at his watch. "We have approximately seventeen hours left to hope for the best—that Sauron's Eye explodes prior to noon. If so, the flare will hit an intact magnetosphere, and most of its energy will not hit Earth's surface."

"And you believe . . . ?"

"What I have been telling you all along, sir."

"The way you answer my questions, Richard. No nonsense, I appreciate that. I remember a case I sat on early as a judge," the president said, smiling at the memory. "Relatively minor charge—one guy slugged another guy out cold. I started the usual process, asking the lawyer how his client would plead. The lawyer said, 'Not guilty,' but then the defendant just stepped around his lawyer and asked to speak directly to me. I said, 'Go ahead,' and he said, 'Judge, I'm as guilty as hell, so I'm ready to take my sentence. But I'll tell you this: if that guy says the same thing again about my wife, I'll be back here again.'

"My God, what a difference that made. I asked the defendant why he slugged the other guy. He said, 'If he insulted your wife the way he insulted mine, in front of our kids, wouldn't you have slugged him too?'

"He told me what the guy said, and that poor son of a bitch was right. I'd have knocked the guy out cold and gladly gone to jail afterward. I let him off with the lightest sentence the law would allow, just some hours of community service. Rare is that kind of case. Rare is that kind of man who just gives you the truth straight out, no embellishments."

He smiled recalling that memory. "That guy went on to become mayor—a damn good one, no nonsense, tells it like it is. And it's why I asked for you to sit with me right now." He nodded toward the side table where a couple of Richard's articles now rested under the weight of Thucydides' tome.

"I've got a lot to think about to decide on in the next few hours. Most times when facing those things, I would retreat into this little side office they fitted out for me when I moved into this house. Kind of a replica of my private library room at home, just that it misses a real fireplace and a view. My sanctum sanctorum. Richard, help here. Give me a best-case scenario and then a worst-case scenario regarding a full-out hit of radiation."

"For how long, sir, and its duration? There are so many variables."

"I know that, but just run with me here for a few minutes. Start with shelter. How deep?"

"Even half a dozen feet of good barrier would help, but that means a solid, well-constructed barrier, not just piling some dirt up around the basement windows."

"I understand that. We're talking deep shelter. I think you figured it out rather quickly that the conference room we met in is nearly two hundred feet down capped above with a dozen feet of reinforced concrete. You didn't see what is on the other side of that conference room; you've been brought down the main corridor. Take a side corridor, though, and you will suddenly come up short at a sliding steel door, proof against nearly anything short of a high-velocity armor-piercing round. Then after that, two doors that are an airlock to keep radioactive dust out, and then the usual metal detector. Once through all of that, you are truly inside and safe from virtually everything short of a direct nuclear hit on top of you. There are enough rations in there to last a year, a small armory; they've even got digging tools stashed in case we have to tunnel our way out through the debris. I'm told every contingency has been thought of. When I got my first briefing and tour, I asked, 'Dig our way out for what? Ruler of the rubble?' The head of that shelter didn't like that one. It was impossible for him to think of a world without a president, even if the president was the only one left alive.

"Anyhow, it was built in secret when they were doing a major overhaul of the White House back in Harry Truman's day. They figured that unless a well-aimed nuke landed right on top of the White House and dug a crater 250 feet deep, the president and his staff down there would survive."

"Survivable down there if that is what you are asking, sir?"

The president shook his head. "Already know the answer to that. Everybody who works here, including me, if they are given a green alpha card on their first day of orientation, is taken to that shelter and briefed on what it is and what they should do if the stuff hits the fan."

"Green alpha card?"

The president chuckled and reached into the vest pocket of his blazer, pulling out a sealed envelope. "I carry this 24-7. Nuclear launch codes, and yes, there is still a serviceman within thirty seconds of me carrying what is still called 'the football.' As for everyone else, on day one working here, a very select few are given a green card the size of a credit card emblazoned with a code—which is changed every month, by the way. If things hit the fan and impact time is imminent, wherever they are, they know they have ten minutes or less to get down to the secured area. One minute late, well, then . . ." He laughed a bit sardonically. "As used to be said, you are shit out of luck, because the doors will have been sealed and you are on the outside. Oh, there is one exception, though. If I am on the outside, banging on the door and hollering to be let in, they'll open it for me, at least."

"But no one else? Say, your own family?"

The president seemed to glaze over a bit.

"Sorry, sir. I know it must hurt. I'm sorry."

"It's okay," he replied, voice tight. "I was told no, once the doors are sealed and I am on the inside, that is it; open them and you risk the lives of everyone inside. At the entryways, there would be a Secret Service agent detailed to stay outside the door. And if anybody tries to force their way in, or if in that terrifying confusion of so many rushing to get in there are those trying to bluff their way through without the alpha card, they are to be shot."

"Merciful God."

"I have such a wonderful job, don't I? Men and women like samurai guards of old ordered to stay outside the castle to defend me, which means suicide for them. But to answer your question: I would have stayed outside that door until Sarah went in ahead of me. I already had that agreement with the security team responsible for me, and they would have respected it. Who holds or does not hold one of those alpha green cards is a matter of great prestige in this building. It means you are one of the chosen few, only a few hundred out of the thousands who work here. Kind of funny in a strange sort of way to think about reactions to that. It is top secret if you have the card—except, of course, for me. But breathe a word that you have that precious green card in your wallet and the Secret Service will haul your ass in for one hell of a chewing out, perhaps even then losing that card, so everyone stays mum about it."

"What about all the rest?" Richard asked.

"Oh, there are blue beta cards as well. That's next priority level down. If the warning time is not a few minutes but hours, they'll be evacuated up to shelter areas in Maryland, Pennsylvania, West Virginia. About 15 percent who work here have those cards. It includes their immediate family if they have the time to bring them in. And ironically, a select few of the White House press corps have those cards as well. Rumor is that we dole those out or take them away dependent upon how their network is treating us, but we even have thought of the so-called fifth estate and their survival."

He chuckled over that. "At least one of my predecessors did indeed pull the card of a reporter who worked for a network that was definitely on that president's personal crap list. My press secretary told me a few hours ago that more than one of that fifth estate has approached her with an appeal to be issued a beta card. All sorts of amusing arguments with how important they are, how their audiences trust them more than anyone else, more than a few self-serving bastards just shouting they deserved one, and one who even tried to blackmail us that they will 'blow the truth' how the government is scrambling to cover its own ass and to hell with the rest. Think of that. Give me a card, let me into your club, and I keep my mouth shut."

"What happened?"

"She told me that, and I had the bastard stripped of his credentials and shown the door and made sure some of his peers knew the truth of it."

"Did anyone get a card?"

"Just one. The deciding factor: she has four kids. She asked that they just be given a slot and she would stay behind. All five of them have already been evacuated to a site in West Virginia. There are all sort of plans and contingency plans for CG. Billions have been spent on it across the years. Back at the start, it was like Churchill's war room. The key personnel and not one person more. Then the list just keeps expanding, even, at least, occasionally leavened with compassion. What about families? Why? To keep personnel morale and functionality up. Otherwise, too many would be breaking down, so that adds in a few thousand more to be saved and the need to stockpile and build yet more. Add up those numbers and then divide that by the amount of space and supplies to tell you how many can get saved in a certain amount of time. Then of course everyone else. Who shall be added? Add you, Richard; you are our top expert on that."

Richard bristled, insulted by the inference. "No, thank you, sir."

"Sorry; don't get riled up. I was just putting out an example. And by the way, yes, you were added to the list when this whole thing started. When you go back to your room to get some rest, the agent escorting you will hand you your alpha card."

Richard stood up, preparing to leave the room. "Mr. President, I am not here to maneuver to get one of those damn cards that I didn't even know existed fifteen minutes ago."

"In other words, I can take the card and shove it, which is what you wanted to say." The president motioned for Richard to sit down.

There was a tense moment of silence between the two, Richard breathing hard, hands trembling slightly as he picked up his cup of tea.

"Relax, Richard. I already had a gut feeling of how you would react. If your wife were alive, you'd give it to her, and if she was like my Sarah, she'd have been insulted and torn it up to stay with you if you refused to go."

Richard's emotions began brimming over.

"I've come in here to cry by myself more than once," the president said reassuringly, "especially while Sarah was dying and afterward. Can't cry in the Oval Office or even up in what was the bedroom we shared, but in here . . ."

Another moment of shared silence.

"The rest of your question, sir," Richard finally said to break the uncomfortable quiet. "What is the best-case and worst-case scenario after we are hit?"

"Go ahead."

"Best case. The duration is short, a flare that is narrowly focused with a minimum tail, meaning continued expulsion off the sun's surface ceases within a few minutes. That means that given whichever side the planet is facing the sun and therefore most directly exposed will be hit hard in those few minutes. What is left of our magnetosphere due to the CME strike that allows all this to happen will still be there, bent back from protecting the earth. The energy is highly prone to magnetic fields, and therefore some of it could be bent around enough to strike the far side, or at least part of the far side of the planet as well. So even then, no one will be really safe.

"The dose level on the surface will most likely be fatal for anyone exposed for more than a few seconds, just like with anyone out in the open when a nuke is detonated. Beyond the flash burns, which a CPE will not produce, the direct blast of radiation a person receives in that first microsecond is enough to kill if it is much more than 250 to 300 rad or so—and 600 is a 100 percent death sentence. If it is that bad, better to get a dosage of several thousand at once."

"Why?" Then the president nodded in answer to his own question. "You go unconscious within minutes and dead shortly thereafter. Is that it?"

"Yes, sir. Also, the so-called fallout that everyone worries about with a nuclear bomb going off is actually irradiated debris thrown up clear through the stratosphere by the bomb itself that then drifts downwind to kill. That will not happen with this."

"There is one aspect of that only a few are discussing," the president said.

"And that is?"

"Nuclear power plants. The waste storage areas. If the power is shut off entirely for more than a few weeks, shutting down those massive cooling towers, the waste will eventually heat up to the point that it burns through the containers and starts fires that will spread radioactive plumes heavenward."

"I never thought of that."

"I have; some good people have, and they are trying to figure out solutions in the little time we've got left. Now in the best-case scenario, what about food supplies?"

"No problem with anything stored properly, even canned foods and such, but longer-term? The same fate we face if on the surface is true of any animals. Unless sheltered, they will be dead. That article you have on the table there, the thesis that a flare might have been the trigger for wiping out entire species during the end of the last Ice Age now seems more plausible. Between that and all those who were left behind on the surface? Even in that best case, it will be horrific, with potentially hundreds of millions dead, and those coming up out of the shelters will have to deal with that ghastly nightmare. With so many dead, sir, their bodies still exposed out in the open where they fell . . ."

His voice trailed off for a moment, emotions still on edge. "Burying the dead, the trauma of it, high potential of disease spreading because of what has to be done during the cleanup. More will die; that must be assumed. But beyond that, life on this planet will continue, but only barely. Not as we know it now, and it will most likely be years before the global ecosystem returns to some level of stability."

"I see."

"Now worst case."

"As if what you just told me is not bad enough."

"If the flare is exploding off the surface of the sun for days, long enough that Earth goes through one or more full rotations while engulfed, it will most likely be the endgame for 99 percent of the population."

"Why so?"

"Those in deep shelters of course, they'll get through it, but everything on the surface irradiated for a day, even days? Animals, even plant life will be pretty well wiped out as well. I don't even want to speculate on possible climatic effects since anything related to that seem fraught with politics, but I would assume it most certainly will have an impact. Those that survive? What do they come up to? Especially if they've only got enough reserve food for a few weeks to a month? Oh, there might be a lucky few in very deep shelters, completely stocked for a year—years, even. Sit back, watch videos, drink some good liquor, maybe eventually plants will start to come back to life when the survivors finally crawl out of their holes a year or two later."

"I remember that huge forest fire at Yellowstone some years back," the president interjected, and there was something of a hopeful tone to his voice. "The National Park Service just let it burn—said it was a natural process, and that got a lot of people very upset. The land was absolutely scorched, and critics were screaming that a fair part of the national park there had been totally destroyed. But then a year later, new life began blooming up from deep seeds and roots that across millions of years have always survived those kinds of fires."

"Maybe something like that," Richard replied. "At least hope for that, for the few that do come out. But that might take a whole season or seasons if it is going to happen at all. In that case, I think they'd have to wait out a year or more, and best to stay underground while they do so."

"Why?"

"Would you want to come up above ground after a maximum event to see the millions of dead around you? To perhaps have to face those who might have survived but did not have sufficient supplies stockpiled and are driven beyond desperation, ready to kill for a single meal?"

"I see."

"Anything else on that, sir?" Richard asked, sneaking a quick look at his wristwatch and noting that in about five minutes the president would be dragged into yet another meeting.

"Just some thoughts I now have to deal with. So, continuity of government. Who gets the priority, who gets the nod to live? Government, of course. Beyond that? If planned long in advance, some certain few would be getting snatched up as we speak, people valuable for us after the event. In fact, some already are."

"Is there such a plan?"

"Yes, the CDC had one in the event of a fast-moving pandemic. Military, of course, for things military. But for this? No, there is not some prime list and then we play out some sort of 'bomb shelter' game of who gets to go—the doctor, the nurse, the pregnant woman, the genius, of course throw in a few artists, maybe even a philosopher or two, and obviously a bunch of scientists. But then if high enough up the chain, everyone will want to add in an extra family member—which is understandable—or a political crony who gave a hell of a lot above and below the table during the last campaign. And let's not forget mistresses and all the rest."

He rattled the list off as if it had indeed been discussed, perhaps even that day or would be at the upcoming meeting.

"My first day in office, who goes and who does not if everything goes bad was a top-priority briefing along with a lot of other secret briefings, some of which left me with my jaw hanging."

"Such as have we been visited by aliens?" Richard asked, trying to sound light but actually dead serious.

The president just smiled and continued, "As I was saying, it has always been about CG—continuity of government. Not continuity of people, of the soul of a nation—instead, just the government as if that is the nation. In this federated republic of ours, of course each state, modeling on our federal plans, developed its own plan and shelters right down to cities like New York, Chicago, Boston . . . even this city.

"Surprised, Richard? What some city governments have prepared for themselves would turn your stomach while the rest of her citizens huddle in subway tunnels, freezing or sweltering with no water or food, and slowly die. Or people cowering in the basements of million-dollar high-rises and within a few days going berserk. Oh yes, but everyone rejoice, for the city government will come out intact and ready to lead just as they so effectively did before the shit hit the fan. You should see the plans that the good mayors and city councils have spent millions on over the years. There are some real gems, such as New York, Chicago, and San Francisco, for starters."

He sighed, finished the last of his coffee, and looked at his wristwatch. "My next meeting is about to start, and this will be the topic—continuity of government. You've given me a lot to think about and the ability to vent a bit as well. Stay close; I hate to interrupt your sleep, but that's the way it is."

"Just one question, Mr. President."

"And that is?"

"When did you last sleep?"

"Not since you started scaring the shit out of me."

PART VII

Children are the living messages we send to a time we will not see.

—Neil Postman, *The Disappearance of Childhood*

15

"IT is absolute chaos out there!" Darla cried as she staggered in past the open steel doors of the Underground, now renamed the Ark.

Darren, who was huddled with a handful of volunteers, looked over at her, nodding wearily and motioning her to wait for him. Around them, hundreds of children were streaming in, nearly all of them frightened, more than a few crying, some of them hysterical. At the sight of that long, semidark cavern awaiting them, many recoiled in terror, even turning around to run back out.

Darren finally broke away from the group he had been giving a pep talk to, appealing to them to just herd the kids along and if need be to push them along down toward the Kraft Foods warehouse area.

"Darren, this is out of control."

"I know. Don't you think I can see that?"

He turned away from her and back to the small group he had gathered in what was increasingly a vain attempt to bring some semblance of order to their efforts. "Everyone please shut up for a moment!" Darren shouted, but with the overwhelming din, echoing in the entryway to the tunnel, his appeal for quiet was not heard.

He had suddenly realized within minutes after General Perry had thrown in with them and ordered his troops to let the civilians and their children come through that no one had really thought about the next step: what to do with the soon-to-be thousands of children pouring in, most of them distraught and frightened. He was so focused on just seizing the place and then fending off the countermoves to take it back that what to do later was not really on his radar.

It was now upon them, and their efforts had already disintegrated into chaos.

At least Perry had thought some of it through from his end, which was to keep control of the facility from the outside. The M1 Abrams remained parked smack in the middle of the open gate so that there was only a narrow passageway of several feet to either side of the tank for those entering.

The general then positioned the Bradleys to the far side of the parking lot, blocking the approach road and then radioing that all vehicles from the government were to remain out on the highway or parked at the Hyatt located at the exit. He had passed along disinformation that he was negotiating an agreement with the "renegades" holding the underground. Once the children had been cleared, government authorized personnel would then follow no later than by the end of the day. He'd added a caution that parents and community members several thousand strong would riot if any attempt was made to seize the place by force.

He had adroitly thrown in that just suppose all this wild talk about a so-called extinction-level event was just that: talk. Politically, how would it then look if hundreds of civilians had been killed? While on the other hand, to nobly agree that children should go first would make the governor look like a hero.

It was actually not a lie when it came to the threat of fighting. Hundreds of parents who were armed, at Darren's request, remained out in the parking lot after ensuring their children were safely inside.

Bizarrely, the vast parking lot out beyond the chain-link fence had some of the aspects of a tailgate party, with campers pulled up, more than a few grills cooking, and meals being served out, while several noisy generators provided electrical power.

Darla commented that the biggest motivator for why they were armed and staying was the decades of building mistrust for their own government and that this was a way to vent it at last. A sort of middle finger extended with the statement *You bastards know you are just like us and will die like we will.* The only fear for Darren was that as the hours counted down, panic might set in with them as well.

There were too many variables. How long would the governor and crew accept Perry's disinformation game and hold back? Would the parents and the rest of the community accept the fact that certain adults would be allowed in to help take care of the children while the rest of them were excluded? Or, for that matter, in the final hours and minutes, would panic finally take hold? It was said that even on the *Titanic,* such was the case in the final minutes. It was all a precarious balancing act, and Darren knew that the slightest thing might upset that balance and chaos would ensue.

Military police from the local National Guard barracks continued to maintain a cordon on the far side of the fence and pass the word that parents were to say goodbye to their children a distance away and then move them forward quickly to the fence, where they were then to pass alone through the cordon, past the tank, and into the Ark.

It was, of course, a wise move; otherwise, parents would have been coming into the Underground, which would have quickly degenerated into a few at the start, and then more and yet more trying to push their way in and vanishing down into the rabbit warren of side tunnels.

General Perry had left to Darren and Darla just what in the hell to do once the children were inside the facility, and most of them entered dazed, confused, and nearly all were frightened. Mass hysteria was taking hold out beyond the fence and was then carried into the Ark. How could it not be?

For every mother who knelt and gave her five-year-old daughter a reassuring hug, parting with the words "It will be a fun adventure, sweetie; you get to live underground just like a hobbit, and in a few days, we'll be back to pick you up," while just a few feet away would be a father or grandmother hysterically screaming or crying for the child to be good and remember them. More than a few completely broke down, backing away at the last moment and, still holding on to their children, turning about and fleeing, some shouting it was better to keep their kids with them if they were all going to die.

Darren had arbitrarily set a cutoff age of eighteen as the upper limit, while some argued it should be sixteen, fourteen, or even twelve given how many might show up. His counterargument was that they would need those seventeen- and eighteen-year-olds to help run the place in the months ahead and when they finally emerged back to what was left of their world. When word was passed as to the age limit, more than a few tried to slip their nineteen-, twenty-, even twenty-one-year-olds through the barrier.

Perry therefore had ordered his MPs to check IDs when in doubt before letting them approach the gate, and thus more than a few who were but sixteen or seventeen were turned back, their family shouting protests when told that some identification had to be provided.

The matter of the age cutoffs was a truly heartbreaking decision. Darla openly wept when presented with the question of how young the children could be and finally gasped out that two years old had to be the minimum. Otherwise, who would take care of them when there were thousands who would need seeing after? A compromise finally accepted was that if a brother, sister, or family friend older than twelve would take responsibility for a younger child, then there would be no lower age limit, and thus scores of frantic parents were bargaining beyond the gate with those they knew—or did not even know—imploring their neighbor's fourteen-year-old daughter or sixteen-year-old son to take their nine-month-old child.

Darren finally approached Darla, and she wrapped her arms around him, holding him tightly and weeping uncontrollably.

"I just can't take it out there!" she sobbed. "Bear, it is too much. I kept seeing my grandbabies out there. I keep seeing . . . I never thought about this part . . ." Her words shuddered out between sobs. "Those parents, my God. Bear, are we even doing the right thing? Maybe families should stay together—"

Her point was emphasized by a fight breaking out at the gate. A hysterical woman being physically restrained by several MPs after nearly forcing her way through, crying that she had changed her mind and wanted her baby back.

Suddenly, there was a shot, those near the conflict dropping to the ground. Cries of panic rose, the crowd surging back. The woman had a gun, and an MP struggled with her to keep the gun pointed up in the air. Another MP ran up, pistol drawn, leveling it at the woman.

Darren ran toward the fight, sprinting to get in front of the MP, sparing a glance toward the other two struggling with the woman. She let go of the pistol, which clattered to the ground.

"Stand down!" Darren shouted at the MP. "Holster your weapon and stand down!"

The man looked at him nervously, weapon aimed straight at Darren's face. He could see the young MPs eye behind the sight, squinting, finger coiled around the trigger of the Glock.

"Son, just stand down. She's been disarmed."

The MP looked past Darren, finger drawing away from the trigger. Nodding, he holstered his gun.

Darren stepped up to him and pulled the gun from the holster, ejected the magazine, then, sliding the receiver, ejected a .45 round onto the ground. He felt a tightness in his gut. A few pounds of pressure on the trigger and he'd have been shot. He was still wearing his Kevlar vest, but the weapon had been aimed at his face.

"You stupid son of a bitch!" Darren snarled. "You are relieved."

"My gun."

"Damn you, we're on the same side, and you were ready to shoot me. You are relieved; now get the hell out of here."

Sticking the unloaded Glock into a side pocket, he turned back to where the two MPs had the woman pinned to the chain-link fence. A third MP was holding her pistol, a small pocket Ruger, doing the same thing as Darren, dropping the magazine and chambering out the remaining round. Darren went up to her. There was no anger in him, just a near-infinite sadness as he looked into her eyes.

"Ma'am, you could have been killed," he said, reaching out to put a reassuring hand on her shoulder, motioning for the two MPs to release her.

"I want my babies back," she sobbed. "I just want my babies back."

"Sweetheart, please trust us." Darla had come up by Darren's side. "They're safe with us. Maybe this whole thing will blow over and they'll be back with you tomorrow."

"I want to go in and get them!" she implored. "Please."

Darren gave a sidelong glance to Darla, his gaze indicating a negative, but she did not need his prompting. After what she had just done, to let her pass through could trigger a rush, and to let her go inside in this state would certainly create yet more hysteria with the children.

"Let's get on the other side of this fence," Darla said soothingly. "I'll get their names, you go out to the parking lot, and I'll see if we can find them later."

Darla put an arm around the woman's shoulder as she sagged, head bowed, gasping for breath between her shuddering sobs.

"Can everyone listen up, please!" called General Perry through his loudspeaker, trying to take control of the situation and standing beside his Humvee parked just beyond the gate. "No one was hurt—just a bit of a panic, but everyone is okay. Please listen up. No one with a weapon is to approach the fence. Children might have been hurt, so please work with us."

Darren looked to the MPs who had subdued the woman. "You guys okay?"

"Yeah, just a bit shaken," a sergeant replied.

"You did good." He looked over at the disarmed MP. "But get this idiot out of here. Okay?"

The sergeant needed no prompting, cursing as he grabbed the panic-stricken soldier and shoved him out through the gate.

Darren followed behind them, going up to Perry, who was shaking his head.

"This is going bad," Perry said. "Didn't you think about what to do with the kids? How to get them away from their parents without all this damn hysteria?"

Darren lowered his head. "We were so intent on just getting the place, then dealing with you—"

"I've got my hands full dealing with the government people. The governor's security detail tried to get up here a half hour ago, weapons drawn. I thought it was going to blow then. I managed to bluff them that if they tried anything I'd unleash the Abrams and the Hyatt would turn into a free-fire zone."

"Can you still hold them?"

"Hate to put a worry on you, but monitoring the net—at least what is still functioning or not jammed up—there's a call out for some air support."

"Shit."

"Yeah, in the shit for certain. A couple of Apaches. If they show up and we don't have air support, they can just sit back a quarter mile out, and the tank and Bradleys are toast."

"Would they go so far?"

"Yeah. They've got nothing to lose, and killing a couple of hundred voters won't hurt the next election when it sinks in we're bluffing them and have no intention of letting them in."

"Unless that Sauron's Eye doesn't blow. Answering for that afterward?"

"I reminded them of that again, but that argument is losing its sting. For the moment, it's still working, but come morning and the forecast still is holding that Sauron's Eye will blow? At that point, if it looks like it is definitely going to happen, that's when they'll try their move."

"Darren!"

Darla pushed her way through the crowd, and for a moment, he thought something else was now going wrong and she needed help.

"They found them!" she cried, weaving her way through the crowd that was edging back toward the gate.

Behind her was their minister, followed by more than a dozen men and women, most of them elderly. She was half pulling along behind her a man in his early to midsixties, nearly bald, what little hair left gone nearly to white, slender and diminutive but in excellent shape as if he still worked out for an hour every day. He was wearing just a sweater and light windbreaker with Central High emblazoned on it. By his side, he was holding tightly to a woman nearly Darla's height—slender, gray hair pulled back in a bun, posture absolutely straight and erect like her husband's.

Captain Harrison was at the back of the group shepherding them along. Harrison, out of breath, nevertheless smilingly saluted Perry. "We finally found them, sir."

Perry turned back to Darren. "Don't make me do your job again, Darren."

"General?"

"You need organizational help. I heard you were sending some people out to find a school principal, his wife, some doctors, and others. I sent Harrison here out with a Humvee to lend a hand and, once found, pull them in."

"It's chaos out by the highway," Harrison interjected. "Vehicles all over the place. I spotted your preacher friend here and rounded up a few others who said they knew where this principal lived, and we set out. Figured I could best help by having a vehicle and still acting like I was a government official to bluff our way through their attempts at setting up roadblocks. Anyhow, here they are."

Darren could barely hear what Harrison was saying because behind them, a five- or six-year-old was throwing a tantrum and screeching at the top of her lungs that she wanted her mommy. Without prompting, the elderly woman turned around, knelt, and swept the child into an embrace to soothe her, whispering that they would find her mommy in a little while.

"This here is Jerry Green, sir!" Harrison shouted over the din, stiffening slightly as if speaking about a superior officer. "Principal of Central High."

"You want the man to get things in order," the minister announced, stepping in closer, "this is the guy. If there is anybody in this entire town that is universally known as the best teacher and principal out there, it's Mr. Green."

He must indeed be the best, Darren thought, given how his minister was acting. He could see it, as well, how the crowd pressed in around them was acting. More than a few nodding in agreement with open and obvious admiration.

"Ask any parent who was lucky enough to have their kids at Pleasant Gardens Elementary and you'd hear about his wife, Helen Green."

The preacher looked at her and smiled with open affection. "When I first moved here, she was my daughter's fifth-grade teacher."

He reached over to give her affectionate pat on the shoulder, though at the moment, her attention was focused on the frightened girl, continuing to whisper to her soothingly.

"Jerry here was offered the shot at being superintendent, and he laughed at it, saying his job was walking the halls of a high school and knowing the names of every single student, and not sitting behind a desk getting fat. So they're yours now," the minister announced. "I'm heading back out to the highway to see how I can help out there."

Before Darren could even reply, the minister was gone, making his way back through the crowd.

Jerry called a thanks to the minister and then turned back to Darla and Darren. "Heard what you and your wife did, Mr. Brooks. Noble, and I'm damn proud of you both," Jerry said, stepping forward and shaking Darren's hand.

"Thank you." The praise raised Darren's morale a bit.

"And do you have the slightest frigging idea in the world what you've set yourself up for?" Jerry demanded, the moment of praise gone. "Did you think for just one damn minute how to run this place with five, ten, maybe fifteen thousand kids running amok come tomorrow—if there is a tomorrow?"

"And a bunch of toddlers wandering around crying for their mothers because they shit themselves six hours ago," Helen added in, standing up and still holding the distraught child in her arms.

Darren looked at them, a bit embarrassed and unable to reply, barely able to hear what they were saying.

"Let's take this inside!" Darla shouted, pointing the way to the Ark's entry.

They started off, followed by the dozen who had come in with them. Darren looked at them questioningly.

"They're with us," Jerry announced as if it were already an accepted fact, and Darren did not object.

Edging around the tank, they crossed the open space into the entryway, where the noise level went up even higher as if inside an echo chamber.

Helen handed off the child, who had calmed down a bit, to one of the women following her. She then stood on tiptoe, hands over her head and clapping loudly. "Children! Everyone quiet!" she shouted, her voice as strong as any drill sergeant's. "My name is Mrs. Green! I'm the new principal here."

She paused for a second and pointed to a girl in her midteens. "Mary Anderson. I know you! My, how you've grown. Come over here, sweetheart, and give me a hug."

The girl, smiling, shyly did as asked, and Helen hugged her.

"Mary here is my new student assistant," Helen announced. "I want all you children to follow her. She's going to lead you on an adventure down into that tunnel. I want to hear later who is the bravest. Now go along, Mary, and lead the way!"

Mary looked at her wide-eyed. "What am I supposed to do?" she whispered.

"Just lead them down." She looked at Darla. "Where should she go?"

"All the way down," Darla said. "There's a place there with plenty of snacks."

Mary shouted for the children to fall in behind her while Helen grabbed Darla by the shoulder. "We've got to talk now!" she said sharply. "What are your plans? What do you have here? Just what the hell are you going to do or think you can do?"

"Let's get in our Tahoe; it's quieter in there," Darren said, motioning to the vehicle parked to one side.

Once inside with doors closed, Helen sighed deeply. "Damn, I could use a drink," she announced.

"All right, let's get down to it," Jerry said, sitting in the back seat with Darla by his side. "Helen and I heard some rumblings late this morning that something was going on down here, but we figured it was just a rumor or crazed people were trying to take the place to hide in."

"Figured we go to our cabin down by the lake to sit things out," Helen interjected. "And if it happened, that's where we wanted to be. If your people had pulled up ten minutes later, we would have been gone. Anyhow, that captain, the preacher with a couple of others, rounded us up and told us what they wanted. 'Okay,' we say, but we insisted we stop and grab some teachers we know and respect until that Humvee was packed and came back here."

"It is a madhouse out there," Jerry said. "MPs are keeping the approach road open, but out on the highway, cars are parked or abandoned for a mile or more. Several thousand people are out there and some sort of convoy of buses, some military-type vehicles, and even some limos parked around the Hyatt."

"Those are the people that want in here," Darren replied.

"Yeah, we finally learned about that. Bastards."

"You going to let them in?" Helen asked.

"When there are no more kids coming in, maybe then," Darren said. "At least that's what we are telling them for now."

"There are over thirty thousand children living just here in Springfield," Jerry announced. "Can you hold that many?"

Darren sat silent for a moment. Yes, they could, but for how long? He still had no idea just how much food was stored at the Kraft warehouse and in the shipping containers the state had pulled in here. Beyond that, water, toilets, general sanitation? He looked back at Darla, wide-eyed.

My God, have we bitten off more than we can chew? he wondered.

"Doubt that many will show up," Helen pointed out. "A fair number of people still don't believe that Sauron thing is going to explode. Years of doomsayers talking about climate change, Yellowstone blowing up, the New Madrid fault line cracking wide open, EMP, you name it. A lot believe this is just one more scare."

"Some of them then think they can weather it if it does happen—go into the basement, pile up some food, bottles of water, shovel dirt onto the outside windows. Others, well, they figure it's up to God, and if this is the end, they want to be together. Can't blame them for that. So no, maybe ten thousand children, perhaps a few more, is what I'd figure on, though there might be a panicked rush in the final minutes. Can you handle ten to fifteen thousand?"

"We'll have to," Darla replied.

"Okay, then, it has to be organized now," Helen announced. "Sweetheart, you can't let this go on as it is right now. So if that Sauron's Eye does blow up, how long are they to stay down here? A day? A week? Maybe a year?"

"We don't know," Darren said wearily.

"Just great." Helen sighed.

"Damn it!" Darla snapped. "Sorry if you don't like what we've done so far, but what's the alternative? Turn the thousand or so kids already in here around, push them out, tell them to go find their mommies and daddies, and go die with them? How about we then let the governor and his people in and just call the whole thing quits. Is that it?"

"Honey, you got me all wrong," Helen said as she reached out with a reassuring hand and patted Darla's knee.

"Look, we're all tired and worked up," Darren announced, cop instincts kicking in, defusing people who were upset. "Anyone for coffee?"

"Yeah, sounds good," Jerry replied.

Darren turned on the car and drove the few hundred yards down to the turnoff to the restaurant area, passing Mary, who was shepherding along fifty or more young children. Helen rolled down her window and offered encouragement. Darren turned onto the access road to the restaurant area and saw that Joe was still at the counter of his pizza shop.

"What are you doing here, Joe?" Darren asked as they stepped in.

"Lot of hungry kids out there. Mixing up what I got left, giving out slices as they go by. Slice of pizza can calm them down a bit."

"God bless you, Joe," Darla said as she motioned to the pot in the coffee machine.

"It's been sitting there for hours, but go ahead. Sorry I'm out of creamer, even the powdered stuff. Styrofoam cups are under the counter."

She filled four cups with the thick brew, passing them up to the counter for Darren to pass on to Jerry and Helen, who had slid into a booth.

They all took a sip, Helen and Jerry grimacing; the coffee indeed had been slowly cooking down for hours, but for Darren and Darla, coffee like this had all too often been standard when out in the field.

"All right, you two damned idealists, what was your plan?" Jerry asked.

"It was to hold this place open and only children get in," Darla replied.

"So you stiff the governor, a couple of thousand of his cronies, and hangers-on who think it should be their asses that are saved, then you just let kids in, is that it?"

"Something like that."

Jerry leaned back and laughed. "Damn it, you two are crazy, but you've got guts."

"Jer, we've got to get down to some realities and start planning; small talk about why they did it can come later," Helen said. "First of all, who's going to feed these children, bed them down where it's warm, take care of them, keep them from flipping out, and then—if this thing is bad as some are predicting—keep them alive once it's over?"

"Like I said, we hadn't thought that far ahead," Darren replied wearily, feeling absolutely dejected and holding his coffee cup between his huge hands, squeezing it nervously so that it cracked and started leaking.

"You got a notepad or something I can write on?" Jerry asked.

Darren got up, went out to the Tahoe, and returned with several pads and extra pens.

"To work, then," Jerry announced. "First. Kids only?"

"We thought something like that."

"And then suppose that storm hits as bad or worse than some are predicting—at least that is what I was picking up on the shortwave radio before getting dragged over here. You could be down here weeks, months, before things settle down and it's safe to go out."

Darren did not reply.

"You familiar with *Lord of the Flies*?" Helen asked.

"I saw the movie some years ago," Darla replied, and Darren nodded.

"Kids are the most wonderful of all of God's creations," Helen said with a wistful smile, "but they can turn into monsters if let loose and given free rein to do as they damn well please, especially if there is a group, a gang, a mob of them. That's elementary school teaching 101. Just because they're so damn cute, don't turn your back on them, especially on day one. I had more than one teacher quit on me at the end of their first day. I remember the time—"

"Helen, no war stories, we don't have the time for it now," Jerry interrupted.

She smiled and nodded.

"So what do we do?" Darren sighed.

"We know the game; you don't. My wife and I take over once those kids are through the door."

"What?"

"Why not?" Jerry said with a smile. "Besides, I've always wanted to be a dictator."

"Now wait a minute," Darren said.

Helen reached out with a reassuring hand and patted Darren's. "My husband's sense of humor gets a little twisted at times. Doesn't it, Jerry?"

Jerry smiled at his wife, but Darren could see he was serious.

"Darren, I've been a high school principal for twenty-five years, a teacher for nearly twenty more before that, and coached every sport there is except for cheerleading across forty-plus years. To be a good principal, you've got to be a dictator at times. Don't hand me this educational crap, the latest theory from some damn professor who never actually had to handle a roomful of thirty hormone-driven sixteen-year-olds ready to run amok. Do you understand me?"

A faint smile creased Darren's weary face. "Okay. What will you do?"

"Take over, like I said. You focus on keeping an eye on things overall, but once someone steps through those steel doors, Helen and I are in charge unless we need some of your backup to defend the place or kick someone out."

The mere thought of going back out to the entryway and continuing to try to do what he and Darla had been attempting for the last six hours left him inwardly shaken. Nevertheless, he looked at Darla and she nodded.

"It's yours."

The two nodded without comment as if assuming there was no alternative.

"Fine, then. First off, where's the food supply and how much?" Helen asked.

"We don't have an inventory yet on the government supplies. Let's just hope we find several of those shipping containers packed with MREs. Each of those is a ration of upward of four thousand vitamin-balanced calories. The rest? The other source is the Kraft warehouse, but that un-fortunately is most likely half-empty. But even then, that's a couple of acres of shelves stacked fifteen feet high. At least a million or more meals."

"I hope it isn't all Cheez Whiz," Helen said. "Which leads me to question two, which any elementary schoolteacher would ask. Have you planned on what to do when all that Cheez Whiz starts coming out the other end of them?"

"Oh, God." Darren wanted to bury his head as that thought hit.

Helen chuckled. "What do you have down here for toilets?"

"I don't know. Each warehouse area—there's over thirty different firms with facilities here—has plumbing with running water, flush toi-lets. I don't know. Maybe seventy-five, a hundred tops?"

"Divided by ten thousand kids. Maybe one toilet for every hundred children." She shook her head and sighed.

"There's no time to call up some Porta Potty place," Jerry interjected sarcastically.

"We've got to figure all this out quickly," Helen replied.

"It's like her to be more worried about the fundamentals than I am," Jerry announced.

"Well, you deal with it a lot when they are five and six," she replied.

"Let's hope that government storage area you mentioned planned to include some chemical toilets." She jotted some notes down on a pad. "Next. Water?"

"Two sources—town water, which of course is gravity-fed, so hope-fully that will continue for some time. Also, the quarry operation ran into more than a few underground springs; water coming through lime-stone is very hard, but drinkable. There are some places where they piped it into underground springs, using it to clean equipment."

She checked that off.

"Sleeping arrangements?" Jerry continued.

"Hadn't thought of that yet either," Darren said. "The state has ship-ping containers of stuff down one of the corridors; some of them are packed with cots, and Tyson has a furniture storage facility, a hundred thousand square feet. Must be a lot of beds and such in there."

"We segregate sleeping areas off real quick-like," Jerry announced. "Otherwise, some of those horny kids will start to think this is orgy land. And if this whole thing blows over in the end, we definitely don't want to deal with the bad PR and liability when a couple of dozen young ladies come back with an extra package."

"Jerry!" Helen warned.

"You don't deal with them the way I do every day," he replied. "I've literally thrown a bucket of cold water on more than one couple going at it under the bleachers or out in the parking lot."

"Segregated male and female sleeping areas," Helen continued. "Might sound old-fashioned to some, but Jerry is right, and that's the way we'll run things. Smaller children get priority on the bedding to be found at Tysons. Now, what about the ambient temperature in here? It feels a bit chilly."

"Constant fifty-eight degrees."

"Too cold, especially for the little ones," Helen announced. "We have to get word out to parents bringing kids in to pack a heavy coat, sleeping bags, or extra blankets for them."

The two continued to run down an ever-growing list of what was needed, and to nearly all of the questions, Darren just looked at Darla, and Darla back to him, both of them shaking their heads.

Finally, Jerry sighed and fixed his gaze on Darren. "We're going to need maybe upward of a thousand adults in here."

"What?"

"You did think of that, didn't you?" Helen asked.

"Not to that number. I assumed maybe a couple of hundred. You know, teachers like you, and of course medical personnel."

"Who's going to run this giant nursery, elementary, middle, and high school? Because that's what this will have to be turned into—a giant boarding school, pre-K through twelfth grade. And from what little we know so far, it could go on for weeks, even months if things outside are bad with desperate survivors—if there are any—scrounging for food. Even concerns about residual radiation if the waste storage at nuclear power plants cooks off, so we'd better plan for months. So afterward? When it is safe to go outside? Then what?"

"Okay, I can see that," Darren replied. "When Darla and I decided on this, we knew there had to be some adults, but if we started granting exceptions—parents with two or more kids, parents with a child under five—it would turn into a riot."

"I understand that, and no, there will not be exceptions," Helen said. "I agree, but we've definitely got to choose some adults to go into the lifeboats as well. Consider it people who will do the steering, rowing, and keeping the kids alive."

"So who chooses?" Darla asked.

"We do—we and the parents outside," Helen said. "It's flattering to know so many people out there trust my husband and me. What the hell? Chances are we taught more than a few of them across the years as well. Let us get it moving by going out there for a while, pick out folks we can trust to stand with us to the end, and move them in close to the gate to stand guard. We then pass the word that the adults we let in will be the best of the best of our community—those whom the parents can trust to do the right thing for their children."

"Kind of an idealistic order, isn't it?" Darren asked.

"You've got to be an idiotic idealist to get into our business," Helen replied sharply. "Jerry and I know the reliable ones that we get to help guard the entryway. We pass the word out for the type of adults we want to let in. But we have to do that now and do it fast."

"And they will be?" Darren asked.

"Mostly teachers, some staff. Did you even think we might need a few school janitor types who don't get sick when having to mop up some kid's puke? That's what we want, and the parents out there will help us figure out who because quite a few of them Jerry and I used to address as Mary Lou, Billy, and Jimmie."

"They're right, Darren." Darla sighed. "We've got to get adults in here to help with all these kids."

Darren nodded.

"Okay, Helen and I are going outside," Jerry announced. "We'll start by talking to the parents out there. Start running off names of teachers we know and trust and then have parents go fetch them and bring them here."

"With or without the rest of their families?" Darla asked softly.

"What do you think, honey?" Helen asked. "Any one of them who agreed to just save themselves, claiming some bullshit altruism motive and then leaving their spouses and kids behind, I wouldn't give two cents for. They come with spouses and kids or no deal."

Darla looked up at Darren and nodded. "Okay, then. Go to it."

"You two have additional problems—you know that, don't you?" Jerry said.

"Go on."

"Medical for ten thousand kids, for starters. You've got to accept doctors, nurses, and such."

"We've already been told there are two doctors at the top of everyone's list in this town, named Sarbak and Donkervoet. There are people out trying to bring them in now."

Helen and Jerry nodded. "Sarbak did a hell of a lot for me and also for a lot of other women in this town, so he is in," Helen said. "Donkervoet's a good choice as well. Folks outside the gate will approve of them running the medical side of things. The parents will want the best, the ones they already know and trust, and they will help find them and then step back when those people are let in here."

Darren warmed to that.

"Realize if this scheme is to work," Helen continued, "we'll need doctors, nurses, medicine, maybe even operating equipment, because sure enough, some kid on day one is going to have an appendix ready to bust or get a compound fracture."

"Can those two take care of the logistics once we bring them in?" Darren asked.

Jerry nodded. "Sarbak is on the board of our main hospital. He'll know what to get and who to pick out to bring along with him as well. He's the type that would have the guts to loot the hospital for what will be needed and will know what to take."

"Better send some MPs along with him," Darren said.

"No need."

"Why?"

"Darren, Darla, don't you get it?"

"Get what?"

"We've got to get those thousands of parents out there working for us; the best chance for the survival of their children if that Sauron thing blows is right here. One of the people I dragged along with me today, Kevin Malady, was head of security for my high school, a football coach as well. Gentlest guy in the world as long as no one is threatening his kids. Let me put him in charge of helping out with sending search teams out to bring in people we want. Beyond that, pick out some well-armed parents to run with those two doctors to help them in any way possible. The MPs are of better service where they are right now if the state government people try to pull anything. Do we understand each other?" Jerry asked.

Darren smiled and offered his hand. "The job is yours. You are a blessing, and may God help you."

"Why don't you two try to get a little rest?" Helen said with a smile.

"Later," Darla replied, "when this is all done. Then we can rest."

PART VIII

The world begins at a kitchen table. No matter what, we must eat
    to live.
The gifts of earth are brought and prepared, set on the table. So it
    has been since creation, and it will go on. . . .
At this table we sing with joy, with sorrow. We pray of suffering
    and remorse. We give thanks.
Perhaps the world will end at the kitchen table, while we are
    laughing and crying, eating of the last sweet bite.

      —Joy Harjo, "Perhaps the World Ends Here"

Dawn. That moment of returning consciousness. Is this still the dream? The dream is still real for a few more blessed moments, at times eliciting a tender sigh, a long-lost memory of innocent youth, or a cry of fear of the nightmare you were running from with feet mired in clay. Consciousness taking hold, so many times regretted because the dream was so wonderful, at times embraced to escape the terror that walketh at night.

Reality. Reality takes hold again. For a moment of disbelief, surely it was just a nightmare, like some bad movie or book that ended with "But it was only a dream." Is this really happening? Did she really leave me for someone else? Did the doc really say I have cancer? God, let me go back to the dream, please, if this is now reality.

As dawn swept over the East Coast of America, millions stirred to wakefulness. For many thousands, their first thought was, Why in the hell am I waking up here? Their consciousness returned so that they found themselves in such strange surroundings—an apartment filled with others still mostly asleep and nearly all of them strangers, or behind the wheel of a wrecked car overturned in a ditch, or shivering naked in a field, or just pulled to the side of the road, the highway ahead and behind jam-packed with cars filled with others just coming awake.

And then full reality floods in. The sun is just breaking on the horizon. Nothing happened while I was asleep. It is still there, isn't it? Turn on the radio; maybe it has gone away. Maybe it has all gone away.

But it hasn't. Listening to the radio, there is full consciousness now; it truly is real. A great dividing starts to occur, a primal Rorschach, a Myers-Briggs, a test of each and every individual, all collectively facing the same reality. The test? The realization that I will most likely die today, along with everyone else.

That test now stuns one to full awakening. Not just an awakening that comes with every dawn but a more profound awakening, a gestalt as to reality itself. Today I will most likely die. Not just me but perhaps my entire world will die with me. There will be no memorial service for me, that moment of friends standing up in a church full of mourners and tearfully telling all just how important I was. A long procession of cars to the cemetery, and maybe years later someone still remembering me and placing flowers on my grave. Who will put flowers on the grave of humanity if humanity itself has gone away into the darkness with you? All the moments, all the histories, not just of now, today, but going back thousands of years to be erased away in a flash of light that is coming. Disappearing as was once said "like tears in rain."

At dawn, a couple stood at the middle of the Brooklyn Bridge, and there were hundreds of others around them, nearly all of them couples, nearly all just standing quietly, watching the dawn. "Why here?" they might even ask the couple next to them. "Oh, this is where we first met thirty-four years ago. It was love at first sight; we thought this would be a nice place to watch it all end." And those who questioned understood because that was their reason as well from nearly sixty years ago.

An eighty-year-old farmer in Vermont walks into his barn, already late for the morning milking, and looks around. Why? Because that is what he has done since he walked to the barn with his great-grandfather when he was five years old. And this morning, the cows are crying out because the milking is two hours late. The barn has stood for over two hundred years, made by the great-grandfather of a great-grandfather. Crude initials carved into a beam by a child of each generation with dates next to each set of initials going back to the early 1800s. Next to the initials, wooden rungs of a ladder to the hayloft worn down by generations of his family climbing up there in winter to fork down feed, and on sweltering summer days going up there to stack the fresh-cut hay coming in. Sitting here with my family might be a very nice place to pass the day, he thinks.

In Gettysburg, a historian who drove all night to get there walks the storied field. More than a few wander about in the morning twilight, perhaps drawn here like he was because, as a soldier who fought there wrote, "Where great deeds are accomplished, greatness lingers, and this is now the vision place of souls," and if his soul were to pass today, he reasons, let it mingle with the souls already here. When the historian had first come here as a boy of nine, his imagination was filled with fire and thunder, in his mind and heart seeing and feeling all that had happened here, breaking away from parents, running out into a sun-drenched field, crying, "Follow me, boys! Follow me!" And now? How might this place look a thousand years hence? Maybe the vine-covered monuments will still stand, the same as the Pyramids. Perhaps some might survive, and a thousand years hence, their children's children will gaze upon the weatherworn letters carved in stone, the headstones row upon row, and wonder, What happened here? The thought of that made him weep.

And so it was across thousands of such places, places sacred in memory to each and every one who gathered there.

Others began gathering at their places of worship. Preachers, pastors, reverends, and rabbis after a sleepless night now trying to fix in their minds one last sermon, one that would bring peace not just to their flocks but to themselves as well. To try to explain why God would do this. For surely if the universe was created by God's design, then his hand must be in this final day for a reason? "Have we become Sodom and Gomorrah?" some might then ask. For Abraham, had he not bargained with God, asking at first if but fifty righteous men could be found in those twin cities of evil, surely he would spare them all. Then he bargained God himself down to forty-five, to twenty, and finally to ten. But even then, not ten could be found, and as his brother Lot and family fled the cities, they became pillars of fire and smoke.

For some, that lesson would be the final plunge. For some, to fear, lamentation and begging for forgiveness, for others, resignation, for who are they to question the will of God? More than a few cried out that if ever it were the time to pray, it is now, and in such fervent appeals, surely God would turn his wrath away and all would then have learned their lesson and sin no more. For others, it was resignation that if so ordained that this would be the final day, then so let it be. And for more than a few lost in nihilistic emptiness, what was to come was surely proof that the universe was indeed meaningless, without thought or purpose.

For those who had survived their night of madness, those with the strength rose to continue it. Another shop to loot, a place to burn. Just watch it burn. There goes someone it might be fun to torment, to kill because they are different from us, and now it is time for payback. Surely there must be something to drink, to smoke, to inject to deaden it all.

Many others, though? The millions trapped on highways . . . It is only thirty miles to the ones I love; I can still make it. If need be, I'll get out and walk, run to be with them at the end. To run the final distance to where a door opens and old friends with their families greet you in tearful embraces.

For too many sad others, they had gone through their hope, denial, and rage and landed at resignation so deep that it became catatonic, just a curling up, usually alone, and waiting. More than a few decided not to wait, opening a medicine cabinet or a dresser drawer where the rusting revolver had rested for years awaiting this moment.

Those who still had hope, the ones who believed they could still shape their own fate, frantically prepared. Pile more dirt around the basement windows, place anything that can block death on the floor above the basement, see if anything can still be found at the market. Or, if already having prepared long ago, to inventory yet again, some doing it like the demon of avarice counting his gold, others deciding there was still a bit extra, so go down the street and tell that neighbor to join them.

At a far different level, guards stood at steel doors as helicopters landed nearby, as convoys of trucks and buses arrived. "Please stay in line; we need to see proof of identity and access card. One suitcase only. Please stay in line . . ." And at more than a few such places, crowds stood beyond the gates, and barbed wire–topped fences. Some just bearing silent witness as the chosen were driven past, others cursing, and more than a few starting to kill and be killed in return. In a few such places, mobs won out by sheer force of numbers, storming in, and then there was yet more killing in some places done by the first who had stormed in, now shouting it was their place and for the rest to go elsewhere. In just a few places, order might be maintained, but in those last minutes, what then?

16

"ALLISON, God bless you, where did you find these?"

"One of the staff who has already gone left them behind; he was notorious for sneaking out behind a bush in the Rose Garden. Given how high level he was, nobody really objected."

As she spoke, she handed Richard a well-worn pipe—a meerschaum, no less—and a leather pouch with some tobacco in it. He took the offered gifts, exhaustion forgotten for the moment with the anticipation of leaving the confines of the communications center and enjoying a relaxing smoke.

"With the president's compliments, Richard. He passed the word to try to find one for you."

"God bless him," Richard replied, chuckling. "So where do we go?"

"Outside, of course, but with everything going a little bit crazy now, more than a few smokers are lighting up and telling those protesting to go shove it. But I think you and I should still stay within the rules."

After another conversation with the president just after midnight, Richard had spent a near-sleepless night in the small communications center where he now had a permanent station, monitoring the situation and talking through the night with Judith, who was staying at her post over at Goddard.

For the moment, Sauron's Eye appeared to have stabilized, its energy levels dropping slightly. Judith hoped it meant that the solar storm was collapsing in on itself, that the sun's nearly incomprehensible field of gravity would wind up containing the explosion and turning it in upon itself. That was a hope, of course, but only a hope. Sometimes it did indeed mean that an anomaly they had been observing was dying down, which did happen at times with CMEs.

But this was a potential CPE. A smaller one that had blown off from the sun nearly a year ago, and fortunately on the far side relative to Earth, had been recorded by *Helio III* and extensively analyzed afterward. In its final hours, it had behaved in the same manner that he was seeing now. A slight energy drop as if it was coiling itself up, until the pressure of an explosion deep below the plasma surface of the sun finally erupted, overcoming the intense power of the sun's gravity to leap forth. He was still running on that analysis, even though several observers in China and elsewhere were claiming the crisis might very well pass, that there would be no massive flare, though the impact of the approaching CME would still have to be dealt with.

Ironic, he thought. Not many days ago, a CME packing the intensity of what everyone called a Carrington-level event was seen as a potential global catastrophe. But now, in comparison to a solar flare? If that alone was the problem the world would face today, it would be greeted with nearly a sigh of relief.

He was hunched over his monitor, reviewing the data yet again, hoping to find some clue that could at least start to change his mind, when Allison had tapped on the open door and held up the treasure she had found.

She motioned to the door, and, stretching with a moan after so many hours hunched over a monitor, he followed her out into the corridor. Their path was becoming somewhat familiar—turn left, then right, second elevator. They came out onto the main floor in the West Wing, and he immediately sensed a difference from just the evening before. There was a tension in the hallway that was palpable, raised voices echoing in the corridor.

A young woman wearing a heavy winter parka, jeans, and boots and dragging a carry-on luggage bag behind her came out of a side office, bumping into Richard and then elbowing past him. Richard looked at her with surprise as she pushed her way past him without even a polite

"Excuse me." It was quite a contrast to the oh-so-formal look and behavior expected of White House staff only the day before.

"Those with beta cards have been ordered to start evacuation," Allison whispered while pointing the way that Richard was supposed to go.

"What the hell do you mean? That bitch has a beta card and I don't?" he heard someone screaming from the office the woman had just exited.

Allison tried to nudge Richard along, but the confrontation was startling, at least for this outsider who was now at the epicenter of power. He stopped at the doorway and looked in.

The half-open door to the office suite where the argument was transpiring swung wide open, and a woman of middle age, dressed casually in jeans and a heavy sweater, pushed an older man a foot taller than she was out into the hall. Richard had to step back to get out of their way.

"I don't make these decisions, Mr. Hanson," the woman snapped. "That's further up the chain than me."

"I can't believe this shit!" he shouted back. "That bitch has a beta card, and I don't? Who was she screwing to get it?"

Allison brought her left wrist up to her mouth, whispered something into her wrist phone while glancing at Richard and motioning with her free hand that he was not to move.

Without hesitation, she stepped into the middle of the confrontation. "Problems here?" she asked, voice neutral and calm.

"Mr. Hanson here is pitching a fit because my assistant is being evacuated and he is not."

"Does she have the authorized blue beta card?"

"Yes, she does. She's a good translator, and we need her. Mr. Hanson, who does not have a card, is objecting."

Allison turned to face the angry man who towered over her by half a foot or more. Ignoring her orders, Richard instinctively stepped forward, coming up behind Allison to lend support. There wasn't much that he could physically do against a man with a build like that and twenty years younger, but maybe his presence would help somehow.

"Mr. Hanson, you have one of two choices," Allison said calmly.

"Settle down, go back into your office, and get back to work, or you will be escorted off these grounds."

"Go back and work? Work for what?" he cried hysterically. "That bitch that just walked out and this one here get evacuated while I stay here to fry?" He leaned in closer to Allison. "Let me guess. I bet you have an evacuation card too!"

Before she could reply, two Secret Service agents turned the corner behind the arguing couple, and to Richard's shock, one of them had drawn his pistol, the other one moving up swiftly and silent, grabbing Hanson by the forearm.

"Sir, you are coming with us, and I advise you not to resist," the agent who grabbed him announced sharply, while the armed agent stood back six feet, weapon raised.

It was beyond shocking to Richard. *This is the White House,* he thought. A day ago, everything was still so orderly, professional. A weapon drawn and now pointed at a staffer?

Hanson tried to shrug off the agent who had grasped him by the forearm and then saw the other agent with weapon drawn and froze.

"Okay, I get it," he whispered nervously. "I'll just stay here and go back to work."

"Sorry, sir, we have orders. Any disturbance like you just pulled and you are to be escorted off the grounds. Now let's go," the agent holding on to him replied forcefully with a tone that indicated there was no room for debate or appeal.

"At least let me get my stuff out of my desk."

"No time for that, sir; we'll give you something warm to wear on the way out."

"Fuck you!" Hanson cried. "This is the thanks I get for working here for fifteen years? Fuck all of you!"

He tried to break free. "You have no idea of who I've got pull with in here. I'll have your asses fired for this!"

The agent with a weapon out quickly holstered it, approached Hanson, pulled his arm up behind him, and pushed him forward. Cursing loudly, Hanson collapsed so that he had to be dragged along, the three disappearing around a turn in the corridor.

Allison turned to face the woman Hanson had been arguing with. "Ma'am, are you okay? Did he hurt you in any way?"

The woman began to cry. "Can't blame him. Know what I mean? He's got a wife and kid; I guess he was hoping that even though he didn't have an evac card, extra space would be found for them. Tanya, she's the one that just left. She's single, but she is the better translator; Hanson isn't. That's why she got assigned to be lifted out."

The woman, obviously shaken, took a deep breath, struggling to regain composure. "Sure, we're all scared shitless right now. Can't say I blame Hanson, but that's the way it is. I didn't even know Tanya had a blue card until she returned to the office a few minutes ago with her suitcase ready to go and to say goodbye and wish us luck."

"I'm sorry," Allison replied, "but that's the way it is. With luck, this whole thing will never happen, and everything will be back to normal in a few weeks."

The woman looked past Allison to Richard and stared at him with a malevolent gaze. "Not according to him," she said, and her tone carried a message of blame, as if he were the bringer of doom.

"Thanks for helping me out," the woman said, returning her attention to Allison. She hesitated, still glaring at Richard. "And Hanson might think I have one, but no, I don't have an evacuation card." She went back into her office.

Allison walked back to Richard. "Come on, let's go," she ordered, putting her hand on his forearm to lead the way.

A minute later, they were outside, and Richard took a deep breath. It was cold; apparently, a few flurries had come down during the night. He zipped up the parka that Allison had given him and went through the ritual all pipe smokers often take comfort in of filling the pipe and tapping the tobacco down just right so that it burned smoothly.

"Oh, damn. Would you happen to have a lighter?"

She looked up at him with a bit of a mischievous smile as if she were about to say no. *To get this close,* he thought, *and then the torture of not having a light!* More than once at Goddard, when he would sneak out to have a smoke, he'd forget his lighter or the matches he was carrying wouldn't flare to life, and there would be long, frustrating moments until another "sinner" appeared at their secret gathering spot and offer him a light.

Allison finally relented, reached into her pocket, drew out a butane lighter, and handed it to him.

Just as he lit his pipe, there was a blast of wind that snuffed the lighter out. A big helicopter with twin rotors came over the roof of the White House, pivoted around to turn its nose into the wind, and touched down lightly on the South Lawn, snow swirling up around it in a near blizzard.

Even before it was fully settled, the main doorway into the south portico of the White House swung open, and several security personnel emerged wearing black tactical gear, with weapons out in the open, the last of the three turning back, shouting something, and then one after another, over thirty people ran out in single file. It was a strange mix to Richard. One was wearing a well-tailored suit with no overcoat; behind him, a woman carried a squirming and crying toddler in her arms. One after another they emerged, most with carry-on bags, four of them a family with two small children in tow.

The aft access ramp of the chopper was down, two armed personnel having emerged, assault rifles held at the ready, gesturing for the civilians to move quickly. As soon as the last one was in and before the ramp had even fully closed, the rotors picked up speed, snow swirling about. It lifted off, nosed down into the wind, and cleared the fence to the west, climbing fast.

Richard, having turned his back to the rotor blast, looked over at Allison, who had done the same.

"When did this start?"

"Four hours ago. We'd be doing it anyhow given that the CME is going to hit us starting at noon, but now with your solar flare, there is even more urgency."

He didn't like the way she'd said *your solar flare,* and as if sensing his reaction, she offered a wry smile and whispered, "Sorry about that, sir. It's just people around here are either calling it *Sauron's Eye* or *Carrington's Flare.*"

"I'd hate like hell for that to be the way I get remembered by history," he replied. "If there is a history about this is written one day."

A rising thunder was echoing from the Mall; another twin-rotor helicopter was racing by, heading toward the Potomac, followed by another and then four more, diverting around the left and right of the Washington Monument.

"Congressional staff, most likely," Allison announced without comment.

He noticed a fairly large crowd standing on the far side of the White House fence, some just watching, more than a few shouting, making rude gestures, holding up signs: *what about us? sinking ship! fleeing rats!*

Inside the fence, the perimeter was being guarded by military personnel spaced at ten-yard intervals, weapons openly displayed.

"This is kind of way too obvious, isn't it?" Richard asked. "Reminds me of old videos of our embassy being evacuated when Saigon fell back in 1975."

"Yeah, it is definitely a public relations screwup of the first order. The Washington bureaus of all the major news agencies have been urged in very forthright terms not to fuel public panic—that this is just a precaution—but it's not sitting well at all with the hundreds of thousands still in this city."

"What about the internet? Cell phones? Something like this must be going viral and getting plastered all over the country." He paused, knowing the answer.

"Any cell phone service that was brought back up and running after the last storm gridlocked after the president put things out clearly in the open yesterday afternoon. Internet, and cell phone linkage is all but nonfunctional, except for a few government secured systems. Anyhow, people know what's going on. The leaders of the federal government and their staff are being evacuated, and everyone else is being left behind."

She sighed and stared off, watching as the helicopters disappeared from view.

Richard took that in as he snapped the butane lighter, a hot blue flame shooting out, and puffed the meerschaum pipe to life. He took a few deep puffs, inhaled, and felt a slight rush. To whomever had left the tobacco and pipe behind, he offered a silent thanks, though he couldn't think anything positive about the choice of blends with that too-frequently-used cherry added into it. It smelled nice, but its taste never appealed to him.

"Wouldn't it have been smarter to do it by buses or something?"

She chuckled sadly. "Sir, you've been asleep for part of the night or staring at your uplink to Goddard and *Helio II*. Let's get out from the shadow of the building for a moment."

She led the way out onto the South Lawn of the White House, where the helicopter had landed but minutes earlier, looking up to make sure there wasn't any traffic coming in.

He turned to face where she was pointing toward the Capitol and stood in silent awe.

Washington, D.C. was burning.

It wasn't just plumes of smoke here and there; it was a black pall of smoke rising behind the Capitol dome like a dark harbinger of what was to come. The only reason the air around the White House was clear was because a strong wind was gusting up from out of the west.

He stood silent, watching the black wall of smoke soaring heaven-ward, illuminated from within as something exploded, a fireball rising inside the miles-wide inferno, lending an even more hellish light to the spectacle.

It was silent, he realized, just the sound of the wind at his back and then the rising chatter of a helicopter lifting off behind the Capi-tol, racing down the length of the Mall, arcing up over the Lincoln Memorial, and disappearing from view.

"Most of the police force just gave up and deserted during the night," Allison said as if reading his thoughts. "When the mobs realized that most of the city police force was deserting, they truly went into a frenzy. In a way, though, I can't blame the cops, especially those with families still in the city."

He nodded.

"There's that moment when the thought forms, *Why in the hell am I getting killed protecting some damn 7-Eleven from being looted?* I heard that once the cops started packing it in, the firefighters gave up for the same reason, in some cases abandoning equipment in place after being shot at and attacked, without the cops there to protect them. Even the EMTs have stopped going in. They were exempt for a while, but the mobs even started turning on them, thinking they had drugs that might be fun to have. That's why we've had to go strictly to airlift of personnel out of D.C. to wherever it is they're supposed to go. On top of the looting and fighting, every major road out to the Beltway and beyond is gridlocked with people trying to get out. With gas supplies already so low since the last storm, more and more cars are stalling out on the roads.

"The original plans cooked up by FEMA years ago were written by damn fools who really didn't think it all out. The plan on paper was for several hundred buses, commandeered from the city or rolling out from military bases, to handle most of the evacuation. Can you even imagine that?" she said derisively. "Just put the buses on the road; of course everyone will just stand back and wave in a friendly manner as they drive by. The select few then get into the buses while everyone being left behind in their building waves goodbye, then drive out to the Beltway, which of course will be clear of traffic and on out to the west of the city."

It really was absurd, Richard realized.

He looked back toward the inferno and for a moment wondered if maybe nothing should have been said, to let people go through the last two days of their lives without knowledge that all was most likely at an end. Of course that thought was absurd, given all the information sources of a global community. Rumors were springing up days, even weeks in advance that the sun was going into an unusual cycle, perhaps a confluence of a number of cycles tens of thousands of years in length, that now triggered this nightmare. To have kept the reality of Sauron's Eye secret was absurd, but nevertheless, at this moment, he felt it as a personal burden and responsibility.

As if sensing his mood, Allison stepped closer and put a reassuring hand on his shoulder.

"In the hours ahead, we are all going to see the best and the worst of what we are as a species. Out there in that madness is some of the worst. I hope we all see some of the best inside that building." He looked back at the White House and nodded.

"You still think it is going to let go today?" she asked, and there was almost a childlike appeal in her voice.

He nodded.

She tried to offer a reassuring smile in response. "Richard, I'm freezing my butt off out here. Can we go in?"

He tapped what was left of the burning embers out of the pipe and gestured for her to lead the way.

PART IX

How can man die better than facing fearful odds . . .
—Thomas Babington Macaulay, *Lays of Ancient Rome*

17

"LISTEN to me, Darla; let's compromise on this. You go sleep for an hour, then I'll go for an hour."

She shook her head. "Other way around, Bear. And besides, where in the hell are we going to find a place to sleep?"

They had been standing watch at the steel door all night. Dawn was breaking under clear skies with temperatures hovering in the low twenties. With the light of day, they could see the vast crowd of thousands out beyond the chain-link fence that had been pouring in during the night as word spread through Springfield about what was happening.

Gone was the world of internet, Twitter, Snapchat, and Instagram, where one person could reach hundreds of thousands nearly instantly. At least some still had old-fashioned landlines that had survived the last CME or been restored in the three weeks afterward so that friends or family called to pass the word. News of what was happening here had therefore spread as it once did—word of mouth or through a phone call. "Gerda, get your kids down to the underground warehouse; you know the place." Then someone would run across the street to a neighbor to tell them, who called another friend, and so forth so that in the hours before dawn, thousands were making the trek, and what had been a trickle of children coming in during the afternoon and evening of yesterday was turning into a flood.

In response, state police, whose commander was still loyal to the governor, had been detailed to set up roadblocks at all approaches to try to turn the tide back. At nearly every checkpoint, it had finally proven to be futile. What officer was going to actually shoot parents with their children bundled up and in tow? The only dark incident was at a road-block on the north side of Route 64, where an officer did draw on a group, ordering them to turn back or he would fire. Three had died, the last one the state trooper. His partner, not out of fear but in sad disbelief at the stupidity of the man he was partnered with, kept his weapon holstered and simply told people to just keep moving. He then left his post, taking his vehicle and hoping against hope that he could make it to where his family lived just outside of Jefferson City and get them back here in time.

One by one, the attempts at cordoning off the area collapsed. Perry had detailed Captain Harrison to move one of the two Bradleys in his possession down to the highway and keep at least one approach lane open in anticipation that last-minute emergency supplies still might be shipped in, and to keep an eye on activities over at the Hyatt, where over fifteen hundred government officials, their numbers swelling by the hour, were still kept waiting, assuming at any minute they would be let in.

The M1 Abrams had been moved slightly so that its heavy front armor faced down the road rather than the steel doors, pivoted so that it only partially blocked the gate but left an opening several feet wide on its right side. Perry had then parked his other Bradley in front of the tank so that a corridor was created—the tank and Bradley on one side and the chain-link fence on the other side. At the entryway into that corridor, a near solid wall of MPs and armed parents were posted. Behind them, several tables were set up, hand-lettered signs displayed above the tables, announcing check-in points for children, teachers and staff, and medical personnel.

Jerry personally manned the table with a small group of trusted staff to help with selecting the teachers and other personnel to be admitted into the sanctuary along with their immediate families and put to work. It was a nightmarish task. In most cases, candidates who approached were quickly recognized, and the back of both of their hands marked with an ink stamp taken from a nearby bar stating *FREE DRINKS*. That stamp divided those who might survive the day and those who would not. If they had a spouse with them, and only a spouse would be included, their hand was stamped as well, and they were told to quickly move along and head into the Ark, where their work assignments would be detailed.

The hard task was that for each candidate accepted, there would be another who would be met with a sad shake of the head and "Let's wait until midday and see how many more volunteers we'll need," which was a lie that most saw through, and then they were told to please step away from the table.

Darren had stood with Jerry through a fair part of the night to provide backup if needed, and he could see that Jerry, though outwardly tough and appearing absolutely in control of the situation, was torn apart inside with each rejection, especially if it was someone he knew and had worked with across the years.

"You just gotta intuit people by sixth sense and then make a decision quickly," Jerry had told him during a brief pause. "A lot about being a good teacher or principal is about instinct, a gut feeling. Either you got it and keep developing it, or you don't and should get a job doing something else. I have to make snap decisions; there just isn't time for anything more. If I dwell too much on the fact that it's life-and-death—not just for them but their spouse as well—I'd break down. I can't think about it. I just pray I'm being guided to do the right thing. Perhaps far more than the teacher who was the best at honors English or history, I want a respected old guy who taught auto mechanics, a guy who knew how to work hands-on with kids, that many teachers looked down upon when it came to teaching mechanic skills.

"I'm not just choosing the teachers and staff who might have just been good in a classroom. I have to think long-term, given this crazy idea you've handed me about saving these kids, and maybe they'll make a better world of it someday. I want people who can teach about life and living and not just math or auto mechanics or history. That's what I'm trying to sift out."

He offered a wan smiled to Darren. "You stay focused on trying to save the lives of these children. My job now is to think about who can help us to save their minds, hearts, and souls as well after this is over."

More applicants had then come up, and with a painful sigh, Jerry went back to his task. Darren wondered how Jerry had the strength to be the chooser of those who might live and those who would not. He was glad Jerry was doing the task.

He had, as well, worked out a system that so far was holding up under the increasing pressure. Those who Jerry had stamped were told to move quickly along to where Helen would sort them out and assign their work positions.

Once through the outer gate and just inside the steel door, Helen greeted them with a few helpers around her, all of them staff and teachers she had worked with throughout the years. No longer trusting computers, she had reverted to old-style composition notebooks for recording information.

Each new entry was asked the same questions. "Your name? Grade you taught or specialization? Family members with you?"

At times, Helen stood and hugged who approached, addressing them by first name and crying out that she was glad to see them and a minute later ordering them off to get to work.

A photocopier in the main office still worked, and Darren had run off hundreds of copies of a map of the place until the machine jammed up and he didn't know how to fix it. Each new arrival was handed a map, told what to do, and then hustled on through the steel doors and down the access tunnel. Children were to be organized by ages first in various areas down at the deepest end of the Ark, then subdivided by which school they came from, whenever possible teaming them to a friend or those that they knew. The younger children already inside were being tagged with shipping labels taken from one of the warehouses, the labels draped around their necks stating parents' names, addresses, their names, ages, and school they were attending. Finally, labels were taken out beyond the chain-link fence and distributed to parents to fill out on their own to speed the process along. They were learning to improvise as each precious minute ticked by, to keep things moving, for there was no manual or training for what they were now attempting to do.

Nearly everyone—children, parents, those working to sort things out—had been up all night. All were increasingly exhausted, and if they paused and thought about what might very well happen that day, they were filled with anguish and terror. The youngest, so sensitive to the moods of adults, were expressing that anxiety in the loudest ways possible. In the area set aside for prekindergarten, it was turning into bedlam. That location was getting gamy, for no one had thought ahead regarding just how many toilets they would need. One of the few right decisions made about the youngest was that the furniture storage warehouse would be their gathering place; dozens of beds could be pulled out of shipping boxes, even just a mattress put on the floor, and adults could try to get them tucked in at least for a little while. That warehouse did have four toilets for their employees, but out of the four, one was already jammed up because a stuffed animal had been sent on a "journey to go find Mommy," and flushed. It was taking a very strong stomach and nerves of steel to go into that sector. One poor teenage girl drafted to help out finally just fled, crying that she couldn't deal with it, got past the steel doors, and ran off.

So as teachers approached, Helen greeted them joyfully, especially if they were early elementary, and sent them on their way. But for each teacher coming in, dozens of children continued to arrive as word spread across Springfield of what was happening, and some parents made the tough but right decision to try to ensure their children survived.

The first medical personnel had finally begun to show up as well. Dr. Sarbak was still at the hospital, looting equipment and medical supplies, doing it at gunpoint at the start, being backed up by a dozen well-armed parents. Dr. Donkervoet was working at a table next to Jerry, handling the sorting out of incoming volunteers, selecting doctors, nurses, and trained specialists who would be admitted into the Ark. The word was out for pharmacists as well, the first of them showing up just before dawn in a jeep filled with trash bags jammed with medications, vitamins, and other supplies.

Weary and so desperate for sleep, Darren and Darla just stood to one side of the steel doors and watched. Darren had a clipboard with several pages of notes on it. Darla had assigned several volunteers to keep a tally of how many were coming in, and as the flood of people increased throughout the night, both were beginning to worry about just how much food was actually on hand at the Kraft warehouse. The manager still had not shown up, and without the passwords, the office computer was inaccessible.

Darren had yet to get an accurate inventory of what was down there, so all he could do was estimate. With two hundred thousand square feet of area and pallets of food stacked nearly twenty feet high, and deducting space needed for access ways for trucks and forklifts, he was running with a rough estimate of at the very least five million meals. But meals of what? And compounding the question was just how much had been shipped out over the last three weeks so that in some sections the warehouse was nearly empty. The already overused joke was wearing very thin that they would all be living on Cheez Whiz, Velveeta, and Oscar Mayer wieners for months to come.

He was now facing up to a statistic that literally was about life or death. How long would everyone actually have to stay down here? He had talked that over with Captain Harrison, and the answer was grim.

It might not be just a few days. Something he had not even thought of until Harrison mentioned it was a concern about nuclear power plants. If personnel did not survive to maintain safety standards, the waste so imprudently stored at each of those facilities would eventually start to heat up when the cooling pumps shut down. The overheated stored waste would catch on fire, explode, and send out plumes of radioactive debris. People might therefore very well survive the solar flare only to be killed by man-made radiation weeks or even months later.

There would also be chaos resulting from those who did manage to survive and were then scrounging for food and supplies, and all of that, compounded by the concern that they did not want these kids to see what had once been their idyllic city carpeted with the decaying dead. One possible reality that was indeed frightful: that the parents of many of the children might very well linger outside the entryway until they died from the radiation. And then? Weeks, even months later children emerging would confront that horror as their first vision of this strange new world, if indeed above ground was somehow survivable. Therefore, the hope was that there would be enough supplies allowing the survivors to stay underground as long as possible.

So it would be weeks at the very least and at worst maybe up to a year or more. They had to run with the scenario that something would indeed happen for the worst, because to make such calculations based upon something to be hoped for would be a supreme folly.

From brief conversations with Perry during the night, Darren had learned far more than he wished to about the grim triage they most likely would have to face. He'd responded with "We'll cross that bridge if we ever get there." It had been too much to think about at that moment. As long as just children and those vetted to help them continued to come in, he could not bring himself to lock the doors.

He stood silent, looking at his clipboard, eyelids feeling heavy as he tried to keep count of just how many were coming in while wrestling with all those other questions as well.

"Bear, you sleep. Come on. I can take over."

"Other way around, sweetheart." He fell silent as a teenage girl entered carrying a pair of crying, year-old twins.

"Diapers or something; we'll need those as well," Darla said.

"Maybe we should have thought about all of this before we put ourselves into the middle of it all."

She looked up at him, more than a bit surprised. "If we hadn't, who would have? Who could have pulled it off?" Her voice broke. "Let's pray someone is doing the same for our grandchildren."

He knew, of course, that the inability to reach their own children and grandchildren had been something of a motivation for their decision to at least take action locally. It was a surrogate for their own inner crucifixion.

"Sorry. It's just that my mind is going numb trying to think of all the things needed and all the contingencies. Do we even have enough supplies?"

"Lock the doors on them?" she asked as if hesitating to raise the question.

"Could you?" he asked.

"No. Could you?"

"No, not now."

She stood on tiptoe to kiss him on the cheek. "You go to sleep, Bear."

"Okay, let's do this. Paper, rock, scissors. Loser gets some sleep."

A minute later, he sent her packing off to his office where he had a cot stashed in the closet behind his desk. For some strange reason, he had always been able to outguess her at least three-quarters of the time they played that game.

"Darren!" Captain Harrison frantically waved to him to come out to where he was standing by the M1 tank.

As Darren slowly trotted out, he half wished that he had lost the paper, rock, scissors game with Darla, but if he had lost the first round, he would have argued with her for two out of three.

"General Perry needs you now!" Harrison cried, gesturing for him to fall in behind and follow him to the other side of the gate where Perry's Humvee was parked.

Passing beyond the gate where Jerry Green had his check-in table set up, it was at that terrible moment for Darren a step into another world. Hundreds of families were milling about, gathered into their tight little circles. Parents had been handed the shipping labels and were filling them out, tying the labels to a button or zipper of the child's jacket and then guiding them to the gate. More than a few parents, in their rush to get here, had forgotten to pack a bag for the child with at least a few changes of clothes and something to comfort them. In that frigid weather, he could see fathers and mothers, now realizing their mistake, taking off their winter coats and sweaters, handing them to their children to take, and then standing there shivering as they watched their children go through the gate.

He heard snatches of conversations flooded around him.

"Now remember, angel, Mommy expects you to be a good girl. I saw Mrs. Davis just go in; remember her from kindergarten? You go with her now."

"Sweetie, don't worry. I put Mr. Floppy Ears in your backpack, but don't pull him out until later. We wouldn't want to drop and lose him now, would we?"

"Remember how we prayed every night before you went to sleep?

Let's say it together now as one big family. 'Now I lay me down to sleep . . .'"

"Son, you're fourteen now. There was a time when fourteen meant you were a man, and that time is here again. I expect you to behave like a man. Now look me in the eyes and promise me you'll be strong. Now go kiss your mother goodbye. No crying; she's too upset as is."

Parents whose children had already gone through the gate clung to the fence, some trying to smile, waving, telling them that all was okay. "Go on, sweetheart. Do you see your friend Mary? Go catch up with her."

Others just stood silently holding each other. Others disintegrated into tears, crying, husbands having to help wives turn away, wives having to help husbands. A few changed their minds, shouting for their children to come back as they disappeared into the darkness of the tunnel.

"Darren!"

He had frozen in place for a moment, so overwhelming was the pain washing around him.

God, why did I do this? he asked silently. *Why me? Are we doing the right thing? Wouldn't it be better for them all to be together at the end, if this is indeed the end?*

The sun was well above the tree line to the east, and in that morning sky, one could look at it for several seconds before turning away. The answer to his prayer was in his heart as he gazed at the sun and Sauron's Eye, which appeared to be looking straight at him and his world with a malevolent gaze.

He followed behind Harrison. Few in this town knew him, and he thanked God for that as he shouldered his way through the crowd, because what could he say if they turned to him with pleas and appeals as a friend to look out for their child or if there a way they could all go in together as a family? He looked over at Jerry Green's table.

Jerry had been forced to increase the detail around his table, a human wall now, mostly parents; from the looks of them, they must have been one hell of a football squad in their day, helping to keep the crowd back and in some semblance of order, letting a few through at a time after showing their identification before Jerry stamped the backs of both hands.

"Damn it, Darren. Now!"

Harrison was by the Humvee with General Perry by his side, motioning for him to come over. As Darren approached, Perry sat back down inside the Humvee, putting on a headset.

"What's up?" Darren asked.

"It's about to hit the fan, that's what's up," Harrison replied, nodding toward Perry sitting in the front passenger seat. Leaning into the vehicle, Darren could hear what he was saying.

"Bravo Xray Seven. This is General Perry. I am ordering you to disregard George One. Repeat, disregard George One."

Perry turned a switch on the comm unit built into the front dash of the Humvee, and now Darren could hear the conversation both ways.

"General, sir, you are telling me to disregard a direct order from the governor?"

"Affirmative."

"Sir, I cannot do that. And sir, George One has informed me that you have been removed from command."

Amid the chaos surrounding him between crying children, more than a few crying parents, and others shouting for instructions, all of it a sea of anguish and confusion, he now heard something else—the thumping of a helicopter, growing louder by the second.

"Xray Seven, abort! Abort! You are following an illegal and immoral order. Abort!"

"Sir, I cannot; I have my orders."

A National Guard helicopter came in low and hot, just clearing the trees to the south, and behind it was an Apache gunship a hundred or so feet higher.

"Don't do this!" Perry shouted, but there was no response as the Black Hawk passed straight over them, the sound near-deafening, dust and debris kicked up, parents crouching and pulling their children in protectively. The pilot then pulled up sharply into a banking turn, bleeding off speed as he circled, while the Apache swung about and went into a slowly turning hover a couple of hundred feet higher. The sight and sound of it was intimidating, as it was surely meant to be. So much dust was now swirling up that Darren had to squint, turning his back to the down blast, a sharp memory now triggered of Iraq, all the damn dust and sand kicked up by helicopters.

"Your attention, please! Your attention, please!" The Black Hawk had a loudspeaker rigged up, the voice sounding sharp, threatening, echoing above the roar of the engines and rotors. "You are ordered to disperse immediately, by order of the governor. Clear a way so that emergency vehicles can enter this facility. Once that operation is completed, room will still be available for any who wish to enter."

The message was repeated three times.

Darren, looking for a vantage point, finally climbed up on the hood of the Humvee. Some people, those at the edge of the crowd of several thousand, began pulling back, but most still remained in place, crouching.

"You have five minutes to disperse. Disregard those wearing National Guard uniforms who are in open rebellion and attempting to hold an official government facility. They are troops in rebellion and shall be dealt with according to martial law. If you do not disperse, extreme measures will be taken."

As the message was repeated for the third time, the Apache arced up into a high-angle turn, dropped its nose, and thundered down, aiming straight at the crowd.

Collective cries of panic rose, the crowd surging back from the fence. Others lying flat pulled their children in tight to cover them. More than a few shots rang out, parents on the ground taking aim and firing at the Apache but with no effect against its well-armored hull.

"This is General Perry!" Darren saw Perry up by his side standing on the roof of the Humvee, shouting into the microphone linking him to the helicopters. "Don't do it. For Christ's sake, there are children down here!"

The Apache swept over the crowd barely twenty feet above the ground, like a hawk swooping in for the kill. At the very last second, it pulled up into a high-arcing turn, while whoever was on the Black Hawk kept repeating the same message.

"Stand your ground!" shouted Darla, having been disturbed from her nap. Holding up a battery-powered bullhorn, she had climbed partway up onto the Abrams M1, shouting the same message several times. "They are fellow Americans; they will not shoot at their own children down here. Stand your ground!"

The crowd was disintegrating into chaos, but her cries rallied enough to turn back and stay in place.

Perry jumped from the hood of the Humvee and back into the front seat. "Bravo Xray Seven, In the name of God, are you going to shoot at the children down here?"

"Sir, I have my orders direct from the governor—"

"Fuck the orders, man! Are you going to shoot the children down here?"

The loudspeaker on the Black Hawk went silent, the chopper rising slowly while the Apache went into a menacing holding pattern a couple of hundred feet up.

"Sir, I don't want to." Darren heard something of a plaintive note to his voice. "The governor is listening in on another channel, and he has just ordered me to disperse this crowd by any means possible—not to shoot to kill, if possible, but shoot to at least frighten."

"Damn it. You know as well as I do it will go out of control and kids will get killed."

"Sir, I don't want to, but—"

"Make a decision as a man!" Perry shouted back. "All of us might be facing God before this day is out. What will you tell Him about what you did here today?"

There was a pause of only a dozen or so seconds, but for Darren, it seemed like an eternity. He jumped down from the Humvee and unslung his AR-15. It was useless against an armored Apache, but it might sting the Black Hawk a bit.

The Black Hawk's rotors picked up velocity, nose pitching up, and it climbed out, the Apache turning and doing the same.

"God bless you, and thank you," Perry said.

"General Perry, the governor orders you to report to him immediately."

Perry laughed. "You know what to tell that self-centered son of a bitch what he can go kiss."

There was a bit of a chuckle in reply. "Sir, nearly all of us are with you, but there are some who are not. I'm sorry, sir, but it isn't over yet. Bravo Xray Seven signing off."

Perry got out of the Humvee, while in the background, Darla repeatedly announced that everything was okay, for parents to continue to bring their children in, and for adult personnel to report to Jerry Green.

"He's right," Perry said. "It isn't over. It is going to turn bad, real bad."

The sun, climbing well above the horizon, once a source of comfort, now filled Darren with an icy chill down his spine.

PART X

Death closes all: but something ere the end,
Some work of noble note, may yet be done.

—Alfred, Lord Tennyson, *Ulysses*

Once past that obstacle, there were two more security personnel, this time Secret Service. Another showing of IDs, which were cross-checked to a sign-in sheet, which both he and Allison had to initial. One of the agents opened the door into the conference room, an agent inside gesturing to where Richard was supposed to sit while Allison stayed outside. A briefing was already going on as he slipped into his chair; he was a bit nervous and did not want to be noticed. The room was smaller than where he had met with the president and advisors only the day before. About twenty or so were crammed into its narrow confines.

He was noticed immediately by the president, who interrupted a presentation by Secretary Van Buren, who was speculating on long-term environmental effects from a full-scale flare of longer than one day. Richard glanced at the monitor displaying species die-off estimates. It looked grim.

"Dr. Van Buren," the president said, interrupting the presentation, "if we could hold your briefing for a few minutes, Dr. Carrington has just entered the room, and we all want the latest update from him on what is happening with the sun."

"Yes, Mr. President," Richard said softly, voice a bit shaky. This wasn't going to be easy.

He stepped behind the podium, the room so small that he had to squeeze in behind it. He scanned the data and openly sighed, regretting that since it was obvious everyone in the room was hanging on his reaction and what he was about to say.

"Whenever you are ready, Dr. Carrington," the president urged him, making clear there was no more stall time.

Richard cleared his throat, adjusted his glasses, and finally waded in. "The luminosity of the sun has increased over the last seventy-five minutes."

"What does that mean?" the president asked.

"Sir, the sun's output of visible light has increased just over 2 percent, and the rate of increase is accelerating. The point of origin of this increased luminosity is Sauron's Eye. Up until seventy-five minutes ago, Sauron's Eye appeared, relative to the plasma surface of the sun, to be a dark spot more than fifty thousand miles across,

18

HE was almost getting used to the ear-popping ride on the elevator taking them several hundred feet beneath the White House. But this time, as the door opened, he found himself facing four black-clad security personnel openly armed with M4s strapped across their chests.

Allison showed no reaction other than producing her ID, holding it up, and telling Richard to do the same. They were checked against a list and then told to proceed.

"What's this?" Richard whispered. "It wasn't this way yesterday."

"You can tell things are getting a little dicey upstairs; several people tried to slip their way down here," she replied.

This time, she led him down a different corridor; it was narrower and sloped down to a lower level. At the end of that descent, they turned left. A heavy steel-reinforced door, halfway open, was in front of them. Passing through the entryway, Richard noticed that the open door was more than a foot thick, resembling a safe door at a bank, complete with the Mosler logo. Farther in were double doors, glass walled, one behind the other. Allison opened the outer of the two, gesturing from him to go in. She closed the outer door, which sealed tight, and with the inner door opening, his ears popped.

It was the same as the ultraclean rooms at Goddard, except rather than to ensure dust-free environments for rooms with sensitive equipment and computers, it was to guard against radioactive dust. Finally, there was a standard body scanner.

while the outer rim of it was a swirling mass of high-intensity energy boiling up from deep within the sun, thus giving it the appearance of a malevolent humanlike eye, pupil in the center surrounded by a light-colored sclera. That is shifting rapidly as predicted. The most recent close-ups from *Helio II . . .*"

He paused and turned to look at the monitor. Several seconds passed, and a still image appeared on the screen. He looked at the time stamp; it had arrived a little over ten minutes ago, which meant the image was about twenty minutes old. He glanced at a row of clocks that displayed the time in D.C., London, Moscow, and China.

"The CME will start to impact in approximately an hour and twenty minutes. The full impact will reach us in two hours. Regardless of the damage that this CME will do to us—and it will prove to be the most intense solar event to strike our planet since 1859—we are at least in some ways prepared for it. The event of three weeks ago was a wake-up call, but now we enter at least twenty-four of the most nerve-racking hours in the history of humanity once that CME has bent back our magnetosphere and left the surface of our planet exposed."

Looking over to the technician sitting in the corner, hunched over her computer monitors, Richard asked, "Can we get an image of Sauron's Eye from approximately three hours ago?"

It took about ten seconds for the image to appear.

"Put the two side by side, please."

She did as requested. He took it in and shook his head, wondering if this was how seismologists felt when still trying to track down precise warning times for earthquakes.

"Notice the most current shot. Those long, curling streams of intense white light, which are actually advanced streamers of a proton event or flare, spiraling up around what we could call the pupil of Sauron's Eye. The pupil is rapidly contracting as the high-energy storm from deep within the sun is exploding up through it. As the speed and intensity increase, the eye will start to look like it is winking at us as the pupil collapses in and then explodes."

He stared at it for a moment, lost in silent awe and fear. He had spent a lifetime studying the sun, and at this instant, he felt as if he were indeed staring at something malevolent and deadly. That which he had given a lifetime to know seemed poised to destroy all that he knew. He wished the eye of doom would just collapse in upon itself and disappear into oblivion, but of course, like Tolkien's story, that was fantasy, not the reality he was trying to explain.

The president urged him to continue.

"Each of those flares is tens of thousands of miles long, charged with an energy that would make the simultaneous detonation of every nuclear weapon on this planet pale to insignificance."

He glanced at Admiral Brockenborough as if to say, *The power you think you can wield is nothing compared to this.*

"Three hours ago, the gravity of the sun was causing those vast coiling explosions to arc over and plunge back down at such velocity that they punched thousands of miles through the boiling plasma that can be loosely defined as the surface of the sun.

"Now to the most current image. Those coils of high-energy protons are escaping solar gravity and are now streaming outward at nearly the speed of light."

"So it's begun?" the president asked.

"Almost, but not quite yet, sir. What we are seeing there is a foreshadowing, a forward edge, like the outer bands of a hurricane that announce a storm is coming but is still some distance off. Yes, that means they are already hitting our magnetosphere, but it is just the opening move."

"How soon before the full-out blow hits?" the head of national security asked.

"Ma'am, I cannot give you an exact estimate to the minute, but it is all but certain to blow within the next twelve hours."

"If that damn thing blows before the CME fully impacts our magnetosphere . . . ?" asked the president.

"Best case? The flare blows within the next hour and forty-five minutes. The head of it, moving at nearly the speed of light, cuts right through the CME, which is moving at only 1.7 million miles per hour. If so, there is a strong probability that it disrupts the CME significantly

as it blows through; it then strikes our magnetosphere, and most if not
nearly all the energy is absorbed and diverted."

"In other words, we are saved?" someone whispered.

"Yes. Not just from the flare but perhaps even the effects of the worst
CME since what is called the Carrington Event of 1859."

"There will be one hell of a lot of explaining and cleaning up to do
after what has happened in the last twenty-four hours," the head of the
NSA said, shaking her head.

"And some of us will look like total assholes," replied Admiral Brockenborough. Richard knew the jab was directed at him and perhaps
even the president as well.

"I would prefer to look like an asshole," the president struck back
angrily, "if that means we are spared this nightmare. I'll take that mon-
iker any day."

"Sir, if such a possibility is indeed the case," Admiral Brockenborough replied, unfazed by the rebuke, "that we still might be spared from
this nightmare scenario presented by the good doctor up front, that
changes the strategic situation profoundly."

"Admiral, stop right there! I've made my decision regarding our nuclear weapons and have communicated thus to every leader of a nuclear-
armed nation, including Iran and Korea. My order for a full stand-down
is firm regardless of what happens today. Either obey that order without further debate, or I will accept your resignation here and now. Do
I make myself clear, Admiral?"

"Yes, sir," he replied with barely suppressed anger.

The president returned his attention to Richard. "Now give us worst-
case scenario, at least from a solar event and not the insanity of our
own collective suicide."

Richard, shaken, pressed on. "I've already done so several times, sir,
regarding worst case both with this group and you personally. It is still
the same."

"So that's it, Dr. Carrington? We are facing the final hours?"
Richard nodded.

"We have about an hour and forty-five minutes left to prepare," the president announced softly. "Let us all pray for the best but prepare for the worst. Let's get to work as planned, and no one—I repeat, no one—is going to go off half-cocked."

He swept the room with his gaze, and no one dared to reply as he stood up and left the conference room. Richard waited for most of the room to clear, no one bothering to approach him to talk, so he felt truly alone, again the Greek messenger. He followed the last of the group out the door, not sure what to do next or where to go. At this moment, he wished he could simply walk out of the building and find some way to still get back to Goddard, some familiar, comfortable surroundings to sit out the next few hours.

"Sir," Allison said, "the president wants you in the Oval Office now."

"Why? What more can I say or do?"

"Maybe it's just to listen," she replied.

19

"DARREN, wake up! We're moving."

Harrison was shaking him awake. Darren struggled to sit up, completely disoriented for a moment and trying to focus, finally realizing he was somewhere familiar, but familiar from a long time ago.

After the incident with the two helicopters, he thought it best to just stay close by General Perry's side. He was offered the backseat, and that was the last he remembered.

"How long was I out?" he asked groggily.

"Less than an hour; you needed it," replied Perry, up in the front seat and turning to offer him a Styrofoam cup filled halfway with black coffee.

Darren took the cup without comment and sipped it. It was almost cold, and he downed it in a few gulps. The caffeine jolt helped to bring him awake, but at the same time, the raw coffee on a very empty stomach nailed him as well, and he was hit with a sudden wave of nausea.

Feeling the Humvee moving, he was still confused as he looked out the side window. Harrison was driving, backing the vehicle up, trying to turn it, but the crowd of civilians around them was in their way, with General Perry shouting for them to move. And then there was the high-pitched whine of a turbine engine.

Darren was hit by a wave of fear that the choppers were coming back until he realized it was the Abrams tank guarding the entryway through the chain-link fence starting up. The tank began moving slowly forward, the crowd parting for the sixty-ton behemoth. Harrison positioned the Humvee in front of the tank to lead the way.

"Who's going to block the gate?" Darren asked.

"I've ordered the Bradley pre-positioned there by Harrison to stay in place. We've got a problem down by the highway, and that's taking priority now."

The road ahead opened up as the outer edge cleared of the several thousand still packed around the entryway. The local MPs who were loyal to their town and to Perry saw them approaching and stood from the positions they had established behind cars parked to either side of the road, waving for him to keep going forward, some of them falling in behind the tank following Perry's Humvee. Perry had his window down, the icy wind whipping in, truly bringing Darren awake, while Perry shouted for the men on foot to stay in place, to not leave their positions. "If you hear fighting up ahead, any troops then coming your way, shoot to kill!"

Harrison sped up, reached the turn from Limestone Road to Haywood Road, and came to a stop. Fifty yards ahead, concertina wire was stretched across the road, and Humvees were to either side. Dismounted troops stood behind the two vehicles, their weapons raised, pointing straight at them. Darren flinched. The windshield was supposed to be able to take the impact of a 5.56 or 7.62 mm round, but nevertheless, he wanted to duck. Harrison and Perry both remained upright, having expected this.

"Just stay cool, Darren," Harrison said without looking back.

"What in the hell is this all about?"

"Negotiation time."

That sent a chill through Darren, his anger instantly rising. "General, if you've sold out and are letting them in—" He might very well shoot him for such a betrayal.

"Just shut up and listen," Perry replied as he opened his door and carefully got out of the vehicle, holding up both hands to show that he was not carrying a weapon but still hanging on to the small handheld mike for the radio.

"All right, Governor, I am at the roadblock," he announced. "Have your people clear the concertina wire, and let's get this done; there isn't much time left."

"Mr. Perry," the governor answered, "we have an agreement, so now it is your move first. And why the tank with you?"

"You told me we had to move it. Once we get this damn agreement taken care of, I've ordered the troopers in the tank and Bradleys to dismount and turn them over to your side."

"Agreement?" Darren roared, grabbing Harrison by the shoulder and forcing him to look back. "You sons of bitches!"

He now guessed that part of the agreement was to bring out the ringleader who had started this whole fiasco for the state government and turn him over and at the same time surrender the tank and Bradleys. With the tank no longer holding the outer gate, the governor and his people could just roll their convoy into the Ark and take it over.

Darren realized that while he had dozed off, Perry had sold them out. The only hope now was that Darla would slam the steel doors shut and try to hold out. Even then, it was an endgame. The tank could blow the door apart. Darren very slowly unslung the short-barrel AR-15 from his shoulder. He was not going to allow himself to be taken without a fight.

"You'd better not try to fuck me over," the governor's voice crackled on the radio. "We have a deal, Mr. Perry. Clear passage and the ringleader of this stupid insanity is turned over for immediate justice."

"You son of a bitch!" Darren brought his weapon around and raised it. He was not about to shoot Perry in the back. He hesitated, wanting Perry to first turn and face his end before killing him.

"Darren, don't you move another damn inch!" Harrison cried, holding up an old-style 1911 .45 Colt, aimed straight at Darren from only inches away. "Listen to me. You slept through some interesting negotiating. Don't screw it up!"

"Screw up what, damn you? That you betrayed all of us?"

"Just lower your weapon and give me thirty seconds to explain."

Darren saw Harrison's forefinger was wrapped around the trigger.

"Darren, in the name of God, just give this thing a few more seconds, and then you'll understand."

Even as Harrison shouted his warning, Darren could see six 18-wheelers moving up the exit ramp from Route 64 and then onto Haywood Street through the narrow lane cleared of vehicles. Behind the 18-wheelers, the assemblage of buses, limos, and SUVs parked around the Hyatt were starting up as well, scores of people dashing out from the hotel to get on board the caravan as it moved out. The troops blocking the road were pulling the concertina wire back from the road.

"What is going on?" Darren asked as the first 18-wheeler drew closer. When it turned broadside, he saw a cross emblazoned on the side with a familiar logo of the church he attended.

"Listen carefully, Darren," Harrison said, removing his finger from the trigger and lowering his weapon. "Do you belong to that guy's church?"

"Yeah, a lot of us do down where we live at Lake of the Ozarks."

"He's been sitting with those trucks for over an hour and cooling his heels waiting to get in."

"Why?"

"Bargaining chip."

"What?"

"After he left here yesterday evening and helped to round up some of the teachers and doctors, he went back down to his church, where he pulled together four tractor-trailer loads of supplies. The members of your church must either be a bit crazy or have some foresight. Did you know they had truckloads of survival-type supplies?"

Darren nodded. "He believed in the end-times, so yeah, a lot of us tithed, and the money went to emergency supplies."

"Well, he loaded nearly all of those supplies into four 18-wheelers and brought them up here, but then the governor's people blocked them from going in. Those other two 18-wheelers were put together by Doc Sarbak, stuff hauled out of the hospital and pharmacies. They got stopped too."

The first tractor-trailer was almost upon them, Perry leaning out of the Humvee and waving for them to keep on going, pointing the way to the entryway into the Ark.

"And the deal is?" Darren asked, still suspicious.

"A lot of slick negotiating with the governor, who is about to get one hell of a surprise," Harrison whispered. "Now just watch, okay?"

Darren fell silent as the first 18-wheeler approached, led by the Bradley that up until that moment had been deployed near the highway to observe happenings at the Hyatt. If indeed his pastor had stripped out most of the supplies stored in a warehouse behind their church, there were at least several hundred thousand rations in those trucks, along with solid-state electrical generators that could be recharged with solar panels once the solar storms had subsided, water purifiers, survival gear, tens of thousands of small batteries, thousands of low-energy LED lights, emergency medical packs, vitamins, tools, and so many things not thought of until the crisis of this moment that would be priceless if anyone were to survive after the storm had passed.

As he spoke, the other trucks rumbled by, accelerating to fall in behind the trucks from the church. At the same time, out at the Hyatt parking lot, the long caravan of buses began rolling, scores of people still running out of the building and getting into vans and limos. Their procession, led by several Bradleys and a convoy of Humvees, moved to come in behind the tractor-trailers.

Darren took that in. Perry had indeed made a Faustian bargain that he would never have agreed to, and he felt betrayed. All the families with children still waiting to get in would be shoved to one side while these thousands selected for what they called continuity of government piled into the Ark. Once secured, then what? Would the governor honor his side of the bargain and let everyone waiting outside to then come storming in?

He knew the answer was no, and the governor knew that as well. The crowd would be whipped up to a near frenzy just at the sight of the privileged few so easily driving in, relaxed in the comfort of their heated buses, vans, and even the hate-inspiring official limos.

Things were about to degenerate into a riot.

Looking at their convoy, Darren could see they had already planned for that. At regular intervals, Humvees—several modified for urban fighting with top-mounted guns and equipment for firing canisters of tear gas into a mob—rolled with the convoy. Behind the Hyatt, a deep thunder echoed. Two Black Hawks rose, one of them in civilian colors with the seal of the state of Missouri on the side. Without doubt, the governor and his personal entourage were in that one. He would definitely not risk riding with the convoy, and once his people had secured the facility, he would be flown the short distance to the entryway. Behind the two Black Hawks, two more helicopters rose; a second Apache had arrived. They hovered above the convoy like deadly dragonflies.

It was all so well planned, so cynically thought out.

They would show compassion for the thousands of kids already inside. And when it was all over, be it a week, a month, a year from now and it was decided to reemerge, they, of course, would be the rulers—the children cared for, but then raised and taught by whom? What then of the promise to thousands of parents that only their children would be allowed in with a careful selection of teachers, doctors, and those from the community with special skills to help them survive afterward? We will save your child, but the rest of you will die, only then to see this betrayal as the privileged, the elite, motored past you to safety?

It was almost certain to Darren that within minutes, a full-scale riot would ensue beyond anyone's ability to stop it, and then what? It was looking forward, after the nightmare than had been a deeper motivator for Darla and himself. They'd wanted to at least give their children a chance at life, and maybe in the aftermath, when so much had been washed away, they could create a better world. But now it was finished, and he was filled with bitterness.

"Mr. Perry," the governor's voice crackled on the radio speaker, "you're getting what you want, and we're starting to move as well. Now keep the road open for us."

"Yes, sir, Governor. I am getting *exactly what I want!*"

Perry all but leaped into the front seat of the Humvee, pushing the minister as he did so. "Harrison, get us the hell out of here! Hit it!"

Harrison had already shifted into reverse and floored it, nearly ramming into the front of the M1 Abrams, which had shifted into reverse as well, pressing up against the rear of the last of the 18-wheelers. As ordered, the gunner of the M1 fired off a high-velocity armor-piercing round aimed to skim over the caravan. The muzzle blast and shriek of the projectile passing overhead at over four thousand feet per second was deafening, the shock wave stunning the guards who had been manning the roadblock. If not protected by the top cover the vehicle, they would have been fried to a crisp by the muzzle blast.

Several of the guards who had been blocking the road were knocked off their feet, stunned by the blast. One managed to open fire as he lay on the pavement. Fortunately, the windshield was indeed proof against 5.56 mm rounds, the glass getting pockmarked by the bullets but not shattering. The coaxial machine gun aboard the tank was brought into action, again aiming high with tracer rounds snapping out and just clearing the lead vehicles in the caravan.

"Governor!" Perry shouted. "You tell everyone to stop where they are, or I'm ordering the tank crew to tear them apart!"

"You fucking son of a bitch!" the governor cried. "You lying bastard!"

"Yeah, I lied! Anyone advances one foot closer and they're dead. See you in hell, Governor!" Then Perry switched to another frequency. "Okay, back it up. There's going to be a response real quick. Back it up! If any of their Bradleys or anything else comes one foot closer, shoot to kill."

The two Bradleys that had been leading the government caravan came to a dead stop, stalling the hundreds of vehicles that had queued up behind them. They had heard Perry's warning and knew that to advance head-on against the tank was suicide. The crew of the lead Bradley opened their rear hatch, bailed out, and ran for it.

Harrison continued to guide their Humvee back, keeping close to the M1 they were out in front of. The chain gun each of the Bradleys mounted could shred their Humvee in little more than a second, but fortunately, they did not open fire, their crews undoubtedly knowing that to do so would result in a death sentence delivered by the M1 in response.

Once around a bend in the road, Harrison pulled off a sharp maneuver of slamming their vehicle into a tight pivot and swinging around the side of the M1, which was continuing to back up.

One of Perry's Bradleys, regaining its position at the chain-link fence, moved to one side to clear the way for the 18-wheelers. The crowd outside the fence had fortunately scattered back rather than trying to surge in, urged on by the tank opening fire and announcements by Darla on her bullhorn for everyone to get the hell out of the way. Emergency supplies were being rushed in, and the drivers were ordered not to stop for anyone in their way.

As they approached the opening in the fence, Darren could see the taillights of the last of the 18-wheelers clearing the outer gate and continuing toward the Ark.

"This is insane!" Darren shouted, nearly laughing. He had shifted from rage to outright delight at the sheer audacity of Perry's con job. The contents of those 18-wheelers, once driven into the Ark, would be safe and secured and priceless.

The governor had been holding all of that as hostage, and Darren laughed at the thought of the governor's reaction. But at that same instant, it was obvious that Perry was not amused by what he was hearing on his radio.

He switched on the loudspeaker built into the Humvee as they drove into where parents and children still waiting to enter were gathered, several thousand strong.

"Everyone clear this area!" Perry announced. "Get your kids into the tunnel now, then get away from the entry! Move it! Move it!"

Perry looked back at Darren. "The shit is about to hit the fan."

Darren saw the Apache helicopters rising from behind the Hyatt.

PART XI

Seize the day, as little as possible trusting the future.

—Horace, *Ode 1.11*

20

AS Richard, for the first time, was shown into the Oval Office of the White House after leaving with the president from the deep, secured conference room, there was such a mix of feelings and questions. *Why me?* The meetings with the president in his private study were one thing. They were quiet and personal, the president making him feel secure as if they were two colleagues talking about their professions.

This was far different from the earlier meetings. Six staff members were standing about, conversations hushed, reports being given, and six more were seated at the far end of the circular room, two of them military, of which one was Admiral Brockenborough. Allison had shown Richard to an ornate side chair, handed him a laptop linked to Goddard, and told him to keep absolutely current on what was happening with the CME and Sauron's Eye.

The forward edge of the CME was definitely beginning to impact, and the energy levels hitting the magnetosphere began to soar. Watch stations that could still be reached in northern Europe and across Russia were reporting an aurora of stunning intensity, cascading down far outside its usual realm in the Arctic Ring, with a report that it was becoming visible as far south as Israel at a latitude of thirty-one degrees. During the event of 1859, there had been reports of the aurora being visible as far south as the Virgin Islands and of such intensity that it was even visible during the day across northern Europe so that it looked as if the sky were on fire.

Once settled in, Richard stayed glued to his laptop's screen, getting updated photos every minute of Sauron's Eye. At least for a while longer, hardened communications such as satellites were still functioning. But for how much longer?

He could almost look at the eye dispassionately, the way an oncologist could study with fascination a metastasizing tumor that was exploding into a patient's body, even if that patient was a lifelong friend. The sun, the source of their life, was now poised to strike them all—everything, their world, their home, their shared history. Was this indeed the act of God who now willed it so in His anger? Or was it the act of a universe devoid of any true meaning or reason, just a random thing where humanity happened to be in the way? Each thought was equally disturbing and frightening.

"Dr. Carrington?"

He raised his head and looked about. It was the president, sitting behind his desk. All those in the room looked at Richard, and he suspected he had been called upon more than once and had not responded.

"Sir?"

"The latest update?"

"Ah, yes, sir," he replied, looking back down at the screen.

In the last few minutes, the numbers were trending up in a frightful way. Across all his years, he had never seen such readings. All storms of the past, what were now mere CME storms—even this latest, an equal to the dreaded to the event of 1859—had carried but a fraction of the energy he now saw in the readouts scrolling across the laptop screen, the numbers so small that he had to take his glasses off and hold the computer up close to see them clearly.

He looked back up and out the window. Was it psychosomatic, or did it seem brighter out there across the South Lawn where two helicopters had just touched down, armed personnel fanning out around the machines that might promise life while a couple of dozen staff ran toward them.

"Sir, illumination—visible sunlight—has increased nearly 10 percent in the last few minutes."

Everyone turned to look out the window, several whispering they could see it and that it actually was brighter out there.

The president turned back to face Richard. "Which means?"

"I can't say for positive, sir."

"I've trusted your judgment up to now!" the president roared, nerves worn to an edge. "Just give me your best damn judgment, not more qualifiers!"

"Yes, sir."

"Go on, then."

"It is about to blow."

"When?" asked Admiral Brockenborough.

"I can't say for certain."

"When, goddamn it? You're the astronomer. When?"

"Within the hour, two at most, but there is a chance it is letting go even now," Richard snapped. His own anger boiled over. "Damn it, I can't give you a precise minute!"

Several looked at their wristwatches, others to an eighteenth-century grandfather clock forever ticktocking the seconds out as it had for centuries.

"Forty minutes to full CME impact," someone whispered.

Richard nodded.

"Please remember, what I am looking at from *Helio II* is data traveling at the speed of light and arriving here approximately nine minutes later. A flare will travel just under the speed of light, when we see it blow from *Helio II*. Given its velocity, we will have anywhere from one to five or six minutes at most as a warning."

"Therefore, it could already have blown and we haven't seen it yet," Brockenborough deduced.

"Yes, Admiral," Richard replied, his disdain obvious.

"Mr. President," Brockenborough said, turning away from Richard and stepping up to the president's desk, "I'll say it again. The Russians and the Chinese are getting the same data. Perhaps they have already surmised that this flare thing has already exploded, will tear apart the CME before it hits our magnetosphere, and then dissipate harmlessly.

In that confusion, if they move before we do to take their nuclear forces out of deep submergence or overall lockdown, we would be naked to an EMP first strike. I implore you one last time, sir, bring our forces to full alert now."

"Or what, Admiral?" the president said, his voice pitched low, dispassionate.

"Or, sir, you will be remembered as the one who was sitting in this Oval Office when America was destroyed."

The president sighed, stood up, turned his back, and went to the window to watch as the two helicopters lifted off. Seconds later, a heavy twin-rotor Chinook circled in to land.

"Dr. Carrington?"

To Richard's surprise, a member of the Secret Service presidential detail was bending over beside him, voice pitched low, barely above a whisper.

"Yes?"

"Should we move the president now?" he whispered.

"To where?"

"He was supposed to go to a location near Camp David. If not, his fallback position is the shelter beneath the White House."

"How long to fly there?"

"Thirty minutes."

"Don't," Richard whispered.

"Why, Doctor?"

"If there's any delay when you are in transit, unless that helicopter is proofed against nearly everything, it could be dropped by the electrical disturbance created by the CME. Best to stay here."

"Peterson, stop whispering," the president announced. He stood looking out the window facing the South Lawn. He turned back, attention fixed on the agent, but not in anger. There was even the trace of a smile.

"Mr. President," Agent Peterson began, but the president held his hand up.

"Yes, yes, I know. Even over my objections, you're supposed to protect me at all cost. The same way you did during the campaign when someone took a shot at me."

"Mr. President, I and the rest of your team believe—"

"Peterson, who is in charge here? You or me?"

"You are, sir."

"Very good. For your information, I've decided to stay here, in the White House."

"Sir, the plan is that you are—"

"Oh, for God's sake, Peterson. Screw the plan!" The room fell silent. "There is more than adequate shelter three hundred feet below where we are standing right now. All those alpha card holders are heading there now."

"Sir, the plan is—"

"Peterson?"

"Sir?"

"Who is president here?"

"You are, sir."

"Why, thank you, Peterson." The president smiled, a light enough tone in his voice causing the tension in the room to notch down.

"The vice president is already in place at Site R. Continuity of government is . . ." He paused and looked back out the window. "Well, for what it's worth, those who think they are continuity of government have already evacuated and are in place. Maybe a little more than forty minutes from now, they can emerge, the flare having blown harmlessly, disrupting the CME, and by this evening, the entire world will be changing its underwear, and in a week, it will be back to regular news—which Hollywood idiot has cheated on their spouse and who is going to win the Super Bowl."

"We can pray so," Peterson replied.

"You and me both, Gary. And what did we learn? 'It had not come nigh unto thee.' The ninety-first psalm. I read it again this morning. Might be worth all of us reading it if, as Dr. Carrington hopes, that damn thing blows in the next few minutes before the CME hits and then we survive. Because if so, after getting the shit scared out of us, I'd like to believe that God then sits back smiling and thinks, *Scared the crap out of all of you and taught you a lesson, didn't I?*

"If it is indeed possible that he gets persuaded by prayers, I bet he has never had so many prayers sent his way as is happening today. Isn't that right, Doctor?"

"Yes, sir," Richard answered. He had never been much of a man of faith until these last few days. "Yes, sir, I am praying."

"The moment you pick up that Sauron's Eye has blown, Richard, you tell us."

"You'll hear me all right, sir."

There was a round of nervous chuckles.

"Gary, how long would it take to get me and these other folks down to the basement shelter?" asked the president.

"We've drilled it at under ninety seconds," Peterson replied.

"See? No sweat, people."

"Sir, why in the hell stay here?" asked Brockenborough.

"Why not?"

"Sir, this is showboating a little bit, isn't it? The internet is down, and national television is down; therefore, you don't have hundreds of millions hanging on your every word and heroism for staying in the Oval Office. It is just us, sir, and it is time we went to the shelter."

"Admiral, we are staying here because I think it is the right thing to do."

"Really?"

"Yes, really. Admiral, maybe you didn't get a few important lessons at Annapolis. Maybe the old days of the captain going down with his ship are passé now, but at the very least, the captain is the last one to step off his ship and will stay at his post until all of his people are evacuated. At this moment, I am president of a country where, at best, maybe one person in ten thousand has been evacuated to long-term shelters for survival. Therefore, with that in mind, I think I'll stay here awhile longer."

He looked around the room. "Who are they? Who have we in our wisdom evacuated? Ourselves! Maybe if we'd had more time, it might have been different and we'd have picked the best and the brightest to go instead, though I know those who plan such things will usually make sure their names are written in and to hell with the Nobel laureate or brain surgeon. We all know that is the way it is. So, my colleagues and friends, I think in all fairness, we at least stay here awhile longer before running off to the shelter. Richard, how long before the full intensity of the CME starts hitting the magnetosphere?"

"Just over thirty minutes, sir."

"And Sauron's Eye might already have exploded and that the flare is on its way?"

"Yes, sir."

"If so, we might all survive this and will know whether we have or not in just about a half hour or so?"

"Something like that, sir."

"You know, my friends," the president said softly, "this might be a damn good time to really start praying."

21

"THE shit is about to hit the fan!" Perry shouted even as Harrison skidded the vehicle to a stop next to the steel door.

Perry flipped a switch on the comm unit to loudspeaker. Even as he did so, he looked back at Darren.

"Grab this preacher and run!" Perry cried.

Darren needed no urging as he popped open the door on his side, while Perry, with his massive hands and strength, literally picked the preacher up and shoved him out the front door of the Humvee into Darren's arms.

"Get inside, damn it! Run!"

Darren needed no urging. To the west, he could see an Apache arcing up, turning high as if maneuvering into a strafing run. He had seen many a strafing run by an Apache, its firepower so intense that even though he had developed a deep hatred for the foes he was fighting in Fallujah, nevertheless he could almost feel at least some pity for them as they were caught out in the open and their bodies disintegrating into bloodly pulp when struck by the hail of fire from the Apache's chin turret–mounted 30 mm chain guns and cluster of antipersonnel rockets or armor-piercing Hellfire rounds.

There was a holdup at the steel door; the next-to-last 18-wheeler had come to a stop as if the driver were asking for directions, and Darla was frantically waving for him to keep moving.

How many times had he trained over and over for a moment like this?

There would be a primary threat, but numerous other factors would crowd in. Innocent civilians were scattering in every direction, more than a few running with their children through the gate at the chain-link fence and trying to dodge out of the way even as the Abrams backed through it, attempting to reach the safety of the steel door. Several hundred yards to the south, the first Apache was coming out of its turn and lining up.

Unable to gain the steel doorway, still blocked by the stalled 18-wheeler, the commander of the Abrams pivoted his vehicle in an attempt to present its forward armor to the incoming attack. The Bradley did the same, both it and the Bradley firing off smoke canisters to obscure the view along with chaff and infrared flares to confuse the pilot's visual if he was using infrared gear to spot his targets.

Darren had a flash thought. If the Apache was carrying a Hellfire air-to-ground anti-armor weapon, they were all dead. He had seen the effects of it more than once in Iraq, where personnel out in the open were all but vaporized more than fifty meters away from the point of impact of a Hellfire rocket. It would be a massacre not just of their small armored force but of scores of civilians trying to get out of the way.

Harrison was out of the Humvee, shouting for everyone to scatter, while Perry remained in the vehicle, frantically appealing to the Apache pilot to abort.

Darren could see flashes of light igniting from the chin turret of the Apache.

"Down, Pastor!" Darren cried, slamming him to the pavement behind the last of the 18-wheelers that was finally shifting into gear and moving into the Ark.

Darren, crouching, got to his feet and pulled the minister along the side of the truck as if its thin steel-and-aluminum siding could protect him from a tungsten-tipped, armor-piercing 30 mm round.

The impacts stitched across the inner compound, several rounds striking the front armor and turret of the tank, white-hot fragments flying across the compound, but the tank survived. But for one of the Bradleys, it was a deathblow, rounds punching clear through the thin armor, igniting the vehicle into a fireball. Darren watched in horror as the back hatch was flung open and several of the surviving crew members wreathed in flames staggered out.

Several dozen casualties littered the open ground between the chain-link fence and the steel door. The last of the 18-wheelers was clearing into the safety of the Ark, several rounds having struck the aft end of the vehicle, and something within the trailer was burning.

The Apache pulled into a sharp banking turn, tracers from the 25 mm gun mounted on the second Bradley following it but not hitting.

Taking in all that had happened in the last few seconds, Darren realized that those on both sides were National Guard troops. Many had most likely served in the Middle East and Afghanistan and maybe had even seen combat but were long out of practice. The Apache could have just popped up and hovered several hundred yards out and unleashed hell, while the gunner in the surviving Bradley was long out of practice in knowing how to lead a fast-moving target.

Cries and screams now echoed around Darren. People rushed to the aid of the three crew members, one of them still on fire, someone coming up with a fire extinguisher and dousing him.

Too many of the screams were the high-pitched wailing of children who had been hit. The up-close sight of what a 30 mm round could do to a human body was horrifying, especially if it hit a child. Most of the adults and children who still had some semblance of life thrashed and rolled in agony with an arm or leg twisted and pulverized. Those struck in the torso were already dead or but seconds away from oblivion. Several had been hit in the head, and the sight filled him with rage.

Clusters of families and friends were on the ground, crying, bewildered, in shock.

A second Apache rose from behind the tree line to take out the tank and the other Bradley.

"Everyone get inside!" Darla shouted, standing out in the open, urging people to get up and run. Some on the far side of the chain-link fence got to their feet and sprinted through the open gate. Whether doing so to try to reach protection from the attack or seeing a chance to gain entry into the Ark, there was no stopping them short of killing

them, and Darren did not react. If anyone survived this moment, it could
be sorted out later.

Darren grabbed the pastor by the collar, heaved him back up to his
feet, and sprinted the last few feet to the open steel door, slowing for a
second at the sight of a child lying facedown.

Pick her up?

He saw the crimson pool pouring out on to the pavement beneath her
from the exit wound at her shoulder blades. Tears welled up as he focused
on the living, pushing the pastor on while the minister was shouting to
be let go, that he wanted to help the inert child they had just run past.

"She's dead!" Darren gasped, voice tight, fighting back his tears of
rage and frustration. He looked back to the second Apache, which was
now coming in, far slower than the first one.

It was all happening so fast and yet, as he had found with his own
brief time in combat years earlier, each second could seem like an eternity. A memory flashed of seeing a comrade next to him take a head
shot. The man was dead while still standing, having only been talking,
cracking a sarcastic comment a few seconds before. The time it took for
his knees to buckle and collapse to the ground in Darren's memory
and nightmares seemed to take forever, though only a second or two at
most had passed.

The second Bradley, which was still in action, shifted its gun turret
to engage the hovering Apache. It seemed a long, drawn-out moment,
like two gunfighters of old in a showdown, and the Bradley was about
to lose.

At that instant, the second Apache reared up sharply, pivoting as it
did so, and let loose with a long, thunderous blast punctuated by the
metal casings from its 30 mm gun showering down on the pavement.

Darren gasped as he watched the tracer rounds snapping out, streaking across the sky, and striking the other Apache broadside, sparks
igniting as the tungsten-tipped bullets slashed into the other gunship,
tearing into its engine housing.

The first Apache, blindsided by the betrayal, pivoted and fired blindly
for several long seconds, rounds striking randomly into the open area

between the steel door all the way out beyond the parking lot, more than a few impacting into the scattering crowd. The stricken airship lurched sharply to one side at a steep angle, then began rotating down, disappearing from view as it plummeted into an open quarry that flanked the Ark. Several seconds later, a fireball from its impact rose in a coiling black column of smoke.

The second Apache had been damaged as well, and smoke billowed out of the engine housing. Maintaining some semblance of control, its pilot pulled it up higher and turned to face the south, letting loose with a long stream of 30 mm rounds at a target Darren could not see until it had most likely emptied its magazine and added in several air-to-ground missiles. Beyond the parking lot, explosions echoed followed by a rising fireball. Tracers snapped back around the Apache, some hitting, and then it wobbled, directional control failing. It finally went straight down in a barely controlled crash near the steel door.

The whirling thump of the rotors dropped in pitch, the pilot's canopy popping up and the man climbing out, taking off his helmet, and letting it drop as he stepped forward to grab the latches of his gunner's cockpit, struggling to open them. Darren was one of the first to react, crouching to avoid the rotors that were still cutting deadly arcs through the air, running up to the pilot's side to lend a hand. The forward glass of the cockpit had apparently been hit several times but had not been penetrated, the glass a crisscross quilt of cracks, but Darren could see that a round had penetrated the side armor.

Pulling the cockpit open, they could see the gunner was severely wounded, gazing up weakly at them.

Old training and instincts came back to Darren as he turned and cried out, "Medic! We need a medic!"

The pilot unbuckled the gunner's shoulder harness, and then someone was up by their side, saying, "Don't touch him; you might make it worse." From the speaker's features and tonal inflections, Darren wondered if this was the now somewhat legendary Dr. Sarbak, who had shepherded in the two trailers of medical equipment and supplies.

"Rachel! Hey, Rachel! Get my emergency pack!" the doctor cried, looking back over his shoulder and then shifting his attention to the

Apache's pilot. "I've got him. We'll take care of him. Now clear back."

Another explosion fireballed from down the road several hundred yards away, but Darren stayed focused on the Apache pilot.

"Who in the hell are you?"

"Lieutenant Peter Hartmen, Twenty-Third Missouri National Guard Air Battalion."

"Why did you do it?"

"Why what, sir?"

"Bring that pilot over here!"

Darren looked up to see Harrison waving them over to the Humvee parked alongside the Abrams tank. The vehicle had taken several hits; one of the windshields was shattered, and steam coiled up from a hole blown into the smashed radiator.

Leading the pilot, Darren started walking over and then broke into a run. He could see blood splattered against the side window on the passenger side. Several people already had that door open and were gently easing General Perry out of the vehicle while he cursed at them to leave him be.

Darren went up to Perry and took in the sight of blood leaking out of the right side of his torn jacket. From the location of the wound, Darren sensed the general had been hit below the ribs, which would mean his liver. Without emergency surgery, he would surely bleed out in a painful death.

The general's dark chocolate features were pale; he was slipping into shock but trying to maintain control.

"Leave me be! Damn all of you." Perry gasped. "Now put me back in my seat."

Harrison was by his general's side, gazing down and putting his hand on the shoulder of one of the civilians trying to help.

"Leave him be; put him back in the vehicle. He still has work here."

The three looked up at Darren as if for confirmation.

"You heard what the general wants. Now go help the others."

"Thanks, Darren," Perry choked out.

"Second time you've forgotten to wear your Kevlar, General."

"Yeah." He tried to chuckle, but he grimaced at the effort. His gaze wandered to the Apache pilot, who stood silent. "You switched sides. Saved us. Why?"

The pilot stiffened and offered a salute to the general sitting in the Humvee, hunched over and holding his side.

"Shit, feels like I spilled hot soup on me," Perry groaned.

"You need a doctor," Darren urged.

"A few things to do first," Perry replied through clenched teeth. "First, I want a few answers from this pilot. Why?"

"Sir, I didn't join the army to shoot women and kids, sir. I know you were in Iraq; so was I. Lot of the rules of engagement were asinine, but one we tried to stick to was if kids were in the way, hold fire."

Perry nodded. "Is that all?"

"Well, sir . . ."

"Go on."

"I was called in this morning from where I'm based up in Jefferson City, along with the Black Hawk and other Apache."

"Just those assets?" Perry asked.

"Everything is spread thin, sir. Lot of problems over in Saint Louis and up in Kansas City. Plus more than a few pilots have just walked off, saying that if this is the end, they want to be with their families."

"So you got down here and . . . ?"

"Sir, we got called in to the Hyatt where the governor is hunkered down; one of his staff briefed us. You know the type, sir—guy in a tailored suit who thinks he understands the military."

"Bet it was his chief of staff, Fredericks. Can't stomach that bastard," Perry replied, gasping as a spasm of pain hit. "Go on. Then what?"

"Got our orders. We were supposed to preemptively hit—at least that is what the chief of staff wanted—but others protested; at least a few out there have some morals left, saying there were hundreds of kids in the way. Then this thing with those tractor-trailers loaded with supplies came up." The pilot offered a slight smile. "General, I heard your offer and kind of figured you'd pull something off."

"Pretty good, wasn't it?" Perry sighed.

A woman wearing a white medical coat splattered with blood approached the Humvee, elbowing her way through. "What have we got here?" she demanded.

"He's gut shot, ma'am," Harrison replied.

"Let me see." She went around to the other side of the Humvee, ordering Harrison to move aside and climbing in past the driver's seat. "What the hell are all of you doing?" she bellowed. "He needs help now!" Even as she spoke, she was cutting back the parka and uniform underneath with a heavy set of shears.

"Just leave off, will you!" Perry growled.

"I'm in charge here now," she replied. "And it's Dr. Horton to you."

"And it is General Perry to you, damn it," he snarled back.

She ignored him, turning back to Harrison. "There are stretchers in the back of the last tractor-trailer; go get one."

"Harrison, you move an inch and you are fired!" Perry shouted. "I need you here."

The doctor continued to ignore him, reaching into her bag and producing a morphine syrette, pulling off the safety cap.

"You hit me with that, and by God, woman or not, you will be in a world of hurt."

She hesitated as he looked straight into her eyes.

"I'm supposed to be in command defending this place, Doctor. You know the situation; you know what I've got to do. So please go help someone else for now."

"I understand." She sighed, her controlling tone evaporating.

"Go on now; go tend to those who really need it. There's a lot of hurt kids out there; save the morphine for them."

She reached out with her free hand and touched his cheek affectionately. "God bless you. When this is over, I'll come back to help you. Okay?"

"Doctor?" asked Hartmen. "How's my gunner?" He looked back at his downed Apache, smoke billowing up from the starboard-side turbine engine mounting.

She looked at the pilot and shook her head.

He turned away to hide his tears.

"I'll be back shortly, General. You're a fool, but God love you." She reached out to pat him on the shoulder before backing out from the Humvee to help others.

The pain was still hitting, and all he could do was nod. He turned away from her. "Lieutenant Hartmen?"

"Sir?" The pilot turned back to face him, tears streaming down his face from the shock of losing his friend because of a decision he made.

"I'm sorry, son, but I need to know some things," Perry said, struggling for control. "So you got orders to hit what?"

"If things started to go down bad, hit any military assets you people have and try to ensure that the tank and Bradleys didn't block the entry-way, and take down anyone who tried to block the caravan. Sergeant Thu—my gunner—and I headed back to our bird; we're sitting there listening in on the chatter on the comm links, and, well, it finally got to be too much to bear. Then everything just cut loose. The pilot of the other Apache was my superior. Calling him an asshole is an insult to our anatomy. He keeps saying to follow orders, and then when we were done, we'd go inside the Underground like everyone else and we'd live. I followed him, hoping it would still turn into a bluff . . . but it didn't. At least that jerk and his gunner were lousy shots. When we lifted off from our base to get down here, all they could load us up with was ammo for our forward turret guns and several standard air-to-ground antipersonnel rockets. Thank God he wasn't loaded with a Hellfire." He chuckled sadly. "Hey, this is the Missouri National Guard. Baseline cost for a Hellfire is over a hundred grand. Nope, we didn't have them."

"You think he'd have put a Hellfire into the middle of all of this?" Darren asked.

"No doubt."

Darren shook his head.

"I was yelling for that bastard to just hold back on shooting, buzz the place a few times to scatter the civilians, and then, only then if need be, start shooting." The pilot shook his head, cursing under his breath. "Well, you saw what he did. So that's when I made the decision to stop it. Thu, God rest him, agreed. We started taking hits; things began to redline. Plus I knew Thu had been hit, but I didn't know yet how bad."

The pilot struggled to keep control of his emotions. "He was a good man, a good partner."

Perry waited for him to continue despite his extreme pain.

"So I pivoted, locked on to the lead Bradley that was heading this way, and unloaded what ordnance we had left before I had to land. I think I knocked out a couple of their Bradleys, one of them in the middle of the road, so that should block things up for a while longer. But they have at least four more out there."

Perry reached a hand up, which was bloody, the pilot taking it. "Thank you," he gasped.

"Sir, I've been listening in on the radio traffic for several hours while waiting for orders, both from here but also some secured military channels that are still up at the federal level."

"We've been cut off from national-level news for hours," Darren interjected. "What can you tell us?"

"It's all bad. Chaos in a lot of places, but at least one commander of an underground up near Kansas City is doing the same as you—children only. Apparently, word has spread to at least a couple of other places as to what you started here, but they're fighting to take them back, same as here."

"God help them," Perry whispered. "Now what news about the CME and the flare? We really are outside the loop now other than what you can tell us."

"I don't quite understand, but I heard chatter that the Carrington thing is starting; the outer edge is already disrupting radio traffic. If that Sauron's Eye lets go in the next few minutes, something about it could blow the Carrington thing apart and everything will be okay."

That caught Darren by surprise. Everyone had been so focused on the here and now.

"If that's true, then all of this was for nothing," someone standing at the edge of the small group gathered around the Humvee announced.

"And our asses will be in the sling given the declaration of martial law," another replied.

Darren turned, anger brimming over. "Okay. Great. So based on that, you want us to surrender and open up? Maybe tell the kids it was all a bad dream and go home?"

The man lowered his gaze. "Darren, let's pray that all this turns into one huge false alarm. Sorry I phrased it that way. It if is, we thank God, then face whatever it is the governor wants done."

The pilot laughed softly. "Oh, that bastard? He's gone."

"What do you mean?" Perry asked.

"Right after everything blew here, and before I shut the engine down on my bird, I heard the Black Hawk was lifting off with George One on board, outbound to Jefferson City."

In spite of his agony, Perry laughed. "You sure of that, son?"

"Yes, sir. Heard it clear. 'George One outbound to Jefferson City.' So the governor is already out of here and heading back to the shelter at the capital."

"Typical." Perry chuckled even as he grimaced and momentarily doubled over. "He sees the plan unravel here, and he boogies back to Jefferson City; they have some old Cold War shelters under the capitol building and a few small caverns like this."

"And leaves everyone else here and in the lurch," Darren interjected coldly.

"Yeah, doubt they'll vote for the bastard in the next election," Perry announced, trying to laugh but coughing, and a splattering of blood came up. "Leaves behind, what, two thousand or more oh-so-essential government workers and their cronies? I bet they are shitting themselves right about now."

"Sir, this fight isn't over. Those folks are desperate, and their Bradleys are still out there. Doubt if they will give up or the troops with them."

As if in acknowledgment, a long, sustained burst of heavy-caliber gunfire erupted at the far end of the parking lot. Darren looked up and saw tracers sweeping across the parking lot, arcing like a garden hose, civilians running, more than a few with weapons firing back and getting hit. The front end of a Bradley appeared several hundred yards away, re-mained visible for a few seconds, then backed up out of sight, the driver undoubtedly realizing he was facing a tank head-on and retreating.

More gunfire crackled, striking those civilians still out in the open, driving them back, clearing the way for what would most likely be a sprint for the entryway once the other Bradleys were in position and could take on the tank from one or both flanks.

"Those Bradleys, are they carrying TOW rockets?" Darren shouted.

"I think so."

"Christ Almighty!" Darren cried.

"Gather in who you can," Perry gasped, "and send some people to flank out. We back the tank up to just in front of the steel door, Bradley to one flank."

"Sir, I'd advise against that," Darren interjected.

"Why?"

"If they do manage to blow the tank, they might have Stingers with them. If that tank blows near the door, it could smash the entryway wide open."

"Then the radiation gets inside and kills us!" someone cried.

"Doesn't work like that," Harrison replied quickly before someone ran off shouting that even in the Ark they were all going to die anyhow. "It's not like a nuke bomb with radioactive debris from the explosion that drifts down hundreds of miles away even weeks later. It will be line of sight. Yeah, don't let anyone stand near that door when it starts; keep them deep down inside, because a steel door isn't much protection against that kind of radiation load."

"But if busted open," Darren interjected, "a mob could then over-run it. Once we get as many kids in as possible, we close up. Blown open with a burning tank in front and then we can't close and lock the door . . . it will be chaos."

"Okay." Perry sighed, voice slurring a bit. "Tank outside the fence and to one side to block, Bradley we tuck in behind some defilade to cover at least one flank."

"Got it, sir." Harrison saluted but then knelt, putting a hand on Perry's shoulder. "It has been an honor to be with you today, sir." He stood and ran off.

Perry looked up at the Apache pilot.

"Listen to me, son. You went way above and beyond just now. With Darren's permission, I'd like to offer you a place inside the Ark. People like you will be needed afterward to teach those kids something about making the right decisions."

Darren stiffened but said nothing.

The pilot stood silent for several seconds with head lowered. "Thank you, sir, and I know I'll curse myself for a fool later, but no, thank you, sir. I didn't do it for that. I don't want it said afterward that is why I made the decision I did. Besides, chances are my kids are not going to make it through the day. If so, I want to be with them when they meet the Lord."

Perry smiled and extended his hand, which the pilot took.

"Now we get you inside, sir," Darren announced, interrupting the two and motioning for the group around him to lend a hand.

"No!" Perry's voice was sharp and clear as he sagged back in his seat. "Staying right here. I'll be all right. Staying here where I should. How much time, Darren?"

Darren glanced down at his wristwatch. The brunt of the CME would start impacting within a few more minutes. If Sauron's Eye let loose at this moment and raced toward their world at nearly the speed of light, according to the latest info, there just still might be a miracle.

He looked up at the sun and squinted. It was not his imagination; it was indeed brighter, painful to glance at for more than a second.

"Keep getting kids in," Perry whispered. "Now go."

As had Harrison, Darren saluted and then bent over to squeeze the general's shoulder. "An honor to serve with you again, sir," Darren whispered before he ran off to find Darla and to help guide the last of the children still arriving to where safety hopefully awaited them.

He glanced again at the sun. It was so bright now. Maybe it was indeed blowing before the CME opened the door to total destruction. If so, the preacher was most likely saying that perhaps a tenth righteous man had just been found. *Maybe,* he prayed, *maybe.*

PART XII

It's when the world ends that we go back to a new beginning.
—Anthony T. Hincks

22

IT'S more than just a race, Richard thought. Einstein's famous comment "God does not play dice with the universe" kept flashing through his consciousness. However people might interpret what Einstein really meant, at this precise moment, that is what it indeed felt like. This whole thing was now a cosmic crapshoot, and the winner or loser was all of humanity.

The room was silent, the president putting on a good display of sitting at his desk in the Oval Office, feet propped up on a footstool, leaning back in his chair, eyes closed, and Richard could sense he was silently praying.

Some paced, while others looked out the windows as a lone helicopter arrived and suddenly got mobbed as fifty or more people burst out of the door of the South Portico, the thin line of a security team struggling to hold them back. Watching the chaos, Richard thought that the helicopter damn well better have electronics that were heavily shielded; otherwise, it would not be flying much longer as the full effect of the CME hit, which it most certainly would be doing in the next few minutes.

"It really is getting brighter out there," someone whispered, and Richard glanced out the window. It was no longer some sort of suggestion or frightened imagination now; the visible light emitted from the sun was indeed increasing rapidly. *Sauron's Eye.*

He returned his attention to the laptop. The image had frozen up for a moment, the screen blanking to dark, which gave him a start, and then it was back on again, to his connection to Goddard's Helio Observation Center. The image was poor, freezing up for several seconds, then transmitting again. Electronics were indeed going off-line.

The Goddard room was nearly empty; he could see Judith standing close to the monitors, back turned.

"Judith?" he whispered.

The Bluetooth link was still working. She turned around to face the camera mounted on his desk. The visual dropped off again, but audio still worked.

"How are you, Richard?" she asked, stepping closer to the camera, image coming back on again. She was holding her ubiquitous over-sized Goddard cup filled with black coffee. He could see her hands were shaking.

"Me? Just counting it down." He lowered his voice to a near whisper. "Everyone is staring at me, wanting answers."

She shook her head, turning for a moment to look at the monitor that was still receiving from *Helio II,* which was focused on Sauron's Eye, a secondary monitor showing a computer-generated schematic of Earth's magnetosphere. It was distorting, looking nearly the same as Mr. Science's inflated balloon, which had been used only days ago to try to explain to the public what happens when a CME hits.

"Where is everyone?" Richard asked.

"I told everyone except for a few essentials to go home to be with their families. Seemed the right thing to do, but some volunteered to stay."

"Like you?"

She forced a smile. "Captain on the bridge, Richard. Besides, right here is the best damn view in the world, win or lose." Her hand was still shaking as she took another sip of coffee and turned to look back at the monitors.

He clicked up a split screen on his own laptop, one half showing the Helio Center and Judith, the other the schematic of the magneto-sphere, which was peeling back. Earth's protective layer, what some called the "God blanket for Earth," was all but gone on the side facing the sun.

He sat silently, ignoring the chaos out on the South Lawn, the frightened mob of staffers pushing in around the lone evacuation helicopter, ignoring the threats of the security team.

God, he thought, *if your intention is to scare the shit out of us, you've done a damn good job of it. Please let that thing blow now. Please.*

He almost added, *We'll be good from now on; we promise to be good,* but fortunately did not do so, for as he raised his head, he was embarrassed to see that more than a few in the room were staring at him because he had whispered the words out loud.

The president opened his eyes and looked over at Richard. "Prayers answered?" he asked.

Richard looked at him silently. Glancing back down at his monitor, he saw the magnetosphere continuing to distort under the hammer blow of the CME, Sauron's Eye glaring malevolently, growing brighter, the pupil disappearing into a scalding white wall of fire.

Richard mentally ran through the calculations, resetting them in his mind every few seconds to run them again. *How long for the signal from Helio II to arrive at the speed of light? In a few more minutes, the magnetosphere will be fully peeled back from the energy blow of the CME. It will, as anticipated, wreak havoc on the world's electronic and communications infrastructure, but we can live through that, even rebuild.*

"God, let it hit, let it hit now," he gasped softly, no longer caring if his appeal was heard by those in the room, as long as a God he so fervently wished to believe in was listening and would spare his wayward children, granting them this last-second reprieve.

No one spoke, nearly all of them staring at Richard, waiting for what he would say next, praying that he would look up at them with a smile and gasp that all would be well.

He was aware of the ticking of the grandfather clock and the soft, muffled chiming as it announced noon. Another few minutes passed in silence. Outside, the helicopter lifted off, its deep thumping of rotors echoing, drowning out the screams of those left behind and someone holding on to a landing skid as it lifted up. It was an absurd sight—a man in a three-piece business suit clinging to the chopper as it continued rising, until the poor fool lost his grip and fell from fifty feet or more.

The helicopter's engines shifted, stuttering, the machine lurching up, struggling for altitude, climbing out past the high iron fence surrounding the White House. It nosed over as its engine stalled, the pilot trying to right it into a proper autorotation shutdown. The chopper settled down with a heavy but survivable impact just short of the Washington Monument.

"God, it has to be now," Richard whispered. "Now."

Another minute passed, and he looked up, gazed locked on the president.

"Lot could not find the tenth righteous man?" the president whispered.

Richard nodded. "Too late now, Mr. President. Earth's surface will be fully exposed to a flare."

"And the flare? Maybe still a reprieve there?"

He glanced back down at his monitor. Communications satellites were well hardened in anticipation of major solar storms, with extra protection layered into the *Helio* units orbiting the sun, but their signal linked into communications satellites up at geosynchronous orbit? It was taking a beating from the CME slamming into Earth. There was increasing interference, but he could still make out what was being transmitted. He looked back up at the president, not saying a word.

The president stirred and then stood up, looking out the window and then turning back to the small gathering.

"Sounds strange, asking this now," he said. "I assume the National Archives has properly stored the Declaration, Constitution, and other documents in the shelter?"

"Yes, Mr. President," said the secretary of the interior, whom Richard had felt a growing respect for over these last twenty-four hours. He was still here even though he had an evacuation card, stating simply that he hoped his family would find a safe place near their home up in the Grand Tetons, but he felt his duty was to stay.

"National Gallery?" the president asked.

"Preselected pieces are already in the deep shelter along with the items you personally requested."

Richard had never thought of that until just now. So many things of this nation that one would want preserved even if it was just a fraction of the age of his own England. *Preserved for whom, if, in the end, none of us survive? Maybe at least whoever one day comes here will find those things, our voices reaching across the millennia to say, "This is who we were; this is the best of what we strived to be."*

What to save? Strangely, he couldn't think of anything dramatic or rich in the history of America at this moment that would be his first choice. England? Of course the Magna Carta, but then what? A warm thought of the Royal Observatory filled him. The chronometers created by the Harrisons, father and son, that revolutionized navigation in the eighteenth century, enabling mariners to correctly calculate their longitude. He hoped that someone thought to hide those away. He had an obsession with old instruments of astronomy, navigation, and the measuring of time. So many of those treasures were on display in Greenwich—which, at this moment, he prayed would be somehow preserved. For that matter, the ancient fourteenth-century clock at Salisbury Cathedral, and even the wondrous, whimsical clock tower in Wenceslas Square in Prague. How might that be preserved?

In London, there was a favorite place to visit when he was a child, the war rooms and command center of Winston Churchill, and of course someone would think of the crown jewels stored at the Tower of London. And across all of England and the rest of Europe, the great museums—the Louvre, the Hermitage, the Uffizi in Florence—surely someone at this moment was ensuring the survival of what was the best of mankind and not obsessing at this moment about how many nuclear weapons were ready for launch.

America? So many of its wonders were natural—the Grand Canyon, Yosemite, Yellowstone, and those would endure regardless of the passing of man. What best to preserve other than its treasured national documents? He remembered a painting by Whistler prominently displayed in the National Gallery. It was of a young woman in a floor-length white dress, a life-size portrait that was so alive with her youthful vitality and barely concealed sensuality. He had fallen in love with her the first time he had visited that art museum on a rainy winter afternoon and stood gazing at her for long minutes. That painting was so much about life yet to be led and anticipation of that life.

Let that be saved, he thought, not hearing as the president continued to run down his own list: Gilbert's painting of Washington, digital recordings with the machine to play them on. Music, so much music from Gregorian to pop; video, little of what was the darker side of us and instead moments of the best of who we were from the golden age of Hollywood. Surely in all the confusion of the last two days, someone at the Library of Congress had raced to conceal those treasures in the deep vaults beneath that most complete of all libraries since the legendary library of Alexandria.

Both he and the president were now consumed with such thoughts, the president asking the secretary of the interior if such things had been thought of. Richard, lost in his own musings, could only hope that there were good people out there, and surely there must be, who would wish to see the best of humanity preserved for whomever might survive or, in millennia to come, would visit this world and wonder who we once were.

He was startled back to reality when a red flash appeared in the upper-left corner of his monitor, while in his earpiece a high-pitched shriek of feedback erupted with such startling intensity that he flinched and pulled the earphone off.

"Dr. Carrington?"

"It's starting to blow, Mr. President," he announced, trying to keep his voice steady and doing a poor job of it.

The president forced a smile. "How much time do we have?"

Richard scanned the readout on the monitor even as the flash of light erupting from what had been Sauron's Eye grew in intensity.

"Not much; what I'm seeing is already nine minutes old. Forward edge will start to impact in two minutes or so, the full blow." He shook his head as he watched, mesmerized as the eruption continued to expand out across the surface of the sun. The scale of it! Sauron's Eye had been fifty thousand miles across; six Earths laid side by side inside it would have barely reached from one side to the other. The explosion was already reaching out far beyond that.

Second by second, it continued to expand.

"It's still building," he announced.

"All of you holding alpha cards are to go to the shelter immediately," the president ordered.

Most in the room started for the door, some hurriedly, others pausing, looking about as if taking a final glance at their world, a couple ceremonially going up to the president to shake his hand. The secretary of the interior remained motionless, gazing out the window.

"Admiral Brockenborough, a moment, sir," the president snapped as the admiral started for the door.

Brockenborough turned with a questioning look. "Sir, no time for ceremony now. I'm the member of the Joint Chiefs of Staff required to stay with you and the launch codes. The other members are either in the Pentagon shelter or evacuated to Site R."

"I know that, Admiral."

"Sir? What, then?"

The president turned to the head of his Secret Service detail. "Gary, please relieve Admiral Brockenborough of his alpha card."

There was no hesitation on the part of the agent who walked the few feet to the admiral's side hand extended out, silently waiting.

"Mr. President?"

"I have no time for you now, sir," the president said. "Admiral, I am still commander in chief, and I am relieving you of command."

"You can't—"

"Yes, I can, damn you!" the president shouted. "Gary, if he doesn't hand that card over in five seconds, break his arm and take it."

Richard stood awestruck by the confrontation unfolding in the middle of the Oval Office.

"Why?" The admiral mouthed the question, features going pale as he woodenly removed the card from his pocket, the passport to survival two hundred feet beneath the White House, and gave it to the Secret Service agent.

"Why, sir? Because you are a loose cannon; that is why, sir. I should have removed you on the day the first CME arrived and you were all set to consider changing our policy of decades that we would only launch our weapons after an enemy strike impacted within the continental United States and you wanted to go to 'launch on warning.' I know without a doubt, Admiral, that if given the chance, if something should happen to me, you just might attempt such a thing or even go preemptive. That is why I am relieving you of command."

"You are a traitor to your country! If anyone is going to survive this, I want it to be us and not them."

"Admiral, better a traitor to my country than a traitor to all of humanity. I'd rather someone—Russians, Chinese, whoever—at least survive even if it is not us. I'm placing my bet their leaders are thinking the same thing I am at this moment and not trying to jockey for position if anything survives the day."

"History will remember you as—"

"History, sir?" The president chuckled, and he looked back out the window, the light growing more intense like a blindingly hot summer day under a high-noon sun. "Admiral, I will not waste one more second on you. Gary, show the admiral out, please. Admiral, if you hustle, you just might make it to the Pentagon in time, but your counterpart from the army who is in the shelter there already knows my orders regarding you."

The president looked back at Brockenborough, who seemed to just deflate. "God save you, sir." The president sighed as Gary showed the fallen commander out of the room.

"Mr. President," said one of his security detail. "Time you moved, sir."

The president looked over at Richard, who was so startled by the drama that had just played out that he had yet to follow orders and head for the shelter.

"Richard, if you can get a visual of that thing when it fully blows, we'll still have a couple of minutes, won't we?"

"Yes, sir, but it will be cutting things close."

"I'd like to stay here just for a few moments more," the president said softly.

Richard did not ask, nor was there any sense of sacrifice within as he remained in place, still holding the laptop, gaze fixed on the screen, focused on where Sauron's Eye had been only minutes before. Intensity growing bright, and yet brighter . . .

Another piercing tone sounded in his earpiece, the screen going blank as the explosion off the surface of the sun raced outward and an instant later destroyed *Helio II*. The last image transmitted the screen overloading with a blinding flash as the full explosion finally ignited. It had actually happened nearly nine minutes earlier, and in little more than a minute—two at most—the full fury would strike.

Richard looked at his watch; it was 12:35 local time. If only it had blown but forty-five minutes earlier, there might have been a chance. He sighed and looked up.

"Mr. President—"

"Yes, I know."

Those final minutes. Some, the lucky ones, had reached a goal—family, friend, lover long ago lost but remembered, both realizing that they should at least be reunited one more time.

Highways were still packed with millions who would not reach their goals on this, the final day. As the CME hit forty-five minutes prior to the explosion of Sauron's Eye, the energy blow of gamma rays peeled back the magnetosphere with an intensity more than a magnitude higher than the December 1 event. As the stream of gamma rays cascaded down to Earth's surface, triggering a near-global electrical disturbance in the atmosphere, most cars that had survived the prior storm now began to short out. Engines so completely dependent on the microsecond management of electrical impulses flowing out of the array of computer chips inside nearly every car suddenly became erratic, like the final terrifying arrhythmias of a heart shutting down. For more than a few in such cars, it was indeed their last moment as vehicles began to wreck, one into another, into chain-reaction accidents blocking roads. In the minutes afterward, some looked upon those who had thus died and thought that, yes, indeed, the living might very well envy the dead.

Those now stuck, sitting unmoving inside stalled cars or trapped by wrecks all around them, began stepping out of their vehicles, looking up, squinting, whispering, "Honey, the sun, it's so bright," "Daddy, why is it so bright?" and those with courage and love would embrace with a reassuring word. "Oh, it's okay, it's okay, sweetie."

Among the ones who had gone feral, some did not even notice what was happening to the sky with its intensity of light, so lost were they in their orgy of destruction, and they continued in their madness, though more than a few paused, looked up in wonder and then terror, and cried out that they were sorry for their insanity of the last two days, falling to their knees and begging, crying out to be forgiven. As to so many lost in drug and alcohol stupors, the most dramatic moments of their lives would never even be noticed.

As for those in churches and synagogues, or for some a beloved grove of trees, a mountaintop, or a quiet stretch of beach? Some would look up and fear would take hold. Others looked up and the fear was there, but to embrace someone at that moment, even if a stranger, and offer a smile of reassurance and love and comfort. In the churches, some would be in silent prayer, others listening to words of comfort as the twenty-third psalm was recited, and sadly for some, a final word of denouncement and anger against those who had brought down this wrath of God upon the world, never registering in those moments that it was they who were the ones filled with wrath. And such would rage, not at the dying of the light but instead at the coming of the light, not grasping the reality of their own hypocrisy.

For those who had still sought to live, there were cries that it was time to go inside, to go down deep, as deep as possible. Some, knowing they were ill prepared, frantically threw a few last shovelfuls of earth against a basement window. Some stood gun in hand, shouting at those who were once friends and neighbors that there was no room within their shelter and to back away. But for others, before closing and locking the door, there would be a pause, a final look at friends and neighbors, before saying with and outstretched hand, "Give me your kids; let's get them inside."

For those blessed at this moment to be with someone that they loved far more than their own lives, there was a smile of reassurance, a gentle kiss, and then a tight embrace while awaiting the hoped-for dream that in a very short moment they would awake upon a far distant shore and still be together. At that moment, never had they loved life and the one they were holding as much as they did now as they whispered reassuringly, "I'll see you on the other side."

23

"DOWN!"

There was no need to shout the warning as the antitank TOW rocket streaked in from the far side of the open quarry, impacting the more vulnerable side armor of the M1 Abrams.

Those huddled on the far side of the tank were still sheltered by its bulk, but those on the side of the impact were struck down up to fifty meters away. The blow from the weapon burned into the aft-mounted turbine engine, shutting it down. Flames licked up out of the exhaust grates. Acrid smoke poured out, spiraling heavenward, even as the vehicle's commander activated the internal fire suppression system, hoping to keep the fuel from igniting.

"Everyone back away from the tank!" Darren shouted. In Iraq, he had seen the horrific destruction created when an M1 blew. The fire suppressant appeared to be doing its job, though a black plume continued to billow out.

Another TOW missile streaked in, this one fired from a Bradley that had just raced into the edge of the parking lot. It went high by a dozen feet and to the far side of the tank, impacting a split second later against the limestone wall, far too close to the still-open steel doors into the Ark.

Is the son of a bitch trying to put one into the entryway? Darren wondered. A TOW round going in like that and exploding deep within the tunnel would be devastating.

Harrison was crouched down by Darren's side, handheld phone wired into the tank, shouting instructions. The Bradley that had fired off the first TOW was backing up, racing for concealment as the M1's main gun fired, the armor-piercing round slicing into the Bradley's turret, sheering it off, the vehicle bursting into flames.

There was no cheering, though, from the hundreds sprawled out on the pavement, now caught in the crossfire as 25 mm rounds from the Bradley down in the parking lot swept the ground, rounds sparking in brilliant flashes as they struck the front of the M1. Their own surviving Bradley tried to maneuver along the road to bring its own weapon to bear but was impeded by the hundreds of civilians trapped between the opposing sides.

Now unable to move but still capable of fighting, the M1's crew stayed at their post, playing hide-and-seek with the two opposing Bradleys down in the far side of the parking lot, dashing out to lay down fire with their 25 mm and 7.62 mm guns and then pulling back into a narrow ravine to the west side of the access road before the main gun of the Abrams could be brought to bear.

The deadly game ended for a moment when, after firing several rounds, the Abrams crew nailed another Bradley, which fireballed from the impact.

Even though many around Darren cheered, the sight sickened him. Those who had been vaporized or were still alive and trapped within the burning vehicle might very well have been a friend or neighbor.

"Up, everyone up!" Darren shouted, trying to stay focused on those around him. "Keep moving inside!"

Even as he did so, he kept looking up at the sun, which was now so much brighter. The orderly process of keeping parents and children out beyond the fence and handing out name tags had completely broken down in the last few minutes. He felt numbed, watching parents now just pushing their children forward and telling them to run for the tunnel. A few nevertheless were still trying to follow the system, squatting down and hurriedly jotting down names onto ID tags before sending their children in.

"Forget the damn name tags!" Darren shouted. "Just get them inside!"

Scurrying low to the ground, he went up to a husband and wife, now on their knees and fiercely hugging their two small sons.

"Move them! Move them!" Darren cried, reaching out to grab the boys. He caught a glimpse of a name tag fluttering on the lapel of one of the boys, the sight of which gave him pause.

"Carrington?" he asked.

"What of it?" the father cried, defensive as if the name were now somehow a curse.

"Are you . . . ?"

"No, my father and great-grandfather. Is that a damn problem now?"

"No, I promise you. We'll make sure they're safe." He looked down at the two, turning them about. "Go on, boys, just run inside. It's okay. Now run!"

He looked back up at their parents. Both were crying. "I promise they'll be okay. You two had better clear out, though; it's getting ugly."

The father offered a nod of thanks, forcing his wife to turn around and running for the opening through the outer gate.

An increasing tempo of small-arms fire ignited from down in the parking lot. The one Bradley still trying to hold back the attack by moving forward suddenly erupted into flames as a TOW rocket sliced into it, the secondary explosion inside the vehicle blowing the Bradley's top turret off.

The fighting vehicles on the other side now raced into the parking lot, regardless of the threat posed by the M1, opening up with their 25 mm guns, the rounds slamming into the tank's reactive armor. The crew in the M1 fought back, a single armor-piercing round cutting clear through the lead Bradley from front to rear, molten metal vaporizing all those within and setting off the fuel tank and ammunition on board.

Two Humvees raced out into the parking lot, and Darren could see that one of them had a TOW launch system mounted to it.

"Darren, get out of here!" Harrison cried, huddled beside the tank. "Keep the kids moving!"

Whoever aimed the TOW knew his business, the wire-guided rocket streaking out, its engine boosting up to full velocity and racing across the parking lot to impact the right-side tread of the tank, blowing it off. The tank crew fired back, ignoring the Humvee now that it had launched its main weapon, continuing to focus on the Bradleys. Another was hit with the same disastrous results for those within, the remaining Bradley again pulling back into defilade.

Incredibly, one of the buses carrying government civilians rolled into view. Had they been mistakenly told that the tank had been knocked out and it was safe to advance? Darren peered heavenward. It was now impossible to even try to glance at the sun, and he realized the entire area was being bathed in a brilliant, surreal light. To those still waiting out in the government convoy, it was clear that the end was at hand and there was nothing to be lost if they tried to rush the gate.

No, that bus and those now rolling behind it were coming forward in spite of the threat of being killed by the tank. Facing them as well were hundreds of civilians who, having fled from the parking lot and were still armed, now unleashed a fusillade at the convoy in blind panic and rage.

All knew that Sauron's Eye was exploding, and time had run out at last.

"Children only! Children only!" Darren cried. "Just run for it!" Jerry Green and his team who had pulled back to just outside the steel door were still trying to cull those few adults allowed to go in, shouting out names, telling them to run for the entryway. Helen up by his side, helping to pull the few remaining volunteers being admitted in, ordering them to go with the children and get them down the tunnel.

What small semblance of control that had existed even just thirty minutes earlier completely unraveled into blind panic.

The lead bus, fired upon by angry civilians, started burning, those still alive within it piling out and running toward the Underground. The thousands that the governor had abandoned to their fate were not going to sit by passively and die. More and more piled out of their vehicles when the way ahead was blocked by burning vehicles. A vast crowd of them, with more than a few armed National Guard personnel who had stayed on the governor's side, surged forward, crossing into the outer perimeter of the parking lot.

At least some had thought ahead, and during the last few hours before the firefight had erupted, they had urged their children to go forward, sensing that even if their own fate was sealed, their children still had a chance to live. Tragically, though, Darren could see that some still had their children in tow, some still clutching luggage, dragging it along even though it slowed them down. He wondered what in God's name was so important even now that they had to cling to those possessions.

Mixed in there were still children from Springfield. Darren's rough estimate now was that nearly ten thousand had taken shelter here since yesterday, but there were nearly as many more living in Springfield but a few days earlier, and of course so many more from as far away as Branson and even down to the Arkansas border.

He felt caught in a terrible duality at this moment. Get as many in as possible, but along with the roughly one thousand adults allowed to stay, each additional person meant a thousand more rations would have to be on hand, with water, medicine, bedding, clothes. Would there be enough of them and enough supplies for all to survive?

But even as that side of the equation hit, there was the other side: the faces of desperation of parents surging toward the torn remnants of the chain-link fence, shredded in quite a few places by the firefight. They were now pushing their children forward, sobbing, crying out that they loved them, more than a few offering a lie that would at least comfort for a moment until their child was safely inside. "Mommy will be right behind you, angel! Just run in, I'll be behind you . . ."

"Darren, over here!"

Harrison stood by the Humvee, which had remained parked just on the outside of the steel door. Darren ran over to join him.

Perry was within it, barely alive, the seat soaked with his blood, refusing all treatment other than a pressure bandage wrapped around his waist. He was still at his post, radio mike clenched tight in his hand.

Darren knelt by his side. "Sir, at least let's get you inside the tunnel, stop the bleeding, get some plasma in you."

"Why?" Perry asked.

"Sir, come on."

"Kiss my ass, Sergeant. I know what I'm doing."

Darren offered a reassuring smile and rested a hand on the general's knee. "Yes, sir, you know what you are doing."

"There's radio chatter," Perry whispered, then pressed his headset tight against his ear. He gasped as he reached over to switch the radio speaker on.

"It's blown! It's blown!" The voice was edged with hysteria. "This is K2GEC, picking up a broadcast from Washington that it's blown! My God, have mercy on us! It's—"

The signal disappeared under a wave of static.

"Darren?"

General Perry looked up at him, eyes wide, features firmly set, still in command. "It's time to close it up, Sergeant. Close it up."

He was right. They only had a minute or two before the radiation overload would fully hit with lethal intensity.

"Harrison, grab him," Darren snapped.

"No, I'm staying here. I want Harrison in there, Darren; you'll need him."

"I'm staying with you, sir!" Harrison cried.

"No heroics, no bullshit. Follow my last order, damn it! You're going to be needed by them even after this is over. Now run!"

Harrison filled up, reached down to take the general's hand, and impulsively leaned in and kissed him on the forehead. "God be with you, sir." He turned, head bowed, and staggered into the tunnel entrance.

"Thank you, sir," Darren whispered, coming to attention and offering a salute to a commander who had made the moral choice to sacrifice his own life for what was right as a soldier and as a man.

"Go, Darren. Take care of Darla now! Go!"

Darren did as ordered, turning about. Seeing Jerry and Helen, who were still at their tasks urging children to head for the tunnel, he simply grabbed Jerry, nearly lifting him off his feet, shoving him toward the tunnel entrance. Darla was outside as well and, following his lead, did the same to Helen, who had scooped up a lost toddler. Together, they ran.

"Pack it in!" Darren cried. "Pack it in!"

It was the agreed-upon code signal to finally seal up the tunnel.

Those who had understood the full meaning of the cry "Pack it in!" were responding, but just out beyond the fence there were thousands, many of them who only hours earlier had assumed they were indeed the chosen ones and now indeed saw that they were not. Parents of children within, who had volunteered to stay to the end, struggled to hold the gate as the mob pushed forward, and yet more gunfire erupted, rippling along the fence line into a crescendo, the mob breaking through the cordon and surging in.

The steel doors were closing.

"Darren!" Harrison grabbed him by the shoulder, trying to yank him back inside. Darren pulled himself free, looked at Harrison, and smiled wearily, shaking his head. As he did so, Darla stepped out of the shadows as the door continued to close.

"Inside you go, Harrison."

"Darren?"

"Remember, Darla and I said no exceptions at the start—that applies to us as well."

"What!"

"If we stay, what we did would be a lie. Besides, we think our children and grandchildren will be waiting for us."

He pushed Harrison the last few feet just as the door closed behind him.

"Bear?"

"Yes, angel?"

"Scared?"

"A bit."

"I'm not, as long as I'm with you."

Holding hands they turned away from the door as it locked shut. Darla leaned in close as he kissed her one more time, and then together, hand in hand, they walked out into the light.

24

"MR. PRESIDENT, now!"

His security detail was closing in, and as trained to do, even if the president struggled and protested, they were now taking charge.

"All of you stop!" he snapped, voice filled with authority.

"Now, Mr. President."

"Richard, it's blown, hasn't it?"

"Yes, sir."

"And the last data, how bad?"

In that last few seconds of data that had streamed back from *Helio II*, he knew what it would mean. "It's the end, sir," he whispered.

The president turned to his head of security, who had returned from ejecting Admiral Brockenborough. "Richard, how many Americans are about to die?" the president asked while looking at Gary.

"The vast majority, sir."

"Gary, my last gesture as president. How can I hide while so many die?" He put his hand on Gary's shoulder. "Do you read me, son? I want you people to get below now."

"Sir, we're staying!"

"No!"

They were frozen like a tableau, and it was Richard who broke it. Pulling out his alpha card, he walked up to Allison, who throughout the last hour had stood silent watch by his side.

"You're not alpha listed, are you, young lady?"

"No, sir." She kept her emotions in check.

"You said you and Gary there are engaged."

She nodded.

"I want both of you to live." He pressed his card into her hand. "Marry, love each other always, have lots of babies and someday tell your grandchildren how your friends faced this moment with honor."

She began to break.

"Gary, the rest of you," the president announced. "We've got a good vice president, and she is safe up at Site R. Report to her once things settle down. Now go!"

The four agents stood, not sure how to react. Allison approached Gary and slipped her hand into his.

"You heard our president," she whispered. "Come on."

She turned Gary around, still so torn.

Richard caught his gaze. "Marry that girl."

That broke the moment, and with head bowed, Gary went out the door, Allison by his side, the others following.

The president looked back to where his secretary of the interior sat, staring out the window. "James?"

"Think I'll just go outside for a walk, sir."

"Of course," the president replied, patting him on the shoulder as he slowly walked out of the room.

The president then turned to face Richard. "Richard, get out of here."

"No, sir."

There was a trace of a smile. When all of this had started, he had made the decision. His only regret was that he would never know the fate of his son, daughter-in-law, and grandchildren. As to his wife, he wanted to believe this was the day they would meet again. "Sir, I've studied the sun my entire life. I'd like to see what it can do today."

He stepped up to the president's side, and they both gazed out across the South Lawn. The panic-stricken crowd had scattered, though a few stood with heads bowed or were on their knees praying.

"The country will come back someday," the president whispered. "Maybe next time, we really will do it right." He looked over at Richard and extended his hand. "I'd like to think our wives are over there on that far shore, waiting to greet us."

Richard smiled, unable to reply, and held on to the president's hand.

He looked out at that nearly blinding light washing over the city with a startling radiance, the Washington Monument standing out starkly clear, the pillar illuminated as if by a thousand spotlights. *It will still be here in a thousand years,* Richard thought, *as will the Pyramids. They will endure and perhaps one day again inspire to reach, as Lincoln once said, to the "better angels of our nature."*

As he stood silently by the side of the president, a thought struck him. He had never thought that the end of his world would look so beautiful.

AFTERWORD

I believe nearly every author has that "first novel" experience, believing in the Cinderella Fantasy, that our wonderful opus will of course instantly become a bestseller. Then we find out the hard way, the real hard way, that even if you write science fiction and fantasy, life usually ain't a fantasy. Then you do one of two things. Quit, and many do, or write another one, then another and another, which would become me.

I was in my early thirties, had just finished building a small lakefront home up in Maine. Building that first house, at a time of 12 percent interest rates, only became possible by using the advance for my first book, and a small advance for a yet-to-be-written second to get a down payment together.

A month or so after moving into my new home I'm watching a PBS show, created by one of my all-time favorite authors. In this episode, he was going to take us on a drive from New Jersey to Maine, commenting on various sights along the way in that rich and sardonic voice of his. He had written scores of short stories and long before his television series on PBS he had a late-night talk show out of New York City.

I'm a Jersey kid, living in Maine, so of course I'm glued to the show. When he gets over the Kittery Bridge into Maine, of course he stops at a gift shop to buy an ashtray shaped like a lobster, proudly holding it up and defining it as a true example of American art. He drives on and finally gets off Route 95 at the Waterville exit and the show finishes with him pulling up to a lakefront cottage that looked really familiar. The show over, I go out the door, and take a look at the cabin near mine! OMG, I think he's my neighbor!

It can't be true!

This neighbor had an ear and an eye for working-class America, the kind of world I grew up in. One week a show was about beer, not the craft beer of today, we're talking about suds like Schaefer and Schlitz and the joy of popping a cold one when home from the factory. He often took his camera crew and wandered the American landscape; a favorite episode, driving along Route 22 in New Jersey and commenting on its supreme ugliness yet somehow kitschy, surreal charm. You never knew what he would serve up next.

I had just discovered one of my favorite authors owned the cottage next to my new home. Beyond just being the new neighbor, I had the perfect excuse to show up at his doorstep as a gushing fan because I was now part of "the club," I had just seen the publication of my first novel.

I had heard rumors that unlike his television and radio persona the guy could be a real curmudgeon but I had to meet him. The following day I gathered up all of his books, which were collections of his short stories and a brand-new copy of my first novel, worked up my nerve and walked over to his property. Sure enough a car with Jersey plates was parked next to the door. A nervous knock on the door which opens seconds later to a woman who obviously was not in a pleasant mood with this stranger at their door.

I asked if this was the right residence of one of my favorite authors while nervously holding up his books. I'm your new neighbor and hey, I'm a writer too, here's my first book that just came out!

A silent gaze, a sharp reply that she had no idea who or what I was talking about and she started to close the door. I made a final effort, apologizing for intruding, got her to take my book as a gift from a neighbor, turned and walked away, absolutely embarrassed and crestfallen.

I was halfway back to my cottage, tail between my legs and then I heard his voice, his distinctive voice. "Hey kid, damn it, come back here!"

I turned and there he stood in the doorway: Jean Shepherd.

Jean Shepherd? I think most reading this, unless you grew up in the

New York region in the 1950s and '60s, are wondering "who the hell is that?" Jean was the king of late-night radio talk on WOR 710 AM. A raconteur second to none. From politics, especially politicians on both sides of the fence who obviously were idiots, to the bizarre aspects of Americana, to nostalgia, he truly was radio's "theater of the mind." He was the one who introduced me to the Klondike poet, Robert Service, and at times did dramatic readings like "The Cremation of Sam McGee."

Jean's short stories? Amusingly nearly all of them were published in *Playboy* of all places. Yup, I actually did buy some editions "for the articles," at least that's what I would claim when, to my embarrassment, my mom found a stash. If the name still doesn't connect, there is a line Jean penned that is an iconic part of American culture "Hey kid, you'll shoot your eye out," from his movie *A Christmas Story*.

So, anyhow, there he is standing in his doorway, gesturing for me to come back.

He doesn't seem all that amused at first as I approached.

"So you own that house over there?" A nervous reply yes. "Damn, I hate that place, ruined the view."

A pause.

"My wife says you're a writer?" and he holds up my first science fiction novel with the garish cover.

I squeaked out a yes.

"Okay kid, come on in. You want a beer?"

Ten in the morning with Jean Shepherd, sure I'll have a beer!

We talked for a couple of hours, warm in my memory thirty-five years later. He graciously took my little paperback, even asked me to sign it, of course I pressed him to sign all of his books, and peppered him with questions about his radio days when my dad would allow me to sit up late and listen to Jean hold forth.

Then it finally turned to writing, and that's why I started this essay writing about Jean Shepherd. He took a look at my novel, my precious first novel, asked me what it was about, listened patiently as I nervously held forth about a future earth, an ice age, iceboats as warships, the rise of a religious cult. And I sensed it was just not connecting.

Silence for a moment.

"Bill, want some advice?"

Hell yeah, I wanted advice. This was going to be words of wisdom from on high.

"Bill, write about what you know."

What?

"This stuff, sure you thought it up. But do you really know it?" He said, or something like that and I had no reply other than I grew up on science fiction, along with a lot of the great classics, and Shepherd of course. But other than that, what could I reply.

Across the years there has been a lot of debate amongst Shep's fans as to how much of his material was autobiographical and how much was, well, just made up. You watch a *Christmas Story*, and part of you just wants to believe it was once, long ago, real. We'll never really know because Jean was cryptic about it his entire life. Regardless, real or not, Jean Shepherd was a master at writing "about what you know." Reading his stuff, he connected to any kid growing up in a working-class community. He knew what he was writing about.

The conversation drifted to an end. We shook hands, he offered a gracious wish of good luck as a writer and I started back for my place.

A few days later his car was gone. A month later it was back but I didn't go over again. Just a sense that the cabin on Snow Pond, Maine, was the hideaway not to be disturbed. On occasion I'd see him out on his deck as I was working my small sailboat around the point of land, we'd wave and that would be it. Several years later I sold that house, moved on, and never saw Jean again. He passed away just before the year 2000, I remember hearing the announcement and yeah, I cried.

I continued to write science fiction and gradually moved up the ladder. I went back to graduate school as a full-time student at Purdue for a Ph.D. in history and out of that my writing style and subjects began to change and mature.

So how do I link Jean Shepherd's advice to "write what you know kid," with this book *48 Hours* and to the three bestselling John Matherson novels about a war that devastates America?

I believe it started in October 1962 when I was in seventh grade trapped in a junior high school I truly detested in Millburn, NJ. From some of the classrooms, on a smog-free day, you could see the Manhattan skyline, less than fifteen miles away.

It was the time of the Cuban Missile Crisis.

I remember watching Kennedy addressing the nation, my mother going out to the kitchen after the speech, my father following her, whispered conversation, my mother starting to cry but then putting on the brave face and just saying it was time for me to pack off to bed.

Then school the next day. Walking through downtown, newspaper headlines were on display stands out in front of stores with bold print warning we could be facing a nuclear war. Homeroom period was different that morning as we did a duck and cover drill. No joking about it this time. This time it felt real. And then off to Mr. McSorley's history class, a guy I already disliked intensely. The type of history teacher who was a coach first and teacher a distant second.

McSorley starts the class and goes straight at it. A few minutes of what I guess every teacher in America was doing that morning. Answering questions, talking things through and reassuring, the same way we did on 9/11. But not "Coach" McSorley on that day. Of course the first question, someone asked. "Is there going to be a war?"

His answer, "Yup, this is it."

Great, just great, to a room full of seventh-graders darn near ready to wet their seats.

But he couldn't leave it alone at that. He pointed to the windows, the view of NYC and asked "Do you know what would happen if a megaton nuke blew right now, right there over the Empire State Building?"

He then went into lurid detail. Every sickening detail of catching on fire from the radiant heat, blinded by the flash, shock wave blowing in windows, the building collapsing and even if you survive that radiation, sickness with all its horrors would get you anyhow.

Rather than being in a classroom he should have been locked up in a psych ward for what he did.

The days that unfolded afterward? My father was the neighborhood civil defense coordinator, complete with the surplus WWI helmet painted white with the CD insignia on it. He was out late to meetings almost every night. Within a another day at least a quarter of the kids at my school were absent. Nearly all of them lived in the wealthy part of town and had been hustled off to vacation homes up in the Poconos and Catskills.

At dinner that evening I started asking questions. Other kids were getting out of the area, wasn't there anything we could do? Get jugs of water in the basement, maybe a bunch of canned food, stuff like that?

That wouldn't work, dad gently explained. Our house was a hundred-year-old row home, wood, not much protection. Then what about our locally designated fallout shelter, a brick building that was a switching station for Bell Telephone and only just a block away?

He was flat-out honest.

If NYC gets hit, it will be over for us in a matter of seconds and then we'll just simply be with God. The fallout shelter? Sure it would survive the blast but no one ever got around to stocking it with emergency supplies. That wasn't in someone's budget though he had been hollering about it for years. Sure it might buy a day or two for those inside but then what? No food, no water, and everything covered in fallout. As to the rich kids up in the Poconos and Catskills? Sure, they might live it out, for a while, but eventually it would be the end for them as well, as either fallout, or food shortages, or looting mobs got them as well.

I can still remember the way he looked at me and only after I had a child of my own could I fully grasp what he was feeling inside. He chose to be honest that night. Some might disagree, but I love and respect him for telling me the truth.

Of course it didn't happen, the weeks and months passed, a president was assassinated, the crisis disappeared from national memory, but not completely from mine.

I wanted to understand why. How did we get to this point where humanity, including me, could be wiped out in a flash of madness?

I went to the town library and found, *On Thermonuclear War*, by Herman Kahn. (Not the pizza guy and candidate, the scientist one.) The cover, all black, was in and of itself ominous, it was a thick tome of more than six hundred pages. Heavy reading for someone who had just turned twelve. Someone suggested Pat Frank's classic *Alas, Babylon,* written in the 1950s, a novel about how a small town in Florida struggles to survive in the year after a nuclear war. And yes, as I openly stated in the foreword to *One Second After,* it was my model for how I would shape the story of how Black Mountain, a real place where I live, would try to survive after an EMP strike.

My already passionate love for history, especially military history of the Civil War, still came first but I was no longer just learning about the past. I was becoming a student of a possible future history that leads to "Gotterdammerung."

After college I finally landed a teaching job up in Maine, my desire to move there fueled by a love of winter sports, skiing, and iceboat racing, sailing in the summer, the incredible autumns and yes, in part because of anywhere in the eastern United States survivability in Maine was at least slightly better than New Jersey if the crap ever hit the fan.

During those years I wrote my first science fiction novels, had a beer with Jean Shepherd, and in the late 1980s became a full-time graduate student at Purdue University for a Ph.D., specializing in military history and the history of technology. During that time I first started reading about EMP as an "asymmetrical, first-strike weapon," which in non-military talk means you blow out your opponent's power and communications grid as an opening move.

During my third year at Purdue an event happened that definitely helped to shape *One Second After,* something that I lived through and therefore "knew about." Northern Indiana got clobbered by an ice storm of epic proportions, one of those storms meteorologists call a once-in-five-hundred-year event. Within a few hours, trees were snapping, power lines going down, transformers arcing off in stunning blue-white flashes, actually exploding so the town of West Lafayette looked like it was under an artillery barrage.

Power was down in most areas for up to seven days. Outside the Lafayette area there were communities still off-line three weeks later.

As the storm passed the following afternoon, the road I lived on, which was a major crosstown thoroughfare was impassable, downed wires weaving back and forth on the ground or hanging suspended a half dozen or so feet in the air, entire trees down from one side of the street to the other. It did have a battlefield look.

We were truly a disaster area, the only sounds, that of chain saws, and some cop cars, trying to weave their way around the wreckage with loudspeakers on, telling everyone to stay inside, don't touch any wires, emergency power crews were coming in to help.

By the end of the first day a pathway through the road was cut, a power crew at least clearing the wires. Now just sit back and wait. Right? It never took more than a day or two before this one. So just keep on throwing armloads of wood into the fireplace, heat food on the grill outside. Having the foresight of filling the bathtub meant the toilet flushed and I wasn't reduced to giving my yellow lab beer to drink rather than water.

Fortunately Purdue University had its own power system with all wiring buried so the campus was suddenly what I would one day call "an island of recovery." Classes had been cancelled for the rest of the week, but it was still the place to go, get a cooked meal, even grab a shower at the athletic center.

Gradually we'd all find out that everything from just north of Indianapolis nearly up to Chicago was down, truly down. Not just your local wiring or substation; gone as well were those high power transmission towers that look like giants striding across the landscape. Many had collapsed under the weight of ice. It meant everything clear back to where electricity was generated was down.

By day five or so, that's when it started to get freaky. That is when I found myself observing human nature, if just a few props are pulled out from under us, things start getting a bit weird, and you can see how it could quickly slide into dangerous.

We're not talking about some massive urban area, this was a midwestern university town with a heck of a lot of very intelligent people who you should assume would just be mellow and wait it out.

A repair crew showed up in front of my house around day five. Hooray, the juice is coming back! I went outside to say thank you and as I approached the crew chief gruffly announced they were just restringing wire, there was no electricity coming in.

I put on a smile, replied politely that I kind of figured it was that way, and acted friendly, saying I could cook up some coffee for the crew on the grill if they wanted and joked I still had some cold beers they could stash for later.

One of the guys lightened up a bit and we started to talk. They were a crew all the way from Kentucky and had been at it for days. I got a quick education how most of the grid was still off-line, the worst any of them had ever seen.

Then the question and reply I can still remember clearly. I asked him how was it going for them. How were folks reacting. And with that the laughter started.

I heard how bribes had been offered; twenty bucks, fifty bucks, one guy waving several hundred dollars if only they would hook him up then and there. No matter how much they tried to explain to him there was no electricity flowing he refused to believe them, then started cursing at them and stalked off. Police and National Guard were starting to accompany power company trucks so people would be kept back and stop harassing the crews. One crew drove into a cul-de-sac to begin restringing wires, but when the residents were told they were not there to actually turn the electricity back on, they went ballistic, a couple of them driving their cars down, blocking the way out and announcing they weren't moving until power was turned back on. It tooks cops with threats of arrest to get the crew out of there.

And so it went. At least Purdue had power. In the smaller towns, people were just packing it in and moving to where friends or family still had power. Local stores were shuttered. Pharmacies got priority for hookups to portable generators providing enough juice for that corner of the store where you could get medications refilled. No credit cards, cash or check only. Local supermarkets took huge hits, when they ran out of fuel for their emergency generators and everything frozen and refrigerated had to be condemned.

One final memory which was like something straight out of Rod Serling's classic *Twilight Zone* episode, "The Monsters are Due on Maple Street."

Early evening about six or seven days into it and suddenly half a dozen houses across the street lit up.

Think of what just a week or so during a midwest winter without electricity was doing to us.

My side of the street and the surrounding block was still without electricity. Within minutes everybody was out of their homes, pulling on jackets, standing around, asking one another questions the way a crowd will when of course no one really knows the answers. It was just that the lucky few across the street had a functional wire back to a transformer that had just been replaced and was feeding them the precious juice . . . but not the rest of us.

Someone knocked on a door of one of the blessed ones. "Hey Jim, how come you got power and we don't?"

"Don't know, just lucky I guess."

More people were wandering across the street, standing in the yards of the chosen few with electricity. Someone came trotting up carrying a long coil of that orange colored outdoor wire, asking if he could hook in to an outside plug. "Come on Jim, can't you share some?" Someone else actually approached with a power strip, like the indoor type your computer is hooked into, suggesting why not just plug that into an outside socket and half a dozen houses could get wired in as well.

I didn't know Jim, but I could see he was getting nervous. And in that crowd the writer in me could just see Rod Serling standing to one side, in his cool Brooks Brothers suit, cigarette smoke coiling up, and saying "Presented for your consideration, a university town about to turn ugly . . ."

I just went back home, sat by the front window, watched the circus and finally a cop car actually pulled up. I guess one of the chosen ones with electricity was getting nervous.

Finally, a day or two later, the lights came back on for me. And, yeah, it felt like a miracle. The juice, the ubiquitous juice that runs our lives, had miraculously returned! I could hear the blower for the heater kick on and turned the thermostat up to seventy-six. The fridge, empty of food, hummed back to life. At least the town had the water system up and with that juice just ticking in to my little single-story ranch house the meter was again spinning round. A few hours and it would be hot bath time. Even my freezing cold water bed, (yes, I'm from the '70s and '80s) would begin to warm up. Television, is the cable system back up? Damn it no, but I can still get out the rabbit ears, hook them up and get a fuzzy signal from Indianapolis. And OMG, my computer!

Before the power blew off I had the good sense to disconnect everything, in case a surge hit first. I reconnected, took a deep breath and pushed the on button and that screen came back to life!

The notes for what would be my doctoral dissertation, were waiting for me. The next book in my Lost Regiment science fiction series, ready for another chapter . . . but my first priority? A raid on a German airfield in that glorious game "Secret Weapons of the Luftwaffe," called for me. So there was the rest of my first evening with the electricity back on. A cold beer that I had stuck into the freezer for an hour, my contented yellow lab curled up by my feet, the house blazing with light, while I tangled with a couple of Me-262s in my computer generated P-51 Mustang. (I won of course, the AI back then was predictable.)

Thus was the great ice storm and power failure of Indiana in the early 1990s. Did anyone die? Yes, a few. The poor guy with a bad heart trying to scrape the ice off his driveway, or cut off downed limbs with a chain saw, the usual idiot or two who did touch downed power lines. Some broken limbs from falling on the ice and that was about it. But mass starvation? Actually freezing to death? Disease from failed sanitation and untreated water? Rioting and civil breakdown?

Nope . . . but the experience was certainly stored away by this author.

After grad school I landed a professorship at Montreat College and moved to the wonderful Norman Rockwell–like town of Black Mountain and had been there for eleven years when it was the summer of 2004. A couple of years earlier I teamed up with Newt Gingrich to write a series of historical fictions about the Civil War. On a hot summer day we were scheduled for a meeting to start planning our next novel. Newt had lined up a suite for me in a hotel near where he lived, since his house was getting torn up with remodeling. I got there early, settled in, and waited. He arrived for our meeting a few hours later and it was obvious he was furious about something.

"I'm sick of it. Damn it, when will Congress or anyone wake up about EMP?!" he snapped at the guy accompanying him who at first I assumed was an assistant or something.

"EMP? You mean electromagnetic pulse?" I butted in.

He later said that caught him a bit off guard, at first firing back, "You know about EMP?"

I answered yes, shrugged, commented that I had picked up on it when reading stuff on nuclear war fighting strategy.

We settled down around the suite's kitchen counter, and was introduced to the gentleman with him, Bill Sanders. Not an assistant, Bill was a lieutenant commander in the navy who was considered a top theorist on nuclear warfare strategy and technology. Bill would eventually go on to write the technical afterword for *One Second After*.

I then got the rundown on what had happened. Earlier in the day a Congressional study group had released their report, about the threat to America sustaining a deathblow from an EMP strike.

The terrible irony of that day. Some idiot had scheduled the report and open hearing for its release to be scheduled on the same day as the long-anticipated report by Congress about the attack on 9/11. Result, not one media source showed up for the EMP report. It was like the tree falling in the forest routine, or whatever television show gets scheduled opposite the Super Bowl. We talked late into the evening, the three of us going over copies of the report.

It was a long drive home the following day. We never did get around to talking about our next Civil War novel. Instead, Newt challenged me to write a book about EMP. Maybe what was needed was a novel that could raise public awareness and eventually help create political action and preparedness.

That challenge was a life-changing moment.

Once home I carefully studied the report, the declassified section about a hundred pages or so. After finishing the Congressional report, like any historian trained to do research, I started to dig into the addendums, tracked down technical reports cited in footnotes, which led me to more obscure articles with yet more footnotes.

What did I learn? The report, the analysis of how our high-tech society would break apart within hours if the nation's power grid went down from an enemy attack was accurate. The most chilling statistic: the casualty rate.

No electricity means a total breakdown: no water, sanitation, nursing homes become hellholes, disease runs rampant, loss of heating and cooling, safe food and medication distribution go down, the list is numbing . . . it becomes a cascading nightmare, along with the breakdown of social order. Conclusion: upward of 90 percent of all Americans would die within a year. The greatest disaster in the history of humanity that would transcend the two world wars, and even the great plague of the fourteenth century.

I had to take the challenge. I had to write a book that would help raise public awareness, but how?

A long frustrating year followed. A story line was just not coming together. I started to fall into what I came to call the "Jack Ryan trap." Yeah, we have our hero, bad guys have three nukes, get them close to the continental United States on a shipping container boat or maybe a North Korean sub. Our hero races to spread the warning, even stops a couple of them and then . . . and then? The story line sucked. I knew it and I was dead-ended.

A frustrating, long winter and spring followed of absolute writer's block and it would just not come together. It can be a near insanity triggering experience for anyone striving for a creative project. You almost catch glimpses of it at times, like the movement of a shadow you thought you saw in the corner of the room. But it just won't come, that golden moment, that instant in time when it suddenly falls into a sublime pattern, that true "OMG" moment.

Winter slipped into spring with no idea what I was going to do.

I am blessed to live up in the Smoky Mountains. My college, tucked into a narrow valley below Mount Mitchell, is such a beautiful, unique community. We average about five hundred full-time students. It is a small tight-knit community. From my first days as a teacher, at a small boarding school in Maine, I've always believed that teaching is about far more than the fifty minutes a day in a classroom. It is all that surrounds that time: the chance meetings in a hallway, who you sit down with at lunch, noticing a student that just seems down and since you know their name you go over to them to have a chat and find out what's going on. Those are the real moments of teaching and learning and often building lifelong friendships.

Graduation day therefore is a day of some mixed emotions. Sure, the professor side is there, that after a few hours of sweating in one's ceremonial robes it was out the door, head for home, and three months of freedom!

But there always was another side. At our college all the professors sit up on the stage. From that vantage point you see not just happy families and friends, you see the students in their robes, ready to take the big step. After four years you know every last one of them and at times it does leave a lump in the throat. More than a few had become "my kids," and on this day they are leaving, and chances are that for many I'll never see them again. Memory of them will eventually blur into the memories of several thousand students that have passed through my life since I first taught a high school class back in 1978.

The day was hot, actually downright sweltering and that vast octagonal-shaped assembly hall had no A/C. The robes you get to wear as a prof might look cool, but believe me, they turn into sweatboxes when it is ninety degrees. There was the usual procession to start, a couple of hymns and prayers since we are a Christian college and can do such things. Introductions and then finally, the graduation speaker.

Does anyone actually remember who spoke at their graduation and what they said? I've sat through dozens and frankly cannot remember a single one, except this one, on that particular day.

I've always said that a great graduation speaker, when stepping up to the podium, should pull out an old-fashioned egg timer, hold it up, announce he was setting it at ten minutes, and when it started to ring he'd shut up and sit down. Whoever does that will get a standing ovation not just at the end, but at the start as well!

On that particular day I knew such would not be the fate of anyone in that sweltering room. Within five minutes the speaker, clutching the podium, was just beginning to warm up to his subject while two thousand in that room were sweating and already silently begging for mercy. Five minutes went to ten, ten to twenty, and it was obvious he was nowhere near finished.

About thirty minutes in I leaned over to a professor next to me, a darn good friend and whispered, "how about you fake fainting and I'll carry you out." I was dead serious and she later said if he had gone on for another ten minutes she would have fainted for real.

So there I am sitting, no longer listening, the speech just a drone of noise, soaked in sweat . . . and gazing out at the audience, watching "my kids" and how they were reacting.

At that moment, it was as if Jean Shepherd were sitting behind me, and whispered "Kid, write what you know."

The story that would become *One Second After* formed within me at that instant and it did indeed seem like but an instant in time.

At that moment what did I know? I knew those kids, I knew more than a few of their families. I saw and knew neighbors, friends, a beloved elderly couple, kids who had graduated several years earlier, married and were back with their newborn baby. I saw an old honored friend, an Omaha Beach vet, and had just gone there with him the year before. They, us, our town, my town. That is what I know.

And in that knowing a deep sadness swept into me as well. What would happen to us, to all of us, to these people I love, if the lights went out and in one second the America we knew ceased to exist?

Jean's advice came home to me at last. I will write about "us."

If you've read my John Matherson series you might have learned that where the story is set in North Carolina, the village of Black Mountain and Montreat College, they are real.

I wrote a book about what I knew, which is simply about us. Along the way I interviewed dozens, from my friend the chief of police, to the pharmacist who actually broke down in tears as we thought out the questions. Doctors, my UPS driver, my auto mechanic and my neighbor, a buddy who can darn near build or fix anything. "What would you do if the power turned off and never came back on?" My father had passed away only months before I started to write the book. I went back to his nursing home, interviewed the director and the nurses, all of whom I saw as guardian angels and asked "What would happen here if the power went down and the emergency generator shorted off as well?" If you've read *One Second After* you know how that particular interview inspired a scene that was painful to write.

As mentioned early on, Frank's *Alas, Babylon,* was in my thoughts and with respect for him I'll say again that I saw my book as taking a concept and moving it into the real-world threats of the twenty-first century.

The book finally came out several years later, hit the *New York Times* Best Seller List, two more would follow, and now this book, *48 Hours.*

I know more than a few might be asking now, "Hey wait a minute, *48 Hours* is a whole different story, it's not even about EMP, so why this essay?"

I was completely unaware of the issue of how solar storms can effect our electrical grid until a few weeks after *One Second After* came out. A friend called me up to congratulate me and then asked if I had ever read a book called *The Sun Kings.* It was about the early days of solar astronomy and how the astronomer Richard Carrington first connected solar storms to the impact, several days later, on the electrical infrastructure of 1859, the spreading web of telegraph lines. Across parts of northern Europe, England, and the United States, systems shorted out, wires even caught on fire and melted off the poles.

I read the book, and there was another OMG moment that infrastructure security was not just about EMP but about something else, coronal mass ejection (CME), as well. That stayed with me and finally would lead to this book.

Has what I have written had an influence on things? Some say I was the trigger point for the sudden emergence of the "prepper movement."

I'll step back from that; there were a heck of a lot of others writing about the subject and my book just seemed to hit at a moment when it could be most helpful (even if after nearly fifteen years there still has been no federal-level action to harden our nation's infrastructure against such an event).

A couple of years back my publisher asked me to write a book about CME. I finally agreed and thus started over a year of staring at the ceiling at one in the morning, getting really good at beating my computer at level-eight chess, and going nowhere fast. Whatever I tried seemed derivative of the past, what I had already written. The only difference being there'd be about forty-eight hours warning that the grid was about to go down, but then where's the story? The usual running around by some characters, our heroes getting ready, the cadres of bureaucrats screwing things up, we already know that would happen and I felt, sure I could write it, but in a big way it would be a cop-out. A serving up of just another helping of what I had already done before with my Matherson books.

And then there came that moment yet again, that OMG moment. I was in a greenroom, ready to tape a television interview out in Springfield, Missouri, and chatting with a close friend of mine. I told her my lament of yet another bad dose of writer's block, she made one simple comment and the entire story hit me in that instant. A day later I was back home, at the computer, and writing.

48 Hours presents a moral question, a true "what would you do if . . ." Dare I say maybe it presents the ultimate question to all of us if a solar event more powerful than a CME ignited, and humanity, or at least 99 percent of humanity, knew it could be facing the end of their world in the next forty-eight hours.

I wrote it in part out of frustration as well. I believe in America, I believe that as Abraham Lincoln once said we are indeed "the last best hope of earth." But of late how we all seem to have turned on each other is heartbreaking. Being left or right, liberal or conservative, believer in God or not (at least as you believe in God) is tearing us apart as a nation. So thus a question: If *48 Hours* ever did become a reality, what would we do; what would you do? Maybe at such a moment we would see that which separates us has become all but meaningless and that all of humanity has far more in common than whatever divides us.

I wrote *48 Hours* with a belief, a hope that this is something "I know," that at least some of us, would indeed reveal, as Lincoln once said, "the better angels of our nature."

William R. Forstchen
July 2018